NanoCorporate

A Novel of the Near Future

Rob Preece

BooksForABuck.com
2012

BooksForABuck.com
March 2012
ISBN: 978-1-60215-170-3

Olivia

Olivia Jardan's phone chimed and she answered without checking her display. "Talk."

"Detective Jardan?" Police central's standard mechanical voice.

"Confirmed."

"We have evidence of biometric failure by an ensured ratepayer." The Police Corporation's intentionally robotic voice rattled off the policy number, then the name of the failed individual, Hank Merryweather. "Standard rates apply. Please accept or reject."

As if a cop could afford to turn down jobs. "Accept."

"Confirmation noted, detective. Assess and Avenge."

"Assess and Avenge," Olivia echoed before signing off.

Biometric failure could mean anything from a split fingernail to the outbreak of some designer-plague. Regardless, the number indicated that Merryweather was a centercity ratepayer. All ratepayers demanded instant response, but centercity ratepayers were the worst.

Olivia checked her police tunic to be sure it was fully charged, then headed to the rail.

As she trotted toward the station, she double-checked Merryweather's failure location on her phone. He'd apparently suffered the failure at his place of residence in centercity. Unfortunately, he lived a fair distance from the nearest rail. Which meant delay or expense.

The train arrived just as she did so she boarded before calling Merryweather. Woe to any detective brash enough to call a ratepayer without being able to promise they were en route to a summons. If the ratepayer didn't tear them a new one, police central would.

Merryweather's automated response system refused to put her through even with her police override code. Which wouldn't have been odd under normal circumstances—ratepayers didn't go out of their way to respond to low-status cops. Still, with a declared biometric failure, Merryweather should answer if he could.

Trying not to think about the cost, which would be subtracted straight from her completion bonus, she requested a system override. Perhaps she could break through Merryweather's phone's blocking software even if he were intentionally offline.

The override worked—sort of. The phone block went away, but Merryweather still didn't answer. So she sat back in her seat and tried to catch up on routine police work.

An old man got on at the Richardson Center stop and claimed the seat next to her despite the largely empty train.

She considered moving, but realized he wouldn't be on for long. No mere citizen could go into centercity.

On a long shot, she scanned her seatmate, noting three violations, none coded for anything violent. Which meant no bonus for Olivia. She went back to her ever-present voice codes.

The stranger studied her, apparently unwilling to let her mind her own business. He must finally have realized she wasn't going to initiate a conversation, because he finally spoke in a croaking whisper. "Never stop to admire the scenery, do you?"

She turned down her phone's video display, projected directly onto her optic nerve, so she could study the elderly citizen.

She tried to remember the last time she'd seen anyone with thinning white hair, epidermal blemishes, or decayed musculature. She'd seen old video, of course, but nothing like this in real life. Even a premium system flush didn't cost much and the Interfaith offered a flush almost as good for free—if you didn't mind sitting through a few sermons.

"I'm a police detective going about authorized business. I'm not a—" she subvocalized, looking for the word, and got the answer from Google. "—not a tourist."

"That's exactly why I thought you'd be checking things out. In the Infoweb sims, detectives are always—"

"Those sims are entertainment, not reality."

"Thought so. But still, you need to know what's going on, don't you?"

Olivia waved a hand at the small windows where transparent cells were cut into the rail car's solar-panel-walls. "What would I look at? Miles of solar panels? Infrared heat release? You know just about everyone is sitting quietly in their homespace, plugged into the Infoweb or the Interfaith, not doing anything and not making trouble?"

The old man seemed nonplussed. "But—"

"Dallas looks like every other corporate city in America—nothing but solar panels as far as I can see. Seen one, seen them all."

He turned, looked out the window as if actually looking for the first time, then shook his head slowly. "I'm sure that's not right."

"And I'm sure you need a flush, Citizen…" a follow-up scan, "Roberts."

He looked uncomfortable. "I don't have—"

Sure enough, his credit balances registered near zero. She hoped he wasn't scamming the rail because the robots monitoring payment were programmed to deal out harsh penalties.

"It's on me. So's your ticket." Olivia selected his code, transferred the cash, and gave the transaction her biometric okay. Like everyone, Roberts already had the scrub nanobes inside of him. The payment would activate them, let them do their job.

It would take at least twenty-four hours to complete the flush, but he'd start feeling better in minutes.

Olivia hated to think that anyone was wandering around Dallas looking that old. It wasn't as if they were back in the twentieth century. Still, it was annoying that he hadn't gone to the Interfaith for the free scrub. It wasn't as if she had a lot left over at the end of each month.

The old guy got off the rail at Midway, just as the tracks crossed the old Interstate that created the centercity border.

She could practically feel the scans as she went through that largely invisible, but very definite barrier. As a cop, she was a nominal ratepayer. Even so, she could only enter centercity, the heart of the corporate city, on business. The Merryweather project code meant not having to answer questions posed by polite, but cheerfully violent, security bots.

As the rail neared Mockingbird Station, Olivia checked with central, which reported continued failure in its system override.

Merryweather's autoanswer was less polite this time, reminding her that she had already left her priority code and that Ratepayer Merryweather would get back to her in his own good time.

The train slid to a smooth stop and Olivia stepped off—into the heat of a Dallas summer.

Although her uniform wicked perspiration from her skin and its black surface converted seventy-three percent of the sunlight into electricity rather than heat, she still wilted. September in Dallas was plenty of reason for anyone to huddle in the air-conditioned comfort of their homespaces.

She considered taking a car from the station, but decided to jog. It wouldn't take any longer and, despite what she'd said to Citizen Roberts, it might help to look at the neighborhood and determine if biometric failure had breached the bio-barriers of Merryweather's homespace. Besides, she didn't want to lose money on this assignment and cars were expensive, especially in centercity.

Reflecting the wealth of the ratepayers in this part of the city, the homespaces were larger than those in outer rings, with glistening solar panels maintained by armies of tiny cleaning bots. A thousand tiny hums indicated that the houses were active, sucking water vapor and carbon from the air. Other than the size, they were little different from houses on the other side of the barrier. What shocked her were the trees: huge biological trees, their leaf canopies soaking up water and carbon that could be used in construction, and blocking direct sunlight from reaching solar panels.

Olivia had seen plenty of conspicuous consumption in the four years she'd served as a cop, but she'd never seen anything like this. Of course, most police jobs involved citizens rather than ratepayers and the rings rather than centercity. She'd been downtown several times, but this was her first trip to the residential segments of centercity.

Considering her problems with the autoanswer, she wasn't surprised when Merryweather's homespace rejected her Police authorization code. Biometric failure enabled another option. Olivia uploaded the override provided by Merryweather's insurance company. That got a grudging approval from the house's artificial intelligence. Even computers were smart enough not to mess with insurance companies.

Before she stepped inside, Olivia stretched the fabric of her uniform tunic over her eyes, nose, and mouth to create a biochemical barrier. Biological accidents and attacks were unusual, but they weren't unknown.

The second she saw Merryweather, though, she knew that no weird toxin or bioengineered bacteria had created the bio-failure. Failure came from cranial trauma and loss of blood.

Olivia reached for the large man's wrist and felt for a pulse while her sensors attempted to contact Merryweather's implants and determine if anything remained system-operational.

It took her fifteen seconds to reach the obvious conclusion. Hank Merryweather was terminally dead. From the blood spatter and the deep bloody gouge carved in his forehead by something heavy and sharp, he hadn't met with an accident. Ratepayer Merryweather had been murdered.

The Avenge half of the Police Corporation motto, "Assess and Avenge," went into immediate effect. As the detective assigned the case, Olivia would track down those who had killed Merryweather and ensure that they paid the price for their behavior.

She confirmed that her phone had uploaded the biometric detail to police central and verified that her account had been credited with both a completion fee (discounted for a supposed delay). A credit had also been applied for the murder investigation—a disappointingly small credit.

Unluckily for Merryweather, but luckily for Olivia's bank account, his biometric failure had turned into a two-fer.

Looking for evidence rather than cause of death, Olivia checked the victim more carefully.

She'd seen death before, but only among cits. Ratepayers were supposed to be beyond that. Not that they were immortal, but crass violent death just wasn't a part of what the sims showed of their world. She couldn't help being sickened by the contrast between Merryweather's obvious wealth, and the violence of his death.

His homespace controller displayed more bad news. Merryweather's file system had been plundered.

Olivia connected to central and dictated her preliminary report. "Ratepayer Hank Merryweather is dead due to trauma to the brain. A sharp heavy object, such as an ax, believed to be the weapon used. Such weapon was not, confirm *not*, found on location. Multiple files have been removed from Merryweather's computer. Some of these appear to be unsigned creations. I am unable to ascertain the purpose of the unsigned codes."

"Assessment?" the robotic voice demanded.

The assessment was obvious. Stolen code, especially naked code lacking digital rights management overlays that limited their use, could rocket a citizen into the kind of wealth that would make him an Infoweb celebrity.

"Somebody plans on living high off of Merryweather's intellectual property."

"Report accepted," the computer at central relied after an infinitesimal delay. "Assess and Avenge."

"Assessing and Avenging," Olivia promised.

Julia

Julia Turnboldt didn't need to check the time—her phone projected it directly onto her optical nerves. She did it anyway. Merryweather was late. Again.

Free-code was supposed to be a good time, not to mention an opportunity to meet guys her mother considered suitable. Well, her mother might consider them suitable, but Julia found everyone she'd met so far impossibly dull and sometimes not too bright. The one exception, Hank Merryweather, was too caught up in his causes to be interesting. Still, he was one hell of a coder. Julia had learned a lot from him—when he bothered showing up for his appointments.

She exhaled, pasted on a smile, then called him.

Instead of Merryweather's autoanswer, the logo of one of the big insurance companies filled her optical system. "Final benefits for Ratepayer Hank Merryweather are now being processed. If you have financial claims on his estate, you must file these claims within three days. Do you wish to leave a message?"

Final benefits? Merryweather wasn't even fifty. Sure that seemed old to Julia, but a ratepayer could expect to live to at least a hundred and fifty before body scrubs began to fail.

A chill trickled through her. Merryweather wasn't just late for their meeting, he was terminally late. She'd never get the chance to explain her most recent project to him, make him eat his flippant dismissal of what she knew was solid code. She'd never learn more of the sneaky tricks he used to cut the components he used down to the bare minimum, meaning that his code was not only clean but offered higher profit margins than anything the big shops turned out.

She crushed the carbon-fiber cup that had held her latte, dropped it into a public constructor for reshaping, and headed back to her office. Without Merryweather's help, she'd be working late for the next couple of nights.

Olivia

Olivia tried to organize the data pouring out of Merryweather's homespace controller.

"Number and codes of anyone entering the homespace in the four hours between Merryweather's last access and reported biometric failure," she demanded.

Five individuals had entered, although Merryweather had authorized only the first. The fifth was herself, which left three unaccounted for. Apparently those others had been manually admitted. That wasn't a contract violation, but it was unusual. If Merryweather hadn't been a centercity ratepayer, his insurance company might have fought payout due to that irregularity.

Olivia checked for fingerprints on Merryweather's fully stocked constructor, found none, and used it to fabricate a forensic scanner.

As she'd suspected, the scanner indicated massive trauma to Merryweather's skull. Mixed with the shattered bone, sub-molecular flakes of buckyball carbon suggested that a constructed device had been used in the murder. Her initial theory of an ax attack was holding up well.

She added the detector's information to the readouts from Merryweather's biosensors. Together, they formed a complete autopsy report.

Her credit balance clicked up slightly, but only very slightly. The price of the scanner had been deducted from her fee.

She shook her head. She was done here. All that remained was to track down the killers, avenge Merryweather's death, and report back to central.

She grabbed Merryweather's arms to drag his remains to the constructor for recycling but an alarm flashed from her phone. "Ratepayer Merryweather has requested specific biological handling."

Right. Real ratepayers weren't bound by the rules ordinary people had to labor under. She dropped his arm and summoned the body disposal team. She wouldn't get paid for the wait, but at least the insurance company would pay for the disposal.

She used the delay to log into central's database and track down the homespace locations of the killers. Motive and means were obvious. Citizens clearly wanted the kind of code a first-class designer like Merryweather would stock. That gave them motive. And they'd constructed a carbon buckyball ax to do the job. That was the means. When she found them, she'd have to determine how they'd gotten into centercity. After all, centercity existed to keep citizens out and ratepayers safe. Someone higher up in police corporation security was going to be answering some tough questions.

That, though, was no skin off her nose. She'd find the facts and see if she could end her day financially ahead of yesterday.

The body disposal team arrived shortly after she'd discovered the killers' locations and she turned the corpse over to them and headed back to the rail, catching the train to the outer rings.

She dictated her tentative conclusions and next steps as the train floated out of centercity.

"Data is consistent with your conclusions," central admitted reluctantly. "Do you wish backup for the apprehension? There will be a twenty-five percent fee waiver given the number of alleged assailants."

Not happening. Even with the partial waiver, bringing in hired help would drain her balance quickly, leaving her hanging if everything didn't go well. Besides, if she couldn't handle a few lowlife cits from the outer rings, she needed retraining.

The outer rings looked pretty much like centercity or her third-level ring. Acres of solar panels pointed hopefully toward the sky. A few narrow nanobe-implanted roads, and the occasional remnant of twentieth century architecture-inorganic materials too expensive to reclaim but too impractical to actually use, marred otherwise straight lines of mirrored panels.

There were no trees out here, of course. Sunlight, carbon and water were basic feedstocks for both trees and people. The resources sucked up by the small forest in centercity could have fed, clothed and sheltered thousands of citizens.

Figuring that the killers might be enjoying the fruits of their raid, Olivia headed toward the apartment two of Merryweather's last visitors had shared.

It was a dusty little place, which didn't make a lot of sense since dust interferes with solar collection and the code for constructing dusting robots was free, but the suspects were guys in their early twenties. Maybe filth was a fashion statement.

She walked up to the door and input her police override, not even bothering with a polite interrogation.

The door's AI refused to accept her code. Which was odd. It cost money to ignore an override, and nobody with money would live in a pit like this.

Cops don't get paid to give up, though. Olivia turned her police tunic down so it was less obviously a uniform, switched her surface codes to reflect a cit lifestyle, and smiled into the greeter, politely requesting personal access.

"The household is accepting no visitors at this time," the greeter AI replied.

"Oh, that doesn't mean *me*. The boys invited me over. They said they had got some cool new codes and it was time to party."

"The household provided me with no exception list. I am sorry, sir or ma'am."

Sir or ma'am? A greeter so dumb it couldn't do basic human sex discrimination should not be able to defeat a police access request.

Olivia tore a single buckyball strand from her tunic, touched the two ends to her tongue, and used the natural adhesion in her saliva to hang it between the door and the frame. It wouldn't keep anyone in, but it would let her know if someone left.

Her makeshift detector in place, she jogged down the narrow alleyway to one of the few open courtyards in the neighborhood.

No matter how desperate people were for space, they left room around public constructors. Those were the last resort of citizens who'd lost everything. Given enough time in line, a citizen could construct the solar panels and miniconstructor that would let him or her start a new life. Code for miniconstructors was provided as a public service by corporations who planned to recover their investments by selling designs for final product, but most necessities were available from the Interfaith, at the price of a few hours of sermon-listening.

Public constructors also served wandering police officers who needed equipment they didn't carry in their pouches. Which is why Olivia had noticed this one when she'd mapped the neighborhood.

She cut her way to the front of the line, let the machine scan her ID, then selected the tube of dissolver she needed. Her account balance dropped and she shuddered at the cost. This job would turn into a money-loser if she wasn't careful.

The constructor hissed a little. Two seconds later, she had the tube of dissolver.

Equipped and ready, she returned to the apartment.

"Report change of status," she ordered the greeter.

"I am not authorized to report to you."

Her buckyball strand remained in place, though. If the killers had been there when she'd arrived, they were still inside.

She plucked the strand from the door and brought it back to her tunic, letting the self-assembling nanobes reclaim any molecules they might need from their orphan.

That taken care of, she gave the solar panels near the door a good soaking with the dissolver.

Like every modern homespace, this one was constructed of solar panels. These panels were constructed using the codes the Interfaith made available for, literally, a prayer. They weren't designed to stand up against a police-strength dissolver—and they didn't.

In less than two minutes, a door-sized chunk of wall fell in.

Unlike Merryweather, the four guys inside didn't *look* dead.

No blood trickled over the floor. No brains showed through split skulls. No squawks from disgruntled computers complained to the world.

They looked completely happy, enraptured by their codes.

A faint spatter on one of the men's shirts scanned blood. That blood, her scanner said, was Merryweather's. In the corner, an ax, constructed from diamond-hard buckyballs, deteriorated, its purpose served.

The same could be said for the guys. No sound came from their mouths. The slight rise and fall of their chests was absent. They were dead. Almost certainly killed by whatever they'd stolen.

She'd entered Merryweather's homespace with proper caution against biological contaminants. Here, though, she'd been more concerned about a violent objection. If whatever had killed the suspects was biological, she'd likely killed herself, too.

* * * *

It was too late to do much but hope her expensive police immunity, which had so far turned out to be more of an insurance company fundraiser than a real help, would protect her.

In the meantime, she had a report to make.

"Citizens Roper, Sheriffe, Diamond and Brown confirmed deceased," the bloodless tone of Control agreed. "No insurance. Confirming assess and avenge completed."

"I need a scan analysis for danger to myself."

A brief pause. "Cause of death, simultaneous heart failure. No unexpected biological components detected."

If it wasn't biologicals, it had probably been drugs or psychoactive code. They'd used what they'd stolen and Merryweather had struck back at his killers from beyond his grave.

Which created another problem. What if they'd sent the codes elsewhere before using them? Dallas could now be filling with corpses.

"I'll need to determine whether stolen code has been released outside this homespace's firewall," Olivia reported. Wrapping up the murder had been predictably easy, but the cleanup might be more difficult than usual. She knew what central would pay for that job-zero. Still, it had to be done.

To her surprise, central didn't accept her input. "Infoweb monitoring is in place. Return to your routine assignments."

She blinked, then checked her phone. Amazingly, police central implemented a 100 percent completion payment for the avenge. The general rumor among cops was that central *never* calculated a job more than eighty percent complete.

"Instructions confirmed," she said. "Returning to stand-down status. I will order this homespace, and the deceased, dissolved as a warning to others. Standard policy per directive 1e728c2084."

She grinned as she broke through the keeper's emergency access panel and set the homespace self-destruct code. This would take care of the bodies as well, saving her the body disposal fee and providing a nice bit of organic matter for the neighbors' systems.

Control had gone quiet and she thought their conversation was over, but it crackled back to life just as she reached to press the 'activate' button. "Negative on the destruction. The four are adherents to the Holy Father segment of the Interfaith. They have special body rituals."

Like insurance companies, you didn't argue with the Interfaith.

"Confirmed. Structure and bodies are left for Interfaith disposal. Proceeding to stand-down."

Acting on an urge and a hunch, though, she scooped the suspects' computer from its slot in the wall and took it with her.

Vinson

An alarm jerked Chief of Police Harles Vinson from a 3-D sim concerning four beautiful female citizens and a horse. He, of course, played the part of the horse. What those cits did with their tongues and bodies was definitely something. This particular sim was the latest thing among sophisticated ratepayers and Vinson liked to think of himself as among their number— even though police work, even at the highest levels, put a man just barely above a citizen in social standing.

"What?"

"We have a code 729," a sexy contralto reported. Being chief of police meant he didn't have to put up with mechanical voice ordinary cops got.

Vinson shook off his chair's caress. "Details."

"Ratepayer Hank Merryweather was executed by four citizens, apparent objective, theft of unsecured intellectual property."

Which wouldn't create a code 729. "But?"

"These four citizens were found dead by our investigating officer, one Olivia Jardan."

"Commendable. *Found dead*. I love that wording."

"All four are coded for Interfaith Extreme Traditional disposal."

Vinson put his head in his hands and swallowed down the hard knot in his stomach. "That means—"

"Chief Vinson, that means we have a code 729."

Promotion in the Police Corporation was based more on background than on talent, but you didn't make it to Chief without having both. And you didn't remain at the top of the corporate structure if you didn't understand power.

One person choosing IET disposal meant nothing. But four out of four sounded like an Interfaith Enforcement Squad. And Enforcement Squads didn't murder ratepayers—ever. That, more than anything, was at the core of the Great Compromise back fifty or more years ago. With economic war about to break out between Corporate Dallas and Corporate Houston, the last thing he needed was a meltdown in the Compromise.

"Put me through to Reverend Ariel," he ordered. "And head Officer Olivia Jardan off the case. Give her some sort of plum assignment but make damned sure she doesn't dig any deeper into the Merryweather thing. Oh, and before you give me Ariel, who's Jardan's supe?"

"That would be Sergeant Paul Shenker."

"Connect me to him, now. And then perform a probability analysis. I want to know why Interfaith enforcers are killing ratepayers and I want to know now."

"Conducting analysis," central said.

Vinson flipped through his feeds, reluctantly switching off the citizens and horse. He wasn't sure human females could really do that with a horse and had some thoughts on how he could find out. After all, nobody cared if a few cits vanished. None of that would matter, though, if the great compromise broke down on his watch.

Olivia

"**Priority** override." Central's voice spoke directly into Olivia's brain. "Stand by for a new assignment."

Her heartbeat accelerated. While she was sorry for Merryweather, she was a professional. Death was just death, but an assignment meant money. A second assignment so soon after the first could just mean that she'd taken a big step up in the queue, might even mean she'd start making the kind of money her mentor, Paul Shenker, talked about when she'd been his apprentice.

"Accept," she said, even before she knew the job.

Central rattled off the details—an intellectual property dispute this time.

Olivia could hardly believe her luck. IP paid, and was therefore usually reserved for the most senior cops.

According to central, two ratepayers had gotten into a dispute over a piece of code they'd each worked on. Idiotically, their intellectual property contract failed to allocate proportions of ownership and they couldn't agree on whether the man who'd provided most of the code, or the woman who'd written the small but clever algorithms, should receive the majority of the royalties.

As a potentially invaluable bonus, Olivia's assignment included five one hundredths of a percent of any eventual royalty stream. She'd heard of cops who had retired on the basis of royalty streams earned during their work but she'd never been offered one herself.

For once, timing actually worked for her. Since she was already out on assignment, police central wouldn't have to spring for an extra transportation allowance.

She rerouted back to centercity, heading to the arbitration courts jointly owned by the insurance companies. Once she left the train, she re-programmed her police tunic from its usual solar-absorbing black to a more fashionable dark red color—despite the sacrifice in solar efficiency. When dealing with high-status ratepayers, it was important to be seen as an equal, someone whom they could talk to without excess condescension, and black was such a citizen color.

The mediation turned out to be easy—and she got another 100% completion bonus. She grinned as she took the rail north, away from centercity. This had to be a sign that her life was turning around.

She couldn't think of anyone she'd rather share her fortune with than her family and, rather than return to her own small homespace, she connected through to her mom. Time to provide the whole family with a first-class meal construction. Family was just the thing to get the ugliness of five deaths out of her mind.

Julia

"**But** you have to come over for dinner tonight. I invited this nice young man who's invented the most wonderful wine flavorant." Julia's mother was in full matchmaking mode.

For just a moment, Julia considered it. She was a food designer herself. It would be fun to brainstorm with a guy. Then there were the possibilities for stirring up design variations on the whipped-cream-on-naked-body theme. One thing she could count on, her mother wouldn't try to hook her up with anyone who wasn't physically perfect—not that any ratepayers weren't physically perfect. Not a lot of point in having money if you didn't use it to take care of yourself.

"Sorry." Julia pulled up her calendar in hopes she could manage a convincing excuse. Perfect. "Can't do it, mom. I've got a free-code meeting."

"Oh, honey. You aren't still doing that? It's passé."

"You talked me into it."

"Last year." Her mother made that sound like the ultimate insult.

"I've got something I want to show them." She paused. "Hey, I've got an idea, how about you try it on the guy you invited over."

"What is it?"

"Self-warming pizza. You never have to worry about it getting cold, so you don't have to heat it so much you burn your mouth."

"But that's brilliant. You can't give it away for free."

"Hank Merryweather made us all try Citizen Slop last week. It's horrible. And those people can't afford to spend their money on IP."

"Maybe they should get jobs, then. When your grandmother was a child, nothing was free."

Julia shook her head. "Mom, I've got to go. I'm already late for the meeting."

She networked to the free-coders, looking forward to finding out if anyone knew what had happened to Merryweather.

"Late as always." Joe, a nerdy guy who'd gotten dramatically less friendly when she'd refused to date him, gave his usual greeting.

"Where's Hank?" another demanded.

Nobody answered, which meant they didn't know even as much as she did.

"Forget Merryweather," she said. "I've got something I want you to try."

She pushed the code for the pizza to the other designers through the network. Obviously they'd have to approve it before it would be fed into their constructors, but she didn't have much doubt they would. She might not be the best food designer in Corporate Dallas, but for sure she was the best in their free-code group.

While the others uploaded their constructors, Julia checked eBay for anything exotic and new. Despite her mother's claims, she wasn't completely indifferent to fashion and everyone knew that natural was in. She entered a bid for a pair of genuine lizardskin thigh-high boots just as her phone signaled that the free-code group was gathering again.

"Good pizza," one of the other women in the group admitted. "I like it that it won't dry out sitting around."

"Complete waste of time." Joe's rejection, a copycat of how Merryweather normally responded to her creation wasn't hindered by his mouth being full of pizza. "You used all sorts of proprietary IP in this. Even if you made your code free, it would still cost users for the underlying modules."

Julia laughed. "Probably ten credits for the whole pizza. Anyone can afford that."

"You're missing the point, Julia. Merryweather's idea is that we work on the underlying modules. That way, we could offer completely free design, or we could create code where we'd get to keep all of the revenue since we wouldn't have to pay for all of the core functionality that everyone needs."

"I'm a food designer, Joe, all right? I designed a pizza that's as good as anything you could make even if you used real tomatoes and cow-udder cheese—"

A chorus of 'eeews' interrupted her.

"Sorry, but that's where cheese originally came from as the rest of you would know if you designed food." A part of Julia's training had involved tasting various 'traditional' foods including even meat, although the animal flesh thing was something she'd never told anybody, especially not her mother.

"Free-code doesn't need self-warming pizza," Joe lectured her. "I'll send you the current library with my annotations on what is needed before we can have even a basic set of capabilities."

"Sure, whatever. Send me the whole thing." It sure seemed like her mother was right. free-code *had* been taken over by losers. Now that Merryweather was gone, she didn't even have a chance to learn his clever coding tricks. It was time for her to back out and get on with her life.

Olivia

A genuine frame and brick house still lay at the core of the Jardan family homespace.

Her great-grandparents had it built in one of Dallas's expansion booms, back when the exploding metroplex had swallowed increasingly distant farming villages and incorporated them into the energy-consuming maw of an early twenty-first century city. But it had been built late enough that retrofitting solar panels, CO_2 collectors, and assemblers hadn't been especially difficult.

Now, of course, a solar panel array covered the entire quarter acre of the property.

She hardly recognized her mother although she'd visited only a month previously.

The blonde held out her arms and pirouetted." Do you like it?"

"What have you done?" She was used to her mother's short dark hair and angular build and could hardly believe the waif-like child with blonde hair down to her knees was actually the same person.

"You know your mother. She always likes to change things." Olivia's father rarely changed at all. He wore the same black citizen coveralls he'd worn ever since she could remember, had the same hairstyle—half-inch spikes of hair sticking straight out from his head like porcupine quills—and the same muscular build that had been in style when he'd been a kid but was so completely out now that the slender dandified look was in.

"But she didn't just do her hair, I mean, she's three inches shorter." That kind of body-mod was more than just a scrub, and it cost a fortune.

Her brother, Sammy, nodded. "According to the Interfaith, that kind of tampering reflects the sin of vanity."

Sammy was one year older than she, but they'd been like twins growing up, sharing games, studying together, and exploring the forest of solar panels that surrounded their homespace.

They'd even applied for police training together but Sammy had scored just under the cutoff. He'd been happy for her, but she couldn't deny their closeness had lessened as she'd moved out on her own and he'd been stuck looking forward to fifty or more years living with the parents.

Perhaps trying to do her one better, Sammy had sworn that he'd become a designer—a forlorn hope if ever there was one. If an entire family chipped in, citizens might, possibly, be able to raise the money needed to pay for designer training sims. But actually becoming a designer required an apprenticeship. And no master designer would ever take a citizen apprentice when there were plenty of ratepayers lining up for the job.

Like so many others his age, Sammy had retreated into the Interfaith, relying more and more on it for guidance and for friendship.

He scowled from Olivia, to their mother, and then back to Olivia.

Their mother seemed oblivious to Sammy's harsh words. She spun around to give Olivia another look.

"It's a brand new sculpt. Fully customizable with painless nanotechnology reconstruction. Want to know the really cool thing? It was *free*."

"Free-code," Sammy interjected. "The Interfaith offers Free, but their code is licensed and tested. Any hacker could throw together free-code and you'd never know what side effects it might have."

"Lucky for me this one worked, then," their mother said. "I'm beautiful."

"I worry that she won't be able to change back," her father admitted.

"Why would I want to go back to my old self? If I get tired of this sculpt, I'll just pick a new design."

"Free-coders are all perverts," Sammy grumbled. "Why do you suppose there are more female sculpts than male?"

"Because women care more about how they look?" Olivia guessed.

"Because they're perverts who plan to grab sexy cits and force them into their fantasies."

"Who cares what they're thinking," her mother fired back. "Besides, Olivia pays our premiums. We're not cits, we're insured."

Sammy glared at her. He didn't need another reminder that his sister had become the family success and Olivia felt vaguely guilty, as if getting a job and earning a few credits was a bad thing.

"Hey guys," Olivia said. "Can we stop the arguing?" She couldn't stop her cop instincts, though, and made sure her mother's transformation hadn't altered the sensor chips implanted in every citizen and ratepayer at birth. Police work was challenging enough. Without secure identification, it would be impossible.

"I got two 100 percent accomplished bonuses today," Olivia said. "So dinner is on me. I thought we'd try something new and different. Top-notch design stuff, even. Live a little."

"Are you sure you can afford that?" Sammy asked. "Ratepayer stuff. Come on. Besides, Interfaith constructs ensure all essential trace element needs are met."

"I'm happy with Interfaith twelve," her father grumbled.

Her mother wrinkled her nose. "Meat and potatoes. Boring. *Bambi and Shamu Rowans* sim-constructed a Roman Orgy meal with stuffed hummingbird, boar raised on acorns, sherbets, and wine. And other stuff, too, I can't even remember. And the entire thing is coded for easy construction even in a citizen-sized constructor. That's what I want."

Olivia suspected her mother had just recited most of an Infoweb advertisement. But if the ad targeted citizens, the meal couldn't be *too* expensive.

"Maybe some wine with the number twelve, dad? To celebrate?" She did a quick look at the royalty rate for the Roman Orgy code, confirmed it was within the budget, and gave her mother a wink. "I'll set the constructor to set up the orgy to you, Mom. And Sammy, don't worry about the money. Tell me what you want—I'll let you know if it's too expensive."

He tousled her hair. "So you've become a success, have you?"

She practically burst with pride. Maybe she needed to come home more often. She'd forgotten how close she and Sammy had been. "Can you believe two 100 percent completion bonuses? In one day?"

"I thought they never gave those out, they always found some way to nickel you down."

"Maybe there was a system bug. I'm enjoying it while I can. What's it going to be, Sammy?"

Despite his platitudes about Interfaith meals, Sammy decided on a Real-Feel™ steak, The Dallas Real-Feel™ Corporation claiming to offer *the ultimate in constructed meat*. Olivia programmed cashew chicken over rice for herself, blowing her budget on spices that were supposed to be close to the complexity of the original recipe from Thailand.

The high-powered constructor she'd coded for her parents earlier that year whipped up all four meals in less than twenty minutes and she carried the packaging to the carbon fiber table.

Olivia had her hand on the heat seal ready to rip it open when her brother put a hand on her arm. "Let us pray."

She glared at him to see if he was kidding, but he looked dead-serious.

"Your brother has been studying on the Interfaith," Olivia's mother cheerfully announced. "No tuition at all. Thanks to his guidance, we've all been praying a lot lately."

"Yeah. A lot." Her father didn't sound nearly as cheerful about it as her mother had.

Like everyone, the Jardans had always used the Interfaith for free code. You could survive with what was free on the Infoweb, but anything beyond bare survival cost—and the Interfaith charged only time and energy.

Evidently Sammy had given a lot more. He droned on for a good five minutes, listing just about every sin, with a bonus stress on gluttony and drunkenness, before letting them finally enjoy their meals.

The food was worth the wait, so Olivia tucked in as soon as Sammy shut up, hoping he wouldn't call for another prayer break once she'd broken the heat seal.

Her father waited until the frenzy of eating had settled down, then smiled at his daughter. "So, Olivia. We want to know about the jobs you did. Two in one day? That's got to be some sort of a record, right?"

"A murder and an intellectual property dispute."

"Anyone famous in the IP?" Olivia's mom was hooked on entertainment sims. The often-wild lifestyles of the rich and famous designers made them perfect subjects for full-body emersion entertainment.

"Neither has done anything big. But the hot pepper flavoring they came up with might be worth something."

"Oh, flavors." Her father shook his head, looking up from his mostly flavor-free Interfaith #12. "Amazing what people will waste their time on. What was the other one? Oh, yeah—someone with insurance got murdered?"

"I'd never heard of the victim, but he was a big-time ratepayer. Lived inside centercity. Four cits somehow got into his homespace."

"Oh, Olivia, that's horrible," her mother said. "Did you have to terminate them yourself? I know how hard that can be on a sensitive person like you."

"I found all four of dead from abusing codes they'd stolen."

Her father belched, then belatedly raised his napkin to his lips. "Excuse me. Ol' Interfaith 12 does give me gas. Drug codes, were they?"

"I assume so."

Sammy's eyes got the faraway look of someone consulting the network, but he snapped back before the conversation headed off in another direction. "The victim's name isn't Merryweather, is it? Hank Merryweather?"

"That the only murder posted today?" The four cits wouldn't be classified as murder. After all, they didn't carry insurance so their deaths had no consequences.

"Only murder in centercity. Good riddance, I say."

"You knew him?" She loved Sammy, but he didn't run in ratepayer circles.

"Of course I didn't know him. You're the only real ratepayer I know. Merryweather was a free-coder."

"More power to him," Olivia's mother interrupted. "People like him are how I could afford this sculpt."

Sammy's knuckles whitened, and he visibly forced himself to relax. "Free-coders aren't just dangerous to themselves, they're dangerous to you, Olivia. Be careful."

She laughed. "One thing for sure, Merryweather isn't going to hurt anyone."

He shook his head. "Free-coders are messing with the Interfaith, with the compromise. If you get caught up in that fight, your career could go down in flames."

Bingo. That was the connection Olivia had been looking for. All four of the cits had requested IET disposal. Now she had a second motive for the murder, which just might be one too many.

"Olivia's received her completion bonus," her mother said. "She doesn't need to get any more involved in this case. Now, can we talk about something more pleasant?"

Shenker

Sgt. Paul Shenker woke up feeling great. Which wasn't especially unusual. His nanobe scrubbers kept him refreshed and his body, at thirty-five, was as healthy as when he'd been in his early twenties.

After stretching, he realized his mood didn't just reflect physical wellbeing—the danger had apparently passed.

He hadn't enjoyed getting a call from Chief Vinson himself. Hadn't wanted to think about Olivia Jardan in danger, and he certainly wasn't comfortable with Vinson's decision that Shenker monitor Olivia's behavior.

Still, Olivia had gone on to her next assignment, apparently forgetting about Merryweather's killers.

He constructed himself a simple breakfast. He'd never admit it to his fellow sergeants, and especially not to the more senior officers, but he enjoyed basic citizen and Interfaith meals, spiced up, at most, with a dab of TrueButter™.

A small alarm chime, played directly on his inner ear, completely disrupted his sense of calm and comfort. That idiot girl hadn't gotten the lesson after all. She was interfering.

He requested a connection.

"Paul." Her smile just about split her face in half. "I was just about to call you."

"Olivia. I've got to—"

"I've been working on a murder case. I tracked down the immediate killers, but I have evidence that indicates there may be more involved."

"Stop." Didn't she know police calls were monitored?

"What's the matter? I thought you'd want to know how I'm using what you taught me."

"You're not to do any more investigation into the Merryweather case. It's closed."

"Come on, Paul. The man is a ratepayer. His premium insurance package justifies a complete investigation. I cracked the AI of the guys who actually killed him. How do you suppose they got into centercity? Four cits? Sure it *looked* like a drug deal, but you and I both know that cit drug deals happen in the outer rings. Even if Merryweather designed them, he wouldn't deal with cits from homespace."

"Olivia, you've got to stop. You're in over your—"

"So, I hacked their AI. These weren't random cits. They're Interfaith Enforcers. They constructed Identikits that included Ratepayer identifications for getting past the centercity barriers. Did you know that could even be done? What I don't understand is why they dropped those Identikits before entering Merryweather's homespace. I never would have been able to track them down if they'd still had those fake IDs."

Whoa. Shenker was intrigued despite himself, and he couldn't resist learning more. "Do you have the Identikit Codes?"

"Sure. Police Pattern Recognition doesn't have anything on them if you can believe that. I'll transmit."

Her PPR might not have identified them, but Shenker had more access than she. "They're CyberNinja™ Specials. One-hour usage only. They may have wasted time before they got to Merryweather's."

"But CyberNinja™ is ratepayer grade. Interfaith Enforcers shouldn't have that.

Cold dread had been growing since he'd heard that chime. Now he could barely keep his voice from shaking. "Don't do anything else until I get there. This sounds like it might be important."

"You think we're onto something here?"

"You have no idea. I'll get there as quickly as I can."

He broke the connection and called Vinson.

"We have a problem."

Martin

"**Dad**. You were right. Your buddy Merryweather's death looks like it's getting complicated."

Martin Reynolds studied his thirteen year-old daughter, Angie. He'd come to depend on her because of her weird ability to travel through the Interfaith, but he feared he might be damaging her by asking too much. "What sort of complicated?"

"Way too many wiggles between Corporate Police and Interfaith Enforcement. Not just Enforcement, either, all the way to the top."

"Does it feel like war?" The Great Compromise had limited it, but friction remained between profit-obsessed corporations and the prophet-obsessed Interfaith.

"I think the cops are going to sacrifice one of their own. They're too worried about Corporate Houston to want to take on the Interfaith."

Martin's grandfather remembered an era where all Texas was united, but that was when people had to ship natural resources around the world. Now, just about anything could be constructed out of a design, energy, carbon, hydrogen, and oxygen—along with a few plentiful trace elements. As a result, the need for larger economic/political entities had vanished, and corporations certainly wouldn't pay for what they didn't need.

"All right. I guess we'd better move, then."

"Again?" Angie had picked up some strange ideas about settling down from her time on the Interfaith. They were ideas no Free Citizen could afford. And Martin and his family had to blend with the Free-cits.

"Again."

"I suppose you're going to try to rescue that cop." Jimmy, at five, was okay with their constant moving, but he couldn't understand why Martin didn't just put on his cape and right wrongs like a masked avenger.

"I have to try."

He scrambled a call through to Olivia Jardan, the cop working the Merryweather case, but her autoanswer refused to accept. He left a message but suspected it would be lost in spam forever.

If her autoanswer was any indication, Jardan was an attractive woman, with short dark hair and olive-colored skin that matched her name. She was also likely to be dead within the next hour and there was nothing he could do about it.

Not that Martin had much use for cops—or time for women. Since he'd taken his job for the Corporate Houston External Relationships Co-Op shortly after Jimmy was born, he'd been on the run, hunted by Corporate Dallas cops. Still, there would be a certain poetic justice in helping a cop escape from her fellow officers.

He shook his head. For that to happen, this Officer Olivia Jardan would have had to take his call, heed his warning. It didn't sound like that was going to happen. Which meant he'd better start thinking about other alternatives. Without his help, Olivia Jardan was dead.

Olivia

Paul Shenker was a smart guy, but he'd apparently forgotten that interns watched their mentor at least as closely as he watched them. His voice had shifted when he'd announced he was coming. He wasn't planning a friendly visit, and he wouldn't stop by and help out.

Abruptly, Olivia remembered her brother's warning. Shenker had called her, not the other way around? She'd *planned* on calling for his help, but she hadn't gotten to it. So he'd known about the case without her telling him.

Her phone recorded everything, of course, so she ran through Shenker's call again, this time noticing the way Paul had tried to shut her up, had practically begged her to keep her words off the air. She'd ridden roughshod over his objections.

"Free-coders aren't just dangerous to themselves, they're dangerous to you, Olivia. Be careful." Her brother's words had turned prophetic.

Somehow she'd gone from investigator to suspect, and she didn't even know what she was suspected of. Being somewhere else when Shenker arrived sounded like an excellent idea.

Olivia forced herself to breathe deeply, sucking in oxygen when she wanted to pant, panic and run. She looked around her homespace. It wasn't much—a hundred and fifty square feet of living space—but it was her home, a space she didn't have to share with anyone. Renting her own homespace in the inner three rings had been another mark of being a ratepayer. Citizens tend to stay with their families unless they're actually kicked out like those enforcers in the outer rings.

Abandoning her home would hurt. Staying, though, seemed likely to hurt even more.

Forcing herself to stay calm, she gathered what few essentials she could carry.

Years before, she'd gone on a weeklong camping trip, way out in the dead southern towns that had once been included in Dallas's sprawl. She'd kept the backpack hanging on her wall as a reminder that she'd wanted to do something like that again—if she ever got the funds.

Now, she yanked the pack down and tried to decide what she'd need if she went on the run.

The computer she'd salvaged from the dead Interfaith Enforcers went first. Her uniform would do well enough for clothing. She hoped there wouldn't be any need for ballistic protection, but the buckyball fabric was memory-enhanced, meaning it would harden into a shield if struck by a projectile. Its officer locator chips would be a problem though, so she constructed a diamond knife and a superconducting breadboard.

Willing her hand not to tremble, she cut out each pin of the implanted chip, connecting them, in turn to the breadboard. The momentary breaks in connectivity shouldn't matter as the suit's natural flex and the nature of the self-actualized wireless packet network meant that lost packets would be retransmitted transparently. As long as no lead was cut for more than two seconds, she was safe.

She stared at her naked body in the mirror and touched the knife to her arm. Her implanted identity chips were grafted to the bones of her upper arm, the interior of a rib, and the pelvic girdle. Cutting them out would be a major operation—one that would incapacitate or kill her, especially as most of her nanobes would cease operating when they detected the lack of an identity signal.

Leaving them in would invite anyone with a scanner to identify her and call the police.

But those chips were designed to respond to a proximity ping, rather than be used for tracking purposes. She'd just have to stay away from cops, and from centercity, of course.

She input a code she'd borrowed from her mother once to make her hair darker and curlier and mashed the resulting nanobe cream into her hair.

The nanobes went to work instantly, entering into the cellular structure of the hair strands, reshaping them, moving mass around, and altering the optical characteristics of the chemical makeup.

As disguises went, it was something out of ancient history.

Her phone warned her that time was getting away from her. She checked her supplies and added a water bottle and assembled a couple of dehydrated foodbars.

Everything fit into the small knapsack with a bit of room to spare.

She hefted it, decided she could lug one more thing, and tossed in the diamond knife.

Central could detect or deactivate her powered police weapons so she couldn't risk them. But she had been a cop for long enough to feel naked without a weapon.

And speaking of naked. She pulled on her butchered uniform, molded the self-healing fabric around the deep cuts where she'd stripped out the identity chips, slung the pack over one shoulder, and sealed her door from the inside, telling her greeter to deny access to anyone, regardless of override.

Shenker had taught her the importance of an escape hatch and she'd made homespace solar panels detachable. Rather than using the door, she went through a panel, then sealed it behind her. A competent police trace would discover the backdoor, but her trick should give her a bit of time.

She'd just finished applying the sealer when Shenker called. He was only a few blocks away.

Olivia forced herself to walk calmly away from her home.

Although a cop has priority, Olivia joined the line at the public constructor less than a block from her homespace, pretended to pay attention to people trying to cut ahead of her, but really watching to see what happened.

"Looks like someone is in trouble."

The hungry-looking man in line behind her pointed at two police vans that pulled up three doors from her homespace and disgorged eight uniformed cops.

They had their masks activated, obscuring their features but also providing a degree of protection from a gas or nanobe attack. As if they feared that *she* might come after *them*.

They surrounded her home but made no effort to enter it.

"Never seen that before," the hungry man said. "Usually they just push their way through. Must be someone important."

"Maybe."

She was a nominal ratepayer, or at least she'd been one until an hour or so earlier. But Olivia was under no illusions of her importance. Through a lot for work, and some serious sacrifice on the part of both her parents and herself, she'd managed cop training, which let her make the huge leap between citizen and ratepayer. Seeing how *real* centercity ratepayers lived the day before had pointed up how trivial she was in the corporate consensus. To a ratepayer like Merryweather, or even Hall and Arndt, the litigants in the dispute she'd moderated, she was indistinguishable from a citizen—just another nonentity with minimal resources and no creative training.

Two minutes after the first cops surrounded her homespace, a small car arrived and Paul Shenker stepped out.

He quickly took over, repositioning the cops who'd secured her homespace's exterior, then walked up to the door.

"I've sent a courier to pick up the IE computer," he lied over her phone. "He should be there now. Go ahead and check his identity, then admit them."

Almost everyone else in the line was looking now, so Olivia hoped she'd be seen as just another morbidly curious citizen.

"Olivia? There seems to be a problem with the connection. It's critical that you open your door and allow us, I mean the courier, access."

The hungry man nudged her. "Line's moving."

Walking backward, she took two steps toward the constructor, but she kept her attention on the police raid.

Shenker, in his courier suit, glared at her greeter, then shook his head and gestured to the other cops.

He must have confirmed through her greeter that she was still inside—at least as far as it knew.

Which told him that she was aware he'd arrived, and that she hadn't bolted.

That seemed good enough for him.

On his orders, the eight lower-ranked cops pulled aerosol containers from their packs, tightened the fastenings on their masks, and sprayed a heavy gray mist over her entire homespace.

"Seen that on the Infoweb," the hungry man told her. "Them's self-replicating nanobes. They'll eat the entire homespace. Anything made of carbon is just chewed up and turned into CO_2. Sort of like a fire, 'cept controlled. Any person in there, well, they're made of carbon too. Enough, anyway that the nanobes will eat them."

Shenker came back on the phone, telling her that they'd send the courier back in half an hour and for her to just sit tight.

Which led her to believe her hungry new friend knew what he was talking about, even if he had learned it from watching entertainment.

It took about half a minute for the self-reproducing nanobes to reach critical mass.

Then, one by one, the homespace's support structures sagged, and the normally rigid solar panels drooped into what had been her home.

When they didn't find her calcium-based skeleton, they'd learn she was still alive. She needed to be somewhere else when that happened.

Vinson

Chief Vinson watched the building collapse on his sim viewer. Shenker had moved quickly and efficiently to eliminate the threat to the consensus. Sure, the Sergeant hadn't been happy about killing his student. Well, Vinson wasn't happy, either. If word got around that cops were killing cops, recruitment could drop and the Police Corporation's profit margins would plummet. But a battle with the Interfaith was unthinkable. Merryweather might have been a ratepayer, but he was still a free-coder. It wasn't just the Interfaith that objected to giving citizens access to code. There were plenty within the CC who believed that free-code was somewhere between a mistake and an abomination.

With Olivia Jardan taken care of, there was the little matter of Paul Shenker. Should he co-opt or terminate the one remaining cop who knew too much?

Vinson brought up the Sergeant's file.

Two minutes later, he smiled. Shenker was desperate to be accepted into ratepayer society. He seemed to believe in the fairy tale of having a ratepayer heiress fall for the hardworking cit, whisk him into the upper reaches of centercity, and surround him with the luxury his citizen family could only have dreamed of.

Vinson nodded to himself, then called his wife. "I need a Junior League type to pay a little attention to a Sergeant Paul Shenker."

His wife wrinkled her nose. "A citizen? You must be kidding."

"Technically, he's a ratepayer."

"Oh, give me a break."

"Come on. You've got to have friends who wouldn't mind slumming, finding out if what they say about cit males is true. We're not talking permanent, just give him a taste."

Maudie frowned. "I'll see what I can do. But you'll owe me."

He sighed. "Add it to your account," then winced when he saw the size of the withdrawal she'd made. Damn.

Olivia

"**Guess** the show is over." The hungry man nudged her to move up in the line. "If I was the type to settle down, I'd use the PC to construct me a couple of solar panels and a miniconstructor of my own. Then I'd put down stakes on that piece of land the cops just cleared. Plenty of good sunlight there. Not too many ratepayers want to move this far from centercity, so a clever citizen could have himself a property for months, maybe years before anyone knew. You'd get evicted eventually, most likely. But a year or two of being left alone is worth a lot."

"Why not go for it?" Olivia suggested. "Wouldn't it be nice to be able to avoid the lines at the public constructor?"

He shook his head as if she'd tried to fly a trick question by him. "Person gets to be my age, they realize lines aren't so bad. Call me old-fashioned. Still, I'd rather talk to real people from time to time than always sit in my chair and sim my day away. 'Sides," He gestured at the cops waiting for the last of Olivia's homespace to evaporate. "'Sides, that particular space is generating a bit too much corporate attention. Know what I mean?"

"I'm with you."

"Must have messed with a ratepayer," the hungry man guessed. "I remember right, was a pretty girl lived there. She looked something like you, come to think of it."

Olivia forced her heart to still. "Maybe we use the same sculpt."

"That's probably it. Used to be only ratepayers could sculpt." He examined her more closely. "I'm thinking that dead woman had better hair than you. Always kept it neat and shiny the way a man likes. Costs a few bucks to get that natural look, don't you know?"

"I guess."

"Maybe she thought she was too good, shot down a ratepayer."

"You think something like that could have happened?" Olivia was pleased that her trick with her hair had worked, but she took the comment about her airs to heart. She'd need to look more servile if she were going to fit into the lower stratum of citizenry, which was what she'd just become.

"Hell, yeah. They pay the police salaries. Like the ratepayers say, there'll always be more citizens."

Paul Shenker strode around her ruined homespace shouting out orders, urging the cops to complete the job and find her remains. She couldn't see his face, but he looked like he was treating this like any other job. The year she'd spent as his trainee apparently meant nothing at all. The sense of betrayal almost overcame her composure.

She inhaled, then expelled all of the air from her lungs and stepped forward another space in the line.

She dared not cry. Cops might ignore citizens at the public constructors, but a woman balling her head off would attract attention. Shenker's actions were his problem, she reminded herself. His betrayal wasn't about her. She had been doing the job he'd taught her to do.

"Think she got out?" She tried to keep her voice casual.

The hungry man shook his head. "They surrounded the place. You saw the lead cop check to make sure the seals were still in place, didn't you? She's dead."

When Olivia's turn came at the public constructor, she requested a pair of roller blades. She was going to need to move and getting on the rail meant being scanned, identified, and caught.

The constructor was pumping out the last of the glossy black footwear when her phone signaled.

Paul.

Her tongue started to shape the accept code, but she cut off the word before she could vocalize it. They couldn't know they'd missed her this quickly. The cops would have to wait for the nanobes to self-disable, and then they'd need to check through all of the inorganic remains in her destroyed homespace. But Shenker had always stressed one thing: double-check. And that was almost certainly what he was doing now.

She listened as he dumped his message into her system.

"Listen, babe. Central seems to be overreacting to my decision to send them information on the Identikits you located. If you get this, get away from your homespace and contact me so I can keep you safe. I just got word that the police have gotten a CC override allowing them to vaporize your entire place—with you in it if possible."

She resisted the temptation to laugh. If she hadn't seen Paul taking the lead in destroying her place, she might have fallen for the fake concern of his call.

She stepped into the constructed blades, let them mold themselves to her feet, and rolled off. Fortunately, blades, along with citizen slop, were available for free.

Shenker

Paul Shenker shut down the connection and glared at the eight cops he'd brought for what should have been a routine job.

Olivia Jardan was a good cop, but she wasn't the goddamned Invisible Woman. She couldn't have left after he'd sealed her homespace, but she certainly wasn't inside. The eater nanobes were specifically designed to leave undamaged skeletons for identification. Only there hadn't been any identification because there wasn't a skeleton.

Olivia was still out there.

He'd left a message on the off-chance she'd run an errand, but the odds of that were somewhere close to zero. She had picked something up in his voice and run.

"Can't find anything, Sergeant," one of the cops reported. "I'm starting to think there's nothing to find."

Shenker had been thinking that for a good five minutes, which might be why he'd made sergeant and this cop hadn't. Unfortunately, because he was sergeant, he was the one stuck calling Vinson.

The chief of police answered immediately. "Is she taken care of?"

"She must have taken warning."

Vinson narrowed his eyes. "Meaning *you* warned her?"

Shenker stiffened. "I relayed a copy of the call to central for semantic analysis. As you can see, I did hit stress level three once, but this isn't out of the normal range when dealing with a murder case."

Vinson looked like he wanted to tear someone a new orifice and Shenker figured the guy on the other end of the line was the lucky winner. Instead the chief shook his head. "Okay, I think I've got it. Jardan's brother, Sammy, is working his way up in the Interfaith. They had dinner together last night. During that dinner, he searched Merryweather and link-connected him to—"

"May I ask how this helps, sir?" Interrupting the boss was high-risk, but Shenker didn't want to know about whatever political crap was happening. Chief Vinson had said that silencing Olivia was essential in heading off a civil war when Corporate Dallas needed all of its resources to fight Corporate Houston. That was enough for him—more than enough unless he made himself highly useful.

"It means you're off the hook," Vinson said, "at least partially. Jardan's brother, Sammy, could have made her suspicious. Your unusual request would have tied to that."

"I see. So, she ran."

"So she ran." Vinson leaned forward until he seemed about to pop out into Shenker's optical nerve. "Now, Sergeant, here's the deal. Track her down, silence her, and silence anyone she contacts with whatever information she has. We know now that she stole the computer from the Enforcers who killed Merryweather, and we know that computer might tie them back to the Interfaith. We can't have ratepayers worried that the Interfaith will hunt them down like citizens if they violate any of those silly religious prescriptions, can we?"

Shenker's heart dropped. Vinson shouldn't be telling him this. "No, sir."

"Oh, one other thing."

His heart dropped further. Was he now disposable? "Yes, sir."

"My wife is giving a little party this evening."

"You want me there to provide security, sir?"

"I want you there as a guest, Lieutenant."

Lieutenant? Not likely. Former citizens didn't become Lieutenants.

"Don't look surprised, Lieutenant Shenker. We've been watching you. Hunt down Jardan and you'll be confirmed in rank, with back pay, including membership in the profit sharing bonus pool effective January."

Vinson didn't have to tell Shenker what failure would mean. Being busted back to private was best-case. Taking Jardan's spot in the recycler seemed a lot more likely.

"Thank you, sir."

"Don't thank me in words, Lieutenant. Thank me by getting the job done."

"I will, sir."

While his cops continued to comb through the empty ruins of a homespace, Shenker nudged a couple of citizens off a bench near the public constructor and sat.

He'd taught Olivia everything she knew so he should be able to figure her out, predict her moves. If he were Olivia and he were on the run, where would *he* go? Olivia knew he'd monitor her phone and her spending. She'd stay off the rail because she wouldn't want to be scanned. But traveling on foot would be too slow. So, she'd need personal transportation. Perhaps a bicycle?

His phone beeped, a low priority code indicating a call from an AI and he almost sent it to storage, but it was coded as related to Sammy Jardan. Considering what he'd learned from Vinson, he took the call.

Twenty seconds later, he had his answer. Her brother, supposedly, had just downloaded roller blades right outside Olivia's homespace.

Shenker pulled up a map of the third ring, calculated how far she could have traveled since the blades had been constructed, and signaled for more cops.

Then he entered the code Vinson had sent him, adding Lieutenant bars to his police tunic. Not bad.

Martin

"**Your** duck is heading due north. Approximately twelve KPH."

"Thanks, Nate." Martin Reynolds set a virtual pin on the map his phone showed. It wasn't the official map. Or rather, it had once been the official map, but he'd overlaid it with those parts of reality that the CC either ignored or refused to believe existed—like thousands of free-cit homespaces out in what the CC thought of as desert.

Olivia Jardan didn't know it, but she was heading into a cul-de-sac. Streets the CC had marked off as available had been overrun by squatters who ignored the CC, betting that the cops wouldn't bother enforcing their rights of way out past the fourth zone.

Martin made a couple of calls, had three more paths blocked off, and hurried his kids along the small creek that fed into what had once been the Trinity River.

When they got there, Angie stopped and stared. "Look at all that water. Why doesn't someone just take it?"

"Someone does," he said. "Dallas Water and Hydrogen Corporation has a dam downstream a bit. Anyone tries to take more than a gallon or so will pay it back to the cops, with interest."

"Seems to me we have as much right to it as some corporation. Water just falls from the sky."

"When you're a grownup, I'll let you take that message to the CC. For now, though, keep walking."

"Oh, dad. My feet hurt."

"Yeah," Jimmy echoed. "We've been walking all day."

"You've been walking for an hour. Come on, we're almost there. I'll let you play in the creek. You can even go fishing."

"Fishing?" Jimmy looked hopeful, but Angie rolled her lip up with a sneer. "That's disgusting."

"Pick up some dead branches as you go," he said.

"For fishing poles?"

"For the carbon. We won't have time and I want to construct someplace we can rest."

"Sounds better than fishing," Angie agreed. "It's hard to sim into the Interfaith while we're walking."

"Don't spend too much time listening to that stuff."

"It's fun."

Martin worried about her. Teen years were hard for any child, but they were especially hard for a girl without a mother. Then again, the life of a spy wasn't exactly safe for any age.

"They're trying to load memes in your brain," he said.

"I don't let them."

He didn't think it was that easy, but Angie had helped him so much with what she'd learned over the Interfaith, he could hardly complain. "Well, be careful."

Olivia

The further north Olivia went, the more she felt like an invader, the more eyes she sensed looking at her from out of tiny homespaces with barely enough surface area to power even the most basic construction.

Not all ratepayers lived in centercity, but not even a nominal ratepayer like Olivia would live out past the fifth ring.

She'd had to duck under cover a few times as police drones passed overhead. Even so, she'd covered some serious distance and was now out in the ninth ring—the last ring. From here, Corporate Dallas sort of petered out, drifting into dry prairie, studded with the crumbling remains of ancient homespaces from the previous century.

She paused to wipe the sweat from her forehead and heard the burble of a nearby stream, mingled with the screech of birds, and suddenly realized how hungry and thirsty she was.

Walking carefully through unfamiliar foliage that might have been something edible, but might also be something poisonous to the touch, Olivia dipped her water bottle into the creek's cold water and sucked a long drink through the bottle's nanofilters.

It was lucky she'd taken that long-ago hiking trip, because entertainment sims tended to leave out practical realities like filtering contaminants from the water. From the indicators on her bottle, this stream wasn't as deadly as some, but it certainly wasn't healthy.

Her thirst satisfied, she refilled the bottle, munched on one of her foodbars, and settled down on a large flat rock shaded by a stand of bamboo.

She hadn't gotten away, but she had traveled far enough and fast enough that she'd left Shenker a huge area to search. Slowing down now would give him time to catch up, but she needed to recover, and this was as good a hiding place as any, at least for a while.

One thing she felt practically certain of-nobody was going to stumble across her by accident.

While her body craved the rest, her mind raced like a taxi stuck in the mud—going like crazy but moving nowhere.

In just a couple of hours, she'd gone from an admittedly low-status ratepayer to a free-cit.

Unlike even the lowest scrub, she couldn't approach public constructors because they'd scan her and send out an alarm. She wouldn't get away with listing herself as Sammy again, she was certain of that. And she couldn't call on her family or friends for help. Even if she trusted someone, her phone was certain to be monitored.

Thinking of her family turned the shakes into shudders. Until now, she'd known she could always return to her parents' home. They'd welcome her in, give her a bit of energy from their solar array, and share code with her. Even her brother would welcome her—maybe more now that she'd failed and he wouldn't have to worry about being compared to an actual ratepayer in the family.

For the first time in her life, Olivia had no one to turn to for support.

Her shudders threatened to turn into enormous sobs and Olivia sucked in a breath and lectured herself on self-control. She didn't have time to waste, and couldn't afford to squander salt and other trace elements by crying.

Her talk did about as much good as would lecturing the Texas sun to beat a little less intently.

The incongruence of worrying about salt while sobbing her heart out pulled Olivia from her funk.

Free-cits didn't all starve. As a cop, an ex-cop, anyway, surely she had survival skills.

First, though, she needed a plan.

She closed her eyes and tried to think. Plenty of free-cits would turn her in for half a credit, or sell her to entertainment corporations that seemed to have an unending appetite for attractive women who could be forced into unnatural acts. She had to find some way to completely disappear.

She was thinking so hard, she didn't even hear him approach.

"You slumming, rater? Looking for a little action?"

Olivia fell off her rock and grabbed for her diamond knife, opening her eyes in time to see a little kid, a big stick in his hands, no more than two feet from her. He could have hit her with that stick before she'd even been aware she wasn't alone.

"I don't think a kid can provide the kind of action I need."

The child couldn't have been more than five but his eyes looked like those of a hundred-year-old, holding too much knowledge, too much worldliness.

"Lots of raters like 'em young. 'Specially the ones who come out this far."

"I'm not a ratepayer."

He laughed. "Nice jacket. You don't get code like *that*, you're not a rater."

Admitting the truth could get her killed. Lying, though, seemed like an even worse approach. "I'm not slumming, I'm running. I need a place to stay. Is there anyone I can talk to? Can you help me?"

"You going to pay? Got any code?"

If she'd thought about it at all, she would have known free-cits would be desperate for code. Given code and energy, anything was possible. Without code, Texas's abundant sunshine meant only sunburn and carcinogenic rays.

But she hadn't thought things through, hadn't even considered downloading practical codes to exchange for help before she'd run.

"I've got some food. Some foodbars."

"Code for foodbars?" His smile made him look younger, something closer to the age he'd probably attained.

"Not code. Fully constructed."

The kid's smile disappeared. "That's not as good. Show me what you got."

She displayed the tubes and he shook his head. "We get those from the Interfaith. My sister Angie *likes* listening to the sermons. She orders up the food for everyone so *we* don't have to listen to it. Guess she's not so bright, huh?"

Olivia tried to remember if she'd been so precocious, so articulate when she'd been five. She was pretty sure she hadn't been.

"I still need to talk to someone. An adult."

The kid shook his head firmly. "No pay, no play. That's rule one. If you weren't a rater, you'd know that."

"That's rule number one for the ratepayers, too. Guess you guys aren't so different after all."

He worked his mouth a bit, but must have decided he didn't have a smart answer for her. Instead, he turned and ran off, ducking into what she'd thought was an abandoned shack. Although no solar panels showed, apparently it wasn't abandoned after all.

She followed him to the door, but couldn't find anything that looked like a greeter.

Which was odd. Even if they didn't want visitors, most people would put their greeter someplace conspicuous. That way, the greeter could tell prospective visitors to go away.

"Hello." She tried a generic opening, hoping that she'd be able to spot the greeter when it answered.

Instead, the door opened and a young-looking woman stepped out.

"You bothering Jimmy?"

"Is that the little boy who just ran in there?"

"Yeah. So?"

"I didn't mean to bother him. I need to talk to an adult."

She scanned the young woman and came up with an out-of-Dallas response. No help there.

She decided to hazard a guess. "Are you Citizen Angie? Citizen Jimmy's sister?"

"What did Jimmy tell you about me?"

"Just that you listen to sermons on the Interfaith."

The girl pouted. "He thinks it's funny, but it's not. If you spend time on the Interfaith, go deeper into the mesh, you earn soul credits. You can use them for code that isn't available for just anyone."

Angie's eyes took on a dreamy look. "Besides, it's like they're talking just to you. They make you feel special, like you're part of something big, something that makes a difference. The Interfaith isn't like the sims city-cits waste their lives on, where all they do is pretend to be someone they're not all day. I mean, life is boring enough without that. And who'd want to be a boring designer?"

If Olivia hadn't been sure Angie was a kid before, the emphasis she put on the *boring* would have persuaded her. Only a teenager thinks of boredom horrible. Adults know there are far worse alternatives.

Martin

His kids were doing a good job.

Martin Reynolds hadn't been too worried about that. He'd accessed Olivia Jardan's records and she'd come up relatively clean, for a cop. But people act differently around children. Before he trusted her, before he took the chance that this entire caper was a setup, designed as a trap for anyone organizing free-cits, he wanted to get a good look at her.

If he was wrong about her, Jardan was going to find herself at the bottom of the stream learning to breathe water.

"I'm in trouble and I need a place to stay," Jardan told his daughter. "Could I talk with your parent or supervising adult?"

"Got any code? Nothing for nothing, you know."

A cop on the run wouldn't have much. If she agreed too easily, Martin would know she was lying.

Olivia shrugged. "Your brother asked me the same question. I may have a few codes on an AI I have with me. It might be dangerous, though, unregistered stuff."

Angie squinted at her. "Any designs in particular?"

"Don't know. It didn't belong to me before yesterday. Do you *need* anything in particular?"

Angie pawed one bare foot on the ground, as if contemplating whether to run. "You aren't a free-cit are you, you're a rater. You look like a spy, too. What's that tunic you have on?"

"I'm not a spy. I lost my homespace and I have nowhere else to go."

"You used to be a rater? Do you know how to code? Dad says we're always willing to take in designers."

"Do I look like a designer? But maybe I could talk to your dad. Maybe there's something I could offer him."

Martin grinned to himself. She was cute, spunky, and she'd survived a police crackdown. If he were looking for some fun, there was a lot she could offer him. Unfortunately, this wasn't the time for fun. Corporate Dallas was lurching toward an economic war with Corporate Houston and that always meant shutting down whatever free-cits they could find. Considering how raters treated free-cits, they were right not to expect a lot of loyalty from them.

"Gonna have to search you," Angie told the cop. "It would be like a rater to sneak in and then assassinate my dad."

"A rater? You're kidding. They wouldn't bother dirtying their hands."

"That's what you say."

"Whatever." Olivia held out her arms and let Angie approach her with the hand scanner Martin had constructed for her.

Martin leaned forward. If Olivia was part of a trap, she'd have to react to Angie's scanner.

Olivia did nothing, although both women jumped a bit when the scanner beeped.

"What's that?"

"Oh." Olivia opened an invisible pouch on her tunic and removed a deadly-looking diamond blade. "Just—"

The second the scanner had given its audio alarm, Martin had leapt for the back entryway.

He knocked the knife away from the cop, protecting his daughter.

"See, I was right," Angie said. "You are here to kill him. Right, dad?"

Olivia

Olivia struggled to subdue her automatic reaction, which was to counter the free-cit's attack, disable him and make sure he wouldn't attack again.

Two daily hours of biofeedback training, plus two weekly hours of live sparring against other police candidates and sparring robots honed a cop's reactions until she could move without thought.

She pulled one hand short just as her fingernails brushed against the free-cit's eyeball, and turned her armbreak into a simple submission hold.

"What's this about coming to assassinate me?"

"Sir, you are guilty of assault."

"From what you told my daughter, you aren't a cop any more. No crime without insurance, right?"

"If I were still a cop, you'd be a blind guy with one arm. So, what was that attack about?"

"You pulled a knife on my daughter."

Olivia took a calming breath. "I was giving it to her. Her scanner located it. It isn't intended as a weapon, just as a useful tool."

Angie's father had chosen a rugged mountain-man sculpt. She'd seen designs like that in the sims, although the muscle bulk was generally seen as decadent and wasteful—qualities not welcomed among cits and considered gauche among ratepayers.

Still, she had to admit it held a certain appeal. Perhaps that was because, as a cop, *as an ex-cop*, she reminded herself, she appreciated the benefits of muscle more than the average citizen.

She released his arm and stepped back, waiting to see if he'd attack again. That's when she noticed that little Jimmy, the kid who'd led her here in the first place, held a projectile weapon of some kind. He might be only five, but his two-handed grip and wide stance hinted he'd used a weapon before—and that he was likely to hit what he aimed at.

"Want to put that down, Jimmy?"

"If my dad says so."

Mountain-man nodded. "Let's hear what she has to say before we do anything rash."

Jimmy kept the weapon pointed at her until his dad had backed away.

"Now," the mountain-man said, "suppose you tell us your story."

It was a test, of course. For whatever reason, paranoid or practical, this stranger actually thought the cops would waste their time tracking down a free-cit. Still, she had nothing to hide.

"I was a cop following up on a murder investigation. Something about the murder of a ratepayer didn't make sense, Citizen, uh," she wasn't going to call him Citizen Mountain-Man to his face.

"Martin, Martin Reynolds."

"Citizen Martin."

"Just Martin."

"Right, Cit—uh, Martin." All her life, first names had been reserved for family, for mentors, and for best friends. And of course for sims, where citizens could emulate the strange lifestyles of those who'd lived hundreds or thousands of years before them. "You can call me Offi… uh, just Olivia."

His smile would have melted the mythical global icecap, but Olivia was too canny to fall for physical sex appeal. Anyone with a few credits could dial themselves up a sexy physical body. A new face cost even less.

That thought reminded her of her mother. Abruptly, the tears she'd forced down threatened to well up again.

She swallowed hard.

"Look, Martin. I want to be honest with you. The cops will probably continue looking for me. If you help me, you might be in trouble. But if you don't want to help me, at least tell your children to stop harassing me."

"I didn't say I wouldn't help you, Olivia."

"Oh. Well in that case, I'm sorry I overreacted."

"But the kids say you don't have any code and you aren't a designer. I'm wondering what you have to trade."

She sighed. "Just tell me what you want."

Yep, his expression was a definite leer. "How about, I take a rain check? You can owe me for later."

"You want me to just promise to do whatever for you? Without even knowing what it is?"

"You have a better suggestion?"

She was dead if she didn't get help. A night, or even a week as mountain-man Martin's sex slave didn't sound too bad in comparison. "All right. Hide me and I'll owe you whatever, whenever."

"Deal. First thing, we need to do something about your ID tag."

"Sure. Then we'll whip up a cold fusion generator so we won't have to leave out telltale solar panels. I don't know what your game is, Martin, but

I'm not stupid. ID chips are forever, short of nanosurgery. And that kind of nanosurgery is an economic capital offense."

He grinned. "Is that what they told you in police training?"

"Are you saying it isn't true?"

Martin's smile was nice, but Olivia didn't have much use for nice, and didn't have any trust at all for guys who tried to use physical charm to get what they wanted. "Oh, it's true all right. Except that nanosurgery is so simple anyone with two weeks of training could code it."

"Assuming—"

"Exactly. Assuming they didn't mind violating C.C. rule number one."

For a crazy instant, Olivia let herself hope. With a new ID tag, she'd be invisible to Shenker and the hordes of cops he had out looking for her. But the instant faded. "Two weeks of designer training is two weeks more training than I have."

"Two weeks more than any citizen gets," Martin said cheerfully.

"Luckily for you, I come from a ratepayer family. I had a month of design training before I washed out."

"Well, Mr. Reynolds, how surprising that your family isn't listed in the Corporate Dallas ratepayer roster."

"I didn't say I was from Dallas."

Olivia's heart dropped. There had been rumors about a possible economic war with Corporate Houston. It certainly made sense that Houston would send agents provocateur to stir up free-cits. "I'm not a traitor."

"Corporate Dallas turned on you, Officer Jardan."

Okay, he'd known who she was all along." Even so—"

"I'm not asking you to fight against your city. Corporate Houston didn't pick this fight. We're closer to the equator than C.D. We've got the ocean in our backyard for minerals and water. We're prepared to live and let live. Is it really treason to want to be left alone? If so, maybe you should have stayed in your homespace and let your fellow cops turn you into gray goo."

Olivia felt as if she should be waving her hands in the air to retain balance. One way or another, her decision now would determine the rest of her life—but it didn't seem likely she'd have a very long life, whichever decision she made.

Julia

Julia couldn't believe Merryweather had been dumb enough to get killed by a bunch of drug or sim-addled citizens.

Unfortunately, the Infoweb made it clear he'd not only been killed, but that his free-code project was somehow responsible. The ratepayer forums seemed filled with people criticizing free-code, pointing out the dangers of allowing non-corporate code into the hands of citizens and then using Merryweather's death as proof of their concept. If Julia had been the paranoid sort, she would have believed the whole thing was orchestrated.

Not that it mattered. In this environment, being associated with free-code could cost her job. She called Joe to let him know she quit—and got a 'code not known' message.

Joe might not put her on his call-through list, but even spam should be sent to autoanswer. *Code not known* was an error message that meant someone was in serious trouble—and Julia suspected she might be the one.

It was time to get away from her officespace. Besides, there was supposed to be a physical shop in Cityplace where you could buy actual spider-silk tops and cow-leather shoes. She was up for her year-end review in a couple of weeks, and the committee would be impressed by that kind of display. To make partner, it wasn't enough to be an excellent designer, you had to show that you were the kind of ratepayer who could mingle with the elite and negotiate with the hardest-nosed in the consensus.

A bit of conspicuous consumption was just the thing to cheer her up.

Because it was a beautiful day, she walked the two kilometers. First, though, she turned her dress to a brilliant shade of white and silver. Reflecting all that sunlight would be a perfect way to proclaim to the world that she didn't have a concern.

She smiled at the ratepayers she saw about their leisure, ignoring the few citizens allowed into the city for physical labor.

She could have sent one of her sponsored citizens to shop for her, stayed in touch by phone so she could see whatever the woman was looking at. With so much going wrong, Julia needed to feel the textures and smell the leather. Besides, she'd been outbid for the boots she'd wanted on eBay. Maybe she could find the perfect set in a physical shop. Nobody would talk about free-code if she showed up in a pair of thigh-high genuine slimy-lizard-based snakeskin boots. Even thinking about it gave her shivers. Completely cool.

Shenker

Paul Shenker studied the sun. At eight in the evening, it was a fiery ball of red sitting glumly near the horizon.

This far out, sunset meant danger. With darkness, ratepayers would come slumming, looking for action their TrueEros™ robots couldn't deliver. And the lowest elements of society, scrubs and free-cits, preyed on those ratepayers—and were preyed on in turn.

But darkness also brought out the rats. Within an hour of darkness, some scrub would sidle up to a cop and betray Olivia's location. It was as certain as the sunset itself. Scrubs had no sense of honor. Shenker, with the citizen past he tried so hard to obscure and forget, was painfully aware of that. It was no wonder ratepayers looked at citizens as practically inhuman—many of them acted that way.

His phone chimed a warning he needed to get ready if he was going to attend Vinson's wife's soiree.

Shenker had his uniform tunic expel all of his collected sweat and dirt into a nearby public constructor, checked his reflection in the glossy black of a solar panel, and grabbed the rail into centercity.

Even on the rail, his lieutenant's bars made a difference. Citizens moved away, made room for him in ways they hadn't that morning when he'd been a sergeant. Ratepayers nodded, treating him not quite as an equal—he was still a cop—but as something they recognized as being a part of their universe.

And it only got better when he stepped into the magical atmosphere of Maudie Vinson's party.

Actual living plants, fed by a water mist, cooled the atmosphere and added a scent that ordinary citizens, and nominal ratepayers like Shenker knew himself to be, could only imitate with designer products. Beautiful women mingled with attractive men, many of them wearing clothing that might have been hand-produced from sheep hair, caterpillars, or actual cow skin. Revulsion warred with envy as he watched the confident way they spoke.

Well, they *should* be confident—they were centercity ratepayers. They were the children of stockholders, the designers who created the fads. He even recognized a couple from an Infoweb reality sim.

From Shenker's perspective the variety in the people was almost shocking. He tended to forget that ratepayers generally stuck with their own faces, their own bodies—enhanced and scrubbed, of course, by the best in nanobe technology but still recognizably unique. Only citizens favored full sculpts, which tended to make them fairly uniform.

Hostess Maudie Vinson chose to display the mature beauty of a woman in her thirties (although Shenker thought she might actually be quite a bit older than that given she had a twenty-year-old daughter). She welcomed him at the door, introduced him to her daughter, Maurissa, and pointed him to the buffet.

The buffet defeated him. His lower-class morality was showing, but those were obviously unprocessed plant life. And honeycomb? What if he found a bee stuck in the middle of one of those little cells?

To avoid the embarrassment of an empty plate, he took a couple grapes and a strawberry dipped in chocolate.

"I hope you're getting ready for the corporate war, general."

Shenker spun in recognition of a voice familiar to citizen and ratepayer alike in Corporate Dallas—Reverend Ariel, head of the Dallas Interfaith.

"Lieutenant, sir. I'm a Lieutenant. Surely it won't come to actual war, though."

The Reverend laughed. "You're thinking of short-term losses. But Corporate Houston has been a thorn in our side for decades—they need to be taught a lesson. And I know I'm talking out of school, but their Interfaith is not up to standard."

"I thought the Interfaith was pretty much the same everywhere." The Great Compromise hadn't been a Dallas thing. Ratepayers were to be left alone, and they in turn would allow the Interfaith free run in managing the citizens—as long as they provided basic services. Nobody wanted citizens rioting.

"The Interfaith has the same content everywhere, yes," Ariel said. "But in Dallas, the Interfaith is a partner to the Corporate Consensus. In Houston, it's a lapdog, rolling over whenever the corporate leaders tell it to."

Shenker smiled. All his life he'd fantasized about rubbing elbows with the most elite ratepayers in the city, discussing the key issues of the day and here he was. "Well it is the corporations who generate the city's wealth, after all."

Reverend Ariel shrugged. "So far as that goes. But think how much your insurance rates would rise if the Interfaith didn't provide something for the average citizen. How easily they could become like the Roman mobs of ancient days."

"Or maybe they'd work harder, make something of their lives rather than just sitting around watching their reality sims."

A new group of guests swept toward the buffet table and two of the newcomers buttonholed the Interfaith leader while an attractive female caught Shenker's eye. "Well hello. I haven't seen you around before."

He barely resisted the urge to pinch himself. Beautiful ratepayer women did *not* flirt with ex-citizen cops.

He sipped a glass of champagne that didn't taste quite right, until he realized it was made from actual grown grapes rather than constructed. Then he set the glass down in a hurry and danced first with the woman who'd flirted with him and then with two more. He was living his dream.

He was almost tempted to ignore the alert when it finally came. But he made his farewells and headed out. Sure enough, Jardan had been seen.

Olivia

Martin's nanobes hit Olivia harder than a kick from a boxing bot.

The Corporate Houston spy grasped her shoulders and held her still as she convulsed and her stomach spewed everything she'd eaten in the past week.

"The worst is over," he promised. "Keep breathing."

"I'd rather just die. I thought you said this was simple."

"I said it was easy to code, I never said it was easy to endure. Now try to relax. I'll teach you to burn new IDs into your phone. You've got to ensure a valid checksum. One of the dumbest mistakes a free-cit can make is to ignore the checksum and walk around with a random number."

"I can't—"

He ignored her objections, overrode her phone's firewalls, and poked a tidy little algorithm into its memory.

Hearing his voice in her phone despite her refusal to accept the call felt like rape to Olivia. But the only alternative was to wait until her fellow cops tracked her down.

Martin had shown her he could help but she didn't believe their meeting was coincidence. The odds that a Corporate Houston spy just happened to run into a Corporate Dallas cop on the run were lower than winning the citizen lottery and being made ratepayer for a year.

She gritted her teeth and implemented the override.

Ten minutes later, her body stopped twitching.

Half an hour after that, Olivia felt vaguely human. Some other human, perhaps, but a member of the species and very much alive.

"That was—"

Martin had been coding his constructor but stopped. "If you're solid enough to talk, you're connected enough to walk. Let's pack up. We've got to get out of here,"

"But—"

"People noticed you as you skated through the rings. The cops are offering a nice reward and someone will try to collect."

She pushed herself up from the ground, then sagged back down. "I can't move. Maybe tomorrow."

"You've been too busy to tune into the Infoweb, but you're something of a celebrity. Cop gone rogue. There's a new sim out called 'Cop Chase.' Citizens get to play the hunter tracking you down, or play you trying to get away."

"My mother is probably playing it. She loves those games."

"You don't get it, do you? This is a cop trick—a hundred thousand players are looking for you and the game algorithms automatically assess their strategies and transmit the best to police headquarters. It's called a Monte Carlo simulation.

"So," he concluded, "it's the four of us against however many tens of thousands they can trick into playing. And one of us hardly counts."

She smiled. "I guess Jimmy is still a little young for spy stuff."

"Jimmy is fine. I was talking about you. How many times have *you* been on the run?"

"I have experience on the other side."

"You only *think* you do. Do you really think they'd let a junior cop play with rule-breaking stuff? Now, let's go."

Martin made her eat a couple of foodbars and drink a quart of water before they actually went. Then he insisted on checking her knapsack, loading her down with some of his stuff—water, more food-packs, a solar-collecting blanket, and an assortment of small plastic tubes that could only hold active nanobes.

"What are these?"

"Just don't let any break." He carefully molded the fabric of the blankets around the tubes.

"Got it." She'd already come close enough to being turned to gray ooze that morning.

Martin loaded down the kids, then pulled his computer from a socket in the wall, stuck it in his own pack, and walked away from his homespace.

"Step along," he said to both Olivia and his children. "This place will disintegrate soon—there might be some danger."

Two hours later, after three short rail rides and a lot of walking, Olivia decided that the mountain-man build had its advantages.

Martin bulled his way through barriers that would have stopped her—a field of bamboo, a tangle of bois d'arc trees that had once marked a property division, and a rusty barbed wire fence, clearing a path for his children and for Olivia.

Only when they stopped for a rest did the magnitude of the changes in her life hit her.

She'd lost her home, her identity, her savings, her resume, her records. She no longer had access to anything but the most basic phone, Infoweb, and Interfaith services. She wasn't even a real citizen—she was a hunted free-cit.

Martin lifted Jimmy over a concrete retainer wall, affection and concern reflected in his too-handsome face.

Seeing Martin interact with his family reminded her of her own family, now lost to her. She and Sammy had squabbled, her father had driven her to distraction, and her mother's dependence on sims for self-value worried her, but she couldn't imagine life without them.

"Do you think they'll come after my parents and brother?"

Martin set Jimmy down and offered a hand to Angie, but his daughter ignored it, and shot him a dirty look when she scraped her shin on a piece of rusty rebar climbing out of the crumbling concrete.

"Check your systems. There could be tetanus out here."

"Yes, dad." The girl's frustration reminded Olivia uncomfortably of her own attitude.

Martin turned his attention back to Olivia. "I suspect the cops questioned your family closely. Do they know anything about the case you were working on?"

"Only that I got a one hundred percent completion bonus. I bought them a premium-code dinner."

"Then there shouldn't be—"

"Oops. Except my brother knew something about the victim."

"Which victim? The ratepayer, or the four scrubs?"

Now that was a strange question. "The scrubs weren't victims. They were killers. If they hadn't been killed by their greed, it would have been my job to terminate or mind-sculpt them."

Martin shook his head slowly in the darkness. "Are you sure about that, Olivia? Because it seems to me that something, or someone, killed them. Are you absolutely sure it was bad code from the ratepayer that did them in?"

"Of course I'm—" She cut herself off. "Erase that. I'm not sure of anything. I grabbed their computer but haven't had a chance to check it. So, I haven't seen any solid evidence that they'd sent any illicit code to their constructor at all beyond some high-end identikits."

"So maybe they were victims as well."

"They can't be victims. They didn't have insurance. They're just collateral damage."

"I'm going to pretend you didn't say that, giving you the benefit of the doubt of a piss-poor educational system."

"What else is there?"

Martin muttered to himself, then ducked through a doorway opening and into what appeared to be the ruins of an early twenty-first century home.

Brick, mold-damaged actual wood studs, and disintegrating drywall still stood although the roof had long before vanished.

"Are we stopping here?" Angie whined. "I'm tired and sore and I've overloaded my systems. She's got new codes on her computer. Why can't we just go someplace more comfortable?"

"Yes, we're stopping here," Martin said. "For a little while."

Angie opened her pack, took out a water bottle and enjoyed a drink, then directed Jimmy to clear a space for her to rest.

Martin watched the interaction between his children for a moment, a smile playing across his face.

The smile faded when he turned back to Olivia. "I want you to think about what you just said."

"What?" She tried to remember what they'd been talking about. Right, the scrubs. "All I said was they weren't insured."

"So they didn't have any right to call for police help, right?"

She shrugged. "How could they? You don't pay the rate, you don't get the cops. It's as simple as profit and loss." If she'd ever been in doubt, the fees and sliding reward schedule would have cleared up any uncertainty.

"That doesn't mean they aren't victims. Someone killed them."

"Okay, someone killed them. I'm sure their families are very unhappy. I'm sure they wish they'd bought insurance. But they didn't and it's too late now."

"You don't think someone should do something? You don't think there's a need to 'assess and avenge?'"

He said those words like they were a curse.

"You're kidding, right? Who'd pay police corporation rates if the police would investigate whether you paid or not. That's basic economics. And don't tell me it's different in Houston. People make choices. If they want protection, they buy insurance. Sure it's too bad when ratepayers kidnap citizens or force them into sex 3-Ds, but that doesn't happen too often. Besides, thanks to the Interfaith, dealing with citizens at all is gauche. Social disapproval prevents abuse from above, and police enforcement prevents it from below."

He shook his head. "I was hoping for a bit more fervor when I heard a cop had gone rogue."

Tears threatened to spill down her cheeks. "That's the problem—I didn't go rogue. It's all just a big mistake. All I want is to go back to being a cop, pay my premiums, and keep my family safe."

Martin shook his head. "You're not going to get any of those simple dreams. So, maybe you'd better start dreaming about something bigger."

"Like maybe being a cop under Corporate Houston rule?" she asked hopefully.

He shook his head. "You've been tagged as undependable. You're out no matter who's in charge."

She slumped her shoulders. "I might as well have let Shenker gray-ooze me this morning."

"Give it a rest, Olivia. When the rules don't let you win, change the rules."

"Like that's so easy."

"Would being slowly consumed by eater nanobes be easier? Because that's your alternative."

Martin

Sometimes Martin wished he was the type who could just go along. If he'd been the type to go along, he would have stayed in Corporate Houston with his nice ratepayer family, finished his apprenticeship in design, and spent his life figuring out how to duplicate, ever so much more minutely, the taste of chocolate.

Instead, when his wife had died, he'd gone a little crazy, started looking for ways to make difference. That's when he'd found Merryweather and the two had planned big, plotted changes that would alter all of North America. After that, he kept his children close. Because when Corporate Houston learned what he was doing, they would be as anxious to shut him down as Dallas was.

Olivia broke his thought train. "So. Now that you have me, what do you intend to do with me?"

"You don't think I just wanted to save someone Corporate Dallas wanted to, uh, liquefy?"

She looked him straight in the eyes. "No."

He failed to suppress his grin. The ex-cop was terminally standard when it came to her belief structure, but she still had him revving his engines. Which was unfortunate because he couldn't imagine anything dumber than a relationship with a woman he needed to view as an expendable tool. "Okay, you're right. I do have plans for you. It's about Merryweather."

She laughed. "I knew you didn't really care about the scrubs who offed him."

"Okay, you win. But not because I think their lives are any less valuable."

"Now who's been spending too much time plugged into the Interfaith?"

"Faith is not what motivates me. Merryweather was working on something important. That's why he was killed."

Olivia narrowed her eyes. "He was working with you, wasn't he? For Corporate Houston."

Despite being stuck in CC propaganda, Olivia Jardan was sharp. Martin reminded himself to keep that in mind. If he could get her to commit to his cause, she could offer a lot. Of course, she just might also betray him, thinking that would let her back into the graces of Corporate Dallas.

"Not in the way you mean, but what he was doing was important, and was the kind of thing that the CC would want to shut down."

"I thought he was a designer."

"He was a free-coder."

Olivia shrugged. "So he made it possible for my mom to get a new mod, or for my father to get a different flavor of Interfaith meals."

"He wasn't just coding odds and ends. He was creating a system." Martin searched for the words that could describe Merryweather's vision to someone who didn't even understand the most basic elements of design. "You know just about everything we construct is built from carbon, oxygen, and hydrogen."

"Everyone knows that," his daughter interrupted.

"Thank you, Angie. But I was talking to Olivia."

"She's still right," Olivia answered and Angie stuck out her tongue at him.

Great. All he needed was two women ganging up on him. "Designs are also based on building blocks."

"I'm a cop," Olivia interrupted. "I know this. Modular coding. Self-contained objects. Got it."

"Merryweather was working to make the basic modules free. With that, anyone could snap together a new creation without paying licensing fees for all of the tasks everyone needs."

She shrugged. "And this helps Corporate Houston, how?"

"He also proposed a set of training modules, so anyone, even a citizen, could become a designer."

"Anyone, like my brother." She spoke softly, almost with reverence.

"Imagine Dallas with a million designers rather than five thousand. Imagine the changes in the social structure. Imagine—"

"You're trying to create a revolution."

"Merryweather was trying to create a revolution. I was helping."

"But now he's dead."

"He's dead, but not everyone who worked with him is. And that's what I need you to help me with."

Julia

Another boring party, another boring male.

Julia Turnboldt watched the cop wander from Maudie Vinson's party and wondered what that woman thought she was doing. Sure her husband was a cop, but he was the <u>chief</u> of police. He didn't have to associate with his lower-downs. And this Shenker had all of the earmarks of citizen.

Julia helped herself to a chocolate-covered strawberry, then set it down on a robotic waiter's tray. Hothouse grown strawberries and high-cocoa-butter chocolate cheated the taste buds. A decent designer, say herself, could code up something that tasted as good as this. What was the point of natural if it wasn't unique? Nothing but ostentatious consumption, which was to say, a lack of class.

"Did you check out that cop?" Maurissa Vinson, Vinson's daughter and a one-time fellow apprentice giggled when she saw where Julia was looking.

"You and your sick fantasies. If you don't know by now that male citizens are only better hung because they sculpt themselves that way, you never will."

Maurissa preened, letting her leather vest gape to display a nicely sculpted pair of tits. Maybe Julia should break down and tweak herself a bit. There was such a thing, after all, as too natural. "Who cares *how* they do it. It's *that* they do it."

"Unfortunately, to get to the meat, you have to listen to them talk."

Maurissa giggled again. "I generally put their mouths to better use."

Julia wasn't a prude. She enjoyed athletic encounters of the sexual kind as much as any girl, but she preferred men with something between their ears as well as between their legs. Finding both at once was the challenge. Clearly Maurissa had given up—or maybe she'd never cared about intelligence.

"I didn't see your dad here tonight." Time to change the subject. "Is he off worrying about the war?"

Maurissa shrugged. "You're not with the free-coders any more, are you? Because something bad is happening to them."

Julia been trying to deny that but couldn't any more. "But they're *ratepayers*."

"Daddy says that in war, everyone needs to make sacrifices."

Julia looked around the party. Second-rate strawberries notwithstanding, it didn't look to her like anyone here had made any sacrifices. And the whole point of being a ratepayer was that you paid your rate. Every month, Julia transferred more money than she wanted to think of to her insurance company—exactly so she'd be protected. Maurissa must have gotten something wrong because there was no way her premium should pay to hunt ratepayers down.

Maurissa took Julia's silence for shock and pressed ahead with her revelation. "You heard about the guy who was murdered yesterday, right, Hank Merryweather?"

Olivia froze. "Yes."

"It was political. Assassination. And he's not the only one. They're going after all of the free-coders."

"The police?"

For the first time Maurissa looked uncertain. "Dad has his guys looking the other way. It's something to do with the war, that's all I know."

Julia nodded, thanked Maurissa and Maudie for inviting her, and headed out. On impulse, she decided to spend the night at her mother's homespace. Not that she really believed anything would happen to her if she went home—Maurissa often got things wrong. She'd gone through the design program, but when it came time to get a job, she'd only managed to line something up with a sim developer, which had to be humiliating. Surely she was jerking Julia's chain.

Except there were all those out of service phones. Something was going on and Maurissa had the only explanation Julia had heard.

Vinson

"**I'm** afraid I'm going to have to insist on your help, Chief Vinson." Reverend Ariel still held a wine glass and a plate filled with strawberries. A trickle of melting chocolate meandered down his cheek as he puffed himself in Vinson's office up like the self-important prick he was.

Vinson looked up from his work. He'd hoped to make it down to the party, if only to humor his wife, but he could have gone all day without having to deal with the reverend. "You're going to *insist*? We're talking about killing ratepayers, Ariel."

Ariel showed his teeth, proving that Vinson had somehow walked into a trap.

"I spent the day meeting with shareholders. If you open for a download, I'll demonstrate."

Vinson knew he'd regret it, but what could he do? He accepted the download. Sure enough, Ariel had the proxies to force the Police Corporation to do what he wanted.

"What do you want from us?"

"Just what I said. Help our enforcement teams track down those free-coders."

"You know you're violating the Compromise? Your enforcers are limited to dealing with citizens."

Ariel smiled. "Which is exactly what you'll be if you don't help me, Vinson. Do you think the beautiful Maudie will have any time for you if you lose your job and have to beg her to make your premiums?"

Vinson didn't like being threatened. But if he refused to go along, he really might find himself out on the street. Ariel was exaggerating when he said Vinson might drop down to citizen, but he certainly risked having to move out into one of the rings, away from centercity, away from power, and away from his wife and daughter. Maudie really would dump him if he couldn't give her the lifestyle she deserved.

"I'll have the police coordinate locations and make sure they don't interfere. But any assassinations are up to you."

Ariel nodded. "That's exactly what I'm looking for, Chief. From the beginning I've recognized the danger of those free-coders. It's about time your stockholders realize that ratepayers can't be coddled any more than citizens."

Vinson forced himself to nod, although what Ariel said went against everything he believed. If paying your premiums didn't buy you protection, what was the point of paying—and how long would ratepayers fund the police?

"Tell your wife I had a wonderful time at her party," Ariel said easily, as if the previous conversation had never taken place. "I met a nice lad from your force. A lieutenant something. Looks like a boy on the rise."

"He's handling the Olivia Jardan investigation."

"Oh? Well, that's not as high a priority anymore."

"I'm not so sure. Mind if I transfer some files back to you?"

Ariel looked at him suspiciously. Not that Vinson blamed him. A decade before, a group of rogue ratepayers had developed a system for uploading viruses into phones—with catastrophic and catatonic results for the recipients. Phones had been upgraded since then, but people remained cautious. Finally the man nodded.

Vinson sent him a summary of the latest informant reports.

"She's hooked up with a Corporate Houston spy," Ariel said. "That's one hell of a coincidence assuming she really was just caught in the middle."

This time it was Vinson's turn to smile. "We don't think it's a coincidence at all. The spy had to be monitoring your activities against the free-coders."

"He'll try to create a split among the ratepayers."

"And a split between the CC and the Interfaith, Reverend." Exactly as he'd warned the stuffed shirt when this case had first rolled out of control.

"In that case, Chief, I suggest you hunt her down quickly. Because she'll be able to move a lot more freely through the city than some Houston spy ever could."

"Funny I didn't think of that, your holiness."

"You're pushing it, Vinson."

"Enjoy the party, Reverend. I've got to get back to work if we're going to head off a disaster you created. There've been free-coders mucking around since before the CC. Whatever harm they might cause, it isn't half as serious as what your enforcement squads have done. So allow me to do my job and try to clean up your mess."

Olivia

"**You** awake?"

Olivia blinked. Her body dumped an adrenaline load at the unexpected voice before her nanobes got to work cleaning out the mess. "I am now."

Angie looked down at her. "I've been doing some work on the Interfaith."

"I didn't know you did work on the Interfaith. I though you just simmed and got the payoffs."

"That's for losers. I told you you can find secrets if you know where to look."

Sammy had told Olivia much the same thing a million years ago. "Okay. That's interesting."

"What's interesting is that enforcement teams are hunting lots of free-coders down. Not just Merryweather."

"Huh?" Interfaith Enforcers existed to protect the intellectual property the Interfaith dispersed to its members. Anyone attempting to appropriate Interfaith products from a valid user could expect an unfriendly call by the enforcement teams. Enforcement teams also punished any citizen who stepped outside of the conventional morality that the Interfaith preached. But they didn't touch ratepayers. Ever.

"Yep. Last night they killed a bunch more free-coders. And the police are helping them."

"Your information must be wrong. Enforcers don't touch ratepayers."

"Now they do."

From across the abandoned cabin they'd appropriated for the night, Martin stumbled to his feet, splashed water over a face that looked like it could use a good nanobe wash to get rid of those scratchy whiskers, and pulled a couple of foodbars from his pack. "Just as we suspected, huh, babe?"

Olivia felt the beginning of the blush and ruthlessly flushed her system. He wasn't calling *her* babe, he was using a pet name for his daughter. Olivia's reaction to him was a normal physical response to danger—there was no reason to make it more than that.

"It's a lot worse than we thought," Angie said. "The cops are working with the enforcers, giving them the information they need to find the free-coders. Enforcers aren't even faking things like they did when they killed Merryweather."

Olivia's brain raced. If the police were cooperating with Interfaith enforcers, that meant whatever secrets she'd stumbled on were no longer important. She could—

"If you're thinking you can go back," Martin said, reading her mind "You've learned some more important secrets since then."

"You mean that you're a spy for Corporate Houston?"

"That's one problem. But I meant you know about changing ID codes— you're living proof it's possible."

"If you can just change me back," she wheedled, "I won't tell them what you're doing here."

"Right," Angie said. "Just join back up with the police and help them go kill a bunch of ratepayers who want to let citizens have access to new skills and new stuff."

"Are the police actually killing?"

"They're providing the information to the enforcers," Martin said. "That makes them responsible."

"But what am I going to do? Being a cop is my only skill. I appreciate you rescuing me, of course, but we both know you don't want me hanging around."

"You're going to help me rescue those free-coders who are still alive," Martin said. "I thought they'd stop at Merryweather since he was the guy driving the plan, but I was wrong and my mistake has gotten, uh, how many Angie?"

"Nine."

"Nine designers killed."

Olivia considered. She could take Martin, overpower him and get away. But where would she run with her counterfeit ID? Besides, he had a point. As a cop, it was her job to protect ratepayers. That the rest of the police weren't doing their job didn't remove that responsibility. In fact, it made her mandate even more essential.

She took a deep breath. "How do we start?"

Julia

When she'd awakened that morning, her mother had brought her a glass of fresh-brewed coffee, made from actual beans shipped in from some exotic land.

Coffee was something of a holy grail for designers. Recreating the buzz was easy—a mix of caffeine with antioxidants, with a dash of molecules to hit the tongue's bitter receptors. But the drink's full complexity continued to elude everyone. Like all food designers, Julia had spent some time working on the problem—she even liked to think she'd contributed to making it better. But *better* remained far short of the real deal.

Still, real coffee, from beans, was for special occasions. Especially with the looming economic war with Houston. Coffee beans just didn't grow in Corporate Dallas.

She took the cup and inhaled the drug's aroma. "Okay, mom, what's the problem?"

"I think you'd better leave."

If the caffeine hadn't done its job, her mother's words would have. "Leave?" She sounded like a dolt repeating her mother's words but this was shocking. Her mother *always* wanted her to stay, as if they were some citizen family, all sharing a single roof.

"It's the free-code stuff. I warned you to get away from them."

"You talked me into joining them."

"We've already had this conversation, dear." Her mother could be counted on to turn snippy. "That was when they were doing good things like making the citizen's basic allotment more palatable and designing free toys for the children. When that Merryweather took over, things took a dangerous turn."

"I didn't know you were so up on the movement."

"I keep everything about you on my news feed, Julia. You are my only daughter."

"Well, Merryweather is dead so I guess you don't have to worry anymore."

"They're all dying. That's why you need to run."

Coffee exploded everywhere when Julia's hand slipped and the cup landed on the floor. She stared as a zillion nanobes sucked up the moisture, feeding it into the home's constructor.

"Was that necessary?" Her mother made ineffectual dabbing motions at the fast-fading coffee.

"What do you mean, they're all dying?" Although a part of Julia knew. There was a reason nobody returned her calls.

"Eighteen were killed yesterday."

"Jeez. That's—"

Her mother nodded. "I'm a shareholder. I'll put this on the agenda for the CC, but you've got to stay alive until then. And I can't protect you. Security doesn't even slow them down. The police say they're assessing and avenging, but I'd rather not have to avenge you."

Julia was in motion, already. She scooped up her AI, some of the best bargains she'd picked up while she'd been shopping, and ran to her mom's constructor to build some basic food she could carry with her.

Her mother followed her. "I'll try to slow them, of course."

Julia hefted her bag, realized she couldn't carry everything, and dumped about half the food back into the constructor where it could be disassembled back into its basic components. "I'm a ratepayer. I've paid for insurance every month since I turned eighteen and you paid for it before then. I'm not supposed to have to hide. And I don't have a clue where to go."

"Maybe," her mother blinked, "maybe out in the rings."

"With the scrubs?" Julia didn't dislike citizens, exactly. She just didn't know any, and wouldn't have anything to talk about if she ever did meet one. While some centercity women slummed, taking advantage of male citizens who oversculpting their sex organs, Julia had never been interested.

"If you stay in centercity, they'll catch you and kill you."

"They who?"

Her mother wrung her hands. "I don't know."

"Of course—" an alarm cut her off.

"Intrusion at your homespace," her phone reported in the sexy male voice she'd programmed into it. "Your greeter AI was bypassed via a backdoor authorization designed for maintenance operation only. A.I. operations are being compromised and…" the phone connection died.

"Oh, shit, mom. They're at my place. When they find out I'm not there, they'll come here next. Maybe you should head out also."

Her mother stiffened. "Nobody will hurt me."

"You think they'll leave you alone to report them to the Police Corporation? Please, mother, take care of yourself."

Her mother hesitated. "Well, I supposed I could make your father take me to lunch. I understand the Old Warsaw has some genuine deer venison in."

"That is so gross. I can't believe you'd eat that."

Okay, Julia had done some experimentation. Still, eating Bambi?"

I was just kidding, of course."

"I love you, mom."

"I love you too, Julia. For goodness sake be careful whom you associate with from now on. And don't tell me it's my fault—I feel guilty enough already."

Julia hugged her mom, then stepped out into the street that ran by her mother's homespace.

The canopy of green trees partially diluted the solar energy, but also served to cool the exterior of the neighborhood. A deserted public constructor, available for any citizens brought in for day labor, trickled water for anyone to use.

To Julia, the bucolic scene reeked of danger.

She was alone, facing an unknown threat. Merryweather had been practically paranoid about his security and he'd still been killed. How was she supposed to get away when he hadn't?

She set off walking.

Martin

"**Julia** Turnboldt?" He couldn't believe a free-coder was returning his call.

"Yes. I was searching my news subscriptions for information about the free-code massacre and came across your call. Who the heck are you?"

"I'm Martin Reynolds."

"I don't know any Reynolds's."

"Which is why your phone blocked me when I called, I suspect. I'm trying to warn free-coders about the danger they're in. You're the first who's returned my call."

"I see." There was a definite pause that Martin suspected had nothing to do with the packet delay in the distributed phone system and everything to do with suspicion on the part of this ratepayer.

"You're probably wondering if I'm one of the people who's hunting you. That I'm trying to trap you into some sort of mistake."

"Look, Mr. Reynolds. I have to be suspicious. Why would you want to help me?"

"Let me connect someone." He linked Olivia into the conversation. "Olivia, tell her about Merryweather."

"Who is this?" Julia demanded.

"Hi Julia. This is Olivia Jardan. Formerly Police Officer Olivia Jardan of the Dallas Police Corporation."

Martin heard the brief pause again. "You investigated Hank Merryweather's biometric failure."

"Initially I investigated his biometric failure. Then investigated his murder."

"And this means I should trust you, why?"

"Do you have anyone else you can trust?"

"I can get by on my own."

"For how long?" Martin broke in. "If you leave centercity, your ID will trigger an alarm and they'll be after you. If you stay in centercity, they'll have you by nightfall."

"So you're just trying to help me out of the altruistic goodness of your hearts?"

"Julia," Olivia interrupted, "Merryweather was killed with an ax to his head. It crushed his skull. Interfaith Enforcers are doing the killing and the police are letting them do it."

"I wasn't that important to free-code. I mostly was interested in pizza."

Martin hoped Julia underestimated her value and her skills. Merryweather had thought highly of her—when he could get her to focus.

"Do you think Merryweather's murderer cares?" Olivia asked. "They started with Merryweather because he was the lynchpin, but they're cleaning up the rest now."

"Come to us." Martin tried to make his voice a beacon across the miles. "We'll help you, stand together with you."

"Uh, who is us?"

"You know who I am," Olivia said. "I'm just an ex-cop, Julia. Because I investigated a bit too deeply into Merryweather's death, I was scheduled as the next victim. So far, I've gotten away. Right now, that makes two of us."

"If you're telling the truth, you're a rogue. Joining up with you would make me an even better target."

"*They* call me a rogue. If you'd like to stay alive, let us help you."

Martin listened to Julia breathe for several seconds.

He was about to speak, but Olivia held up a hand, muting her phone. "Julia has to make her own decisions."

"No offense, Martin," Julia finally said, "but you're a guy. From what I've picked up, the killers were all guys. I'll meet with Olivia Jardan. Nobody else."

Martin shook his head and muted his phone as well. "There's a reward out for you, Olivia. You'd be in danger if you leave my protection. It could be a trap."

"I'd hardly be in more danger than Julia is." She punched off the mute function on her phone. "Let's do it quickly, Julia. We need to get you away from your ordinary surroundings before they move."

They were using sophisticated public key encryption, making it difficult, but not impossible, for anyone listening to eavesdrop. Still, sooner or later, the cops would locate and decrypt this conversation. Olivia was saying as little as possible.

"Can you get into centercity? Martin said I'd be tagged if I tried to leave."

Martin shook his head. "Centercity scans both ways. They'd catch you going in. Even my checksum thing won't help."

"Then we're—"

"If you can meet her quickly in the first zone, change her codes, you could get away before they catch her. Maybe."

Olivia stared at him and he used that as an excuse to check her out.

She was unusual for a citizen. For one thing, she hadn't bothered with a sculpt. For another, she seemed less anesthetized by the mind-numbing

entertainment sims that kept most of the citizen population under control—
the late twenty-first century version of the bread and circuses used to placate
the Roman mobs in the days of Caesar. Of course, she wasn't completely a
citizen. Still, it wasn't just her police training that made her different.

"What?" She put her hands to her head. "Is there something crawling in
my hair?"

"Uh, well..."

Before he could get himself into more trouble, Olivia spoke into the
phone. "I'll meet you in the first ring, at the Spring Valley rail station."

"But—"

"Martin says we can beat the alarms if we move quickly."

"Olivia, do you trust Martin? How long have you known him?"

"I've met his kids. If they think he's okay, he's not a complete jerk."

"All right. Tell me which rail you want me to catch."

"Well done," Martin said after he'd disconnected. "I'll go with you, of
course."

"You stay here and try to contact the rest of the designers. I'm a cop. I
don't need a male to protect me."

"But—"

"You do your job and let me do mine."

Martin knew she was right. That didn't make it easy.

Shenker

It had taken longer than it should have, but Shenker finally stood at the gaping doorframe to the ancient homespace where Olivia had gone to ground—and vanished.

His scanner promised nothing was alive inside—nothing larger than a small rodent, anyway. How had those people managed to live in days before a homespace would consume invading critters and turn them into something useful?

He turned to the officer guarding the door. "Any cops enter?"

"Just me, sir. A foot or so to place the scanners. As ordered."

He didn't have a lot of use for many of the cops coming into corporation these days. The corporation had started auctioning slots rather than picking the best of the tested shortly after Olivia's group. Still this one seemed competent.

"Make sure no one comes in until I give the all-clear." He stepped further in.

Olivia hadn't been here alone. It had taken him a while to piece together the details, but traces of temporary roadblocks remained. She'd been herded almost certainly by the Houston spy.

A small buckyball tube should have disintegrated by now but in the cool darkness of the old brick structure, it retained its integrity. Shenker made certain his biohazard gloves were intact, then stooped, picked it up, and placed it in his hand sensor.

The red alarm on his phone startled him so much he almost dropped the damned thing. He was a nominal ratepayer and had been working for the Police Corporation since he'd turned sixteen, almost twenty years earlier. He had every security classification he knew about. The alarm told him he'd just touched something even more secret.

Which was impossible. Even if this had been a bioengineered plague substance, the sensor should have told him rather than setting off alarms.

"Is everything okay, sir?" the cop asked from just outside. "I'm receiving an emergency withdrawal code."

"Go ahead and step back. I'll try to get to the bottom of—"

"Sergeant, I mean Lieutenant Shenker?" He hadn't accepted a connection, but his phone put it through anyway. Which meant—

"Sir?"

"You have attempted to scan a restricted substance. Would you care to explain your motivation?" Vinson made it sound like Shenker was trying to steal the keys to the Corporate City.

"Pursuant to my investigation of Officer Olivia Jardan's disappearance, I tracked her flight to an ancient and abandoned homespace in the outermost ring. There I found evidence that Jardan had linked up or perhaps was abducted by someone, probably our Houston spy. I located a buckyball device of the type used to contain biosculpt nanobes and scanned, attempting to ascertain from its contents any physical changes Olivia, or her captor, might have chosen to implement. Instead, I received an alarm."

He knew he sounded stuffy. But his own mentor, eighteen years earlier when he'd first joined the force, had taught him well. When higher-ups demand an answer, give it to them in the bureaucratic language of pseudo-professionalism. They might not like it, but they can't argue with it.

"I see." Vinson paused for long enough that Shenker wondered if he might be ordering the cop outside to finish him off. Instead, Vinson picked up the conversation as if he'd never dropped it. "The substance you've requested an analysis of is a forbidden scrub. It erases permanent identity codes and converts the ID memory tags to rewritable."

Shenker almost dropped his scanner again. No wonder this was classified. "So she might be anyone?"

"If we detect multiple simultaneous instances of the any person, this will, of course, set off alarms. It's more likely she'll use unassigned numbers. Citizens do keep being born, Lieutenant Shenker, despite what we can do to minimize the population pressures. And they do need to be assigned IDs. We can't exactly do a King Herod and exterminate all the babies born lately."

"If we find a baby walking around with an adult body, that might be a sign, though. Uh, sir."

Vinson grunted. "Exactly. Still, it hides her better than her own code would. Anyway, production or use of this type of sculpt is strictly forbidden under terms of the Compromise as unanimously ratified by every Consensus and every Interfaith across North America. You've stumbled on something a lot larger than one renegade cop, Lieutenant. So, get to the bottom of it."

"I'll do that, sir."

"Don't go easy on her, Shenker. There's a reason why any ID-altering substance is classified as secret. Obviously Corporate Houston is using her to undermine us—and the Consensus."

"I understand." He didn't understand spying, the economic war, or the troubles with Houston. What he did understand was that Paul Shenker now knew *way* too much. A successful and loyal Lieutenant Shenker might get away with knowing dangerous secrets. The death of an unsuccessful Sergeant Shenker would be a small price to pay for a bit of corporate security.

Olivia

Olivia caught the rail and rode out to Spring Valley station, where the zones butted against centercity.

She arrived a few minutes ahead of her scheduled meeting with Julia, using that time to scope out the station.

It seemed unlikely that whoever was behind the murders could decrypt their telephone conversation quickly enough to beat Julia here, but it wasn't impossible.

She forgot about that, and just about anything else, when the designer stepped off the rail.

Julia Turnboldt—even the name dripped ratepayer class. The designer wore a sleeveless tank clearly machine-woven from actual wormspit. Disgustingly, her slacks appeared to be created from cow skin, somehow buffed to a black shine. The scales on her shoes looked just a little too uneven to be the usual hydrocarbon construct although Olivia did *not* want to believe she was wearing lizards.

Programming those types of fabrics from a constructor wouldn't have been hard, but these weren't constructed. That was actual worm spit and actual dead animal hide. Olivia did a quick Google and determined the technical terms—silk and leather. The names sounded more pleasant than the reality.

Julia looked exactly like a centercity ratepayer slumming.

Although the station had been nearly deserted, by the time Olivia got near her, a mob of screaming children quickly surrounded the designer.

"Do you have any code, lady? Who you looking for? We can find you a man. Or maybe a lady? Need a tour? I can take you to where you can have some fun."

Olivia used her cop scanner to verify that it was Julia rather than a police replica with an identikit, then stepped toward the designer brushing close to her but pretending to be going about other business.

"Remember Merryweather and get back on the train."

She spoke under her breath, avoiding eye contact with the pretty but natural-looking woman she'd decided to save.

"Are you Olivia?" Julia demanded. "You don't scan right."

Since Olivia had kept walking, Julia practically shouted into the crowd.

The whispered message while walking gambit always worked in spy-sims. Apparently Julia hadn't grown up playing the same games. Olivia tried to reach Julia on the phone to avoid attracting attention, but even adding

Merryweather to the subject head didn't get through Julia's blocks. She turned back toward the designer.

Just in time to see one of the kids push the others away and take ownership of the designer.

"You've come to the right place for drugs," the kids told Julia as Olivia closed the distance. "I got what you're looking for."

Anticipation chilled Olivia.

"Don't talk to him."

The kid snarled at her. "Back off, citizen."

"Any problems on the rail, Julia?"

"Just a minute," Julia told the kid, being polite to the little cit. "How'd you know? We were delayed a few minutes."

Olivia grabbed the designer, trying not to think about getting dried wormspit on her hands. "Move."

"What the—"

"Citizens buy drugs from designers, not the other way around."

"Got it." Julia turned to the child. "Sorry. I don't need any drugs."

"But look at this." The kid reached into his bag and pulled out an aerosol delivery system.

An aerosol could be used to dispense drugs, but ingestion or skin contact were more common and more reliable. Aerosols were more commonly used for nanobe deployment.

Olivia jumped in front of Julia, grabbed the kid's arm, and twisted it back toward him just as the kid pressed the release button.

Instead of hitting Julia, the bright orange stream of fluid flew hit the supposed drug-pushing street vendor in the eyes and face.

"Oh, shit." The voice sounded young, but something in the tone sounded horribly old.

"Hey, lady, what the heck are you doing?" Another kid grasped for her.

Olivia grabbed Julia and tugged, but the designer seemed rooted, watching the nanobe do its job.

The liquid looked like a drug dose, and for an instant or two, Olivia wondered if she'd done the right thing. Maybe he had just been a misguided teen trying to score a few hundred bucks off of an obvious ratepayer.

Then the kid's body shuddered.

She watched with horror as his face softened, the nose drooping down into the sinus cavities, then the eyes vanishing, and finally the entire face falling in on itself. The drug pusher wasn't just dead, he'd been slimed.

"You killed him. Someone call the cops." Two of the not-so childlike-kids grabbed her.

"I'm going to be sick," Julia said.

"Good idea. Puke on these kids. They're trying to stop us and they'll get us killed." Olivia pulled out the Houston-model police prod she'd made Martin construct for her and dispersed the kids. They had come for an ambush, not to face someone who knew what they were doing.

Unfortunately, they'd be bringing their big brothers soon. "Julia. We've got to get out of here."

"But what about him?" The designer gestured at the disintegrating quasi-child.

"Considering that all that's left of his head is some hair and a couple rotting teeth, He won't bother you anymore."

"But—"

"It was supposed to look like you'd gone slumming and decided to try IE-forbidden drugs. They probably planned on running your head over with the rail so they wouldn't have to face any questions about just how bad a drug you took. But it didn't happen and you're still alive—for now. Let's keep it that way."

Considering the kids were watching from what they thought a safe distance, and considering what Julia had said about the delay, Olivia abandoned her idea of getting on the next rail and riding away. Instead, she grabbed a car and tried to open the door.

The car remained locked and a couple of cop-looking bystanders were heading her way. Well, duh. Her new identity didn't have any credit so of course nothing happened.

"Julia, would you authorize our usage fee? Quickly."

"Some rescue."

"Just do it." Olivia took a deep breath. "Please."

A long-suffering sigh. "All right."

Two seconds later, the car doors popped open.

Olivia instructed the cab to drive straight east, away from Dallas and from the northern ring where Martin and the group of free-cits he'd gathered around him waited.

She let the car speed ahead, the whine of its electric motor competing with the soft whoosh of displaced air as it rolled across the smooth solar cell-infused roadway. When they had gotten away from any possible witnesses, Olivia cancelled the drive instructions and pulled over to the side of the road.

"Are we there?"

"No. Everybody out. Move."

"This doesn't make sense. They could shut down free-code a lot easier than this."

"I'll help you figure out what's going on," Olivia said. "But first we have to stay alive. Come on, we're got a long walk ahead of us."

"Walk?"

"You know, with your legs."

"But my boots."

Olivia knew about boots. Cops spent their lives in them, protected from contamination and with their ability to mold to whatever they touched. Boots were practical, not decorative. What Julia wore had nothing to do with practical. Six-inch heels and toes that came to a spear-like point were only the most obvious differences.

"If you can't walk with them, leave them behind. Whoever tracked you on the train can follow this car."

"But I can't leave—oh, you were joking, right? These shoes cost more than you earned in the past ten years."

Olivia didn't need to ask how Julia knew how much she'd earned—obviously the designer had Googled her.

She reached into her tunic and pulled out the small drug dispenser Martin had given her. "Get out of sensor range from the car, then drink this."

Julia stared at her, then at the container. "You know what happened last time someone tried to drug me."

"If you don't trust me, why don't you go back and see what happens?"

For an instant, Julia's composure crumbled. "You know that's not fair."

Julia

Julia considered sims low-class.

She'd never understood why people would play games that simulated extreme danger, even situations that would lead to biological termination. Compared to what she was going through now, a sim sounded positively relaxing.

They hadn't just tried to kill her, they'd used a nanobe eater that would have consumed her face and gnawed straight into her brain. Maybe she should have spent more time playing sims. If she had, maybe she'd know what to do next. As it was, she had to follow Olivia or give up.

Olivia reached into the car, coded a new destination, and let it go.

"What is this drug going to do to me?"

Olivia's smile was completely false. "Okay, it might hurt a bit. It made me sick. But they'll track you by your ID code. This will reset it and make it writable."

No wonder this woman was renegade. "Permanent IDs are part of the Compromise."

"So you'd rather die?"

If she lost her ID, she *would* be dead. Julia Turnboldt was a ratepayer, a qualified designer who could name her price in any of a dozen top design corporations. She had her own centercity homespace and a mother and father who were also ratepayers and who loved her. If she took this drug, she'd become nobody, a free-cit without even record of making minimal payments for solar space.

Olivia obviously read her hesitation. "It's writable. After this is over, you can reconstruct your old code. In the meantime, you'll be assigned one from the queue."

She hated it, but Olivia was right. She'd have to settle for staying alive.

Her hand shook as she reached for the tube, but she swallowed every drop.

Olivia gave her a few minutes to recover, but not nearly enough. "From here, we walk."

She'd been certain Olivia was joking, but the woman looked dead serious.

"I told you I *can't* walk." It was all she could do to talk with that drug tearing through her, mangling carefully designed linkages between phone and brainstem, and eating away at the bone in which her ID tag was implanted like acid. Logic told her that her body didn't have pain sensors inside her brain or deep within bone. Logic was wrong.

"It's that or die."

"I still can't walk with these." Clearly her new outfit had been the wrong thing to wear, but she'd been in a hurry and had only thought about how much she'd spent on the clothes and how, if she didn't take them, someone might paw through them.

"Leave them or put them in your pack and carry them. Five seconds."

Considering this woman had just poisoned her, Julia wasn't feeling especially grateful. "I'm a designer and you're a cop. People like you don't give me orders."

"Two seconds."

"I'm coming." The ratepayer tottered out of the car, then leaned against it and removed her footwear.

Olivia looked smug, completely confident even though she wore a constructed black tunic and trousers that had to have been designed by some misogynistic no-talent. They didn't do a thing for Olivia's figure.

"I'm going to die."

"You're *not* going to die. I took the same drug yesterday. You just *want* to die."

Maybe Olivia wasn't a complete loser after all. She had a sense of humor. But Julia still felt like crap and it was Olivia's fault even if she was doing it for Julia's good. "Uh, I don't have a practical pack like you do. Would you carry my shoes for me?" Julia pushed them at Olivia, not waiting for an answer.

"Where's your AI?"

Julia sniffed. "This had better not be about stealing code from me."

"You do have your computer, don't you?"

"If I didn't bring it, are you going to leave me for those killers to find?"

Olivia sighed. "I can't tell you how much I'm tempted to leaving you. But no, you can come with me whether you brought it or not. Now, let's go. We can talk while we walk."

"All right."

Julia did her best, but there weren't any trees outside centercity, only acre after acre of solar panels. Solar panel houses, solar panel-covered yards, and even solar receptors built into the streets. Which would have been fine if anyone had invented perfect collectors. But not all of the sun's energy got turned to electricity. A lot became heat—and Julia's bare feet ached.

Olivia set a fast pace and Julia would have been hard-pressed to keep up with her under the best of circumstances. With her feet blistering and her stomach rebelling, she fell behind.

"Come on, Julia. Keep up."

"My feet hurt and I'm puking every three steps. Why not give me *your* shoes. They look more comfortable and you cits probably sculpt yourself tough soles anyway, right?"

Olivia looked like she wanted to stuff her shoes up Julia's nose. She nodded, though, stepped out of them and handed them over.

They were the ugliest shoes Julia had ever seen. But they sensed new feet being placed inside of them and resculpted themselves to provide perfect support for their new owner. Even better, they were cool.

Unfortunately, they wouldn't stay cool. That capability came from being integrated into the solar energy collected by the rest of Olivia's outfit. Julia's beautiful silk top and form-fitting leather pants were designed for style, but couldn't generate a volt if her life depended on it—which maybe it did.

If she was going to hang with citizens, Julia was going to have to construct herself some basics. One thing for sure. She'd design something a lot more attractive that still got the job done.

Olivia didn't limp at all as they walked what seemed like miles. Julia wasn't sure how she felt about that.

"Self-defense training, not sculpting" she explained when Julia asked. "A lot of our training is real fighting against real bots or even humans, and conducted with bare feet. That hardens things up."

Still, the Texas sun baked the streets. Julia had to admire Olivia's willingness to bear it.

Vinson

Chief Vinson was proud of his patience. He was letting Interfaith enforcers run roughshod over the Corporate Consensus and he'd promoted a man who wasn't getting the job done. A lesser man would have fired Shenker and told the Interfaith leaders they could go pound silicon. But Vinson kept his eye on the bigger picture. He didn't have anyone better than Shenker to go after the girl, and the lieutenant knew her habits and weaknesses better than anyone else. As for the Interfaith, he'd gotten his marching orders from the consensus chairs themselves. Until the war with Corporate Houston resolved itself, he could let them go after free-coders, or he could kiss his career goodbye. For Vinson, that wasn't any choice at all.

Not to second-guess but to help, Vinson pulled up the files on Olivia Jardan.

A couple minutes later, he had an idea. He brought Shenker up on his phone.

"Yes, Chief?"

Vinson pretended he didn't hear Shenker's sigh. "What do you know about *Sammy* Jardan?"

"Not much. He's Olivia's brother. She's fond of him but not fond enough to give herself up if we torture him."

Vinson shuddered. Cops use whatever methods necessary to assess and avenge. Torturing citizens could be cost-effective. But Vinson had been raised a ratepayer and didn't want to hear about that kind of operation. "Fond is all I need. Thanks."

"Before I let you go, I took your advice and looked for newborns showing up in strange places. I've got a record of a code that's supposed to be assigned to a newly registered citizen at some kind of dustup."

"So someone brought their kid to a fight? Citizens don't have any sense of the appropriate."

"This particular newborn took out an Interfaith enforcer wearing an illegal preteen sculpt, dissolved his face."

Vinson inhaled sharply. "Interesting."

"What's more interesting is that there was a ratepayer involved. Looks like the enforcer was trying to grab a designer."

Vinson licked his lips. "A designer associated with Merryweather and his band of kooks."

"Exactly. One Julia Turnboldt. Expert in food and flavor design. I couldn't get much on her from the Dallas F&F Company, but she seems to be one of their rising stars. Looks vaguely familiar."

"I know Turnboldt. She's a friend of my daughter's. You might have seen her at the party. I didn't know she was on the list."

"Apparently."

"This supposed baby got Turnboldt away from Interfaith Enforcers?"

"Maybe not their first-string talent. They're pretty busy with all of the assassinations they've been asked to handle."

Vinson nodded. "I'll take this as confirmation of your theory, Lieutenant. Renegade officer Jardan has taken up with Corporate Houston terrorists and is now actively attempting to interfere with an authorized Interfaith operation against rogue designers."

"I recommend we pull the Interfaith enforcers off any surviving free-coders."

Ariel would hate that. Vinson grinned. "You have a plan?"

"We have no evidence Jardan was even award of Turnboldt until recently. If Jardan wants one free-coder, why not more? If we guard the designers—"

"As bait in a trap," Vinson concluded. "An excellent plan, although getting agreement from Ariel is very much an issue."

"I understand, sir. In the meantime, I could use a list of any free-coders who haven't been assassinated yet and their locations."

"You'll get it. I suspect the enforcers will want their own men on the spot but I'll make sure you're in overall command."

Shenker grimaced. "If those losers are on location, the chances of being detected go way up. Enforcers are not exactly known for their low profile, which explains how Jardan turned around an attack that was supposed leave her and Turnboldt dead."

Vinson sighed. He knew that. But Ariel wouldn't agree to back off. "Deal with it, Lieutenant."

Even over the phone, Vinson felt Shenker stiffen. "Sir."

Vinson broke the connection and walked down to the West End rail station. He'd been stuck inside too long. It was time for him to go outside centercity himself. If he happened to run across a 3-D outfit manufacturing sims involving equines and beautiful females, that would be excellent. But his expectations were more modest. Sammy Jardan wasn't just renegade cop Olivia Jardan's brother, he was also an Interfaith true believer. Which gave Vinson a nice lever to use against the ex-cop. It was even possible that no torture at all would be required. Not likely, but possible.

A personal visit to Sammy Jardan might be just the thing to get him to play along.

Martin

The free-cits wouldn't play along.

"Why should we trust you?" Free-cit leader Justin demanded. "If anything, Corporate Houston treats its free-cits worse than Dallas."

Martin studied Justin. The man had white hair and wrinkles so deep you could lose a memory chip in there. His voice quavered when he talked and his hand actually shook. It didn't seem to Martin the man had much to lose. Clearly Justin didn't see it that way.

"I'm asking you to help create something that will last long beyond one silly economic war. Who really cares, after all, whether Houston or Dallas collects the road tolls? Who cares whether Houston licenses its intellectual property on a company-by-company basis or uses its consolidated IP partnership to negotiate the deals?"

He'd cultivated Justin and other free-cit leaders since he'd arrived in the outer rings around Corporate Dallas two years earlier. Now was supposed to be the time when that cultivation would pay off.

From the angry frustration he saw on Justin's face, Martin feared he'd made a mistake.

"*You* may want to create something that lasts," Justin said. "I'm sure you mean well and you don't intend to shaft the dupes who do your dirty work. But we both know that Corporate Houston will dump us as soon as the war is over. You said it—the war isn't about important stuff, it's about who gets a bit more money out of the trade between the cities. If we throw in with Houston, both sides will see us as traitors, neither side will trust us, and we'll be worse off than if we did nothing."

Fortunately, there were plenty of free-cits who saw Justin as horribly old guard. Martin had hired many of these with code from Houston or, when Houston got nervous about what he was doing, with code his daughter had hacked off high-security regions of the Interfaith. What he hoped to accomplish, though, could not grow from a few hired thugs. He needed the support and enthusiasm of the free-cit leaders.

"Suppose things were different? Suppose *anyone* could be a designer without having to come from an approved ratepayer family? Suppose *you* could design a food, a solar blanket, a children's toy, a nanobe scrub. Suppose—"

"Suppose you tell me where I can get me some of this excellent drug you're smoking," Justin interrupted. "What you're suggesting will never happen. First, it would take designers to create that kind of system and we already know that you don't get to be a designer unless you come from a ratepayer background. Second, Corporate Houston won't let you play that kind of game. And third, you're talking about something that strikes at the very core of the compromise. Why would anyone need the Interfaith if they could design their own stuff?"

Martin waited the older man out. That Justin was arguing with him at all had to mean he could see the potential, feel the dream. Once they had agreement on that, it came down to implementation.

"I don't have the answers on the second half of your problems. I agree that we can't count on Corporate Houston's full support and that the corporate consensus—

"And the Interfaith."

"—and the Interfaith will both have a lot of problems with the plan. As far as the coding, though, I've got an answer. My friend Hank Merryweather launched a program two years ago to design free-code replacements for all of the building-block modules. He was going to put together a training system that anyone could use to become a designer."

Justin held up a hand in the universal 'stop' gesture. "This the Merryweather recently assassinated?"

"I've got an associate working to gather the surviving members of Merryweather's team. Sure, the Interfaith enforcers struck when they figured out what Merryweather was doing, but he and the other designers got a lot of work done first. If we can finish it—

"You want our help keeping a bunch of rich ratepayers alive while other ratepayers are looking for them?"

"I don't like to look at it that way."

"You seem like a sincere kid, Martin. That's why I'm going to be dead-straight with you. You can't turn cits into designers. If even one percent of citizens can read, that'd be a miracle. Cits sit in their chairs and play their sims. The closest they get to design is pretending to go to designer parties. Ratepayers say we're lazy and they're not completely wrong. How are you going to change that? Are you going to tell a citizen he has to learn to read, then he has to study a really boring training sim to learn to design, then if he's lucky he'll be able to design something half as good as he can already get from the Interfaith?

"But—"

"And oh, by the way you've ruined the market for intellectual property so he'll never be able to make any money with his code no matter how good it is. We may be lazy but we aren't stupid. You're not going to have a lot of cits lining up for that chance."

Martin felt his heart sink. "You won't help me?"

Justin shook his head. "Give me a reason to help, some possible scenario where helping won't just get my people hurt. Right now, getting involved looks like the worst thing we could do."

"Think about the upside," Martin pleaded.

"You *find* me an upside, one that is actually possible in today's world, and I'll consider the hell out of it. Until then, you're wasting my time, spyboy."

Olivia

Martin had been busy.

In the few hours it had taken Olivia to collect Julia, he'd gathered a small group of free-cits and set up a camp on the bottom of a dry lake or abandoned reservoir.

Solar panels, camouflaged to look like the barren countryside, covered most of the sand, and the few structures he'd set up could have been scrub bushes if seen from the air. The irony that living trees and bushes survived in centercity and out here in the furthest rings, didn't escape her.

"You've got an army," Olivia said.

"Twenty." Martin sounded pissed. "And I'm paying them. I was hoping to have hundreds. The only reason I have the few I do is that there isn't a public constructor anywhere around and I'm letting them use mine. What does a guy have to do to get people to trust him?"

Olivia examined the neatly laid out camp. It looked like progress to her. "Why *should* they trust you, Martin? Once Corporate Houston and Dallas work out their tiff, you'll be moving on and they'll be hung out for Assess and Avenge."

"I'm not going to abandon them."

If she hadn't known Martin had been raised a ratepayer, she could have guessed by his plaintive complaints. Citizens learned that trust had to be earned.

Oddly, Martin's offended innocence convinced her more than would a stack of paid invoices. She didn't completely understand concepts like idealism and altruism, but she was vaguely familiar with the words. Martin, it seemed, had absorbed their full content.

He was also probably the only spy in history who traveled with his children. With someone else, that might have been a calculated attempt to pretend he was invested in whomever he was living among. But Olivia didn't think Martin made that sort of calculation. She'd seen the way he looked at his children and she couldn't believe he'd use them—not in that way, anyway. He really was as naive as he pretended.

"Of all the people in Corporate Houston, how did they happen to decide on someone like you?"

He drew himself up to his full height, something well north of six feet.

"Merryweather and I knew there'd be another war and planned on this. I studied revolution and resistance for years, then told Corporate Houston I'd work for them for nothing. As far as they're concerned, I'm reporting on economic activities and trying to organize demonstrations among the citizens. They don't know about the free-code project Merryweather and I cooked up."

Olivia wasn't so sure. *Someone* had found out about that project. Someone had been sufficiently worried that they'd broken the Compromise to kill Merryweather and many of the others involved.

"Speaking of which," Martin continued, "where is the designer? I located a couple who happened to be out in the rings and had them brought here, but none of the ones in centercity will return my calls."

"They never got your calls." Julia, looking refreshed and with a towel around her head, stepped from the shower facility. She'd put back on her tight leather pants, her slinky wormspit top, and her high snake boots. She looked like a sim ratepayer more than anything mundane enough to exist in the real world.

Martin did a double-take. "Ah, I'm Martin Reynolds. Thank you for joining us, Ms. Turnboldt."

"It's Julia. And I guess you're the one who deserves the thanks. I'd be dead if I hadn't responded to your call."

Which was a lot more gratitude than Olivia had gotten from the woman.

It dawned on her that Julia was flirting with Martin. Which made sense, in a way since he was an obvious ratepayer. Still, an uncomfortable sensation trickled through her gut.

She pasted on a grin. "So, we're all happy now. And the other free-coders are history?"

"That's the funny thing," Martin said. "The attack on Julia seems to have been the last. Maybe they're keeping things off the Infoweb, but we had twenty-one reported deaths before and none since."

"They're not all dead?" Olivia repeated.

Martin looked back and forth between the two women. "As I said, they wouldn't answer my calls so I can't be absolutely certain that anyone is alive. Still, it's hard to keep news off the Infoweb. And Angie is trolling the Interfaith and not finding anything recent there."

Julia wrinkled her cute little nose. She had to be aware of the way her freckles jiggled when she did that, Olivia decided. Not that Olivia had a problem with flirting at appropriate moments, but this didn't seem like one to her.

"I guess they don't have to kill us. They've wiped out the project."

Martin's smile looked evil. "I've rescued nine designers. You're the tenth. As far as I'm concerned, the project is still on."

Julia shook her head. "Ten? Not even close to what we need."

Martin stared at her. "Well, that's all I have."

"Then maybe we'd better locate some more and drag them out here."

"By *we*, I assume you mean *me*?" Olivia couldn't believe that the precious little ratepayer would get her hands dirty. For that matter, she wanted her shoes back. She was tired of wandering around barefoot.

Julia glared at her. "I meant us, including me. If Martin can set up nice homesites for them, they might as well continue working on the project."

Like that would be possible. "We barely got out alive when I rescued you," Olivia pointed out. "And the cops and enforcers have to be more prepared now. How the heck are we supposed to rescue anyone else?"

Julia put her hand on Olivia's shoulder and stared into her eyes. It was a gesture that Olivia would never have made. Citizens reserved their personal space, interacted with sims rather than with other people and, like it or not, Olivia had the thought patterns of a cit, no matter that she'd spent a few years as a nominal ratepayer. "You're the one who knows how to get around. You're the cop. You'll do the rescuing. I'll stay here and coordinate the communications. Even without my ID, I think I can figure out keywords to get my calls through."

Unfortunately, that made sense to Olivia. It also meant Julia's "we" only went as far as a phone call. Olivia was the one who would have to risk her neck—again.

Julia

Julia could hardly believe the squalor. Even free-cits, she felt certain, could have dirt-repelling nanobes in their garments. And medical implants all contained automatic deodorants to keep the stink down. Martin's pathetic little army seemed to have neglected these basic precautions. If he actually tried to invade centercity with them, the security robots would be able to track them down using only scent detection.

She was tempted to give it up, head back to town to throw herself to the mercy of whoever was behind the free-code massacre. She couldn't forget that kid's face, though, when it dissolved. Putting up with the stink out here might not be easy but it seemed her only option.

Maybe if she could bring more developers in, they could create a place where living was at least possible.

Fortunately, Martin's phone reprogramer hadn't deleted her phone's memory. She still had the distribution list for free-code.

Julia created a message, loaded it with keywords that would scream for attention, and mailed it to the list.

Then she walked around and met with the nine designers Martin had rescued.

A couple had some talent, but most were kids. Like her, they'd joined to meet people rather than because of any special belief. Unlike her, they weren't hardcore coders.

Still, they were what she had to work with.

She stopped a couple from squabbling, suggested a common workplace and development environment, and uploaded them the track-change system she'd created as a project during her training.

That, and maybe a million years, would let them complete the huge programming base Merryweather had in mind.

She tried to explain this to Olivia. Tried and failed.

Then again, Olivia didn't like her. The cop seriously thought that Julia might be interested in Martin and had all of her jealousy hooks going. It was funny that Olivia didn't even recognize she was interested in the Houston spy.

Stupid plan or not, continuing the project was Martin's big idea—and Julia didn't have any better suggestions. It was up to her to figure out a way to turn this idealistic claptrap into something that would work.

"We need a minimum of thirty developers," she told Olivia and Martin.

Martin shook his head. "Considering twenty deaths, that leaves about fifteen more on Merryweather's entire team. We'll have to make do with less."

Julia bit her tongue to keep herself from saying something nasty. Instead she smiled. "Have you ever been involved in a big design project, Martin?"

"Some class projects. I didn't complete the study course."

"Well, I did and I have. So trust me on this. I don't know if we could do it with thirty, but that's a minimum. We need a design group, a separate testing group and a third group to design training sims."

An old man had wandered up, and he sat down under the solar panel awning hung over a tent-like structure that was pretty much all of the camp that Olivia had dragged her to.

"What sort of talent do you need for the training sims?" the old man asked.

Julia gave him her frostiest look. "Full emersion stuff. We're starting from scratch here."

"We don't know the content, but we have people who do sims."

"Who the hell are you?" Olivia demanded. "And what sort of sims are you talking about?"

"I'm Justin Ritler. I happen to be a free-cit."

Julia grimaced. "Free-cit sims are about sex, not training."

The old man shrugged. "We'll need help with the content, of course."

Martin looked confused. "I thought you weren't interested, Justin."

"I'm not interested in Corporate Houston's sabotage efforts. But I just might be interested in working with local coders who know what they're doing. I've got grandkids, you know. I wouldn't mind thinking they had more choices ahead of them than which sim to dope themselves with."

"That'll help," Julia admitted. "Next we need access to a verification authority."

Martin shook his head. "We're talking about a new way of doing things. Why set things up the same as they already are?"

Boy, he was naive.

"Suppose you're a designer, Martin. Suppose you can download a module that *says* it will interface with a constructor. Do you just take that on faith, assume nobody would, maybe, code something that would twist a protein just a little to make it toxic? Even if everyone trusted you, what's to stop someone else, someone like Corporate Dallas, from taking our tested modules and hijacking them, turning out fakes that destroy rather than do the job, and shipping them with our labels? We want to produce something everyone could use, not just some tools for internal development."

It bugged her to have to explain this. For one thing, they should know it already. For another, she knew she sounded way too much like her father.

"But incorporating perpetuates the nineteenth century financial structure that led to this mess," Martin said.

"If you're ever going to be a revolutionary who amounts to anything," Justin told him, "you're going to have to give up on utopian ideas and face reality. This lady knows what she's talking about and you don't. Maybe you and this Merryweather fellow came up with a dream. It'll take hard-headed realists like your designer here to make it happen."

Martin didn't like it. But that didn't bother Julia much. There was a lot she didn't like, either. Like nearly having her face eaten off just because she'd been involved in some project to meet guys. Unfortunately, it looked to her that the only way she was going to get back anything approaching a normal life was to make this project succeed so well the CC would have to admit they couldn't stop it.

She just didn't see how that was possible.

Olivia

Julia had opened Olivia's eyes to a lot of things. At least the woman seemed willing to chip in, although why wouldn't she, considering she'd turned Martin's whole project into something completely different? But Julia figured her self-interest was wedded to making the project work. What if the next coder they brought in thought he would be better off selling them out?

Julia and Martin could haggle over corporate structure, and Justin could worry about turning sex-sim developers into designer training developers, but none of them seemed to have a clue about what really mattered.

She stared at the smug group sitting around the table and decided it was time to introduce a bit of reality.

"I'm not bringing in thirty designers or even one," she said, "until we handle the security side of things. Any designer we bring is a security risk. One call to police central or to Interfaith Enforcement and we're finished."

"Tear out their phones," Justin suggested.

"That way they won't get any work done at all," Julia said. She moved a bit closer to Olivia, as if aligning herself with Olivia's concerns. "Designers need to communicate, upload files, integrate modules. No phone, no code."

Justin shrugged. "Jam them."

"You're living in a past so old I don't remember it," Olivia said. "Anything that would jam enough to help would be the same as ripping them out."

"We won't bring them here," Justin said.

"But Julia said we need—"

"Trust is a key issue in revolutionary movements," Martin explained. "The authorities always have informants, willing to betray the revolution in exchange for a lighter sentence, a few pieces of silver, or protection for their families."

"Great. And the last revolution that succeeded was the Corporate Consensus, right? But only because of the Great Compromise."

"There are some tricks we can use," Justin suggested. "How do you think as many free-cits survive as they do?"

Olivia shrugged. "Because nobody cares about them?"

Justin nodded. "There's some truth to that. But there's more."

"I'm waiting with bated breath."

"Three of the most basic were need to know, the cell system to limit who knew whom, and making sure someone was watching everyone. The free-cits have used those for decades."

Olivia nodded. She knew those same principles from police work. "Can we keep our free-code refugees physically separated in two or three designer teams? We'll need a bunch of mini-camps dispersed around the city's outer rings."

"I can do that," Justin said. "Where do you want them built?"

Olivia looked at him. "I'll communicate directly with the build teams, and we'll build dozens of dummy camps for every pair of designers. I can't see that *you* have any need to know more than that."

Shenker

Paul Shenker yanked the police tunic from the Interfaith enforcer and strapped it on correctly. The idiot was doing his best to get them all killed.

He'd spent hours monitoring his supposed troops, keeping them from spilling into centercity like a plague but it was a losing battle. If one of his informants didn't come through, he was going to have to give up on the entire plan.

Just when he thought the whole plan was a bust, police central connected through to his phone implant. "We have a confirmed communication."

He gestured for silence from the always-gabbing enforcers. "Central, patch me in. I want the informant to be able to hear me but nobody else."

"Patching."

Shenker came in the middle of the conversation but he liked what he heard. He chuckled when he heard his informant complain, "but I'm scared."

Far too many designers had walked and so far his trap had caught nothing but a pair of free-cits who'd been hired by the job. They only knew they were supposed to meet up with a designer, give him the ID switching drug, and link up with a couple of other free-cits outside the fourth ring.

By the time he'd broken the free-cits encryption, he'd missed that link-up.

That was then. Then, he'd been playing blind. With an informant in place, this time his trap was not going to come up empty.

"You don't have to be scared."

Shenker grinned when he recognized Olivia's voice. Perfect. And all so wrong. He'd promised his informant safety, position, protection. And he really intended to do what he could, but he suspected he'd be able to do nothing. Free-code was history.

"Just walk along Old Lemmon Avenue," Olivia continued. "We'll meet up with you when it's safe for all of us."

He'd given the informant plenty of guidance. Since he'd trained Olivia, he had a pretty good idea exactly what she'd demand. Getting the target moving would let her check for tails, put timing on her side. Exactly what he'd expected, exactly what he wouldn't allow.

"Are you kidding?" his informant whined. "If we leave our homespace, we're dead. I don't know how Julia survived, but a lot of others are either dead or missing."

"I survived because Olivia helped me."

Shenker's voice analyzer identified the voice as Julia Turnboldt's at nearly one hundred percent confidence. Unlike Olivia, Julia didn't have any sort of regional accent. Since different branches of large corporations, and even competitors in different cities often traded employees, real ratepayers generally sounded like sim stars on the news channels.

Shenker's southern drawl betrayed *his* citizen background. He was determined that any children he brought into the world would sound like Julia. Not that he had any particular hopes of bringing children into the world. The last thing he wanted was to subject a child to the kind of struggles he'd had to endure.

"You're in with these losers, Julia?" His informant continued following the script.

"I'm alive."

"But—"

"But nothing. You've got to let us help you. We can get you out of there. We have a place for the two of you already. You can continue working on free-code full time."

"Big deal. What about our jobs?"

"When we roll out the completed project, every design shop in Corporate Dallas will want to hire you."

"In the meantime, we can't afford our premiums. We'll be... citizens."

"Considering how much good insurance has done for the designers who've been killed, we haven't been getting our money's worth."

"We can't get a fix on the broadcast," central reported.

Shenker nodded. Nothing else about this job had been easy. Why should anything change now?

"Okay," he told the informant over privacy link. "You can stop stalling. Tell them you're afraid to leave your homespace, but that you'll wait there for them to pick you up."

He listened to his informant weep, whine, cajole, and generally make herself annoying.

If he'd been on the other side, he would have suggested leaving her for Interfaith Enforcement to take care of. But Julia and Olivia seemed intent on making the rescue. Which left them vulnerable.

"Tell them that you need to see Turnboldt and Jardan in person," he added. There was no point in developing a trap this elaborate only to catch a couple of free-cits. "Say you won't really believe it's her unless you see her face."

Two minutes later, everything was set up.

He checked the force listing for available cops, gritting his teeth as he added one Interfaith Enforcer for every cop. He figured the cops would do the work and the Enforcers could take the credit. As long as they didn't get in the way, the job would get done.

Olivia

Her first two pickups had gone off without any problems.

Working with Justin, they'd immobilized citizen-workers who were scheduled to go into centercity, switched the identities of a couple of young free-cits, and sent them in using the authorized codes.

Then things went wrong.

The next pair of free-cits had called in reporting problems and then, ominously, vanished from the airwaves.

Finally, a pair of designers—McKensie Atlas and Kansas Killdit—insisted that Julia meet them personally—in their centercity homespace.

You know it's a trap," Olivia said.

They were riding the rail, each equipped with the identities of a citizen who was so fully immersed in sims they were unlikely to leave their homespaces any time soon.

Julia shook her head. "McKensie and Kansas know the Interfaith doesn't approve of their lifestyle. There's no way they'd turn us over to Interfaith Enforcers. And ratepayers don't take orders from cops, we give them."

"Didn't they sound funny to you?"

"Of course they sounded funny. They're scared out of their gourds."

That made sense, but it didn't feel right to Olivia.

As a cop, she'd learned to trust her feelings and right now those feelings were telling her to run the other way.

"Are they especially good designers?"

Julia shrugged. "About average, unless you want a dynamite handbag."

"So, why are we wasting our time with them?"

Julia sighed. "Because they're all we have. I could just move, get a job with Corporate Fort Worth. But nobody is going to hire a renegade ex-cop. So, maybe it's time you took some chances rather than just whining."

That was so unfair, Olivia couldn't even respond. By the time she'd come up with a suitably flattening answer, they were inside the first ring.

The two changed rails at the Parker Road station, and headed toward centercity.

With each stop, more passengers departed, leaving only ratepayers on board.

"You have any idea how we can get across?" Julia asked. "They're onto the working citizen routine."

Between stops, their rail car hurled south at close to two hundred kilometers an hour—a speed that gave them only moments before they would hit the line—and be scanned by centercity's protective systems.

Which should be fine because they'd reprogrammed new codes right before they left. Except… Shenker wasn't stupid. If he'd caught those free-cits, he'd know Olivia had learned to alter her tags and he'd be searching for newly assigned IDs.

"Turn off," she said urgently. "Go blank."

Julia glared at her. "Deprogram our RFID's? That'll set off every alarm on the planet."

"Just do it. They're tagging on IDs. If we don't register on their scanners, we're invisible."

"*I* wouldn't code anything that sloppy. What makes you think someone else did?"

Olivia shrugged. "The ability to make writable ID codes is a secret. Whoever was designing this security system wasn't high up enough to know that secret so she wouldn't have accounted for it."

"That sounds like a guess."

"I'm open to suggestions."

It wasn't impossible, though. If her mother's sims reflected reality at all, centercity ratepayers loved their pets, and pets were organic, breathing creatures… without imbedded ID codes. Citizens, of course, just got sim pets for their sim worlds. Having a dragon or a unicorn was a lot more interesting than a dog, and impressing your sim neighbors was a lot more worthwhile than impressing a few physical neighbors.

She could just hope that the defenses weren't sensitive enough to notice the difference between a pair of hundred-plus-pound dogs, and a pair of hundred-plus-pound women.

At the last stop before centercity, Spring Valley, Olivia and Julia dismounted, sent cancel codes to their RFIDs, walked down to the next car, and remounted the rail. Rather than take a seat, the two stood in the aisles and did their best to be invisible.

Julia's invisible act was about as unconvincing as anything Olivia had ever seen, but at least the designer kept her mouth shut.

They passed across LBJ, the old ring freeway, which was now an active defense field, and Olivia let herself exhale. None of the active defenses had gone into operation.

Julia brought her face nearer. "I guess we—"

Julia's guess was made irrelevant by what sounded like a thousand alarms going off at once.

Their rail car detached from the train it was on, and shuttled off on a sidetrack, braking hard.

"Arf, arf," Julia said. "That plan didn't work. What next, security chief?"

"Shut up. I'm trying to think."

The car slowed quickly. The ratepayers on board stared at Olivia and Julia with the combination of horror and curiosity that could only be maintained by people so certain of their place in the world that they couldn't imagine anyone challenging it.

"Police," Olivia announced. "Remain calm, things are under control. Our systems have detected an unauthorized intrusion into centercity with this car specifically flagged as at risk. Please keep your hands in sight. Additional corporate police officers will be arriving shortly to process all passengers. Those of you not associated with this unauthorized intrusion will, eventually, be allowed to go about your business. Do not panic."

Spoken with confidence, and that certain tone that real cops had, Olivia's little speech worked. Nobody attacked them, not that she was worried about physical violence from a bunch of ratepayers. Even better, everyone started looking at one another rather than at the two women standing in the aisles pretending to be dogs.

Unfortunately, what Olivia had said about other cops arriving was the only truth she had spoken. They needed to be gone before the police arrived.

"The door won't open," Julia whispered. "I even sent it the fire override code and nothing happened."

The rail was down to walking speed already.

Figuring that a trapped passenger would fake the fire code was elementary.

Police codes were a bit less obvious than fire codes and, although Olivia no longer had her police identity, her phone still held all of the codes. She just had to hope the door was smart enough to understand the cop override, but too dumb to demand officer-specific authentication.

The door hitched slightly when she shot it the code, but it didn't open. Not quite stupid enough.

Rather than try additional codes and wait for the passengers to get up the nerve to mob her, Olivia put all of her power behind a sidekick, right where the latch had hitched.

No human-powered kick could break through a rail's carbon fiber door, but the door was designed to open in cases of emergency, to slide along its tracks whenever an obstruction, like a child's foot or a ratepayer's A.I., got caught. She didn't have to break the molecular bonds, just persuade the servos to do their job.

A follow-up kick completed the persuasion and the dented and mangled door groaned its way open.

"I suggest you disperse rapidly," she announced to the other passengers. "As you've guessed, we're actually dangerous free-cits. The police will be shooting rather than stopping people and asking for insurance information." Fifty ratepayers fleeing for their lives just might distract the cops.

She felt a little guilty when one of the ratepayers tripped and got walked on by three others, but not guilty enough to turn around and help the woman.

Instead, she pointed toward the horizon and ran.

"Should we split up?" Julia's cheeks were red, as if her mediplant had temporarily lost control of her blood flow and was pumping excess adrenaline.

"Let's stay together and try to help each other out."

"Help out with what?"

"Have you forgotten what we're here for? We've got a couple of designers to rescue."

Vinson

Sammy Jardan had been distressingly unhelpful.

A personal visit from the Chairman of the Police Corporation should strike both fear and hope into any citizen's heart. Instead, Sammy had refused to cooperate in the capture of his sister, laughed at Vinson's proposed bribes, and shook his head mockingly when Vinson had threatened to let Interfaith Enforcers beat the snot out of him.

Their meeting hadn't been a complete waste, though. Looking at Sammy and reading Olivia's psychological profile had given Vinson a better sense of whom he was dealing with. Olivia Jardan was an intelligent, capable, and stubborn female. She would have been wise to take advantage of her escape to get as far from Corporate Dallas as she could, but the same perverse sense of loyalty that made Sammy willing to risk his life to help his sister apparently drove that sister to walk into Lieutenant Shenker's trap.

He'd just gotten back to his office when the centercity intrusion alarms went off.

It could have been anything. Since economic war had become inevitable, he'd had those alarms raised to extreme levels and, as a result, delayed thousands of ratepayers, inconvenienced pet owners, and made life a miserable hell for citizens.

This could be just another false alarm, but Shenker had notified him that Julia and Olivia were supposed to be heading in.

"View video," he ordered police central. "Back up to the time of alarm. Double-speed."

The rail's video popped up in his corneal display showing an attractive dark-haired woman with a nice body and an okay face kick out the door. then she and what could only be ratepayer Julia hopped down and jogged eastward, *away* from the designers they were supposed to be rescuing.

He connected with Shenker. "If you're not on it, your troublemakers are just south of 635 and heading east."

"Just called that alarm up myself. I'm pulling every available cop and vectored them in."

"Security video shows the two entering but they went invisible to the rail's telemetry. Meaning they can dynamically change their IDs." Vinson took a deep breath. The shareholders weren't going to be happy about the cost but it had to be done. "Terminate all non-critical missions for any cops currently within five miles and throw them in."

"But... Yes, sir."

"It seems that they've abandoned their mission," Vinson said. "So you can call off the resources you have watching your honeypot."

Shenker considered. "Let me show you something."

A slice of video flickered into his phone and Vinson ran it. "They're going east."

"Did you see Olivia look over her shoulder?"

"Who wouldn't? She needs to know if we're following yet."

"I wouldn't say you're wrong, chief, but you don't know how stubborn Jardan can be. Which is how she got into trouble in the first place. If she has a chance, she'll swing back and pick up those two designers."

"And if you're wrong—"

"I'm not saying we shouldn't seal the border. In fact, I have a great idea. Why not take all of these Interfaith Enforcers and put *them* on the border. Leave me my cops."

That kind of suggestion was one reason Shenker would never rise above lieutenant, why he would never have risen above sergeant under ordinary circumstances.

"If we do that and you're right, Rev. Ariel will accuse us of deliberately misleading his soldiers. If you're wrong, they'll say you put them at risk. Whether you're right or wrong, having that bunch of rogue cits running around centercity unmonitored by cops is a recipe for disaster."

"I hadn't thought of that, sir. I'll send a mix of forces to both locations."

"Do that. I have half a dozen drones overhead. I'm switching them to your control now."

"Thanks, chief. We'll track down these women for you."

"You'd better, lieutenant. I've been handling some pretty rough calls from both Ariel and several high-ups in the CC."

"Rest easy, chief."

Vinson signed off. He wouldn't rest easy. Neutralizing Jardan and Turnboldt was important, but winning the economic war really concerned him. Unfortunately, he had to at least appear fixated on catching the women to keep Ariel off his case. Because Ariel didn't really care who won the war as long as he remained the primary source of intellectual property for Dallas's cits.

Julia

Julia watched the way Olivia moved and tried to imitate it.

She couldn't stretch her legs as far as the ex-cop did, but she connected to her mediplant, instructing it to flush free radicals and carbon dioxide from her system, produce red blood cells, and fully use her lungs.

When it became clear they were going to be running for a while, she toned down her pain receptors, too. Pain could be a useful warning, but it got old in a hurry.

"I thought you said you were going to go ahead with the rescue," she gasped when Olivia slid into a rundown section of what had once been a highway but was now just a hill lightly dotted with solar panels.

"We need to set a trail, throw pursuit off the scent." Olivia wasn't even breathing hard, which wasn't very fair considering Julia had the best ratepayer mediplant.

"I don't have access to a design that would change my smell."

"I was speaking figuratively. You really could build a scenting device?"

"Sure. It'd be easy. Base it on the existing deodorant modules. A lot of that's proprietary code, but we could hack around that."

"Well, let's hope nobody else thinks of it. I meant we'll head this way long enough to confuse any pursuit, then double back to the south and west."

"What makes you think we can get there without being sighted? We already saw one drone overhead and where there's one, there'll be others."

"From up there, one person pretty much looks like another. Besides, that's where the trees are."

"Trees?" They couldn't disguise themselves as trees. Although, given time, a good AI and a constructor, Julia could turn out a resemblance of the two women using tree biomass.

That was the kind of idea that would be put into a sim rather than the real world, Julia knew. Actually designing a perfect replica was a lot more complicated than extracting DNA. For one thing, the DNA approach would take however many years it took to grow a human and they didn't have that kind of time.

"We're looking to hide and someplace surrounded by living and rotting things is the place to do it. Beneath a canopy of trees, they won't be able to detect our respiration from the drones."

Julia nodded. It was better than getting caught right away. It also sounded like a cul-de-sac where the enforcers could track them down at their leisure.

"At least we'll be alive for a while," Olivia said, apparently reading Julia's mind.

"I'm not arguing, I'm just a bit, well, apprehensive."

After that, Julia saved her breath for running.

In far north Dallas, the trees were a good distance from the rail. Still, centercity wasn't *that* big. Sirens were still converging on the sidelined rail car when Olivia and Julia reached the tree canopy.

"Now what?" Julia grabbed the smooth trunk of what looked like a birch tree and leaned against it. Her throat moved convulsively as she fought to hold down her lunch. Fought and lost.

"Oh, gross," Olivia said. "I thought you'd resculpted yourself for conditioning."

Just what Julia needed. Critiques of her mediplant code. "I did what I could with the body I started with. I'm not muscle-bound like you, you know."

"Having some muscles hasn't hurt me any lately."

Julia nodded, pretending she was just too tired and nauseous to argue.

Her stomach gradually settled and finally she let go of her tree. "Are we still going to try to bring in the designers, or should we concentrate on staying alive ourselves?"

"I..." Olivia paused. "I'm been acting like I'm the boss here, but the reason we're doing this is because Kansas and McKensie don't trust anyone they don't know. So, if you want to bail, I guess we bail."

Which put the ball in Julia's court.

If anyone had asked her, even a couple of days before, what she'd decide, she wouldn't even have had to think. Kansas and McKensie weren't her friends. The two were so into themselves and each other, Julia had never figured out why they'd bothered joining free-code in the first place. But she'd promised to help and they needed every designer they could get.

"If we run, Kansas and McKensie are going to die. I say we go and get them."

Olivia nodded. "Thank you."

"For what, probably getting us killed? Anyway, if we're going to do this, I have a suggestion. McKensie and Kansas still have valid IDs, and plenty of credit. They're scared, but if they know we're close, maybe they'll take a chance. And realistically, they'd be safer moving around than waiting for Interfaith Enforcers to raid their house. Let's call them, ask them to rent a car, and pick us up."

Olivia slapped her forehead. "Should work. Get them on the phone and reel them in."

Unfortunately, the gap between a good plan and reality bit them in the rear. Kansas and McKensie continued to refuse to leave their homespace until Julia got there.

"God, I thought *you* were the helpless female type," Olivia said.

"Me?" Julia didn't have to fake shock. She was so independent her mother despaired of her sometimes.

"Am I the only one who remembers a certain boot incident?"

"Oh." Julia hadn't really thought about it, but she had been bitchy to the woman who was saving her life. "Sorry about that."

Olivia gave her a strange look. "You're apologizing to me?"

"Don't let it go to your head. I probably don't mean it."

"All right then." Olivia sighed. "I guess we might as well go and get them."

Olivia

Walking in the woods felt weird. Tree bits, "leaves" her phone told her, covered the ground like a carpet, except they hid stuff under them. Strange smells assaulted her nostrils, and strange rustling noises had her jumping every few feet. They kept walking, circling away from the rail.

They'd just stepped into a clearing when a drone passed overhead, its tiny electrical engine whining as it made small search circles.

"It'll pick us up." Julia froze. At least she had the sense to subvocalize into her phone rather than speaking out loud.

Olivia suspected vocalizing was the least of their problems. The designer made enough noise stumbling through the trees to compensate.

"Don't move until it flies on. We just have to hope this biomass hides us from its sensors. Anyway, the drone is probably better equipped to pick up active electronics and counterwarfare measures that a real invasion force would mount."

It seemed barely possible that the mismatch between their capabilities and what the defense network expected would work in Olivia's favor. At least, Olivia let herself hope that—it was about the only hope she had.

They'd veered sharply when they'd reached the trees, changing their course from due west to south by southwest. Doing so both prolonged their time under the cover of the miniforest canopy and moved them closer to the homespace where Kansas and McKensie waited. But while Dallas centercity might be extravagant, it certainly couldn't afford a continuous forest. Eventually they'd have to emerge.

The sun neared the horizon. Solar panels shifted on their pivots, trying to catch the last photons from the setting sun and casting long shadows across the darkening landscape.

Inside their homespaces, Dallas ratepayers settled down for their evenings, constructed sophisticated food designs or even assembled meals from actual ground-grown plants, doing any last-minute heavy constructing before sunset.

The narrow streets were practically bare of humans and completely free of cars. Julia and Olivia would stand out, would be scanned and, when they failed to show a match with ratepayers in the neighborhood, would be questioned.

"I've got an idea." Olivia looked around, then headed toward the nearest homespace, scanning it when she got within ten meters.

Nothing. Those ratepayers were good little rule-followers and had their seals up and operational.

The seals were up on the next couple of homespaces as well, but when she got to the fourth, she lucked out. People, whether citizen or ratepayer, tended to be lazy. Someone had left a window ajar, an antenna improperly grounded, or, most likely, hadn't noticed when one of the kids had run an illicit tap into the Infoweb to get access to materials that his parents' filters denied.

Whatever the reason, the seals leaked like a free-cit's raincoat. Olivia scanned the residents inside and found two females.

She downloaded the IDs, uploaded one to her own system and forwarded another to Julia.

"Poke that in your RFID, smile and look like a ratepayer," she told the designer.

Julia sniffed. "I am a ratepayer."

"You *think* you're a ratepayer. To the cops, you're a free-cit who *used to be* a ratepayer. Believe me, it isn't the same thing."

Another drone passed overhead, scanned the neighborhood, then continued, apparently convinced by their code.

"This isn't going to work," Julia said. "We'll need the time-based algorithm to keep the ID's valid. Next time we get scanned, we'll be expired, unauthorized."

"Next time we get scanned we'd better have new codes."

Julia looked dubious. "Sooner or later, you'll grab one that's about to expire and you won't know it until too late. Then they'll catch us."

Olivia liked it better when Julia came up with clever plans. Pointing out problems Olivia already knew about but could do nothing to resolve wasn't useful, or fun.

"We'd better hope that 'sooner or later' turns into 'much later.' Later enough for us to get out of here."

Although ratepayers spent a bit more time out of their homespaces than did citizens, Olivia wasn't that worried about the system recognizing two instances of a code wandering around at the same time. And she made sure they only changed their codes when they were very near a citizen homespace. An automated system would see one pair of ratepayers approaching a homespace and a second pair leaving. Perfectly normal.

* * * *

The sun touched the horizon when they finally reached the Lovers Lane region of West centercity-Dallas where Kansas and McKensie lived.

They'd changed IDs six times and found an open seal a couple of blocks away to change for the seventh time when Julia stopped and rubbed her ear.

"Something wrong?"

"I was on the phone with Kansas and McKinsey, letting her know we were getting close, when all of a sudden, the phone cut out."

Olivia checked her own phone. She could punch through to Julia, a few feet away, but that was about it. Since she'd researched phone blocking, she knew how difficult jamming was. It couldn't be just a simple precaution. Somebody knew they were coming.

Their odds of survival dropped like a lead zeppelin.

Shenker

The women were getting close.

Lieutenant Shenker didn't know exactly where they were, but he knew Jardan and Turnboldt had stepped into his trap. All he had to do was make sure it didn't collapse on itself.

He turned to the Interfaith Enforcement captain who'd made himself Shenker's deputy but wouldn't follow orders unless Shenker explained everything in language so simple a two-year-old would expect better. "I ordered the drones away but there's one still there."

"That one's an IE drone, not one of yours."

"Which is why I'm talking to you. Do you want to blow this operation?"

"Your trap would work just as well if we went in and finished the designers first."

It would work better if he murdered the Enforcer, too. But he wasn't going to do either. "Get that drone out of here. We don't want them to suspect anything."

Which was when all hell broke loose.

His link to the Infoweb whimpered and died and his phone connectivity shut down, turning into just a miniature AI in his brain. "Cancel what I said about taking them unaware. Somehow they've managed to jam our signals. That should be impossible."

The captain grinned at him. "Them? Are you kidding? It takes a couple of strong antennas every hundred meters to lay down *this* kind of block. Even if they had access to the blocker design, which is Interfaith classified, they'd also have to have access to a couple of dozen constructors. No way they could do it."

Shenker felt like someone had reached into his chest, grabbed his heart, and twisted. "Meaning?"

"What I said. They didn't do it."

"So, who the hell did? I know I didn't do it. Because jamming their phones is like putting a sign out that says we know they're coming."

"It also takes away your last reason not to kill those designers, Lieutenant. You don't have to worry that the renegades will worry about not getting through. So, why don't I send in the boys to take care of that little matter right now?"

"How, exactly, did you propose to give that order, oh-brainless-one. By phone? Jardan and Turnboldt don't need their phones—last we saw them, they were together. But we do if we're going to coordinate our efforts. So get that blocking turned off. Now."

The IE captain looked chagrined for the first time since he'd attached himself to Shenker's task force. "Uh, I hadn't thought of that."

Shenker ground his teeth, but just for a second. "Just fix it."

"I'd need to phone them and, well, my phone is jammed, too."

Shenker checked his mediplant. If he was ever going to have heart disease, this was the time. He'd explained his plan in excruciating detail, created backup and contingency for everything with the enforcer captain nodding and smiling. Instead of making suggestions, the idiot had just sabotaged him. It wouldn't have been so bad if Olivia had just outsmarted him—at least then he could take consolation that he'd trained her, taught her the tricks. Instead, he got incompetence on the part of a supposed ally.

"Send a runner. Or get your ass in gear and visit them yourself. I need communications to find out how much damage you've done."

"What about the designers. Hadn't you better let me send in a disposal team?"

"Turn off this jamming and then ask me questions."

Shenker didn't kick the IE captain in the ass when that know-nothing slowly turned and stalked out of the observation room he'd set up in a homespace across the street from the designer's, but he was tempted. Working with idiots to hunt down a woman he'd trained himself, who'd gotten into trouble only because she'd tried to be a good cop, gave him a headache his mediplant didn't touch.

Julia

"**The** only way," Olivia said, "they could block our phones is to cut off communications for everyone in the neighborhood. People will notice, be pissed."

Julia studied the black and silver sheen of solar panels reflecting the newly risen moon. Her neighborhood looked a lot like this one, with low homespaces covered with and surrounded by solar panels and with the glow of a billion stars shining through the cloudless night. But her neighborhood had never seemed spooky, never seemed ready to reach out and crush her. "Guess this is what it means to be outnumbered and outgunned. So what are we going to do, just walk up?"

"We need more information."

"How are we going to get that if we can't access our phones?"

Olivia grinned. "If *we* can't use our phones, that means *they* can't either. It's time to go cop-hunting."

Julia shuddered. "You're asking to be fried."

"If you have any suggestions," Olivia sneered, "open up. Otherwise, we'll go with what we've got."

Turning and running was Julia's best thought. But she'd already decided against that. "Whatever you say."

Olivia seemed to flip a mental coin. "We'll circle around to approach the neighborhood from the southwest rather than the north-east. Once we start, you'll cut a chord through the neighborhood without going too close to where Kansas and McKensie live. Since you won't be heading directly toward their homespace, it's possible the cops will assume you're a ratepayer out for a stroll and check you out before shooting. Then I'll catch them."

Julia's blood froze. "I don't like the 'it's possible' and the 'with any luck.' I especially don't like the 'you' instead of 'we.' What if we *don't* have any luck?"

"Then you'll be dead and I'll have to think of something else."

"Wha—you know, I normally have a good sense of humor, but somehow I'm not really on tonight."

"Let's just hope the cops take the bait."

"Oh, so you do have a plan How come I'm bait, not you?"

"You're the girlie one—that makes you the bait."

Julia still didn't like it, but Olivia made sense.

They circled the neighborhood, using the intensity of phone jamming as an indication of where surveillance would be heavy, then stepped outside the worst of the jamming and switched codes an eighth time. Julia made sure Olivia gave her the code for a female.

"You're a ratepayer." Olivia ran through last-minute explanations as their phones fritzed out. "You're out for a walk because you've been working on a design and needed some fresh air to clear your head, or maybe to find a connection."

"You told me that so often, my memory overloaded."

Olivia ignored Julia's interruption. "Whatever you do, buy time. If a female-cop stops you, bond. Make her think you're the most understanding ratepayer in the world for recognizing how hard she's working to protect those who pay her. If it's a man, flirt. Cops dream about hooking up with a real ratepayer and moving to centercity."

"You're kidding?" Julia barely bit back an audible 'eeew' at the thought of an actual long-term coupling with a cop, then realized she'd been thinking reflexively. If Olivia was a typical example, she could do worse—hell, she had done worse. Unfortunately, she didn't go for other women, but if she could find a guy like Olivia, she wouldn't say "eeew."

Olivia

As the designer stepped ahead of her, Olivia noticed that Julia's shoes transformed themselves as she walked, their heels extended into the kind of calf-lengthening spikes she'd worn when she met Julia.

Julia was going into vamp mode. Although she probably didn't mean to, she was also showing Olivia the difference between them. Olivia's shoes were practical and cost very little. But when Julia had dumped her fancy natural-material shoes, had she constructed a pair like Olivia's? No. She still had the code to make something that could be either practical or showy, depending on what Julia wanted. That design probably cost more than a year of Olivia's police salary.

She gave Julia a lead, then skulked after her, keeping in the shadows, her dark tunic fading to match the grayness of the moonlit Dallas sky.

For the first couple of blocks, it looked like Olivia's plan was another bust.

Just as Julia turned a corner, though, a cop stepped out of the night, his chameleon tunic fading from a perfect match for the shadows to a light blue.

"I'm sorry, ma'am. This area is closed to pedestrian traffic."

"But it's centercity." Julia's upper-class accent showed a perfect mix of incredulity and disdain.

"With unanimous approval from the T-50, top fifty corporations, as required in the Corporate Dallas charter, the police corporation has been authorized to impose curfews. I'm afraid I'll have to take you to our mobile detention center to have you verified."

Julia put her hands on her hips, pulled back her shoulders, stuck out her breasts and took a deep breath. "How was I supposed to know about this curfew, considering that my phone isn't working?"

"I'd think that the phone problems would make you more cautious, ma'am. Relax and come along with me, please. We'll verify your codes and then one of the officers on duty will make sure you make it home safely."

Olivia edged closer. This would be a good time for Julia to follow her advice, flirt a little, get the guy to drop his guard. Julia could handle the flirting thing, she'd certainly done the job on Martin. Unfortunately, she must have gotten too grossed out by the idea of cozying up to a cop.

"You are being ridiculous," Julia said. "There's no invasion here. I'll tell you, I've never been one of those who thought ordinary citizens should be cut off from the public constructors, but I had no idea *your people* could be so jealous of ratepayer success. Real ratepayers work hard for everything we get, you know. You seem to think you have a right to just lay around, exploiting all of the hard work that we do, watching your sims and sucking up photons and hydrocarbons like they only exist to make your life comfortable."

The cop stiffened, every ounce of his focus on the designer. "I'm a ratepayer, myself, ma'am. All cops are."

Julia's laugh was a masterpiece of contempt. "A *ratepayer*? You pay what, a few bucks for minimal life insurance? You call *that* paying rate?"

Olivia could have stomped her feet on the ground and whistled as she closed the distance. The cop was so mad, he had no attention to share with anyone else.

A flicker in Julia's eyes showed that she saw Olivia approaching. She turned her vitriol even higher.

"Minimal ratepayers? Talk about the biggest jokes in the system. Are your children enrolled in the apprentice programs? I don't think so. Have you designed anything that any corporation includes in their design portfolio? Of course not. And you call yourself a ratepayer. Puh-leeze."

"It may be a joke to you, but—"

Olivia chopped to the side of his neck, cutting off whatever he was going to say.

Julia spun toward her, beads of sweat flying from her forehead." Couldn't you have waited another hour? I only had to repeat myself something like three times."

Olivia knelt beside the groggy cop, her leggings automatically thickening in the knees to protect her from the rough solar fabric that coated twentieth century roads. She patted him down, stripping away a shock gun, a baton, an unmarked spray canister, and several carbon buckyball restraints so thin that they'd cut off a prisoner's hands if he struggled. "You made him so mad he couldn't think." Olivia considered, then decided to let Julia have what she was holding back. "You made me mad, too. Sorry if that made me slow."

"Why would you be mad?"

"You think I like that kind of talk?"

Julia looked puzzled for an instant, then laughed. "I was channeling my father. You know I like you, right?"

"Really? I'd hate to see how you treat those you don't like."

"Watch me with Kansas and McKensie."

"You don't like them but you're trying to save them."

"I don't want to be responsible for getting them killed. Besides, I already told you we need every developer we can get to finish Merryweather's project."

The cop groaned as he regained consciousness. "What happened? Who are you?"

Some cops got a kick out of restraining a prisoner's hands behind his back, and watching him jerk those hands off in his attempts to get free. Olivia didn't have time for that kind of game. She used one of the cop's restraints to bring his hands together in front of him and locked them down. "You know what will happen if you try to get out, right?"

A good body scrub could repair the loss of a couple of hands. But only if he got to a constructor in time. With the phone system down, the cop had to know that his chances weren't great. He might actually die.

"What do you want from me?"

"A little information."

"Tell me what you want and I'll give it to you. It isn't like it'll help you. We've got the entire city locked down."

Nobody could be that bad a liar. He might be telling the truth.

"What were you doing here?"

"Like I told the ratepayer, we've got a curfew in place."

"And shut down the phones."

"I thought that was you. Shenker is all about maintaining contact."

Olivia's blood froze. Paul Shenker had been a cop when she'd been constructing AlmostLive™ dolls. He knew secrets she couldn't guess. There'd be no stopping him.

"Why the curfew?"

"It's a trap. Someone, I'm guessing it's you, is supposed to be heading this way and we're to apprehend them, just like in the old-time cop sims. I can't believe I caught you."

Julia snickered. "Yeah, you caught us all right."

"Don't go counting your completion bonus yet, junior," Olivia said. "If I were you, I'd be more worried about staying alive than how much you might earn."

"I would have caught you if it hadn't been for the phone jamming. How'd you do it?"

"That wasn't our trick."

He shook his head. "Great. I'll bet it's those loser I.E. types."

"You're working with Interfaith Enforcement?" Julia tried to make her question sound casual. From Olivia's perspective, it hadn't worked. She just hoped the cop was distracted worrying about cutting his hands off.

"Not a brain in the whole lot—but they sure like killing."

Olivia didn't need to hear that.

"Here's a heads up," she said. "If you report, they'll know we talked, right? They'll know we told you that police central is violating the corporate consensus, that it's going after paid ratepayers just because they happen to get a kick out of free-coding."

"I don't think I want to hear this."

"Too late, junior." Olivia felt a trickle of guilt. She'd just ruined this kid's life, and she'd done it for nothing more than to gain a slight edge.

She swallowed, trying to swallow the guilt with the saliva in her mouth. "You now officially know too much. Central finds out, you're looking at a brainscrub, minimum. Based on what's happened to everyone else who knew the secret, it could be worse. They'll probably slime you."

Sweat dripped from his abruptly green face. "If I get a brainscrub, I can't be a cop. What would happen to my parents?"

"Same thing that happens to anyone's parents," Julia said. "I told you that you weren't a real ratepayer."

"Come on, Julia. Cut the kid some slack." Julia might want to play good-cop, bad-cop, but Olivia had little patience for the good cop side.

She turned her attention back to the cop. "You want to know what will happen to your family? Maybe they'll *only* be turned out of their homespace when you fail to come up with their rate. More likely, they'll lose everything and have to subsist off of the public constructors. If you hurry, you can save them a place in line."

His eyes showed he'd seen that happen, but it had always been *other* people, never *his* people. Olivia had been the same way.

She let him stew on that for a quarter-minute then pretended she was just getting an idea. "Hey, there is one possibility, one way that things could work out all right for you. No brainscrub, no parents thrown out onto the streets, nothing bad at all."

"What's that?" He seemed to be holding his breath, poor punk.

"You'd better hope that we get away." Julia's voice still held notes of the haughty ratepayer, but she added a subsonic vibration that hit the cop like a palm-heel to the solar plexus. "If we get away, maybe nobody will learn that we talked."

"I've *got* to report it, don't I? I'd be guilty of taking unauthorized financial gain otherwise."

"I thought we were talking to a ratepayer, not some fearful clone of the Interfaith." Julia sighed theatrically. "See Olivia. I was right and you were wrong. I said you'd need to kill him, but you insisted he had at least two brain neurons to rub together."

The cop jerked as if Julia had kicked him. "Wait a second. If I don't talk and you get away…"

"Then who would know?" Olivia finished his sentence for him.

He screwed up his face in a way that could reflect some sort of stomach ailment, but was more likely his way of summoning up his time-stamped memory modules. "I'll tell you what I can and I won't report the conversation."

"Well?"

"We started patrolling the streets a couple hours ago. Forty-two minutes ago, we announced a curfew, advising everyone to stay off the streets. Five minutes later, the jamming went into effect."

"How many cops and how many IE types? Olivia asked.

"There were eight cops from my section, and that eight is all the *cops* I know about for sure. There's one IE type for every cop but they just sit around with their eyes glazed over, mostly. I don't know for sure what other cops are here. Other than Shenker, himself."

"Is this the only area under lockdown?"

Their cop wanted to come up with an answer so bad it hurt him. "Uh, I just don't know."

If Shenker was on site at the Kansas/McKensie homespace, he'd had predicted their moves. That was bad news.

"What's your assigned route? When are you supposed to report? I want a download, now." This close, the jamming wouldn't stop a transmission.

"But those are my personal orders."

"So, decrypt first. Don't let fantasy obscure reality on this one, pretty-boy. They'll brain-scrub you for meeting me or for knowing about the free-coders. They find out you did both, you won't get a bonus, you'll get dead."

"I understand," the cop squeaked. "Here's the download."

Martin

Martin initiated another call and got nowhere. He reminded himself that Olivia and Julia had probably switched codes, but he still felt a heavy weight of responsibility. He'd sent them into danger. He would be responsible if they were captured.

His heart picked up when his phone signaled, but it was his bosses in Corporate Houston.

"Reynolds."

"Mr. Reynolds, we've been hearing disturbing reports."

"Is that good or bad, sir?"

"Don't play innocent, Reynolds, it doesn't suit you."

"If you're referring to Corporate Dallas's crackdown on free-coders, I think this could be excellent for us. We're talking about the potential to split the Dallas CC and the Dallas Interfaith right down the middle. Without the Interfaith supporting the CC, citizens are much more likely to listen to the Corporate Houston message."

A moment of silence let Martin hope his bosses would be convinced. He was, after all, telling the truth—just not the entire truth.

"We understand that you're supporting free-code. You will now stop—"

"You can't begin to understand how much sympathy we're getting through that move." Martin interrupted before he could be given orders he didn't want to hear and kept talking fast. "The Dallas CC seems to have put some kind of filter on information in the Infoweb, but the truth is getting out. Corporate Midcities is responding to my entreaties and Corporate Fort Worth seems completely indignant about allowing Interfaith Enforcers into centercity to murder full ratepayers."

"Don't play games with us, Reynolds. You may fantasize about free-code changing the world, but the world has no place for utopian pipe dreams."

"Maybe not, sir. But you need dreamers to create a revolution, and that's what you asked me to accomplish."

"Follow orders and don't even think about stabbing us in the back, Reynolds. Your children are going to want to be ratepayers someday. You step out of line, they'll be blackballed in every Corporate City in North America."

Martin struggled to keep his voice from trembling. "I'll keep that in mind, sir."

"That would show more wisdom than you've shown in the past, Mr. Reynolds."

He hung up and opened his eyes to see Justin staring at him. "You've been ordered to stop this program. Correct?"

"You monitored my phone?" Although the CC insisted the phone encryption was unbreakable, Martin had never really trusted that statement.

Justin's chuckle ended in a hacking cough. "No," he gasped when he could breathe enough to talk. "I read your lips. You really should learn to phone without using them."

"They're ordering me to can free-code, just as you said they would," Martin agreed.

"And?"

Martin took a breath. Ideals were easy when there was no personal risk. If he ignored his orders, Corporate Houston would cut their support, follow up on their threats and probably betray him to Corporate Dallas.

He breathed again, slowly, cranking his medical implant to control his heartbeat. "The project goes on."

"You're going renegade?"

"I'm not going to *tell* them I'm ignoring their instructions."

"They threatened your children, didn't they?"

"You didn't read *that* on my lips."

"I read it on the wind. They'll use whatever tools they can do retain their power. Their attacks on the free-coders show exactly how much they care about the supposed ideals of corporate freedom."

"But what else is there?"

Justin shook his head. "I'm not that old. But I will tell you one thing."

Martin waited.

"You'd better find an answer. Because if you don't find an alternative, your entire free-code thing will just become another corporate entity. That isn't what Julia meant when she suggested incorporating, but that's the way it'll go."

Martin nodded, then went back to his mapping program. At dozens of locations around Dallas, free-cits built little homespaces for whatever coders they could rescue—and Houston-model special purpose constructors turned out components for self-assembling cruise missiles. They might call it *economic* war, but destruction and death were still part of it.

Olivia

Equipped with their cop's own map and schedule, Olivia and Julia veered toward their goal.

Julia had stripped the tunic from the unresisting cop, its smart fabric automatically repairing itself where it had been cut by the monomolecular restraints that held the cop in place. They'd programmed those restraints to sublimate in ten minutes, once Olivia and Julia were well away.

Olivia didn't dare hope that cops would mistake them for other cops— cops scanned first and asked questions later. But cops might mistake them for Interfaith Enforcers, whose uniforms weren't quite as regimented.

Even without that, the tunics provided a fair degree of protection, not to mention blending with the background.

Walking as stealthily as she could, Olivia led Julia toward the homespace where the two free-code designers might, possibly, be waiting.

"Something about this stinks." Julia had been quiet since leaving the cop.

"Only one thing?"

"A bunch of things. But what stinks most is, why leave the girls alive? Once they cut off the phones, they might as well kill them. They were going to do that anyway, right?"

Well, duh. That was why they were rescuing them. Which meant Julia asked one heck of a good question.

"How would the cops get into their homespace?"

"How did they get into your homespace? They dissolved it, right?"

"You might be right."

Julia followed her for perhaps half a minute. "I might be right, but you're not turning around. How come?"

"I know Shenker. If he *has* to torture or kill, he'll do it. He won't even look at himself funny in the mirror. But he won't kill just for fun. He's got those designers under his control and he doesn't think he's going to lose them, so why should he kill them?"

"So our rescue puts them in danger."

That, unfortunately, was what Olivia was worried about. "He's not the head boss. They know too much and they'll have to be killed."

"Yeah, but—"

Olivia subvocalized a halt command and faded into the darkness behind a solar collector farm.

"What?"

"Our friendly cop's patrols only go this far. We've got two blocks to go. Shenker will have another squad within this perimeter."

"Want me to troll again?"

It had worked so well the first time that Olivia was tempted, but only for a second. If she'd been in charge, she would set up the inner perimeter with every cop in full visual contact with at least one other. If she'd do it that way, Shenker would too, unless he thought of something even sneakier.

"Turn your tunic to full chameleon and pull it up over your hair."

"That cop sweated in it. I've never met so many people with nanobe failure before today."

"It's a smart fabric, dummy. All of the waste will be wicked to the surface for feed. I shook it out before I gave it to you so there shouldn't be any molecular traces from him."

"It's still disgusting."

Olivia showed Julia how to adjust the police tunic's video frequency. Full chameleon was imperfect during daytime hours when the tunic couldn't begin to match the intensity of light from the sun. In the evenings, it worked like a charm.

"Move slowly and stay in the shadows," Olivia subvocalized.

"I'll just follow you," Julia promised.

* * * *

Olivia froze.

She'd spotted a couple of cops as she and Julia had made their way toward their target. Fortunately, the cops couldn't both maintain full chameleon and keep watch on each other, and several of them looked to be getting bored as well, standing and stretching their legs, or using inhalants to give themselves energy jolts.

She'd tried to think of a way of taking them out, but Shenker's overlapping zones and full visual contact made that impossible.

Three men and a women, all carrying sniper equipment and with hoods down but not locked, waited just outside the homespace door. Shenker was the tallest of the three. That didn't mean she'd identified the danger, though. Her former mentor would have snipers hidden somewhere else.

She pointed out the ones she could see to Julia. "Try phoning Kansas or McKensie from here."

Julia stared into space for a second. "Still jammed."

"We'll have to get even closer."

"What's the plan?"

"We bring them out, as promised."

"But there are three cops with sniper scopes at the front door."

"So, we use the back door."

Julia must have thought she was crazy. "They don't have a back door."

"Now that's a problem we can fix. *I hope.*"

"I wish you hadn't added that last part."

Chameleon on full, they crawled the last two hundred feet, finally reaching the homespace a hundred and eighty degrees from where the three snipers waited.

Olivia swept her gaze over the nearby homespaces and solar collection grids. Shenker was waiting at the front, but he'd guard the back, too.

"What should I do?"

"I'm going cop-hunting. I want you to wait for my signal."

"What signal is that?"

Well, duh. Olivia had never experienced a time when her phone didn't work, when she couldn't simply subvocalize a command or order over any distance whatsoever. But if she stepped more than a couple of arms lengths from Julia, the two women would be out of communication range.

"If I'm not back in half an hour, assume the job is blown and head back to Martin."

"I thought we were a team."

Olivia forced a smile. "I said *if.* I'm planning on winning this one."

She stretched her tunic until it took the form of a long hooded duster, covering her legs and feet, as well as her head.

Despite the fabric's wicking properties, this was Dallas and it was still hot. Heat and discomfort were part of the price she paid for the chameleon qualities.

"Couldn't we just go in like this?" Julia whispered. If they can't see us, they can't shoot us."

"We could go in, but we couldn't come out. We don't have extra tunics for the girls. Besides, when those solar panels break up, they'll know we're there. They won't have to see us to shoot. And if they know where to look, their equipment will spot us. These are cop tunics, after all."

"Good points. Never mind that comment."

Olivia nodded, then realized Julia wouldn't see the gesture and shook her head at herself, finally gritting her teeth in frustration that she couldn't stop the head movements even when they were invisible.

This shared journey had been something of an eye-opener. Julia had shown toughness Olivia wouldn't have guessed at. She was in danger of actually starting to like the designer.

"See you in a few."

Shenker

Some sixth sense warned him they were close. Shenker put on an air of nonchalance, but made sure he had a shell chambered in his sniper rifle.

He didn't want to kill Olivia, but that was the only option. She'd gotten involved so deeply, connected with corporate enemies. If Shenker failed, another cop would be brought in. The only difference would be, Shenker would be dead as well.

Once the idiot Interfaith Enforcer went off to turn off the jamming, Shenker actually had a minute or so to think. He took the time to review the video of the two women on the train.

One was obviously Olivia. He recognized Turnboldt from Vinson's party. Had she realized then that she was being sought? Could she have been spying on the police? Not that she'd find anything from Vinson's wife. The woman didn't have a clue.

He checked the time, then slipped into full chameleon mode and made another circle around the house.

All of the cops seemed to be in place. *Seemed*, because he couldn't talk to them with the phones blocked. In his gut, he knew that the two women had made it through the outer perimeter, but he had no solid evidence and no way to contact those cops and learn the truth or share his insight.

The Interfaith Enforcement guy, wearing a chameleon that wasn't even buttoned, bobbed into sight a dozen yards away. "Lieutenant, where are you?"

The temptation to line him up in the sniper rifle sights was overwhelming. He could even blame Olivia for the tragic death.

But that was fantasy. When he fired his rifle, its trigger images would be downloaded into central's AI. He couldn't even snap the guy's neck because forensics would determine that a tall man, rather than a somewhat less tall woman, had done the deed.

Instead, he unzipped his chameleon hood. "Keep your voice down, Commander."

"I wanted to let you know I've got the jamming scheduled to end in two hours. That's six hours ahead of schedule."

He sighed. "I need it off now."

The enforcer shrugged. "Next time, our designers will add more control elements. For now, that's the best we can do."

Shenker nodded, then handed over his sniper rifle. "The two women are somewhere around here. They'll be wearing chameleon and unlike you, they'll know how to control it. The free-code designers they're trying to rescue won't be. So watch for them."

"You seriously think two women can make it through my enforcers? No disrespect to your cops, Lieutenant, but my enforcers are tough."

"Jardan will eat your enforcers with a spoon. Now get under cover and watch the homespace. I put an obvious guard on the front to encourage her to approach from the rear flank."

The enforcer stroked the sniper rifle like he would a woman. "What are you doing while I kill the bitches?"

"I'm preparing for their escape. Thanks to your jamming, they have a chance of getting away."

Martin

Martin gritted his teeth in frustration. Julia had handed over Merryweather's latest library of modules and training just before she and Olivia had vanished into centercity, but he simply couldn't understand the code. After he and Merryweather had come up with the idea, he'd dropped out of design school to become a spy. But that meant this program was out of his hands. If the designers couldn't make it work, there was nothing he could do about it.

He scrolled through one of the simpler modules one more time. He recognized the language, of course. He recognized most of the syntax and had an idea of the logic, but he could no more write this code than he could make spaghetti without a constructor.

Sitting and waiting was not something he enjoyed doing, especially since Olivia and Julia might have been compromised.

"Why don't you ask what we can do, rather than worry about what we can't do?" Jimmy asked.

Sometimes Martin wondered what his life would be like without his children. This was one of those times. He tousled his son's hair, then got on the phone with Ethan, one of the older escaped designers.

"You have what, six months of design training and you want to help?" Ethan asked before Martin could even finish.

"There's got to be *something* I can do."

"If the training sims were made, you could go full submersion and become a designer in a year or so. But it isn't."

"A year?" Within a year, they'd either have won or been crushed.

"It's a five-year program to become a designer. Just one year would take a miracle."

"What can I do without being a designer?"

Ethan considered. "Get us more designers."

"Working on that." At least Olivia and Julia were. He'd brought in all the free-coders he'd been able to locate outside centercity. For any others still inside, he had little hope. But there was something he could do. He'd thought about the free-code crackdown in terms of political support, but maybe he could use it to attract designer support from the free-code communities in Corporate Midcities and Corporate Fort Worth. When they heard about what was happening in Dallas, some of them would probably give up free-code altogether. But not all. He could—

But Ethan wasn't done. "You can set defenses so they can't kill us if they find us."

"Working on it." Now that Justin was supporting them, free-cits from everywhere past Corporate Dallas's outer rings were manufacturing defenses to the specs sent him by Corporate Houston. He couldn't stop a major military effort, but he could make it more costly-and cost was one thing the corporate consensus could understand.

"One more thing. Make sure we have political and authentication cover when we come out with our modules."

"Yeah, there's that." Julia had raised the issue, but Martin didn't know where to go with it. Code modules were never pirated because customers bought them directly from approved vendors who took them through extensive testing and who then digitally signed them, using CC-certified authentication authorities to make certain they hadn't been altered.

"Work on it hard," Ethan said. "It's important. I can't understand how Merryweather ignored it."

Merryweather had ignored it for the same reason Martin had—they'd both wanted to believe they could implement free-code within the existing system. They'd envisioned some resistance, but hadn't even dreamed they'd be subject to mass murder or intentional sabotage. Martin hated to admit it, but he'd been naive. He just had to hope his naiveté wouldn't get too many more people killed.

"What about testing?" Angie demanded. "We could do that."

"What about testing?" he echoed.

Ethan considered. "Every designer tests his own stuff, but since we design it, we subconsciously avoid breaking it. I guess you could set up a test shop."

Martin high-fived his daughter. He didn't know where to start with the political cover angle, but he had a real good idea of how to implement a test program. A few months of design training hadn't made him much of a coder, but it sure made him good at breaking things.

Olivia

Ironically, Shenker's jamming gave her a chance.

Her tunic's chameleon feature worked by gathering images on one side of the fabric and projecting them from the other. The process took a fair electrical current and generated a definite electronic signature—a signature that every cop knew to look for. But multiband jamming meant no electronic detection. The cops would have to rely on thermal imaging, visual target identification, and cop intuition.

She worried about Shenker's intuition, but the man couldn't be everywhere, and she'd seen him out in front of the homespace.

Olivia stayed low, blending with the black solar panels that would glow like stars in the infrared spectrum. Typical panels operated at only eighty-five percent efficiency, which meant that almost fifteen percent of the sunlight hitting them was turned into heat rather than electricity. Infrared vision would see them, not her.

As they'd circled the homespace, Olivia had worked the triangulation and viewed the firing lanes. Two sniper sites met the criteria Shenker had drilled into her brain. He'd position his best sniper team in one of them. The question was which?

He'd only need one, so she figured the other would be trapped, set to send warning signals and ideally to disable anyone checking it out. Given her hurry, traps could be more dangerous than living enemies.

She narrowed her eyes, using cop-sculpted zoom magnification to look more closely at her two potential targets.

The first was a two-story homespace. Most homespaces were limited to a single story, maximizing the amount of space presented to the sun and avoid shading neighbors' property. If you needed more space, you expanded underground. This homespace, though, appeared to have been constructed on top of an ancient twentieth-century residence. It towered over the neighborhood.

Rows of plant material interspersed with solar panels, creating a sort of island-look to the place, as it would have to, since no one would live butted against a sun-blocking two-story residence. The exceptional height provided satisfactory firing angles, while the combination of plant material and solar panels meant it would be difficult for an assault team to sneak up unobserved.

The second possible site was a small grove of trees. Snipers could hide in the trees, their weapons appearing to be merely sticks hanging out of the branches.

After her journey today, *she* would have picked the trees. They were closer to the Kansas/McKensie homespace, would be tricky to approach, and had the added advantage that each sniper could take a different tree. That added degree of separation would equate to safety. Sneaking up on and taking out one cop would be tough. Finishing off the first, then making her way up another tree to a second would likely be impossible. The drawbacks were discomfort and the slightly shaky firing platform.

She didn't think Shenker had spent much more time in centercity than she had, though. And before today, she wouldn't have trusted living plant objects. For a cop-sniper, a structure meant safety, familiarity, and solidity.

She decided to go for the homespace.

Shenker would have one sniper watching the target at all times. The other would be more relaxed, but would also cover the other approaches.

Since most cops were right handed, and since the backup cop wouldn't want to risk getting in the way of a shooter, he'd probably station himself to the left of the shooter.

She approached the two-story homespace from the north, which she hoped would be the shooter's right.

Her tunic heated as its chameleon mode retained her infrared energy. With every step, she half-expected to hear the sharp crack of an armor-piercing projectile going supersonic. With each move, her shoulders tightened from the anticipated impact of a bullet.

She breathed a small sigh when she reached the structure unharmed. She wouldn't be caught in the no-man's land between safety and the snipers.

She pressed herself against the structure, her tunic fabric bonding with the glassy solar panels that formed the homespace walls.

She waited for the chameleon effect to finalize, then began the vertical climb.

If she'd worn cop assault boots, it would have been easy. Those boots would grab the panels, allowing her to walk up a wall as easily as walking up a ladder. But she had gone with shoes designed for walking.

The tunic stuck. But that didn't make this any easier. Unless she was very careful, the tunic would stick to the wall and she'd slip out of it—ending up naked and fully visible on the ground.

She gritted her teeth and inched up the wall, keeping her arms outstretched so that the tunic couldn't slide off her body.

Sweat poured from her body faster than the tunic's wicking action could handle, making her think of one of those steaming things her father would eat as part of whatever Interfaith special he was addicted to these days. Twenty feet, barely over six meters. It didn't *sound* like much.

It *felt* like miles.

A seam between two panels gave her a toehold and she used that to push upwards. After what had seemed an eternity, and was probably a good two minutes, she grasped the homespace's rainwater collector.

Shifting her weight to the collector, though, caused an audible creak in its structure.

She froze.

Seams and creaky structures were both odd. Surely even centercity ratepayers, more concerned about status than efficiency, wouldn't have left up an old gutter as their water collector. Olivia couldn't imagine anyone wasting rainwater.

"You hear something, Frank?" The voice was impossibly close.

"Yeah. This old place is falling apart. Why you figure ratepayers want to live like this?"

"Because it makes them different from ordinary schmucks like us."

"I'm going to check the intrusion system."

"Good idea. Notify the ratepayers inside that they have someone perched on their roof, why don't you?"

"Who cares? What are they going to do, call the cops?"

She heard fear in the second cop's voice. "You're talking about ratepayers, Frank. People living in a place this big, this ostentatious, are either designers or have access to designers. They just might turn anyone standing on their roof, uninvited, into feed."

"Jeez. You're kidding, right?"

"Ever play those old sims about getting the CC started? You know, where you take a corporation and try to make it succeed? All that killing was real."

Olivia took advantage of their conversation to shift her position, bring another toe into the small gap. When she'd recovered her breath, she launched herself over the gutter and onto the rooftop.

She'd expected smooth solar panels. Instead, pipes and external antennae jutted from the roof.

She barely missed being skewered by one of the pipes, then drew the baton she'd abstracted from the kid-cop and kept on rolling across the rooftop until she collided with the backup man, the cop who'd be more immediately dangerous.

He'd been wary from the sound she'd made with the gutter and he had drawn an electronic stunner, but her tunic's chameleon effect, coupled with Olivia's quick movement, confused him for just long enough.

A strike with the butt of the baton to his gut bent him over. She brought her knee up in a short swing to his head.

He went down hard.

No time to finish him. She continued the baton's rotation, driving it forward from her hips, then letting it go, throwing it directly at second cop's rifle.

Reflexively, the sniper used his weapon to parry the incoming baton. That was a mistake. If he'd shot her, she would be dead and he would, at most, have a broken rib or two. But a trained fighter relies on instincts and training. As she'd expected, counted on, the sniper's training had stressed blocking and countering, rather than ignoring attacks and blasting away.

She followed her baton, got inside the long gun's reach and distracted him with a roundhouse kick to his knee.

The sniper either wasn't much of a cop or he wasn't a cop at all. Rather than club his rifle, using it like a staff for close-in fighting, he held onto his weapon, raising his leg to avoid her kick.

Which was fine with her. She drove a back leg front thrust kick directly into his back knee—the one now supporting all of his weight.

The sniper groaned dropped, conscious but injured. She let him fall to the ground, opening distance between them, but an awful realization hit her. She was no longer inside the rifle's firing point.

The cop—or possibly Interfaith Enforcer—gritted his teeth against the pain in his knee and swung the rifle toward her.

She rolled to where the baton had rebounded, scooped it up, and shoving its tip into the barrel until carbon grated with carbon.

"Go ahead and shoot," she said, hoping desperately she was right, that he wasn't a cop, that he wouldn't have the experience to see through her bluff. "See if the bullet drives the baton out of the barrel or if the expanding powder just blows the lock out in your face. I'm betting your face takes the brunt."

He hesitated, then decided to take the gamble and tightened his finger on the trigger.

But Olivia hadn't waited. She used the baton as a lever, shoving the rifle point away from her as she drove a knee straight into his ribs.

As she'd thought it would, the bullet drove the baton out of the barrel with no problem at all.

Or rather, with no problem for the bullet or for her. The carbon baton shattered under the impact of the armor-piercing shell. And the sniper was in trouble because he was still thinking about the gun and too distracted to pay full attention to his opponent.

She dropped forward onto his chest, trapping his arms and then found the carotid artery going toward his brain and pinched it off.

Three seconds later, he sighed, then relaxed.

She looked around to see that the first cop she'd clouted had gotten to his feet and regained his stunner. He took a step forward, wobbled, and only held his footing by retreating. Still, he looked ready to continue the fight as best he could.

Olivia pulled the rifle from the sniper's unresisting arms, checked to see that a new round had automatically chambered, and pointed it at the backup.

"Drop it."

"Go ahead and shoot. You'll just attract more attention."

"If anyone was going to be attracted, the first shot would have done it. If you don't drop the stunner, I'll take my chances."

His brain was scrambled from the hard knock she'd given him, but he logicked out that she had a point and threw the stunner over the edge of the building.

"Very sensible." She grabbed restraints from a pocket in her tunic. "I want you to secure your partner. He's alive and if you're careful, he may stay that way. Completely up to you." She tossed him one of the restraints she'd taken from the kid-cop what seemed like a year before.

"Frank's not my partner. He's an Interfaith loser."

"Cool. You can kill him if you want."

"Tempting, but maybe I'd better not."

He secured first Frank then himself to a pair of the pipes.

"Just so you know," she said in a conversational tone, "things are getting a little tricky. If you're smart, once you get loose, you might think about asking central for some vacation time."

"Or else what? You going to come after me? I don't think so."

She sighed. "Or else things get tricky—for you. How much of a completion payment do you figure to make from this job? Nothing, right? So, was it worth the pain, the knock on the head, the annoyance of sitting up here watching a homespace you know you'll never be able to afford?"

"Well—"

"Your choice. If you're too stupid to make the right one, I guess you deserve the Darwin Award you're going to get."

She left him there to think about it and headed back to Julia and the Kansas/McKensie homespace.

Julia

Olivia had been gone for too long.

Julia lay flat on the ground behind a group of solar panels. Her chameleon tunic tried to dump body heat into the ground, but she felt like an overconstructed potato about to explode from steam buildup.

She gestured her phone into operation, but got nothing but the buzz of jamming.

To stave off boredom, she analyzed the cop schedule she'd downloaded from the kid she and Olivia had waylaid.

The pattern was obvious.

Shenker had everyone on a two-hours on, two-hours off cycle.

They had twenty minutes before someone went looking for a missing cop. Once they found him, or learned he'd vanished, they'd know for sure they had an intrusion and would circle the entire neighborhood with so many cops an ant couldn't sneak through.

Her muscles tried to lock, resisting her certainty that she needed to move, even without Olivia.

Every slide forward, each push with her knees took an effort of will. Five minutes ticked away as she crawled, meter by meter, across twenty meters from the outer solar panels to the actual walls of the homespace. Each meter, she swallowed hard, glad her stomach was empty and trying not to vomit again—now that would be a giveaway.

By the time she touched the solar panels that made up the outer wall of the Kansas/McKensie homespace, she felt like a solid mass of bruises.

But she was alive.

Putting her forehead directly on the solar panel, she turned the entire homespace into an antenna.

"Who is it?" Kansas's voice sounded subdued. Then again, Kansas was always subdued.

Right. The last ID code Olivia had scanned would have expired by now. Kansas's phone would register her as invalid.

"It's Julia."

"Julia? But the phones have been… they're still out. How—"

"Are you and McKensie ready to go?"

"Where are we going?"

"Right now, I'd worry about staying alive, Kansas. I told you that they're killing everyone they can catch from free-code."

"But we've been here for almost a day and nobody's bothered us. Maybe they just wanted the leaders."

Julia forced herself not to sigh. She had to be persuasive when she felt like tearing down the wall and beating the snot out of both women. "Have you made a call lately, Kansas?"

"Something's jamming our connections. Has the economic war broken out so early? I thought we had weeks."

"It's not the economic war and it's not all of Dallas. You're the center of a dead zone about a mile in diameter. Think about what that means."

Kansas was a dip, but she wasn't stupid. "We're alive because we're bait."

"And you know what happens to bait. Now get ready. I'm leaving in two minutes. If you want to come, that's how long you have."

A conference tone indicated that McKensie had been added. "You browbeating Kansas, Julia?"

"I'm trying to save both of your lives."

"Well, you're too late. There's someone camped right outside our door."

"So you just want to give up and die?"

"Why would they kill us?" McKensie demanded.

"They're cops and Interfaith Enforcers. They're threatened by everything you stand for."

"Yeah, but—"

"McKensie, I'm tired and scared and sick and I'm past caring whether you come or not. If you want to stay and die, go ahead. It sounded to me like Kansas isn't ready to die. Maybe I'll take her and leave you."

"If she goes, I go."

"Make up your mind then."

"But what about the guys outside the front door?" Kansas demanded.

Julia wasn't the only person smart enough to make physical contact with the house and set up an antenna connection that way. The less she told the two women, the less they'd be able to leak.

"We're going to create a distraction, maybe even take out the cops you've got guarding it. Grab whatever you need and head to the back of your homespace where you'll be safely away from the explosions. I'll let you know when it's time to go."

She practically jumped out of her skin when something touched her in the back. She glanced behind her and saw nothing—until Olivia pulled back her hood.

Pulling her forehead away from the homespace, Julia subvocalized, "You're still alive?"

"Barely."

"I've got Kansas and McKensie heading this way. I told them we're going to blow up the front of the house or something. If one of them is squealing, that might distract the cops.

"Good thinking."

Olivia crossed her fingers, took out an unmarked aerosol tube she'd stolen from the kid-cop, and sprayed one of the solar panels that made the homespace's exterior walls.

A few seconds later, the panel sagged and Olivia ran what looked like a crystalline carbon knife along the weakened surface, scoring it, then knocking it out.

McKensie and Kansas stared out the hole, eyes bugging.

"Step out, ladies," Julia commanded. "Time to move."

"Who'll carry our stuff?" Kansas gestured at a huge pile of silk, wool, and leather clothing and shoes. Naturally she wore a crimson-bright tunic and a pair of sandals that looked like they'd fall apart if even someone as tiny as Kansas took two steps in them.

Unusually for centercity ratepayers, Kansas and McKensie had selected full sculpts. Kansas was barely five feet tall and weighed less than a hundred pounds. In contrast, McKensie had to weigh in at a couple of hundred pounds and stood a good six feet plus. Compared to her, Olivia looked tiny.

"Julia will carry your stuff," Olivia lied. "Now step through the opening. Either of you raise your voice, we're going to have to assume you're a spy." She gestured the aerosol tube. "These are police-grade eaters. What happened to that panel will happen to you."

"But—"

"Move," Julia said.

The two moved out.

Three meters from their homespace, Kansas turned. "Julia's not carrying my stuff."

"Amazing," Olivia whispered. "Wonder how that happened."

"Shut up, Kansas," McKensie grumbled. "Nobody was going to be able to carry that junk."

"It wasn't junk. Every bit of it was natural, construct-free product. I can't tell you how much I spent on all that stuff and I'm not going to leave it." She spun around and headed back.

Olivia moved more quickly than Julia thought any person could, blocking Kansas and hitting her with a medical dispenser.

The small woman collapsed.

"So you're in league with them after all." McKensie looked ready to run, but like she couldn't decide which way to head and was temporarily frozen in place.

Olivia shoved Kansas's sagging body toward Julia who bent, threw the still body over her shoulder, and forced herself to stand. It was lucky Kansas had picked a small sculpt because Julia could hardly carry her as it was.

"She's not dead," Olivia explained. "And we can't carry you, so you're going to have to come along on your own feet. Do you have a problem with that?"

McKensie looked at her immobilized partner. "No problems."

"Good." Olivia handed over another medical dispenser. "Drink this."

McKensie checked again for an escape route. Seeing none, she drank the medicine, which Julia recognized as a version of the ID eradicator she'd taken herself. She also noticed that Olivia didn't transfer them the codes to establish a new ID. Without an ID, McKensie's phone wouldn't work and she'd be, hopefully, unable to contact the police.

Julia wasn't sure it would be enough, but it sounded like a reasonable start.

"Now let's get out of here."

McKensie stopped to vomit a couple of times, but the three walking and one sleeping women slipped away from the homespace, toward what they hoped would be the safety of centercity.

Olivia

"**Time's** up," Julia reported.

In the few minutes since they'd talked McKinsey and Kansas out of their homespace, they'd covered a couple of blocks. They were nowhere near clear of the scene, so she had no idea what Julia was talking about.

"Huh?"

"Your buddy Shenker had everyone on a two and two schedule. It's shift time. Even if our kid ran, Shenker will now know that something's wrong."

Olivia should have recognized Shenker's pattern. He'd once lectured her before on a cop's ability to keep her attention focused for only two hours at a time.

"Let's hope—"

The sound of an explosion, strong enough and close enough to knock Julia from her feet and rattle solar panels for blocks around, ripped through the night.

"Guess they got tired of waiting outside your front door." Julia dusted herself off, then had McKensie load Kansas back on her shoulder.

"Jeez," McKensie said. "That explosion wasn't just to take out a door—it would have hurt us."

"That *is* what this is about," Olivia reminded her. "They're killing all of the free-code designers they can find."

"But we're ratepayers."

"Guess that's why they're using the expensive explosives. Now, let's enjoy the walk. We need to cover some distance."

Olivia let Julia lead the way, keeping the rear-guard position both to protect the others and to make sure McKensie didn't bolt.

Twenty minutes, and less than a mile later, McKensie leaned against a building, panting, and Kansas wiggled so much on Julia's shoulder that the designer dumped her on a sandy spot on the road.

"I'm tired of walking. Why don't we take a car?" McKensie might be all muscle, but she hadn't wasted any of her sculpting dollars on aerobic fitness.

"We don't *have* a car." Olivia tried not to let her frustration show. She and Julia had risked their lives for these two. Instead of thanks, they were getting complaints.

"How about that one?" McKensie pointed.

The cop car's chameleon effect was on, but it had been sitting still for long enough to pick up a faint coating of dust.

"Shit. Freeze." She patted herself for a weapon, coming up only with the diamond knife.

"If there were any cops in it, they would have done something by now," Julia said.

Olivia relaxed the muscles of her shoulders and back. Julia was right.

"Cool," Kansas said. "We'll leave this place in style."

"Be careful. Once we get outside of the jamming zone, they'll track the car and kill it," Julia said.

For a change, Olivia didn't mind Julia reminding her of the obvious. She was tired, likely to make mistakes. Having Julia second guess her provided a valuable safety cushion—one they were certain to need.

After forcing Kansas to take the identity drug, she drove her diamond knife through the vehicle's greeter, and yanked the door open.

The car's alarm went off, of course. There was nothing she could do about that. But it took less than a minute to cut the electrical lines leading to the alarm and reshunt them around the fail-safe that was supposed to prevent a car from running once its alarm was disabled.

McKensie climbed in and sat in the front passenger seat. "This is more like it."

Olivia let McKensie sit while she programmed a destination into the car's navigator. Heading directly away from their route was too obvious. Since they planned to take the designers east, she programmed the car to go south—directly into the heart of centercity.

"Are the rest of you getting in, or are you going to wait around for the cops to find you?" McKensie demanded. "I never knew cops rode in such style."

"Out."

McKensie looked at Olivia like she'd gone crazy. "You've *got* to be kidding. I've probably walked ten miles already."

"You walked one mile. Now get out before I drag you out."

"You and what corporate enforcement department?"

Olivia barely resisted the temptation to send the car on its programmed pattern with McKensie aboard.

"Here's the deal, McKensie. *I'm* walking from here. Julia is walking from here. Kansas is stumbling from here. But this car is going in a different direction—until the cops blow it up. If you want to come with us, you'll walk. If you want to go to downtown centercity and file a complaint with police central, then by all means stay in the car."

McKensie laughed. "If you-all feel like exercise, go for it. I'll override your navigation and follow you in the car. Temperature control, built-in refreshments, ergonomically designed seating. Yeah, that's a plan."

The woman had pushed Olivia to the point where she really wouldn't mind McKensie committing suicide by cop. What she didn't want, though, was for her stupidity to kill the rest of them.

She withdrew the last of the kid-cop's restraints from her tunic pouch. "If you stay in the car, you're going to be restrained. Because this car is going to police central, and it's leaving in the next ten seconds."

"Says you and what—"

While the woman was talking, Olivia slipped the restraints around the woman's wrists.

"Jeez. I heard about these."

"Did you hear that if you jerk hard you can cut off your hands? It'll be a piece of cake for a woman as strong as you. Then you'd be free. Of course, I don't think you'll be doing any advanced reprogramming using bleeding stumps."

"Jeez."

"Five seconds, McKensie. In or out."

"But—"

"Two seconds. I'm shutting my door."

"I'm coming." McKensie moved quickly, fear of being abandoned giving her more speed than she'd shown before. Once out of the car, she held out her arms. "Get me out of these."

"Sorry," Olivia lied. "I'm all out of dissolver. You'll have to wear them until we get where we're going."

"Jeez." The big woman kept her hands very still, Olivia noticed. Even so, the thin restraints bit into her wrists. Drops of blood fell to the ground.

Olivia slapped the car into motion, then yanked down McKensie's man-style shirt, sliding the sleeves between the restraints and the woman's wrists. She had left the restraints far looser than she would have on a normal captive. Still, McKensie hadn't wasted body-sculpt budget incorporating grace into her system. She couldn't move without injuring herself. Evidently she'd *wanted* to be a strong clumsy ox.

Olivia could only hope McKensie was a good designer. She was a pain in the rear as a person.

Shenker

The Interfaith Commander had lied to him. There weren't hundreds of jammers, there were thousands.

Shenker mobilized the cops who have been used guarding the perimeter to go through the Kansas/McKensie neighborhood smashing every jammer they could find.

Phone service returned—just in time for the IE commander to report the bad news.

"Someone dissolved a hole through the back wall. Sort of toward one side, like you predicted. And those bitches got away. You should have let me kill them."

Shenker's dinner threatened to erupt. "What about the sniper team watching the back?"

"They're gone. So's one of the kids you had in the outer perimeter."

"Gone as in dead, or gone as in not there?"

"Not there. Not nowhere. Maybe that ex-cop of yours dissolved them, too. Who is she, superwoman? And what kind of outfit do you run, Lieutenant?"

"A professional one. Unlike some."

"Meaning what, exactly?"

"Meaning there is a hole in the back flank of the homespace. I ordered you to take my sniper rifle and guard the back flank. Which you didn't do. Want to explain that, Commander? 'Course, you don't have to explain it to me. You can explain it to your own bosses if you'd rather."

"I don't like your attitude, Lieutenant. And—"

"Going to have to cut this off. I've got an alarm coming in."

"What's the alarm?" he demanded once he'd cut off the still-sputtering commander.

"A police vehicle assigned to your team," central reported, "has been detected off its programmed route. We've queried for a schedule change, but have heard nothing back."

"Location and direction?"

"Police vehicle is approaching downtown centercity, which is an exclusion zone. Drones have been scrambled to destroy it."

"That's a negative. Override. Track the vehicle but do not destroy it."

"Your code does not allow override of primary directives, Lieutenant. Aligning with target now. Target acquired. Launching on mark. Mark."

A flash of light followed about ten seconds later, but a distant rumble that could have been thunder, but wasn't, showed that central had done its job.

Two seconds later, Vinson came onto his line.

"Seems like you've terminated your objectives, Lieutenant Shenker. Congratulations."

Shenker ground his teeth. "I'm afraid congratulations are premature, Chief."

"What do you mean?"

"Olivia Jardan is *not* an idiot. She knows which parts of centercity are banned to unauthorized traffic. That car your drones just shot up could only—"

"You had her tired, on the run, and making mistakes. That was what you planned, wasn't it?"

"Yes, sir. But I don't think—"

"Fine, Lieutenant. Continue to look into this. But I'm pulling all but twenty of your cops off of the job. The war with Corporate Houston isn't going to wait."

"Captain, if you can pull the Interfaith Enforcement guys off of the job, I'd be more than happy to continue on with just twenty officers."

Vinson looked like he was sucking lemons. "They weren't as helpful as we'd hoped."

"I never had any hope for them. Even considering my low expectations, they were worse. Their commander thought it would be brilliant to jam the entire neighborhood where Kansas/McKensie lived. It bollixed police communications when we needed them most."

"I have gotten some irate calls about that. I guess that means phone service is back."

"After the women walked out of my trap, Chief."

"Well, they aren't going to walk out of that fireball on Old Pearl Street."

"Because they're nowhere near it." But he didn't say it until Vinson had severed the connection. Cops who don't show proper respect are likely to find themselves next on the list for permanent retirement.

First things first. He'd gotten the list of free-code designers and sympathizers from Merryweather's AI. With his trap broken, he ordered everyone on the list to be rounded up—everyone that Olivia hadn't already managed to extract or the enforcers killed.

That taken care of, he closed his eyes and pulled up a map of centercity, zooming out from the Kansas/McKensie homespace. Arresting the sympathizers cut down her options, but Olivia wouldn't give up. He'd trained her to fight. So, if *he* were on the run, chased by every cop the Police Corporation could throw on the street, where would he go? With only twenty cops to hunt, and with someone as effective as Olivia as prey, he needed to be smarter, to lead the target rather than spend his life playing catch-up.

He opened his eyes and when he did, he saw the forest. Yeah, she'd head that way.

Julia

Julia would rather die than be a cop.

Kansas and McKensie had bickered their way through every free-code meeting, but back then Julia had other things to think about and had simply believed the two were on their way to breaking up.

Apparently not. Apparently they just liked to complain—to anyone who would listen and to each other if nobody else would pay attention.

"You're hurting me," McKensie whined as Olivia tried to lug two hundred pounds of woman along.

"If we leave you," Olivia said, "you'll be dead. That would hurt more."

"It would hurt her more, but it would be easier for us," Julia suggested. "I vote we dump her."

"Trust me, it's tempting."

"McKensie may look tough, but she's really fragile," Kansas insisted. She'd missed being sick because she'd gone back unconscious after Olivia had drugged her. Now she seemed to be enjoying their outing—when she wasn't bickering.

"If the cops find us," Julia said, "they'll scan you. When they see you don't have an ID code, they'll terminate you. And they're looking. How many cops would you say are searching for us, Olivia?"

Olivia went blank for a second. "Four thousand nine hundred and ninety-five."

"That's a lot of people trying to kill us," Julia concluded.

"Maybe you should come along," Kansas said to McKensie. "Julia makes a good point."

It would have been too much to ask McKensie to stop grumbling, but at least she moved.

They walked a couple more blocks, with McKensie developing a limp that seemed to migrate from leg to leg.

Olivia found a couple of civilian cars waiting for a fare, hijacked them as she had the cop car, and sent them out on different paths. A few renegade cars wouldn't distract all of the cops' attention, but they might help.

Keeping cops distracted seemed like a very good idea.

Olivia had just jumped from the last of the civilian cars, launching it into the night, when a helicopter searchlight blared on, slicing through the night like a knife blade. It focused unerringly upon the car.

"Drivers in civilian car 782A5C12." The robotic voice sounded like an angry deity from a low-budget sim. "You must stop now."

The car didn't stop. Olivia had destroyed its wireless receivers so it wouldn't even know the cops were talking to it.

"They'll have to scramble dozens of cops to follow it, chase it down, and check it out," Kansas gloated. "That was brilliant, Olivia."

"Thanks." Olivia grinned.

Julia wasn't so sure. The cops weren't stupid. Shenker knew Olivia would try to distract them—after all, he had trained Olivia on this kind of evasion.

Or maybe the cops were stupid. A flash of light from the helicopter was followed by the shriek of a jet engine. Two seconds later, the unoccupied car exploded.

"I guess they think it'll be easier to check the ashes for forensic data than to manually override the computer," Julia said.

McKensie turned and puked in the gutter. Considering how much she'd already lost after taking the drug to change her ID code, Julia had never seen a woman with so much to vomit.

Julia gave her half a minute, then grabbed her arm and pulled. "Next time, it might be us instead of an unoccupied car. Now let's run."

It wasn't exactly running, but the four women stumbled faster, heading toward the protective wall of trees where Julia and Olivia had hidden after they'd escaped the rail.

Julia didn't need Olivia's grim warning that going back to the same place was dangerous. But neither had come up with a better alternative.

Stars filled the sky but the moon had set.

Darkness was not their friend. The cops could use their night vision to see the women. At this time, the streets would normally be deserted with most of Corporate Dallas asleep or immersed in sims.

Fortunately, burning cars distracted a number of ratepayers even from high-quality sims. Dozens of ratepayers stumbled out onto the streets rubbing sleep from their eyes and checking out the damage police missiles done. The four escaping women blended in, slowing their run to a casual stroll.

Even more than the ratepayers, the burning cars generated enough heat and light to overload police night vision equipment.

Communications had been restored and Julia checked her phone. Three hours until sunrise. Surely they could hide until then. With sunrise, they'd have a chance to blend in, seek a better hiding place.

Olivia led them more deeply into the greenbelt until she found a dense patch of hanging branches that created a sort of living cave and stopped, pointing at the leaf-covered ground.

"Why don't you guys try to get some sleep?"

McKensie kicked at a mound of brown fallen branches and leaves. "You expect me to sleep on biological material? There might be parasitic insects."

Olivia glared at the woman.

"Deal with her, Julia. I've got to talk to Martin."

"Me deal with her? Thanks." Julia built the mound higher, pushing on more leaves with her feet. She wasn't any more interested in sleeping on rotting, bug-ridden organics than McKensie was, but she didn't see any alternative.

"Deal with me however you want," McKensie whined. "I'm not going to sleep there."

Julia smiled. "This bed is just big enough for two. If you won't sleep there, Kansas and I will. You don't mind, do you, Kansas?"

Kansas looked like she might be happy with the swap, which was enough to make McKensie cave.

Olivia

Olivia hoped that Kansas and McKensie were the two best designers Corporate Dallas had ever produced because they were certainly the biggest pains in the rear.

Compared to them, Julia, whom Olivia had initially considered a prima donna, was little Ms. Courtesy.

She tried to suppress her grin at the way Julia used McKensie's jealousy to manipulate her, then linked through to Martin.

"You're still alive."

"More or less. I don't know how long our hiding place will be secure or where we'll go next, but I don't think we'll get out of centercity tomorrow. The police will be too much on guard."

"Hang on a second. I might be able to help."

Martin's pause didn't provide Olivia with any positive feelings. When he connected back in, his answer was worse. "I had the beginnings of a network that extended into centercity. People who weren't designers but who were helping Merryweather and me."

"Great. If we could find a homespace to hide in for a couple of days, we'd be able to wait out the search."

"Uh, as I was saying, I *had* a network. Nobody is answering their phones. I think the cops must have rolled them up."

Just for a moment, Olivia considered dumping the three designers and heading out on her own. Her chances would be dramatically better without them. Sure that would mean Martin's pet project never got completed, but that was Martin's problem. At least she'd be alive.

"Have them bring food when they come to pick us up," McKensie interrupted. "It takes a good thirty-five hundred calories a day to maintain this sculpt and I'm falling behind." The big designer had settled into the mound of leaves. To Olivia, she looked relaxed, comfortable, and not at all in any desperate need of sustenance.

"We'll see you when we see you, Martin." Olivia cut the link and forced a smile.

"Maybe you should down-scale your sculpt a bit, McKensie. Because our friends can't get through right away. Too much police traffic for safety."

"Like I can change my sculpt now? You think I keep sculpts in my phone or something? Besides, I like being big."

"And I like her that way," Kansas insisted loyally.

"If you brought a mini-constructor, there's plenty of energy-rich hydrocarbon feedstuff lying around," Julia suggested. "Whip up whatever you want. Just be sure to switch over from solar to chemical powering."

McKensie looked at Julia with a confused look. "Nobody told us to bring a constructor. And you wouldn't carry our stuff anyway."

"No constructor, no food. Now shut up and go to sleep. You'll burn fewer calories that way."

McKensie grumbled on for a bit, but finally dozed off.

Surrounded by the sounds of deep breathing from the designers, and weird animal noises from the trees, Olivia sat in the darkness.

Her police optical sculpt let her see into the infrared and she watched McKensie's oversized body cool from waking to sleeping temperature. A smaller and cooler glow, Kansas's, snuggled closer to her friend, absorbing warmth as Dallas's CO_2-denuded atmosphere reflected heat back into space.

"If one of the free-coders really is a spy, I sure hope it's McKensie," Julia subvocalized. "That woman is driving me nuts."

Olivia made room on her own mound of leaves for Julia to join her.

"They're both sleeping," she whispered. "They can't hear us."

"Maybe. Don't you think a spy would be able to regulate her body temperature and fool us?"

Olivia hadn't considered that possibility. But she hadn't really thought about spies before, either.

McKensie had done everything she could to delay them. Exactly what a spy would do. Spending the night with a potential spy in the middle of centercity wasn't high on Olivia's list of fun activities, even if she had disabled the woman's phone.

"I'll stay on watch," Olivia said. "She might decide to slip away during the night and make contact."

"You don't think she'd stay with us and try to roll up the entire organization?"

"I don't know what she'll do. I do know I don't want to wake up with my own knife through my heart."

"Good thinking." Julia paused. "I could take a shift, you know, let you catch a few winks."

"You don't have the training to handle McKensie if she decides she wants to get past you. It's up to me."

The designer shrugged. "Let me know if you change your mind."

Staying awake wasn't a problem. Olivia could filter the toxins from her system, use meditation to allow each part of her brain to rest while the others took over the load, and run enough adrenaline through her body to keep a hippopotamus awake. Eventually, of course she'd have to pay the price.

Staying alive long enough to pay the price seemed like the right strategy. Of course, staying alive was also the challenge.

Vinson

At four in the morning, a man should be able to get some sleep.

Harles Vinson checked his phone for confirmation that Julia, Kansas, and McKensie, along with the rogue cop's bodies had been found in the wreckage of the stolen police car. He found nothing.

Maudie moaned when he got out of the bed they still occasionally shared. "You need me to do anything, hon?"

"I'm worried about the war, that's all."

"Oh. Okay."

He padded from the bedroom to his office, the floor automatically warming to keep his feet from getting chilled as he walked. "Visual on the outer rings," he told his AI. "I want an update on new construction over the past seven days."

"Drone coverage has been intermittent," the AI reported, through his phone. "Satellite records are believed compromised by Corporate Houston or Corporate Consensus counter-intelligence measures."

It said something when the Chief of Police couldn't get unaltered satellite data. Unfortunately, what it said was something Vinson already knew—the Chairman of the Police Corporation was not considered a key part of the consensus.

"Scramble some drones, then," he snapped. "I want those images within three hours."

"Nighttime search is contraindicated."

"Starting with sunrise, then, dammit."

"This may compromise drone defenses and Lieutenant Shenker's search."

"Do it." Compared to the threat from Corporate Houston, searching for a couple of idealistic designers hardly mattered.

Apparently, though, Rev. Ariel didn't agree.

He was on the phone less than twenty seconds after Shenker had given his orders.

"What's this about diverting resources away from the hunt for Turnboldt and the others?"

"Do you have any idea what time it is, Reverend?"

"Way past time you should have caught those four. They're women, Chief Vinson. How hard could it be?"

Vinson wished Rev. Ariel would say something like that to his wife. She'd tear him into pieces and spit out the indigestible hunks. "Your Enforcers jammed—"

"If you're thinking of blaming it on the professional teams I assigned to your man, I suggest you reconsider, Chief. Now, I want those drones put back into the hunt."

"How many designers are we talking about here, Reverend?"

"You know as well as I do. Three. Turnboldt, Kansas, and McKensie."

"And we both know they've got at least a dozen, perhaps more, outside. I've heard from my colleagues in Corporate Fort Worth and Corporate Midcities that they're actively recruiting disgruntled designers from those corporate entities."

"What's your point, Chief?"

"My point is, we need to do more than hunt down these three. We need to track down the whole organization. And we're not going to do that in centercity."

"Give me those girls and twenty-four hours and I'll tell you exactly where the organization is hiding. And my boys will have had some fun."

Vinson shuddered. He didn't have a lot of scruples, but Turnboldt and the others were ratepayers. Rev. Ariel's enforcers would get extra satisfaction from having ratepayers under their control. They might or might not turn up useful information, but they'd certainly break some women.

"Thank you for the offer. I believe we have some of the best interrogation drugs in North America at our disposal, however."

Ariel laughed. "Drugs won't work on the renegade cop, though. That's part of the cop sculpt. Find her and give *her* to me."

"We clean up our own messes."

Ariel considered. "All right. You can have some of the drones, but not all. I want a solid hunt kept up for those four women."

"I've got my best man on it, Reverend."

"If your best man is Paul Shenker, you have more problems than I thought, Chief. The man is a jumped-up cit."

"Send a thief to catch a thief, send a cop to catch a cop."

"Remember, if you're looking for our help in the economic war, you'd better not skimp shutting down these free-coders. If Corporate Dallas won't support us, Corporate Houston will."

"If C.H. wins, they'll put in their own man as head of the local Interfaith. You'd be—"

"Do you really think this is about one person, Chief? That's the problem with you corporate types, you never see that some things are bigger than who moves up a notch. It doesn't matter who's in charge of the Interfaith, they'll see things the way I do. Free-code is a danger. It's a threat to your precious corporations, even if they're too blind to see it, but it's also a concern to us. And we're not going to stand for it."

Vinson didn't like threats—and he didn't like them any better when they came from the Interfaith than when they came from a group of ratepayers who might be misguided but were also, as far as he could tell, staying within the letter of the Corporate Consensus. "I intend to shut down their entire operation, Ariel. There's a Corporate Houston angle, a C.H. spy that's behind a lot of what's going on. So, maybe you should get on the phone to your counterpart there—ask him to shut down their operative here. Once he's gone, this thing will be easy to roll up."

"I'll do that, Vinson. I'll do that."

Vinson smiled as Rev. Ariel disappeared. For once, he'd won a round. He headed back into his bedroom and nudged Maudie awake.

"Oh, hon. Do I have to pretend you're a horse again? Don't you have a nice sexbot for—"

"Neigh."

Julia

The going-invisible trick Olivia had come up with for the rail hadn't worked well the first time and wouldn't work at all if they tried it again.

They'd left the forest that morning, done their best to alter the look of their smart-fabrics, and in the case of Olivia and Julia, performed minor sculpts to change their looks.

There wasn't much they could do to change the way McKensie looked, but Olivia had pulled out her crystalline-carbon knife and used it to trim Kansas's long hair—much to McKensie's disgust.

They might look innocent, but they couldn't fool scanners.

Cops seemed everywhere, checking RFIDs of everyone who got near the rail stops and randomly stopping even ratepayers.

On a hunch, Julia checked the news, using the ID code of a ratepayer who was still asleep. As she'd suspected, the police had cut *all* citizen access to centercity.

Blending would be impossible.

Cops also guarded the few public constructors, meaning they couldn't construct anything to eat.

After a frustrating hour, the four trekked back to the trees.

"I'm open to suggestions," Olivia said when McKensie started to complain.

"Maybe we could fly out," Kansas said. "I did some flying before I met McKensie. We could build an ultralight for each of us."

"If we had access to a constructor—"

Julia stopped Olivia before she could go into all of the reasons why that plan wouldn't work. "You said you wanted suggestions. So, let's brainstorm. No criticism until we've listed all the ideas we have. Then we'll solve problems rather than just say it's too hard."

Olivia looked like she wanted to argue, but she backed down. "Okay. So, that's the first one on our list. We construct ultralight aircraft and fly out."

"Maybe we could get help," McKensie said.

"Help would be good," Olivia said. "That's number two. But let's build on that. Who can help?"

"What about Corporate Houston? Aren't we supposed to be having an economic war with them? Wouldn't they like some inside assistance?"

Olivia nodded slowly, apparently not wanting to spill that they already were working with Corporate Houston, in the form of C.H.'s spy, Martin Reynolds. "It's an idea. Other thoughts?"

Julia licked her lips. "We've got a cop here, one of our biggest assets. How about if we just keep it simple. We kidnap another cop, steal his car, and drive out. You're getting to be an expert at taking out cops, Olivia."

"Whatever we do, we'd better do it quickly," McKensie whined, erasing any positive feelings Julia might have been developing for her thanks to her helpful suggestion. "We can't just stay here. My metabolism is cannibalizing my body. The longer we wait, the weaker I'll be."

Julia stared at McKensie for a moment. Something the woman had said triggered a thought—oh, right.

"Hold on a minute. Who *says* we can't stay here? What are we going to do if we get out? Set up a camp somewhere and settle down to work on free-code, right? We could do that anywhere, including right here in the middle of Dallas." She kicked the pile of leaves she'd slept in the previous night. "We've got these biologicals for feed and energy, so we could construct everything we need. Shenker's drones will never find us in the trees. And we wouldn't have to cross the barrier. We could send our code to Martin and the other guys who escaped, and they could send their updates to us. It could work."

"I'll add it to the list." Olivia didn't sound as excited as Julia.

"What about our families?" Kansas suggested. "Even if our corporate employers abandon us, our families would help. We could go to my parents' homespace. They'd take us in, feed us, and protect us."

McKensie grumbled something, but her phone still wasn't working so Julia couldn't understand her.

Kansas must have, though. "It isn't my fault my family doesn't like you. They would if you'd give them half a chance. And staying alive would be more important than petty disagreements."

"Okay, it's on the list," Olivia said. "We've got ultralights, Corporate Houston, mugging a cop and stealing his or her car, staying here, and getting help from Kansas's family. Any more ideas?"

Nobody admitted anything else, which was depressing. Julia had a nasty feeling that every single suggestion had a huge gotcha.

"Let's start with the first, then," Julia said. "Remember, we're looking for ways to make this work, not reasons it won't."

Whatever she was looking for, she didn't find it. Without a constructor, they weren't making ultralight aircraft components. Without a constructor, they also couldn't stay in hiding.

Mugging a cop might work, but they'd seen what happened when cop cars went where they weren't supposed to—nobody wanted to be caught in the explosion.

That narrowed their choices to two—getting help from Kansas's family, and getting help from Corporate Houston.

"We're at war with Corporate Houston," McKensie pointed out. "If we go to them, we're traitors."

"Better traitors than dead," Kansas muttered. Still, she agreed to let Julia start with a discrete call to the Killdit family homespace.

After Julia wasted a couple of minutes chatting up the greeter, Kansas remembered a personal code word—something she wouldn't have needed coming from her own phone, and Julia got through.

The news was not good.

Police had searched Kansas's family home twice and two cops were stationed outside.

Julia let Olivia handle the call to Martin. Olivia seemed to have the hots for the spy, and had gotten the idea that Julia was competition.

Rather than subvocalize, Olivia spoke out loud so everyone could hear what she was saying.

Olivia

"**We're** looking for some Consensus-level help. Can C.H. do anything to save us? Because we're running out of options here."

"If you stay hidden—"

"We *can't* stay hidden. Shenker knows this greenbelt is the most likely place for us to hide. The only reason we're safe right now is Shenker's guys already went through. I suspect they'll be back. Soon."

"What other ideas have you come up with?"

She listed their suggestions.

"I like the ultralight plan."

"That would work. We'll maybe glue together leaves and flap our arms?"

"How about using a constructor."

She sighed. "The public constructors are guarded."

"Understand. Chicken and egg."

"Huh?" Talking about archaic livestock didn't seem helpful.

"It's an expression my father uses."

She still didn't get it. "It'll take more than birds to get off the ground."

"You know, Olivia, I think you've nailed it." Animation filled his voice.

"Nailed what?"

"Corporate Houston, in the person of yours truly, is going to attack Corporate Dallas. In the process, I'll sneak you a little something. Upload me your coordinates."

Vinson

"**Priority** interrupt." Control's voice went metallic. "We have incoming."

Vinson snapped to attention. His drones gave him early warning of the launch, but it still surprised him.

Thousands of small, unmanned aircraft, launched from an almost continuous ring around Corporate Dallas, took to the air in waves.

He triggered the emergency circuit that gave him a simultaneous link into each of the T-50 CEOs.

"As of fourteen hundred hours, Corporate Dallas is under attack by a large number of small aircraft estimated as at least two thousand, with more being launched every minute."

"Who is doing this?"

Vinson didn't recognize the voice, but panic has a way of changing the way normally confident people sound. "I had drones in place at the time of launch and so was able to observe their telemetry. The design matches that of a standard Corporate Houston light-lift drone."

"Payload?" That was the CEO of Dallas Industrial Design.

"Between ten and fifty pounds depending on fuel used and engine selected."

"Enough to do some damage if they're bombs." That was Louis Brandon, current spokesman for Corporate Dallas. He didn't let the announcement rattle his perfect calm.

Vinson nodded. "Many are broadcasting a message from Corporate Houston. That broadcast should reach centercity within the next two minutes."

"Well," that was the CEO of Dallas Spice and Flavors. "Shoot them down."

Because he had his drones up, Vinson was able to get a better lookdown image than C.H. probably anticipated. Still, carbon-constructed miniature drones were notoriously radar resistant and their tiny engines wouldn't show on any but the most sensitive heat-seeking AI.

"I need T-50 authorization to activate Corporate Dallas security measures," he said.

"So, you have it."

No, he didn't have it. Not yet. "Any objections?"

Silence.

"Okay, now I have it. I'll do what I can," he promised. "I'm afraid some of them, maybe many of them, will penetrate centercity. If they're loaded with bombs, there will be casualties."

"Among ratepayers?" the Dallas Spice and Flavors CEO sounded horrified.

"The old expression, *war is hell*, comes into effect."

From the silence, the expression was new to many of them.

"Let me get to work," he said. "Vinson off."

Olivia

The streaks across the sky could have been fireworks from a Corporate Freedom Day celebration. Puffs of smoke showed where Martin's attacking craft met Corporate Dallas defenses and simply disintegrated.

The first few hundred were hit before they reached the centercity line, but more kept coming, broadcasting merger offers for any corporation willing to sever its ties with Corporate Dallas and throw in with Corporate Houston.

She authenticated the message, using Corporate Houston's public key to decrypt their signature. The timing of the invasion had been altered to help Olivia and her crew, but clearly Martin had been planning this attack for a long time.

It was, Olivia realized, typical of the kind of idealistic plan Martin would glom onto. He probably believed that the promise of cooperation would encourage corporations to abandon their local partners and link up with out-of-towners.

Maybe she was cynical, but Olivia didn't have much hope the message would make any difference.

Half an hour into the attack, Dallas's defenses became more porous, partly, Olivia thought, because they'd run through their armaments and the air defense launch tubes were waiting for constructors to deliver new missiles, partly because Vinson wouldn't want to let Corporate Houston know all of the secrets of its defense, and partly, she guessed, because he'd determined this was strictly a propaganda move rather than an explosives or biological attack.

For whatever reason, Martin's drones started making it through, circling around different areas of centercity and broadcasting Corporate Houston's message of love.

When they ran out of fuel, they drifted down to the ground.

From what Olivia could see, no one outside their greenbelt noticed when one of the cheap aircraft piled into a tree a couple of hundred feet away from where they were hidden.

"Martin doesn't believe in doing things in a small way, does he?" Admiration practically glowed through Julia's words.

"Whatever." She ordered herself not to be jealous. Julia was a designer and could pretty much have any guy she wanted. If she wanted Martin, Olivia could lump it or kill one of them. Staying alive mattered more than who got a boyfriend. Still, Julia didn't have to rub it in.

"Let's see what clever-boy sent us, shall we?" Olivia got up, retrieved the lightweight aircraft, and removed a miniature constructor from its body.

"All right," Kansas effused. "That entire attack was all about this? We can build my ultralights now. At least we could if I had my phone and could download the code for its componentry."

"We need to construct some food first." McKensie was a lot more interested in practical applications than in whether Martin had pulled off anything special. "I'm dying for a big juicy rare RealMeat™ steak dripping with TrueBlood™."

Food was probably the last thing they needed if they were going to be flying out of the city, but Olivia was tired of arguing with McKensie. And she was hungry too.

Not wanting to waste time participating in an Interfaith sim, and permanently cut off from her bank account, she downloaded the code for a basic citizen meal, set the constructor on chemical, and shoveled in a mass of leaves and other biomass.

A few minutes later, the latch opened and she took out a steaming bowl of what looked and smelled like sewage.

"What the heck is that?" McKensie demanded when Olivia gave her the first serving. "I wanted RealMeat™."

"Even if your phone worked, what would happen if you tried to access your account? You're cut off, McKensie. So, you don't get to chow down on high-royalty treats. This is what citizens eat if they can't pay royalties and won't listen to the Interfaith."

McKensie snapped off the constructed spoon and dabbed it at the gelatinous blob sitting in the supposedly edible bowl. "People eat this? It smells like, well, I don't know what it smells like but it's horrible."

"Millions of citizens live on this stuff."

"Yuck." She wrinkled her nose. "Still, I guess it's their choice. Even if my family hadn't pushed me, I think this would have been enough to motivate me to study and learn design, become a ratepayer. I tell you, if I'd known *this* was my alternative, I'd have studied even harder."

Olivia felt her back going up. "Like citizens have that choice."

"Insurance is cheap. Anyone who isn't so lazy they just want to sit at home playing in the sims should be able to afford it. Sure training is expensive, but teachers have to eat, too."

McKensie probably thought real wormspit shirts were cheap. Insurance practically bankrupted Olivia each month. Or it had when she'd still had money. "Cheap for you, not for the rest of us. Where would citizens get *any* money, McKensie, let alone the money to enroll in a class? It takes years of training to become a designer, years of training even to become a cop or a sim modeler. And training costs money. Lots of money."

McKensie took a bite of the glop and shuddered. "And citizens are too good to do ordinary labor, right? Labor that doesn't take all that training. Or are you saying that the education corporations don't deserve a fair profit?"

Maybe that *was* what Olivia was saying. Maybe education and training were too important to restricted to those with the money to pay for them. She shied away from examining that thought too closely. Everyone knew that you needed profit to produce. Still, it seemed wrong to doom the majority of the population to permanent citizen status.

"Just eat, McKensie. And think about what it means to be a citizen. If free-code doesn't pan out, you're going to be spending the rest of your life enjoying citizen-slop."

Julia

"**We** aren't going to be able to fly out," Julia said.

Kansas had taken over the miniconstructor once they'd eaten all they could stand of the citizen slop and was busy producing buckyball-carbon structural members for a small fleet of aircraft, getting Olivia to use her phone to input codes Kansas selected. She looked up annoyed.

"This will work. This framework snaps together—Olivia can do that for us. The nanobes in the wing fabric will intelligently adhere to the right spot. It's foolproof. Maybe you're scared, but flying isn't that hard and Martin sent training sims that we could run until we were all perfect."

Julia took a long drink of water to force down the last of the citizen-slop Olivia had constructed for her. She hadn't complained the way McKensie had, but she didn't enjoy it, either.

"You're missing my point. Did you notice how many of those cruise missiles Martin sent got shot down before the cops decided it wasn't worth the effort?"

"A bunch."

"A whole bunch. I didn't do an exact count because early-on those missiles were flying too fast, but I calculated it was something like ninety-eight percent destruction. Not nearly enough if you're shooting down nuclear missiles and it only takes one to destroy a city—"

"Nobody is going to nuke a city. That wouldn't make economic sense," Olivia objected.

"People panic, make stupid decisions. Economics can't explain that. Anyway, what I'm saying is that if any of us tries to fly out, ninety-eight chances out of a hundred, we'll get shot down. Statistically, that's a .000016 percent probability we'll all make it out safely."

Kansas looked stubborn. "You're assuming—"

"I'm assuming they aren't going to be a lot more careful after Martin's attack, and that thousands of missiles didn't overload their AI. Face it, if we try to fly out, they'll scatter us all over the landscape."

"Maybe if we wait a couple of days, they'll give up," McKensie suggested. "If you restored my phone, I could call up some better food."

"We aren't going to—"

Olivia held up a hand, stopping Julia in mid-rant. "Someone is coming."

Julia listened—and heard nothing.

"We've got to hide." Olivia grabbed the constructor, shoveled in a bunch of leaves, and set the code.

A minute later, the door popped open and she pulled out a flexible solar blanket.

"What are we going to do? Electrify them?" Kansas demanded.

"I'm working on it."

It was a smart idea. A sprinkling of leaves over the blanket helped it blend into the forest floor. In the shadows under the trees, the black coloration was a positive rather than a negative. Even better, the blanket would spread body heat from someone hiding under it, defusing any infrared signature and making it more likely any minor hotspot would be decoded as biological deterioration rather than a human entity.

"Hey, that kind of works. Maybe because you citizens are more primitive, you're closer to nature and all." McKensie climbed under the blanket, revealing a huge problem in Olivia's plan. When McKensie shifted the blanket, its camouflage flew everywhere. Then the once-again pristine blanket molded itself to the shape of the woman beneath it—which was great for warmth and protection but horrible for disguise.

"Is it working?" The blanket didn't even muffle McKensie's voice.

"It makes you look sexy," Kansas admitted.

Julia snatched the blanket away from McKensie. "Give me that."

The Interfaith blanket design was straightforward. Better still, it was fully commented. She scanned down the code, made a change, and stuffed the blanket back inside the constructor.

It only took ten seconds, but during that time the noise of approaching cops got louder.

"Looks the same to me," Kansas said.

Julia caught the blanket, opened it to its two-meter-square surface, and threw leaves over it exactly as Olivia had done a couple of minutes earlier.

"Wonderful." Sarcasm dripped from McKensie's voice.

"I think so." Julia picked up the blanket—and the leaves remained in place. She threw the blanket to McKensie. "Now, drape yourself with this and get up that tree. Oh, and if anyone makes a noise, Olivia will kill you before the cops interfere."

"Maybe there are animals." Julia did her best to keep her voice calm as McKensie hesitated at the base of the tree. "Maybe they are dangerous. But they're not as dangerous as Olivia."

McKensie went up the tree faster than one of the monkeys from the sim Julia had seen at the Corporate Fair.

"Don't come down until Olivia tells you it's all clear. You're next, Kansas."

The sound of helicopter rotors slowing from a high-pitched roar to a lower whine told Julia that the cops were covering all their bases, hoping to flush them from the trees.

She fed in material for a third blanket before dusting the second with leaves and twigs and sending Kansas up a second tree.

While shoveled in biomass for the fourth, Olivia picked up a branch and raked over the pile of leaves remaining.

Olivia had the right idea, but the wrong technology. The top leaves were dry while underneath, the leaves were darker and wetter. Raking didn't disguise the fact that someone had been digging there.

She pulled out the fourth blanket, tossed it to Olivia, and told her to get up the tree with McKensie. "One of us needs to watch each of them. You're scarier so I'll take Kansas."

"Deal. But hadn't you better move yourself?" The sound of ground effect rotors was a constant roar now, making it impossible to tell where any on-foot cops might be or how close they'd gotten.

"Just one more thing."

She loaded one of the projects she'd done for free-code, an astringent agent, generated a liter of the stuff, and sprinkled it on the wet leaves.

It sucked up moisture quickly, but the leaves remaining were still a bit more broken, more chewed up by the environment. If the cops knew anything about leaves, they would notice. She hoped cops knew even less about trees than she did.

"Get up the tree now," Olivia ordered. "I hear something."

Julia grabbed the miniconstructor and her blanket and scampered up Kansas's tree. "I *know* you won't make any noise, Kansas," she whispered as she climbed past the tiny designer. "Because if you do, I'll sprinkle some of the nano-eater I just constructed on top of you."

"You're kidding?" Kansas squeaked.

Julia had been bluffing. She hoped Kansas wouldn't guess that.

Shenker

He needed more cops.

Even Interfaith Enforcers might be better than nothing—he needed bodies more than he needed brains. But he'd gotten rid of the IE and he couldn't go back on his decision.

Besides, twenty cops plus himself should be enough. Olivia was good, but she was saddled with three ratepayers who were probably crying over broken fingernails or having to leave their precious sex-bots behind.

"Spread out in a long line, about five meters apart," he ordered fifteen of his guys, all kids with less than a year of experience in the police.

The other five, men who'd been around, who'd faced up to mobs of angry citizens or crazed ratepayers, he held as his reserve.

"Keep an eye on your buddy to the right and left," he reminded the lead team, who would act as beaters, trying to flush Olivia and her designers out of the forest. "And keep your eyes out for any evidence of burrowing. They might have gone underground."

"You told us this already," Jorge whined.

"And I'll keep telling you," he fired back.

"They're letting anyone into the police these days." That was Andrew, one of the more experienced cops.

"Do your job. I'll make sure those idiots do theirs."

None of the cops, including Shenker, felt particularly comfortable walking on biological material. Modern homespaces grabbed any creeping insects falling leaves, or even pollen that made it inside, and turned them into feed for homespace constructors. Which meant many of the guys were seeing grubs and junebugs for the first time. And the leaves moved when he stepped on them. He knew fallen leaves were dead, but it felt like walking on a giant living creature.

"Keep your eyes out for the women," he said. "Your medical implants will protect you from any toxins from the biologicals."

"You mean these things are poison?" That was Jorge again.

"I said don't worry about it." He wasn't that concerned about giving the women warning they were coming—he had armed drones ringing the far side of the forest, so the women wouldn't get away. Still, Olivia was tough. If he gave her long enough, she'd figure some way to fight back.

His phone made a near-audible click as it switched out of conference mode, setting up an override connection—a connection he'd learned to recognize but never enjoyed. "Yes, chief."

"I see you're scouring likely hiding place for those renegade designers."

Renegade designers? That was a new designation. "Correct, chief."

"Excellent. They've just gone up in priority. Central has completed its analysis of the Corporate Houston attack last night."

"And?"

Vinson coughed. "The entire thing may have been a diversion. Many had constructors inside. One lightweight probe landed in the greenbelt you're currently exploring."

"Oh, shit. They may have—"

"Correct, Lieutenant. It's possible that our friend Olivia is now armed with advanced weaponry. I've released another fifty cops to your control. They should be arriving starting in an hour."

Shenker's phone gave him the time—they'd finish flushing the forest just when reinforcements arrived.

"We're heading north by east," he uploaded the GPS coordinates. "Have them assemble in a firing line guarding the northern boundary of this greenbelt. If my flushing operation works, the women will be heading out that way."

"I'll do that. And Lieutenant?"

"Yes, Chief?"

"Don't screw this up. The Interfaith Enforcement team has tendered a competitive bid to replace the entire Police Corporation. If we don't show the CC we can get the job done, we just might be replaced."

If the consensus took up that offer, they'd deserve what they got. But that wouldn't help Shenker. Without police pay, he'd lose his homespace and have to stop paying insurance on his sister and her family. His dreams of rubbing elbows with ratepayers, raising his own children in centercity, even finding a ratepayer woman willing to have children with him would be down the tubes.

"I'll do my best, Chief."

"I was hoping for something a bit more positive."

"Olivia Jardan has already survived longer than I thought she would. She has external help from Corporate Houston. The data on Ratepayer Julia Turnboldt indicates she is a clever and capable designer. I will track Jardan down, but I'm won't promise it'll be easy."

"Just do it, Lieutenant. Whatever it takes."

Vinson signed off.

Shenker considered letting his guys know they might come under fire with sophisticated weaponry but rejected the idea. They were nervous enough about the bugs and the quasi-living organic matter under their feet and around them.

"Keep moving." They guys had stalled while he'd been on the phone. All but Tyler, who'd forged ahead. "Except you, Tyler. Guys, you're creating a gap."

"How are we supposed to see them, anyway?" Jorge demanded. "My scanner shows organic life and respiration everywhere. And the CO2 monitor is bouncing all over the place."

Shenker didn't sigh, quite. "Which is why I told you to set your scanners for *thermal* detection. The rotting material here generates C02, and the living trees spit out Oxygen like it's going out of style. But they don't generate much heat. Human bodies do."

"Oh, yeah. I forgot."

And this kid was a cop. No wonder Olivia remained free.

"Straighten the line. Keep moving."

Shenker drifted back and forth between the beat line and the stealthed second group. Since Olivia's escape, he'd researched hunting in the forest. Old-time hunters sent peasants into the woods to make a lot of noise and run the animals toward waiting hunters. But Olivia and the designers weren't stupid animals. They'd know they were being hunted, know to switch back if they were being pushed in any direction. Alone, the designers would be easy, but Olivia would attempt to get through the line and double back toward where he and the others had started. Which would, he hoped, lead her directly into one of the stealthed commandos.

"Oh, shit." A loud pop was followed immediately by Jorge plunging to the ground.

"He's been hit. They're attacking us." Another idiot cop opened up with his submachine gun, spraying the area with carbon-fiber darts.

Gunfire spread like a plague, transmitted by fear. Two seconds after Jorge fell, all thirteen remaining cops in the beat line were shooting into the woods, ignoring his orders to cease firing.

Two darts slammed into Shenker's chest as he ran toward Jorge. His police tunic, set to maximum armor protection, stopped the penetration, but he'd have bruises on his chest in the morning despite what his mediplant could do.

"What happened to you, Private?" he demanded.

"Uh, I think it was a trap, sir."

"Hold your fire," he broadcast to the group when a slackening in the rate of fire and the sound of reloads gave him a chance to be heard. "Jorge tripped on a dry branch. He's okay. It wasn't the renegades."

"I'm pretty sure it was a trap, Lieutenant."

Shenker handed him the broken hunk of wood. "It wasn't. So get up and get moving."

"And set the safeties on your weapons," he broadcast. "Next idiot who shoots me is going to be standing at a public constructor waiting for a bowl of citizen slop."

The threat settled the team down. It didn't do much for Shenker. He'd had a bad feeling about this since Olivia had called him days before and that feeling had only been getting worse.

Olivia

Olivia shuddered on her tree branch as the sound of gunfire died off. The blankets they hid beneath wouldn't even slow bullets. Her police tunic provided a bit of protection, but not much. And Kansas and McKensie didn't have anything.

Hiding seemed like their only choice, but ultimately it was doomed to fail. Shenker would continue the search even if he lost money on the deal.

Still, given a choice between getting caught immediately and getting caught later, Olivia would pick later every time.

"Keep an eye on McKensie," Julia subvocalized over the phone. "She's being awful quiet."

She was supposed to be quiet—noise could get them killed. Still, Olivia knew what Julia meant. "I think you scared her."

"I hope so. You heard those cops shooting. I don't think they're looking to take us to dinner."

"Shhh." Although they were subvocalizing, even that seemed dangerous.

Beneath the trees, a line of cops that stretched as far as she could see, each separated by maybe five meters, tromped across the forest floor. They called out to each other and kept each other under continual observation. This time she couldn't take out one without being noticed.

"You thought about what you're going to do with your completion bonus?" a cop directly underneath her asked one nearest to him.

"Go back home and get away from all this bio-matter. Can you believe they have these tree-things in the middle of centercity? I mean, it's like a sim. What a waste. They like soak up the sunlight and CO_2 just so ratepayers can have something pretty to look at. Talk about—"

"You two, keep it down. You're messing with the acoustical equipment."

Until two days before, Shenker's voice had always been comforting. Now, it sent ice through Olivia's veins.

Olivia peeked through a tiny opening in the blanket she'd wrapped around herself.

A cop passed directly under the tree where she and McKensie hid.

"Hey, what's that?"

One of the cops pointed his sensor upward—straight toward Olivia.

"McKensie shifted nervously and one of her legs protruded from beneath the blanket.

Olivia reached down, tugged McKensie's blanket into place and froze.

"What you got?"

"Shit, I thought I saw a thermal signature but straight up."

"Straight up is the sun, idiot. Don't point your sensor that way."

"Yeah, sorry."

The two moved on.

* * * *

Looks like they're gone."

Did McKensie's whisper carry relief or disappointment? Olivia couldn't tell.

"Wait." Shenker would have a second wave, smaller, more silent, and definitely more deadly.

"You think—oh."

They heard the new cop more than they saw him. Dry leaves crackling under his feet, the occasional low-hanging branch whipping around as he shoved it out of the way, and the faint blur of edge distortion from his stealth-mode police tunic and hood gave Olivia an idea of where he was.

Unfortunately, she couldn't see his eyes, couldn't guess whether he was checking out the trees or merely following in the footsteps of the cops who had passed a few minutes earlier.

She forced herself not to hold her breath. The gasp when she could no longer do so would be audible. Simple breathing would not.

The stealthed cop passed under her tree, then froze.

Every muscle in Olivia's frame tightened and she had to consciously will herself to relax. Tight muscles help if you're going to get hit, which explained her body's instinctive reaction. They would slow her down if she had to move.

She guessed he was listening intensely, although she couldn't see enough to be sure. Finally, though, he resumed his slow walk.

But only for a second.

What sounded like a sigh of relief came from Julia's tree.

Leaves crackled as the cop whirled. A weapon, some sort of long-barreled slug-thrower from the looks of it, appeared out of the cop's cloak, pointing directly at the wiggling, leaf-covered human-sized mass in Julia's tree.

Without conscious thought, Olivia judged the distance and leapt.

* * * *

The human eye is hundreds of times more sensitive to movement than to still objects. A cop's training reinforces this tendency. The commando-style cop reacted before her dropping body covered half the distance to him.

But Olivia was still accelerating. She chambered her leg for a kick, and struck before the cop could re-target.

His shoulder-held gun swung wildly as her foot connected with it. As she continued to fall, she drove an elbow straight down on the top of his hood. Into a helmet.

She ignored the pain and stuck two thumb-reinforced fingers through his goggles.

She didn't quite make it to his eyes, but the goggles shattered, distracting him and giving her time to drive a knee into his chest.

Before he could bring some other weapon into the fight, Olivia threw an arm beneath his armpit and caught his neck in a choke.

A few seconds later, he slumped, unconscious.

"Get down from the trees. Now. Move, move, move." She fought the urge to pant, to shout. This cop would have been in contact with the others, would be on Shenker's GPS locator, but calling attention to what she'd done still wouldn't be smart.

At best, they had a minute or two before anyone noticed the commando-cop had gone offline. Without luck, they were already dead and just didn't know it. She had to hope for a whole lot of luck.

McKensie remained frozen in her tree but the other two designers climbed down.

"Olivia will cut you down if you don't move," Julia threatened.

"He was going to shoot me like I was a, a design defect," McKensie protested.

"Maybe next time, you'll know what shut-up means," Julia answered. "Now move your fat butt."

"I'm stuck."

When Olivia started up, McKensie miraculously became unstuck. Maybe she didn't know Olivia was really just getting the constructor. If McKensie wanted to stay behind, that would be okay with her.

"What now?" Julia was down and ready to move.

"Now we find somewhere else. This place is blown."

Vinson

Chief Vinson pulled himself out of the city sim and looked around his barren office. How had he missed the big picture? As CEO, he should have anticipated the IE bid to take over police functions within Corporate Dallas. It had blindsided him.

The second he'd gotten wind of it, he'd composed a harsh note to the Top 50 Corporate CEOs, the group that ran Corporate Dallas, nominally representing all of the corporations, but actually dominated by the dozen or so largest and richest companies. He'd documented the way Interfaith Enforcers had violated the corporate consensus, murdering insured ratepayers like Merryweather, and threatening to turn against the T-50 if Vinson didn't go along with them. He'd forwarded his list of accomplishments and the IE's list of failure.

In reply to his memo, he'd heard—nothing.

"You sure you're getting enough sleep, Dad? Or maybe you need a system flush."

He looked at his daughter, saw the concern written in her eyes. "I'm worried about the war, Maurissa."

She laughed. "Oh, dad. It's an economic war. Nobody gets hurt. Like that attack last night. I mean, a few thousand drones and all they could do was make phone calls asking for our corporations to join up with theirs. It's silly."

He tried to match her smile but knew he hadn't convinced her as soon as he'd done it. "You're probably right. Now, shouldn't you be working?"

"I am working. I wanted to show you something."

He sat, opened his phone connection to full sim, and entered the medieval fairy tale world his daughter had created.

It was good work. When he bent down to touch the cobblestones lining the village street, they felt cool and slightly rough to his touch. The stench of human filth was probably lighter than it would actually have been, but nobody wanted *that* much realism. The scents coming from the village pub, marked by a faded double-headed dragon, were completely realistic, evoking images of porks roasting on a spit, and a yeasty beverage—possibly ale.

The people were the best. He knew one of them was Maurissa and the others were sims, but he couldn't tell the difference until a busty barmaid whose top was cut way too low plopped a plate and earthenware mug in front of him. "Well, try it, dad."

To humor her, he took a bite of the pork and a long draft of ale. "Wow. I can actually feel the alcohol's effect."

"It's the latest thing. We can directly stimulate the effect alcohol has on the human brain."

"Beautiful. You'll be rich."

"It's mostly for citizens," she waved his compliment away. "But I thought it was pretty good."

"It's fantastic. The detail is incredible. I think you'll have a lot of ratepayers tuning in, too, and not just in Corporate Dallas. This should be a best-seller across North America."

"Well, anyway. If your Police Corporation goes bust, you won't have to worry about me. As you see, I can take care of myself."

"Your mother put you up to this, didn't she?"

"She mentioned the Interfaith bid."

Vinson shook his head. That Maudie had done so could only mean she thought the IE's bid would be accepted. Considering her job, she probably had more insight than he did.

"Don't worry. The Police Corporation has faced competition before. There should be resistance to turning over so much power to a group that's not really in line with corporate objectives."

"Sure, dad." Maurissa might have found a way to sound less convinced. Vinson wasn't sure how.

"I've got to make some calls," he said. "Maybe I can visit your sim again later."

"A couple of minutes in and I've got a great starter quest lined up. You'll like it."

Vinson would have preferred a relaxing sim with plenty of eating, drinking and horses, and maybe with a bar wench who *wasn't* his daughter, but he nodded. "I'll check it out."

First, though, he needed to check with Shenker. The Lieutenant had to succeed. Once he did that, Vinson would go after the designers and Houston spy hiding in the rings. In the meantime, it was time to follow up with Sammy Jardan, Olivia's brother. If he was as loyal to his sister as he pretended, there might be another way Vinson could use him. Because Sammy Jardan was on the fast track at the Interfaith. When he learned that the Interfaith, and not the cops, were primarily responsible for her troubles, Sammy just might offer some hints on how to derail this crazy Interfaith bid.

Julia

Olivia used her police override to take over one of the cop transports, and the four women piled in and headed south, away from the safety of Martin and the base he'd set up, but also away from wherever Shenker had been trying to drive them.

Unless he'd outsmarted them. Then again, there was the chance he'd outsmarted himself. With each minute that they remained free, their horizon expanded—leaving Shenker more places to search.

"I don't know centercity that well," Olivia admitted.

"Straight south." Julia hoped she sounded more confident than she felt.

Five miles south and ten minutes later, Olivia smashed the transport's memory system, made sure the camouflage blankets remained inside it, programmed it to take a wandering course eastward, and let it go.

"We're even worse off than before," McKensie protested.

They stood in the middle of a street in the very heart of centercity. Skyscraping buildings, memories of another era, jutted arrogantly into the sky like uneven teeth.

"Much though it embarrasses me to admit it, McKensie raises a valid point," Kansas said. "Nobody lives here, it's just corporate headquarters."

Julia motioned them to silence. In her phone, she overlaid a map of ancient Dallas from the very beginning of the century with one of current Dallas, using their GPS coordinates to place them exactly.

"Ten meters to the west," she said.

"Uh, I don't see anything different." Olivia didn't look like she was ready to join the Kansas/McKensie rebellion, but she seemed concerned.

"Can you open this?" She pointed at the rusty steel of an ancient utility cover.

"The Bell System? What's that?" McKensie stared at the logo of a company that had died back in the old days, even before the corporations won.

Olivia just squinted at the letters.

At some abstract level, Julia knew that citizens weren't taught to read. Education corporations couldn't make money teaching them a skill only designers needed. Still, seeing someone whom she knew to be intelligent staring at simple words as if they contained insolvable mysteries seemed wrong. Idealistic Martin probably had some explanation—and plan for fixing things. As it was, it just meant Olivia didn't have the information Julia had—she'd have to make the decisions.

"There's a whole city underneath Corporate Dallas. Left over from the old days when people used copper wires to deliver electricity and phone service, pipes to deliver water and take away sewage, and even little trains to deliver coal."

"People plugged copper wires into their heads?" Kansas looked mystified.

"Phones weren't in your heads," Julia said. "You carried them in your hand. Haven't you ever done private eye sims set in the twentieth century?"

"I thought those were older," McKensie admitted.

History was another subject that wasn't taught much, and certainly never taught to citizens. But there had been more than wires and fiber optics underground. Before solar power and constructors revolutionized commerce and created the corporate consensus, America had generated tons of waste for each resident—and had spewed much of it through pipes and waste treatment. Unable to use the water and organic waste to fuel constructors, massive storm sewer systems had collected the rain that flooded off huge parking lots and paved expanses and dumped the floods into the nearby Trinity River—a now nearly empty trickle used for ratepayer picnics.

Those ancient sewers still hid under the streets of downtown Dallas because no corporation saw a profit motive in filling them in.

Unfortunately, the steel utility cover was welded shut.

"Olivia, can you open this?" Julia repeated.

Olivia nodded, then pulled out her crystalline-carbon knife and cut through the spot-welds that held the utility cover in place.

McKensie surprised Julia by pushing forward then. "I can get it from here." She pulled off her jacket, showing an impressively sculpted abs, tugged the smart fabric until it became a hard rod, wedged it into a small hole on the cover, and leveraged it open.

"You really are strong," Kansas cooed.

"Spare me," Julia said. "Who wants to go first?"

She wasn't surprised that no one volunteered.

Finally Olivia grabbed stepped onto a rusty riser. "I'll go. But all of you had better follow me. And McKensie, you come last. You're probably the only one of us with the muscle strength to lift that heavy steel cover back into place."

"I can do that." Giving her a responsibility seemed to improve McKensie's disposition.

Julia made Kansas follow Olivia, then came down herself.

Daylight faded quickly, even before McKensie closed the cover, but Julia was mostly pleased. She'd feared some corporation would have expanded downward secretly, closing off the tunnels, but that didn't seem to be the case. Admittedly things smelled—a lot—and they would have to crawl thorough big pipes from time to time, but they had entered an underground Dallas that only a history buff, would even guess existed.

She'd expected it to be drier, though.

For decades, Dallas corporations and homespaces had sucked up every free drop of water, using it, along with carbon dioxide from the atmosphere and recycled organic products as feed, to create everything in their constructors.

Still, the sewer continually dripped and a thin layer of wet mud overlaid what felt like a couple of feet of ancient silt. Even in the higher sections, Julia had to duck slightly to make her way forward.

Then McKensie slammed the utility cover closed. Darkness, enhanced rather than limited by the two small beams of sunlight piercing the small holes on the utility cover, slammed down with it.

"I can't see a thing," Kansas complained.

Julia was glad Kansas said that—it spared her having to say the same thing.

Martin

Martin had to face reality—Olivia and the three designers were lost.

Olivia had called him when they'd escaped Shenker's trap, but when Julia had insisted they head south, away from his base, away from where Justin had assembled a group of free-cits to help create the basis for a future society, Martin recognized that he had been holding a false hope.

Olivia, Julia, Kansas and McKensie were serving the future by distracting who knew how many cops who would otherwise be reinforcing the clouds of drones his sensors detected flying over the outer rings, searching for any evidence of what they were building. As long as the women stayed alive, uncaptured, they would continue to serve the cause, but they weren't making it out.

"You have to eat, dad." Jimmy held a bowl of what looked to be one of the better Interfaith meals. He didn't offer to share it, though.

Martin stared at his son.

"Angie has been playing on the Interfaith again. She's got IF credits coming out her ears. If you ask really nicely, she might share."

Martin's stomach gurgled and he realized Jimmy was right—he was hungry. It didn't seem fair to eat when four people he felt responsible for were buried in the tomb of ancient Dallas, but starving himself wouldn't help them and might make him unable to act if there came a time he could do anything to save them or, more likely, at least avenge them.

"They aren't going to make it, are they dad?" Angie had been inputting code into a constructor but she stopped when he stepped into the small homespace he'd constructed in the ruins of an old strip shopping center.

"Nobody's caught them yet."

"Your plan doesn't depend on any one person. So, we go on."

Martin nodded. He'd gotten a better response than he'd anticipated from free-code devotees in Corporate Fort Worth and Corporate Midcities. With a solid core from Corporate Dallas in place, he had close to the thirty designers Julia had believed to be the minimum. But somehow, during this process, he'd lost some of his innocence. Kansas and McKensie had so obviously been a trap, yet he'd sent Julia and Olivia walking right into it.

"Help me finish setting up this big constructor," he told his children. "If we're going to be any help with this project, we need to be ready to test as soon as the designers start sending code."

"Maybe they'll be all right," Angie repeated. "Julia acts dumb, but she's really on the ball. And Olivia is tougher than you give her credit for."

"What makes you so smart?"

His little daughter put her hands on her hips. "I am a woman, dad. Everyone knows women have to do all the thinking if we don't want the species to die out."

He laughed, but he wondered if Angie didn't have a point.

Olivia

She hadn't realized this world was down here. Olivia had to wonder what other secrets Corporate Dallas held, what other dangers or opportunities might jump out at them—and that she might not recognize.

She never would have thought to go underground. But in just about every way, this was the perfect solution to their problems. Shenker's thermal scanners had no hope of penetrating the meters of stone and clay that separated them from the city above. His CO_2 gauges would never notice the addition of a couple more sources when these mixed in with a hundred years rot and the tiny beasts that made up the population of this underworld.

Away from energy of sunlight, the underworld had little value to the ratepayers of centercity, but because it was in centercity, it was inaccessible to mere citizens. Cops would know nothing about it.

Considering the stink, she would have been happy to know less about it, too.

Olivia extended her vision into the infrared zone, but was unprepared for the darkness that had fallen with the clang of an iron utility cover locking them in, trapping them underground.

The blobs of heat that were the three designers stood out in the darkness. Deeper in the sewers, smaller blobs indicated other lifeforms, nasty lifeforms made this catacomb their home.

"This is kind of cool," Kansas said. "Naturally temperature-regulated, enough water to source whatever hydrogen and oxygen we need. But there's one thing I don't get. Why do you figure there's no one else down here?"

"Why would they be? Julia asked. "There's no sun, no energy."

"We're not that far from the sun. We should be able to figure out a way."

"I'm hoping we can," Julia said. "Because I think we're going to be here for a while. Olivia's boyfriend, Lieutenant Shenker, is going to keep looking for us. If we set foot outside, he'll find us."

"But it's dirty." McKensie swished her foot through a puddle lit by a streak of sunlight.

"I downloaded an old engineering diagram of the sewers and major conduit lines just before we came down," Olivia said. "There are underground parking structures that either link in or are close. We should be able to find someplace a bit cleaner and drier eventually. Right now, I'm happy we're alive."

"Well that's not enough," Julia answered. "We need to get some energy here so we can start designing again. Because we're going to be here for a while."

"And get our phones working again," Kansas said. "We can't design without them."

"Here's the thing." Julia's face, even in the near-total darkness, grew serious. "I told Martin this already but he didn't get it. And the rest of us, we're designers, not cops. We're going to have problems with rules. We need to legitimize what we're doing, to coexist with the corporate structure. As a cop, you had to worry about contracts and corporate entities, Olivia. You're the one who has to figure out how to turn this from a simple design proposal into something that can deliver on Martin's idealistic notions of a new future."

Until Julia had said that, Olivia had felt perfectly comfortable deep beneath the heart of centercity. Abruptly, though, tons of earth packed above her head felt as if it was pressing down, about to burst through the reinforced concrete and crush her.

"I don't have access to the legal databases or AI analysis machine cops use to do this kind of thing. How am I supposed to figure this out if ratepayers like Merryweather and Martin can't?"

"I don't know," Julia admitted. "But if you don't, nobody else is going to."

"They broke CC agreements when they killed Merryweather and the others. Why should they stop just because we figure out a way to apply those same rules to us?"

Through the darkness, Olivia sensed Julia shaking her head. "I guess you need to figure that out, too."

"Well how about we figure something to eat?" McKensie suggested. "What we do in a year or two when we finish coding isn't as important as being alive when it happens."

Olivia wasn't sure Martin or Merryweather would see it that way. On the other hand, Martin and Merryweather weren't there. Staying alive was important.

"I, ah, downloaded some better meals," Julia admitted. "I've got them stored in my phone so we can use them even though all the dirt means I have a terrible connection to the Infoweb."

"So," McKensie demanded. "What are we waiting for? We've got lots of water and what looks like bat crap for organics. That has to have carbon in it, doesn't it?"

"What are we going to use for energy?" Olivia answered. "We can't exactly post solar panels outside the utility cover. They might not be able to detect us down here, but they sure could spot any solar panels we throw up. Not that we have any."

Julia patted the miniconstructor she'd lugged from their hideout in the woods. "I don't think there's enough chemical energy in that bat guano to drive this thing. And Olivia's right. The second we start sticking out solar panels, we're going to get spotted."

"We're going to starve," McKensie said. "Surrounded by organics? How sick is that? Maybe we should just surrender. At least they'd feed us."

"Did you hear the way the cops shot up that forest we were hiding in?" Olivia demanded. "It didn't sound to me like they were stopping to feed anyone."

"We're going to die." Kansas echoed her friend without offering any suggestion. "This rescue has sucked from the very beginning."

Olivia would have felt a lot better if she'd allowed herself to punch out the whiners, but that wouldn't be helpful and they had a point. She'd set out for this rescue like it was a sim, confident she could pick up energy points, weapons, and whatever she needed along the way. Reality wasn't so easy. Considering that she and Julia had dragged Kansas and McKensie into this mess, the two had reason to complain a little. Not too much, though, since their alternative was to be killed by Interfaith Enforcers.

"Let's explore these caves," she suggested. "Maybe we'll find something with energy potential."

Shenker

"**They've** vanished," Jorge reported. "Maybe they were never here in the first place."

Knowing he'd regret it, Shenker let himself blow up. "Never here? What the hell do you think happened to Andrew? Unlike some, he didn't trip over his big flat feet."

"I said I was sorry about falling."

Shenker took a breath, let it out, then took another. "And I'm sorry I brought that up. Still, it's obvious they were here. We've got DNA matches where they scraped against the trees. We've got Andrew all banged up, but certain he faced off against Olivia. And we've got a missing car."

"Hey, why not trace the car?"

Hey, why not try using your brain. Shenker had traced the car—at least as much of its path as he could. Although Olivia had destroyed its memory, centercity sensors marked out its route. The only problem was, it had stopped a number of times. The renegades could have jumped out at any of those locations. They might even have split up, although Shenker didn't think they would. Olivia's sense of responsibility would make her ride herd over the group.

The real pisser was, his informant wasn't doing jack. She should have revealed herself while they'd been walking through the trees. She should have let him know where they'd disembarked and where they were heading.

For maybe the millionth time since he'd broken the Interfaith jamming debacle, he tried calling her—and got an autoanswer that hadn't been updated for days.

Olivia wasn't stupid. She had walked into a trap, but she'd been prepared, had obviously disabled the ratepayers' phones.

"They're still in centercity," Shenker decided. "They can't make it into the rings, so they'll hunker down somewhere."

He looked around at his depleted force—Vinson had pulled back his reinforcements when Shenker had admitted he didn't know what to do with them. "Let's start by checking the families again. Go deeper this time. Look for cousins and coworkers who might be friendly. They're going to get awful hungry if they don't get help, and they're certainly not going to get anything from the public constructors."

"Sure boss."

Shenker noticed a distinct lack of enthusiasm from his team.

Julia

A few rats ran over Julia's feet, but none actually climbed higher than the knees of her pants so she suppressed her panic and stood still. Perfectly still.

Olivia and the designers had explored more deeply into the sewers and found an abundance of organic materials. Unfortunately, finding and using were two different things. Persuading living, biting, red-eyes-glowing rats to climb into the miniconstructor so they could be transformed into food wasn't happening. And the slime the rats seemed to subsist on had too low an energy content for the constructor.

"Are they gone?" Kansas asked.

Julia shuffled her feet. She'd turned up a tiny LED she used sometimes when she was coming home late, and it provided the only light they had down here. Small as it was, it was enough to disturb the rats. Fortunately, the miserable little rodents weren't hungry. At least not hungry enough to attack the women.

"First thing we do," she said, "when we do get some energy, is to set up some smart material walls and floors. I don't want to wake up one morning to find one of these critters gnawing on my nose."

"Eeew," Kansas agreed.

"I think we need to figure out our organization," McKensie said. "If we're going to set up a design shop down here, we need to act like a small corporation. Obviously the three of us will be shareholders. We'll have to vote to decide who'll be CEO."

Julia suppressed her smile. Clearly McKensie liked herself for the role of CEO.

"Three? Looks to me like there are four of us. Or were you counting you and Kansas as one person."

"Olivia is an employee, not a stockholder."

Olivia pushed her way forward, past the overhead grating through which most of the rats had vanished.

"We're not just doing design," Julia said. "We're trying to stay alive. It's not like we have any money to pay employees, anyway."

"If you gave us back our identities, we'd have access to money. I could pay Olivia's salary out of what I spend every week on manicure sculpts."

Julia felt Olivia seethe. It was funny in a way. The ex-cop bought into the whole ratepayer thing even more than ratepayers did. She probably thought McKensie had a point, even as she knew the woman was small-minded and trying to get her goat.

"Creating a virtual corporation is a good plan," Julia agreed. "Thanks for suggesting it. But Olivia needs to be a shareholder. I think we should make each of us equal, but Olivia equal plus one. That way we'll have a tie-breaker, but if all of us designers agree, we'll be able to override anything she wants."

"So you and your girlfriend get to outvote me and my girlfriend?" Kansas asked.

Julia laughed. "You forget that Olivia grew up a citizen. The Interfaith Enforcers make sure none of them act out *forbidden perversions*. Nope. Olivia is straight as a board. Which would be good to find about now."

"Someone straight?"

"No a board. Something chemical we can use to drive the constructor. You're not the only one who's hungry."

"But—"

"So we have an organization." Julia overrode whatever McKensie was going to say. "Then come on. I have an idea."

"I knew it. You just happened to get an idea the minute we caved in."

Julia wasn't absolutely sure, but she remembered her grandparents talking about the old days in Dallas, before the corporations had won, before the great compromise. And just maybe, there was stuff left from those days. Stuff nobody especially wanted, but that could be valuable to four hungry women, three of whom wanted to get to work doing some design. She hoped so.

Vinson

"**They're** killing our profits."

Vinson didn't have to check the display glowing directly on his optical nerve. Perhaps ten people could break through his autoanswer in the middle of the night. Exactly one of them talked like that. Louis Brandon was not only CEO of Dallas Industrial Design and his wife's boss, he was also Chairman of the entire corporate consensus. Which made him Vinson's boss, too.

"I assume, Chairman Brandon, that you're talking about Corporate Houston's increase in the price of the nitrogen-fusing connector module."

"Of course I'm talking about that. What else?"

"You had to expect them to strike back after you increased the price of your buckyball fabrication unit."

"I expected a reasonable accommodation."

Reasonable to Brandon and reasonable to his counterparts in Corporate Houston meant different things. Reminding Brandon of that was unlikely to generate positive feelings. Vinson kept his mouth shut.

"With them squeezing our profits, we need to cut costs. Do you have any idea how much our insurance bill comes to every month? And what's it go for? Police who can't even track down a couple of renegade designers."

"Those renegade designers paid their premiums, too."

Brandon sighed. "Their policies were properly canceled and any remaining balances refunded to their accounts. You can't ding me on that, Vinson. Now, are you prepared to match the thirty percent reduction Ariel is offering, or are we going to have to cut your contract, too?"

"It's the middle of the night, Mr. Chairman. I'll have our negotiators contact yours in the morning and we can discuss all of the terms in our contract. But I assume you didn't wake me up just to ask me about a price break. So, what's going on?"

Brandon hesitated, but finally spoke. "Ariel says that the police have ignored the problem of free-cits for too long. Considering we didn't even know they'd been fabricating attack aircraft, I'd have to say he was right. So, what are we going to do to clamp down on them?"

"We did report that Corporate Houston agitators were working with citizens in the outer rings and beyond."

Brandon waved that aside. "You didn't tell us what they were doing. Ariel says he can beat them into shape."

Vinson sighed. "Who cares about free-cits, Chairman? Other than volunteering for a few parts in low-budget sims, they don't contribute to the economy at all. Ariel wants to beat them into shape to force them to use more Interfaith product. He wants us to eliminate public constructors too, so cits will have no one but him to turn to. If you give him that much power, you'll be at his mercy. He'll blackmail Corporate Dallas into doing exactly what he wants."

"You think that's what's going on?"

"I know that's what Ariel wants."

"I'll think about it."

Vinson waited for the semiaudible click that indicated the end of a phone session and headed for the shower.

It was early, but it would take him a while to get out to the Jardan homespace. Sammy Jardan had been avoiding his calls but he couldn't avoid a personal visit. Vinson was an executive and a cop. Sammy was just a citizen. Without Olivia making insurance payments on his parent's homespace, Sammy could easily find himself without a roof over his head.

* * * *

Vinson didn't spend much time outside centercity.

Looking around at the ring where Jardan had grown up gave him all the reminder he needed of why.

Homespaces squeezed together, spotless solar panels tilting to catch every photon as the hot Texas sun peered over the horizon.

Even the narrow roads between the homespaces were overlaid with solar collectors, and the air was almost brutally dry, drained of water vapor by the voracious appetite for water that thousands of constructors demanded to supplement rainwater hoarded underground.

The stink of constructed foodstuffs filled the air, along with what smelled vaguely like coffee but that Vinson, who loved the real thing, knew to be a cheap Interfaith knockoff.

He presented himself to the Jardan family greeter. "Police Chief Harles Vinson for Sammy Jardan."

No point in starting with overrides when politeness might do, and Vinson wasn't surprised when Sammy opened the door and let him in a few minutes later.

"I told you I'm not going to help you." The two were seated at the Jardan table.

Vinson nodded, then entered his personal code for RealTaste™ SimCoffee™ at the Jardan constructor. "Want one?"

"Sure."

RealTaste™ didn't cost much—not by ratepayer standards. It also didn't live up to its name. Out here, it was an incredible luxury.

He waited until the constructor delivered a couple steaming mugs, set Sammy's down in front of the young man, and took a swallow.

Vinson appreciated it, but Sammy practically salivated over the steaming cup. Still, he wasn't that easy to bribe. "You didn't come here to buy me a cup of coffee, Chief."

"I wonder if you want to help your sister?"

"I'd be a big help if I turned her over to the people who covered her homespace with eater-nanobes."

"What makes you think—"

"You don't think the Interfaith has the same kind of monitors the police do? I watched the damned video."

Vinson nodded. "Things have progressed since then. The secrets we wanted kept are no longer so important. In fact, we want your sister alive."

"That's why you were blowing up the cars you thought she was in day before yesterday."

"Those cars were entering protected territory. The police AI was programmed to prevent unauthorized entry."

"That's some prevention."

"Look, Sammy. I can't undo what's been done. But your sister is more important now than she's ever been. I'd prefer to have her alive because she knows the location of a Corporate Houston base somewhere in the outer rings of Corporate Dallas."

"And I should care because?"

"If you don't care about Corporate Dallas, maybe you should care about your sister. Help us bring her in and I'll release her to you, alive, after we've learned what we need to know. If you don't help us, why I should do you any favors."

"But if I don't help you, you don't find her. So, it seems to me that's the best solution for me."

Vinson stood, grasped Sammy's arm, and squeezed down until he felt the man's muscle slide away from bone. "Don't kid yourself, son. Olivia is going to get caught, with or without your help. If you won't help willingly, you'll help unwillingly. But you won't be as happy about the outcome."

Sammy wrenched his arm free, picked up his nearly full cup, and dumped it into the constructor's feed. "I guess I don't want your coffee after all, Vinson. Why don't you just leave?"

"I'll leave, but I'll be seeing you around, Sammy. You're on the team now, whether you want to be or not."

Olivia

They'd found a bunch of branches from long-cut trees and gotten enough carbon and chemical energy out of those to churn out low calorie versions of Julia's codes. So far, they were surviving, but that was about it.

They bedded down for an uncomfortable night in an underground room that had once, according to Julia, held some sort of remote switching center back in the days when phones were connected by wires and optical glass rather than wireless. Olivia chose to sleep next to the door, which wouldn't close all the way. She would be the first the rats would climb over if they came this way, but she'd also be there if McKinsey or Kansas decided to climb the other way.

The two designers were at least partially mollified by a self-warming pizza Julia had constructed for them, and by Olivia's promise that she'd give them some kind of phone service once they constructed a lab.

The cold and damp concrete floor was hard against the smart fabric of Olivia's police tunic, and harder where she lay her head down in what she was certain was a fruitless attempt to get some sleep.

Just as Olivia felt she would never sleep again, she woke up to the sight of gray daylight penetrating through the open doorway.

Perhaps drawn to her body's warmth, a substantial furry animal pressed against her chest, its breath a steady growl.

Kansas's reliance on screams to greet every strange activity had annoyed her. All of a sudden, Olivia was a lot more sympathetic.

She screamed at the top of her lungs.

The furry animal dug its claws into her skin, jumped to its feet, looked both ways, its pointed ears twitching, and then scurried off into the darkness.

"What was that about?" Julia demanded.

Julia and Kansas were stretching and rubbing sleep out of their eyes but McKensie was already sitting up. Which meant she had to have seen that animal before Olivia had awakened—seen it and left it there to spread its germs or gnaw at her body.

"Some animal nestled up against me like I was a nanoblanket. And you saw it, didn't you, McKensie? Were you hoping it would eat me?"

"You're kidding, right?"

"Do I look like I'm kidding?"

The designer rolled her eyes. "It wasn't a wild animal."

"Right. Maybe it was a free-citizen who happened to miss shaving for the day."

"It was a cat, dummy. It was keeping the rats away, until you scared it off."

"Cats are real?" Sim pets included silver aliens, yellow Pikachus, talking plants, bright-colored birds that screamed about pieces of eight, and other fantasy creations. Olivia had always assumed that cats were a part of that same weird fantasy that inspired all those other pets. Why would nature have evolved something so cute and cuddly?

Then again, this visitor was a long step from the fantasy version she'd known on the sims. On the sims, animals never have rat-breath, matted fur, or the bugs she suspected her new friend had been covered with.

"*This* cat was real," McKensie pointed out. "And I know lots of people with actual pets. You can program your bots to take care of them so it's no problem. It doesn't cost much."

"I guess some ratepayer got tired of taking care of their pet and threw it down in the sewers, then."

McKensie looked out their makeshift doorway in the direction the cat had run. "Not everyone is set up to be a good parent. I think the cat is a good sign, though. Once we get set up, my first design is going to be milk because I've always heard that cats love milk."

"Milk isn't good for them," Kansas announced.

"Well the milk *I* design will be good for them. Are you going to deliver on your plan today, Julia, or do we need to waste another day doing nothing?"

"Food first, I think," Julia announced. "Who wants more pizza?"

Julia's pizza had been good but nobody wanted it for breakfast. What Julia coded up instead made at least Olivia wish she'd asked for the pizza.

She sidled over to Julia while Kansas and McKensie ate. "Do you really have a plan, or were you just trying to keep everyone's confidence high?"

Julia opened her eyes wide in affected shock. "You don't believe me?"

"Let's just say I'm leaving my options open."

"Well, I have a plan. Imagine a place where there is so much chemical energy we won't have to risk setting out solar panels, where we can build a larger constructor, set up comfortable loungers to use while we're designing, a place with a roof that won't leak if it rains, and a place protected from the rats."

Olivia looked around. The three-meter by three-meter room they'd spent the night in was a far cry from the kind of utopia Julia had described. "If it were that easy, why didn't we spend last night there instead of here?"

"Because I haven't found it, that's why. I know where I'm trying to go, but I don't know how to get there."

"What makes you think it's even there, whatever it is?"

"Would even a little bit of trust and confidence be completely beyond your ability?"

"So you're just hoping."

Julia sighed. "I'm just hoping."

"I guess we'd better explore, then, and see if we can find it."

"Do *we* have to come?" McKensie demanded when Julia said they were going to continue through the tunnels. "Why don't you leave Kansas and me here with the constructor? Less to carry and we won't slow you down."

Olivia pretended to consider. "What do you think, Julia? I guess we could secure them here. Of course, if anything happens to us, they'd starve to death."

Even in the dim light of Julia's LED lamp, McKensie's scowl was almost poetic. "All right, we'll come with you. But I don't think you're being very fair. We're all in this together, right? Our own little corporation. So, why do you keep treating us like prisoners?"

Olivia got in her face. "You nearly got us killed yesterday when the cops were looking for us. Bottom line, you haven't earned my trust. Change that and I'll change my behavior."

"You did ask," Kansas said when McKensie looked like she wanted to swing a punch.

"I didn't mean to get us caught. The blanket slipped."

Olivia shook her head. "Let's go find Julia's treasure-trove."

Considering all they had was their clothes and the miniconstructor, it took longer than Olivia would have guessed before they were ready to head out.

Finally, though, Julia led the way into darkness, her tiny LED the only thing keeping them from being completely blind.

Julia marked each tunnel as they entered it. Some, they had to crawl through. In others, even McKensie could stand. Whenever she could, Julia headed south and east. She might not know how to get there, but she certainly seemed to have an idea of where it was located.

Time lost meaning in the darkness. What seemed like an eternity took only minutes. At other times, only seconds seemed to pass, but Olivia's phone assured her an hour had gone by. Gradually Olivia slipped into a zone of walking and crawling, of moving forward and then having to turn around and head back when they hit one dead-end after another.

When it finally pierced her zone-state, Olivia thought the sound was an echo or perhaps a regular drip in the ever-dank tunnels. But no drip would follow them through countless twists and turns of the caverns under Dallas. This wasn't an echo and it appeared to be coming from directly behind them.

She connected with Julia on her phone, speaking subvocally. "Do you know that we're being followed?"

Julia

She'd been certain her idea would work. The sewers under the city were forgotten remains of twentieth century technology that no longer served any purpose. Because Shenker came from a citizen background, he was unlikely even to guess that Corporate Dallas held the bones of its predecessor-city under its solar collector-imbued streets.

Evidently she'd been wrong.

Julia looked around—a completely pointless gesture since she couldn't see anything beyond the five-foot circle of dim light shed by her LED.

"We'll keep moving," she said. "You'll have to ambush them."

And if she survived this, she was going to think about a more muscular sculpt and some training in how to fight. She was tired of making Olivia do all the work.

While Olivia held back, Julia chattered at Kansas about the latest ratepayer fashions.

At a major intersection where a couple of clay pipes descending from above and the main sewer made a near-90 degree turn, Olivia grabbed the edge of one of the pipes and pulled herself into it.

Julia pretended not to notice, walking and talking, exactly as if Olivia were still with them.

Thirty seconds later, she heard the thunk of Olivia's boots hitting the ground and hurried back.

Olivia held her crystalline carbon knife in one hand and faced off against... their early morning visitor.

"Mrrr-ow." A longhaired cat stared at Olivia, its eyes glowing bright green in the near-dark.

"You almost gave me a heart attack," Olivia lectured the little animal.

The cat meowed again, then rubbed its sleek body against her calf.

"She must have been someone's pet," Julia said. "A feral cat wouldn't let someone touch it like that."

Olivia looked nervous. "I'm not touching it. It's touching me."

"It's pretty, and if it was a pet, it has nanobes that will keep fleas and other pests away."

"What are we going to with it?"

Julia bent down and picked up the cat, scratching her under the chin. "We'll bring her with us. A cat with us will keep the rodents away."

The ungrateful animal squirmed in her arms until she handed her over to a cautious-looking Olivia. Once Olivia draped her over her back, though, the animal settled down for a good purr.

"Uh-oh, she's growling."

"When cats do that," Julia explained, "it's called purring. It's a noise they make when they're happy."

"Weird."

"Scratch her under her chin. They like that."

As they neared another intersection, the cat pushed her pads against Olivia's shoulder.

"Ouch. If you wanted down, why didn't you just say so?"

"Talking cats are only in the sims."

"I knew that."

Julia wasn't so sure, but she didn't argue.

The cat scurried ahead of them.

"So much for having her protect us from rats," Kansas said.

Olivia rubbed her tunic where the cat had rested. "She seems to like us."

"No accounting for tastes," McKensie offered. "At least it's a little drier where she's going.

"Lower, too." Julia might have missed the corrugated steel tunnel halfway hidden behind a pile of debris if the cat hadn't shown her the way.

Well, a cat would want the same kind of things a human would—someplace dry and far enough from the rats that she didn't have to worry about being attacked while she slept.

"Let's follow her," Olivia suggested.

Julia's knees were killing her by the time they caught up with the cat.

They crawled almost a kilometer, finally ending up at a confluence where three smaller pipes fed into the big one they'd been crawling in.

The cat had some sort of nest halfway up the wall. Her eyes glowed down like green laser probes.

Cautiously, Julia stood, hoping she wouldn't bang her head on any obstruction.

"Looks like the end of the trail," Kansas moaned. "I'm not sleeping in a twelve centimeter-wide ledge with that cat, and I think I'm the only one of us skinny enough to crawl through any of the other tunnels. You know, Julia, this has been a really bad idea from the very beginning.

"You *are* still alive," she fired back.

"Yeah, but when I wake up tomorrow and my legs don't move because I've turned my knees into some sort of jelly, I'm not sure I'll be thanking you for—."

"What's that overhead?" Olivia asked.

Julia shined her LED past some rusty steel rails at an overhead utility hatch.

"We've passed fifty of those," McKensie moaned.

"Are you ready to crawl back," Julia demanded, "or should we try this one out?"

McKensie rubbed her legs. "I vote we try it out."

"Good plan."

Normally Julia would have sent Olivia ahead to do the dangerous work, but her GPS told her they were near the spot she'd been trying to reach for almost two days now.

Testing each link before she put her full weight on it, Julia scaled the rusty ladder leading to the cover.

Sure enough, the steel cap had those same little holes as had the utility hatch they'd come down through the previous day.

When she got to the top, she switched off the LED, looked through each of the holes, and saw nothing.

"What?" Kansas whispered.

"Pitch black."

"We've got enough of that down here," McKensie moaned.

"Darkness means it's enclosed. I don't know about you guys, but I'm not ready to go back into the sunlight and let Shenker kill me."

"That's not at the top of my list either," Olivia said.

"Let me see if I can get this open."

The thing weighed a ton. But it wiggled a little when she pressed on it so she knew it wasn't sealed. Which was lucky since she wouldn't be able to use Olivia's crystal-carbon knife on welds on the wrong side of the inch-thick steel cover.

You could say what you wanted about those old-timers. They'd squandered natural resources, ignored the power of the sun, and hadn't really gotten the whole idea of intellectual property, but boy had they built things to last.

"Hey, McKensie." She climbed down the ladder made of iron bars sunk into concrete. "Want to show us what those muscles can do?"

* * * *

The heavy iron of the utility cover made a loud grinding noise as McKensie grunted and shoved it out of the slot.

"Leave it just slightly ajar," Olivia whispered. "Let's wait a few minutes in case some sound-activated security system called a security bot to investigate."

They waited in darkness, but only the cat's steady purr broke the silence.

Olivia shoved the hatch the rest of the way open and gestured for Julia to lead the way.

It was her paradise—assuming she was right about what was waiting for them on the other side of that opening.

It would be a horrible disappointment to discover that someone had beaten her to it and consumed all of that delicious carbon.

The cat draped over her shoulder, Olivia followed Julia up the ladder. She carried her diamond knife between her teeth and looked like nothing so much as a pirate boarding an enemy ship in a nighttime engagement.

Which was, Julia realized, what they all were.

Julia climbed out next and turned on her LED, sending a focused stream of light in each direction.

It was everything she'd hoped it would be.

At least five meters overhead, pipes and iron girders showed the dated construction of the sub-basement. Paint flaked off ancient concrete walls where moisture had gradually penetrated that substance, but the humidity remained low, and the cool temperature would be perfect for preservation.

Everywhere she looked, cardboard cartons were stacked halfway to the ceiling, with narrow rows cut between them. A steel handtruck even leaned against one of those stacks, showing how the remains of an earlier civilization had been abandoned.

"What is it?" Olivia set down the cat and stood at Julia's shoulder.

"It used to be the Dallas Public Library."

"Which is—"

"Which is where the city kept books to lend out."

"The city rented books? That violates intellectual property regulations."

"They didn't rent them, they lent them out for free. It was paid for by taxes."

"One reason Corporate Dallas replaced City of Dallas." Kansas had followed them up the ladder and jerked open one of the cartons. Sure enough, it was stacked full of beautiful paper books.

All of that paper was carbon, filled with enough energy to power the constructor. And there had to be tons of it here. With this, they could live comfortably for a year or more, until finally the pursuit gave up and they could return to the sunlight.

Martin

"**The** new constructor is finished, dad. Can I go hang out with the guys now?"

Angie had filled out a bit since he'd moved into the outer rings near Corporate Dallas. Martin hadn't really thought about that until he heard the slight emphasis she put on the word *guys*. Was his daughter really old enough to notice boys? It didn't seem possible.

"Be back in three hours," he said. "I want us to eat together like a family."

"Oh, dad. The gang is checking out one of the ghost towns."

"Those ruins are full of scorpions and rattlesnakes."

"Which is why I spent two days on the Interfaith. Everyone has the latest antivenom code."

He sighed. "Five hours. Be back before dark."

"Like anything's going to happen to me."

"Not if I can help it."

She wrinkled her nose at him, then vanished before he could change his mind.

Justin came in before the door could close. "Tough when they're that age."

"It's tough when they're any age."

Justin nodded. "You do any more thinking about how we make it happen if the code actually gets finished?"

Martin stared at the free-cit who'd become his friend. Justin looked better than when they'd started working together. Having a place to stay and enough to eat had made a difference. But he was still visibly aged, still in desperate need of the kind of body sculpt anyone should be able to afford.

"I've been testing," Martin admitted. "Do you have any idea how easy it is for a minor error to propagate through the system and cause a disaster at the back end?"

"I have a pretty good idea that if you don't build a back end to deliver code, you've been wasting a lot of people's time. You've got what, a couple of dozen designers working now?"

Counting three designers who'd finally made contact with him from somewhere beneath centercity, Martin had the thirty Julia had estimated they'd need to make this plan work. And already, just a week after Merryweather's death, those designers were churning out code, creating together modules that could, theoretically, be put together in new ways and let someone design a sculpt for Justin.

Justin shook his head when Martin explained that to him. "This isn't about my health. The CC will sabotage your code, then say it can't be trusted. You *need* authentication."

"We can encrypt using public key cryptography."

"Without verification, how would designers know your key is legitimate? Remember, the CC and Interfaith control the Infoweb. Maybe you can put your stuff out there, but they can bury it in a million look-alikes."

"I'll think of something."

Justin clasped Martin on the shoulder. "I like you, Martin. You've got a good soul. But you're too damned trusting and you think everyone in the world wants to play nice. You need someone in who's faced real evil, who's killed when she had to, who's gamed the rules and knows what they're for."

"I don't know anyone like—"

"You need a cop."

Martin shook his head. He had a cop, Olivia Jardan. But Jardan was only going along with his plan because that was the only choice she had. She didn't really believe in breaking the old monopolies. She'd swallowed all that indoctrination they fed to citizens under the guise of education. Which was frustrating because he found her attractive and his kids had taken to her.

Still, Justin was right. He put through a call to Olivia.

Which wasn't that easy because the four in centercity changed their identities regularly, but Olivia had sent a list with the identity codes they were supposed to be using. With a bit of hunting he tracked it down.

"Jardan."

"Olivia, it's Martin."

"Yeah?"

"You sound busy."

"We're running a lab in the middle of enemy territory. Of course I'm busy. I've been crawling through every sewer in centercity setting sensors to detect the break-in when Shenker finally figures things out."

"Oh."

"I guess I was supposed to say I've got all kinds of time. What do you need?"

Angie had thought Olivia might be interested in him. Clearly fifteen year-old girls didn't understand how grown-up women's minds worked—any more than he did.

"I've got a police question."

"I'm not a cop anymore." Her voice held what sounded like a touch of bitterness. She'd lost a portion of her identity and was floundering, uncertain who she was, what she might become.

"For me, the important thing is that you were a cop, that you have experience applying the rules of contract and the corporate consensus. As Justin reminded me, you're the closest thing to a lawyer we have."

"Closest thing to a what?"

"A lawyer. Someone who argues legal cases."

She sighed. "We call them cops. Why don't you just tell me what you need from me?"

"Remember when Julia told us what we needed to pull this off?"

"I've got it stored on my phone. Do you need me to play it back to you?"

"I wanted to talk about it."

"She didn't say anything about needing a cop."

"She said we need a way to authenticate code if we want to be more than an invisible niche. And I don't want to be invisible."

"I sort of gathered that."

"If we're going to be authenticated," he pressed on, "we need to be properly registered with the verification authority out in Corporate San Jose. But the only way to register is to be nominated by the local corporate consensus."

"And Corporate Dallas is not going to do that for us."

"No."

So we're wasting our time with this whole project?"

"I'm saying we need the perspective of someone who's enforced the consensus and knows contracts, someone who will shake up the rules. If we don't do that, Corporate Dallas will release millions of corrupted versions of the project and nobody will ever know which one is ours."

Olivia was silent for a moment. Then, "Got it. We register it through Corporate Houston. They're your boss, right? They'd love to have Dallas subsidiaries, show that they're the dominant consensus. Two birds."

Martin swallowed. He hadn't lied to the team but he hadn't made clear how precarious their position was. "Corporate Houston is ruled by the same interests as Corporate Dallas. They would no more agree to certify a free-code corporation than they would bark like dogs."

There was no answer for so long Martin worried that Olivia might have gone into one of the dark spots underground where phone signals didn't penetrate.

Just as he was about to break the connection, she came back. "You aren't humoring me, are you? Giving me a makework project because you feel sorry for me having to live with a bunch of developers who are doing the real work on the project?"

"I'm sure you have plenty of real work handling security for your team. But this is important, too."

"I suppose you need this yesterday?"

He laughed. "Thanks to Justin, I'm not that far behind the game. We won't need this until we have a codebase we're prepared to release to the rest of the world, a beta version."

"When is that going to happen?"

"If a miracle happens and everything goes according to schedule, six months."

"Without miracles?"

"Without any miracles at all, the cops will swoop all of us up before we get anything done. But with just a little bit of luck and mostly the kind of stuff that you can count on happening, we're talking a year."

"No way we can survive here that long. We had to restore phone capabilities for Kansas and McKensie and neither can be completely trusted. And Shenker won't stop looking."

"Keeping your team alive is a slightly higher priority than the authentication thing, but only slightly. Because if we don't lick this problem, we're all going to get caught eventually."

"Thanks, Martin. You're all heart. I'm signing off now but if I think of anything, I'll let you know."

"Do."

Martin disconnected, then walked back to the test lab to see what his son had destroyed. A fifteen year-old girl had things on her mind more important than running the latest test case. For a five year-old, though, the chance to blow things up, burn down buildings, and produce really disgusting smells was close to heaven. Martin had put in place all the safety measures he could think of, but he still worried that the kid would manage to turn himself into gray ooze if Martin didn't monitor him all the time."

"How's your girlfriend?" Jimmy demanded.

"Olivia is not my girlfriend. And she's still alive, which is about as good as we can expect."

"Angie says she *would* be your girlfriend, if you weren't completely retarded."

"Your sister is fifteen. She doesn't know anything."

"She knows more than you."

"That's because she's a woman. They're sneaky that way. Now what do you say we test the constructor interface again. I'll bet you it takes us ten minutes to blow up the constructor."

"Sucker-bet. We can do it in less than five. Come on."

Olivia

Cat's nose started twitching a good five minutes before she and Olivia returned from her latest outing. Thanks to GPS and an old software program Julia had dug up, they now had a practically complete map of the major passageways underground.

Sensors Olivia had insisted on, and Julia had designed and constructed, sent a steady stream of messages back to her phone. In the two weeks since Julia had led them into the old library and they'd set up their lab, Olivia had planted thousands of the tiny sensors. Now, she managed sleep in intervals of about five minutes between alarms as rats, possums, rabbits, raccoons, and the occasional feral dog tripped the sensors.

There wasn't a lot to be said for sleep deprivation, but there was even less to be said for being caught unaware when the cops finally figured out where they'd gone. And her team needed time to implement the half-baked escape plan she'd come up with.

She and Cat were almost back in the library before Olivia's nose picked up on what Cat had smelled for minutes.

Food.

"We made extras." Kansas gave her a big grin as they stepped into the now-brightly lit room. "Have some."

It didn't smell citizen slop, it didn't look like any of the Interfaith standard meals that Angie uploaded to them, and she recognized all of Julia's private stock.

"Where'd you get the money to pay for that?"

"Money?" McKensie laughed. "We're designers. We don't have to pay for code, we design our own."

"But—"

"We came up with a creative way to test our code," Kansas said. "If we eat it and live, the code passes."

"I thought Martin was handling testing."

McKensie shook her head dismissively. "He's doing integration testing, making sure nothing bad happens when we put together code from a bunch of different designers. Before we send each module to him, we have to run the real tests."

"So you're designing food?"

"Okay, I confess that a lot of Julia's free-code stuff that we all laughed at before. Now do you want to eat it, or do you want to construct more citizen slop? If you do, take it somewhere else. I never even want to smell that again."

Cat sidled up to the plate they'd left on the floor for it, sniffed at the food, then started bolting it down.

"Guess your animal thinks it's safe, Olivia."

Olivia understood the strange economics behind Martin's crazy free-code plan. She knew the way licensing fees worked, how each module required a payment back to the corporation responsible for the original code, and that each child process created a new revenue flow. Understanding intellectually and understanding viscerally, though, were two different things. For the first time, she really got it.

"You don't have to license modules for all of the components because—"

"Because we already have the base code in our libraries," Julia bragged. "We're already able to program up food that meets our basic health requirements, that tastes a lot better than citizen slop, and that doesn't violate a single copyright or license requirement."

Olivia's head whirled. "Martin said it would take six months or a year before we were finished."

Kansas was still grinning. "Before it's *finished*. But nobody said we had to wait until it was finished to start using it. Besides, like McKensie said, we're designers. We know how to kluge around errors. It's what we do. Making this available for less experienced designers would be dangerous."

"But this smells as good as TrueBeef™ Olivia said. "We could put this out now, let people have something to eat for free."

"Put it out how?" Julia asked. "Now we're back to Martin's problem. When Merryweather was doing this, he could authenticate himself. At least you'd know you were getting something a valid designer had done. But we can't do that anymore, as I know Martin explained to you."

Olivia nodded. Of course Martin would have run things by Julia first. Even though he hadn't finished the design training program, he was a ratepayer from a ratepayer family. Olivia had never been anything but a jumped-up citizen-who had now jumped back down.

"So—"

"There's a lot of bad code floating around on the Infoweb. Probably a billion modules of one kind or another are out there, orphan. Some of it is probably valid code, some of it stuff that needs some work, and a lot of it is traps designed to blow up when a designer messes with it. If you can't tell, it takes longer to verify than it would to recreate it yourself, or just buy authenticated modules."

"I'm not a designer, Julia, but I get the idea. We need authentication. Now let me get some of that stuff McKensie programmed up and then maybe you can give me some ideas on how to get around the problem rather than just telling me it's got to be solved."

"If I had any ideas, I'd share them. Here's what I know, though."

Olivia ate while Julia went through the basic concept of authentication—something that hadn't changed much in the hundred years or more since the invention of public key encryption. Olivia knew most of it, but it was interesting to hear the way Julia explained things. She really had a knack for getting to the core of the concept, abstracting away all the fluff.

A designer, as Julia explained it, encrypted a module or a complete design using a 'private key,' a software algorithm she kept secret. A potential user selected that designer's registered public key to decode it. That it decoded properly guaranteed that the correct private key had been used to encrypt, and provided authentication. The problem was knowing that the public key really did belong to the designer.

Authentication authorities provided the service of encoding the public key. Using the known valid authentication authority's public key to decrypt the designer's public key meant that the designer's public key was now known to be valid.

"It's a chicken and egg," Julia said.

"A what?" They'd been talking about codes and ciphers and all of a sudden Julia was talking about animals again.

"It's just an expression. It means we can't get there from here without some sort of shortcut."

"Which is what Martin wants me to figure out."

"Good luck," McKensie said. "Because you can't go to the San Jose authentication authority without being verified by your local corporate consensus."

"There's got to be a way," Kansas insisted. "I'm sure you'll figure it out, Olivia."

Olivia wished she were that confident.

Cat finished the constructed meal it had been eating and yawned big, showing sharp little teeth and a pink tongue.

It wandered over to Olivia and head-butted her calf until she sat down on a rock and let it climb into her lap.

Its growl-like noise comforted to Olivia now that she knew it wasn't a threat. The animal had become the ally she'd needed to cope with her loneliness. She'd also helped keep the basement where they'd set up their lab free of the rodents that infested the rest of the tunnels.

Julia

Nobody had read paper books for decades. When she'd been little, Julia's grandparents had occasionally waxed nostalgic about books that you held in your hands and read, even promised that one day her library would be Julia's.

Julia had laughed at her at the time. Sharing a book without each reader paying for it had to be stealing. Lugging around big hunks of paper was about as useful as hoeing weeds. Immersing yourself in a story where you couldn't change the outcome seemed weird.

With the Infoweb and a decent phone, nobody had needed books since the beginning of the twenty-first century.

But paper was made of cellulose and similar organic chemicals. And cellulose, $C^6H^{10}O^{5}$, was close to the perfect fuel for a constructor.

Still, Julia felt a bit awkward as she fished out book after book from the long stacks of cardboard cartons and fed them into their constructors. Paper in books was almost as old-fashioned as clay tablets, but there was still intellectual property buried in the cellulose. Someone had worked hard to embed their thoughts and ideas into the paper, to share these with others. Destroying it hurt.

She'd thought Googling the titles would assuage her concern. Surely in the vastness of the Infoweb, that intellectual property was preserved in a more accessible way. Some was. Much was not.

"Hey, we need more books if we're going to eat tonight," Kansas said.

Julia realized she'd been staring at one book for a while, lost in her thoughts. "I want to sort them before we destroy them."

"If nobody's come looking for them in fifty years, I doubt anybody will miss them."

"I know that, but—"

Kansas picked up a thick book and read from the cover, "*Managing Projects with Visual C#*. You might as well ask someone to design using zeros and ones."

"You can have that one," Julia said. "But I want to look through them before they're gone."

"Why not look through those billions of design modules out on the Infoweb while you're at it? Your chances of finding something you can actually use are better. Look at this one, "*Programming the Commodore 64.*"

"Sixty-four what?"

"Let me check—oh you won't believe this. Sixty-four K."

"That's not too bad. My parents had a computer once with only a couple thousand Gigs of main memory. That's really small."

"Not K-Gigs, K. As in sixty-four thousand bytes of memory."

Julia couldn't help giggling. "I guess we aren't going to need that one, either."

"Don't spend too much time on your search." Kansas pulled up a softbound book featuring a woman with an enormous chest. "This one doesn't look that great, either."

"I've never understood why some citizens go for that kind of sculpt. I mean, can you imagine carrying around all that extra weight?"

"McKensie does."

"Not there."

"True. Anyway, check the date on this book. Nineteen something. That was before sculpts."

"Those are real?"

"It's an artist's recreation."

"Got it. A two-dimensional sim. Now that is useless."

Most of the books were like that—technical and business books that related to designs so far in the past that only a historian would be interested, novels that featured people involved in incomprehensible mating behavior, inexplicable battles, or police stories where cops involved themselves in fighting money-making corporations without a clear profit motive of their own. None made sense.

After a couple of days of sorting, Julia wondered if she shouldn't have listened to Kansas in the first place.

Until she found a book about Texas government.

"Hey Olivia, come check this out."

Olivia spent most of her time out in the tunnels these days. After failing to persuade Julia to design fighting bots, she and Cat obsessively patrolled the sewers. Although Julia recognized that kind of behavior, her own mother had a tendency toward obsessive-compulsive activities, she hadn't been able to suggest anything that let Olivia relax—until now, maybe.

"You've got some more fuel you want me to carry?"

"I don't mean the paper, I mean what's written on the paper."

Olivia stared at the book. "Yeah, letters. I recognize them."

"Don't be deliberately obtuse. It's Rules and Regulation of Texas Local Governments, 2015 edition. Don't you get it?"

"That you found an ancient book. Congratulations, Julia. Maybe you can put it up for auction once we get out of here."

Had Olivia always been sarcastic? Maybe she was hanging too much with McKensie.

"2015 was back at the beginning, before the consensus, when the corporations still worked in the context of government."

"I didn't know that. Thanks for the history lesson."

"Read the damned book. You might get some ideas about how to solve Martin's problem."

"Oh." Olivia obviously bit back whatever sarcastic remark was about to fly off her lips, but if Julia hoped for a smile, she didn't get it. "I've already told you I can't read. Reading is for designers, remember?"

Julia had known that, but knowing and understanding were two different things. "But how can you—"

"I understand charts, and I used police text-to-voice capabilities of my phone when I run into a contract dispute. Reading is not that important."

"I'll teach you," Julia offered, without giving herself a chance to wonder when this was going to be happening. She was already down to four hours of sleep a night.

"In your spare time, right?"

"That isn't very nice." But Julia had promised she'd work with Justin to put together training sims for Martin. Sims that would let citizens as well as ratepayers take the design modules they were creating and design useful things with them. For basic design, they wouldn't have to read. Creating something to eat, for example, could be as simple as using a basic metabolic unit, a texture overlay, and incorporating one or more flavor modules. For better than fifty years, any module designer worth her salt knew to 'publish' basic attributes any designer could access. Going deeper, training citizens to design new modules of their own rather than just customizing and snapping together, would be harder than she'd even guessed. She'd have to teach them all to read, first.

"I'll do it when I can," she said.

"Thanks, Julia."

From Olivia's tone, Julia didn't think the ex-cop trusted her, or thought they'd ever have the time. She suspected Olivia was right. While logic told her that Shenker could never find them in an underground city no ex-citizen would ever dream existed, her gut warned that something bad was about to happen.

Shenker

Shenker had to conclude that Olivia was ahead of him for this round. His informant hadn't been the brightest star in the heavens. If Olivia were looking, she could have determined which of the two designers would betray her. Of course, if she had taken his lessons to heart, Olivia would dispose of both designers. Letting two live when one was believed to be a traitor would be false economics and economics was one area where Shenker was firmly in line with the consensus.

His phone alerted. Vinson again.

"Chief."

"Sergeant. I mean, Lieutenant. Any progress?"

Shenker had no illusion that slip of the tongue wasn't intentional. "I have some ideas I'm chasing, Chief."

"I'm going to have to pull the rest of your cops, Shenker. If and when you discover something, give me a call and we'll talk resources."

"But—"

"If and when, Shenker."

"Yes, chief."

"But keep looking. Not only can she point us to the Corporate Houston spies, this Olivia Jardan of yours is a black eye for the department. Your little scheme running sims on her escape earned the department some entertainment fees, but it makes us look like idiots for not finding her. When every third citizen has caught her half a dozen times, what does that say about us? No wonder the Interfaith Enforcers put in a competitive bid."

"That sim gave us some good leads. But citizens don't have the knowledge base to help us in Centercity." Shenker didn't have the knowledge base, either, which was a part of his problem. It was a problem he wasn't going to share with Vinson. Vinson didn't need more reminders that Shenker came from a citizen background.

"Who cares what you *intended* it for? The reality is, we need Olivia captured. The only upside we have right now is that Ariel and his Interfaith goons want her as bad as we do."

"When I find her, I'll use them, then. She'll have set traps I don't want my cops walking into."

"That's the kind of creative thinking I appreciate," Vinson said. "Oh, I do have a little present for you."

Shenker's gut threatened to climb out his mouth. Considering Shenker's record of failure in tracking Olivia down, anything Vinson might choose to give him was likely to be bad.

"I'm all ears."

"Oh, it's nothing I can give you now. It's for when you discover your little protégé."

Shenker exhaled a sigh of relief. He still had a job.

"Speaking of presents, Lieutenant, the corporate consensus has given us a little gift."

"What's that, sir?"

"If we don't find your cop and those designers within forty-eight hours, they're going to turn the job over to the Interfaith Enforcers. The IE has submitted a low bid."

"But that violates the Police Corporation exclusive contract."

"That contract, the CC tells me, has been superseded as inconsistent with our economic war."

"I've only got forty-eight hours?" He'd burned through a couple of weeks already. Two more days might make a difference, but an unbiased oddsmaker would take bets against it.

"*We* have forty-eight hours, Lieutenant. Because if the IE takes over, you can bet they aren't going to be paying my salary."

Maybe. But Vinson would still be alive, still be part of a ratepayer family, still have all of the assets he'd accumulated over a lucrative life as a top executive, a ratepayer wife who earned her own income, and a daughter who'd been brought up with all of the advantages, who already, in her early twenties, had probably earned more than Shenker would if he remained a police lieutenant for a century.

"I'll find them," he said.

"You know, Lieutenant, I believe you will."

Shenker nodded, although his phone had been set for audio only and Vinson wouldn't be able to see his gesture. He broke the connection and started his slow drive through centercity Dallas one more time.

The women hadn't passed the centercity barrier. They weren't in the small forests that made up the greenbelt within centercity. They weren't hiding in homespaces belonging to any of their families. He and his team had raided thousands of homespaces, verified that no one had forced their way inside or was holding the family hostage. They'd even stopped every car on the roads, responding to the unlikely thought that the four women might be riding around in perpetuity.

So far, he'd come up empty.

It was almost as if they'd vanished into thin air.

Which gave him an idea. He turned his gaze upward, looking into the skyscrapers, once symbols of progress and now covered with solar panels. They were still, many of them, in use. Although people could work out of their homespaces as well as anywhere, some corporations demanded that their staff show up at an official office, make a statement that they were one of the power corporations that ruled the city.

Olivia hadn't faded into thin air. But she couldn't be up in one of the corporate buildings without anyone noticing.

He stopped his car and stepped out.

After a few moments, the car whined away, doubtless responding to a call from some nearby ratepayer seeking transportation. He barely noticed.

Here, in the heart of centercity, between the skyscrapers, old Dallas roads remained.

Out in the rings, and even in centercity beyond the high-rise district, individuals and corporations had encroached on the old roads and highways, setting up their solar collectors to grab every photon of energy, every drop of water, ever molecule of carbon as it floated by.

Here, though, in the very heart of the old downtown, conspicuous consumption remained the hallmark. Naked roads, built of concrete and steel bars, gleamed in the sunlight.

Marring the smooth sheets of concrete, iron lids fit over holes in the ground.

They were big, those lids. Big enough to allow even a large person like McKensie to enter.

He put a call through to Vinson.

"They're underground in the skyscraper district."

"You've located them?"

"I know where they're hiding."

Vinson took on the vacant look that indicated he'd turned away and was actually doing something else, leaving only a sim to entertain Shenker.

Finally, though, he returned. "There were extensive underground diggings in the twentieth century and even early in our own century," Vinson conceded. "But it'll be dangerous. Do you think Olivia would set traps, or would she trust you wouldn't guess?"

"Olivia never trusted anyone."

"Too bad she's not on our side. We need more people who aren't surprised when they get stabbed in the back."

Shenker wouldn't be surprised when it happened to him. He knew the knife was coming. He didn't know why it hadn't already happened. "I'll need some guys. A lot of them."

Vinson projected Shenker the best map he had of the sewers and tunnels under the city and they put their heads together figuring where they'd enter, where Olivia and the others most likely would be hiding, and where they would run once they knew he was after them. In his gut, Shenker knew that Olivia had formulated a plan to deal with him. He just had to hope her plan wouldn't account for the desperation Vinson had created in him. This wasn't just about tracking Olivia down any more, it was about proving a point to the CC, about demonstrating that the Police Corporation could deliver.

"Oh, yeah," Vinson said after he'd sent the code activating every available cop and placing them under Shenker's orders. "I promised you a present, didn't I?"

Olivia

At two in the morning, six of Olivia's sensors went off almost simultaneously.

Three of them, those signaling by radio waves, were hit by an electromagnetic pulse and blacked out immediately. The other four, connected back to Olivia's security computer in the library by a maze of molecular-strand silicon-glass, sent back fragmentary pictures of masked cops and clouds of gas before they too blacked out.

Olivia checked the mapping and ascertained that the assault originated from all angles. Her aboveground sensors confirmed that cops were thick on the streets as well. This wasn't a casual intrusion. It was the real thing. Shenker knew where she was and was going all-out.

She woke the others and scooped up Cat, stuffing the animal into the specially designed pouch she'd constructed. "We're being attacked. Time to go." She set off the thermal charge on the utility hatch leading down to the sewers from their subbasement, creating quick welds that would make Shenker call for heavy equipment to break through. If they were lucky, it would give her an extra few minutes of lead.

"Are you crazy? The sewers were our way out," McKensie screamed.

"The sewers are a deathtrap. They've released gas down there and burned out our sensors before I could figure out what chemical it is. Follow the plan. We've got to go up."

"Up? Your so-called plan is wishful thinking. We can't just climb into some corporate office from a basement and walk through their building."

"Watch me."

"I don't know about you guys," Julia said, "but Olivia has gotten us out of scrapes before. I'm going to follow her orders and hope she knows what she's doing. One thing for sure—*we* don't know how to fight cops."

"Come or stay," Olivia strapped on her emergency equipment, prepared against just this eventuality and gathered in Cat. "That part is up to you. I'm going."

"Uh, one thing though," Julia said. "Everyone carry some books. These are the ones I've sorted out" She allocated a stack of about four books per woman, carrying six or seven herself. That done, they were ready. And nobody stayed behind.

Decades before, someone had sealed the heavy steel gates that connected the library subbasement with the aboveground tower.

That hadn't sat well with Olivia. Shenker called any place with only one entrance a trap. Recognizing the need for an escape hatch, Olivia had broken the seal and greased the hinges the day they'd taken residence here.

Now she shoved the gates open and climbed out.

A sudden bang nearly stopped her heart.

"It's just a cleaning bot," Julia reported. "It ran into your open hatch."

"Okay." She gave Kansas a hand out of the doorway, then closed it and weld-sealed it in place. The weld wouldn't fool anyone but it might delay Shenker's minions. They needed every second.

"Out onto the streets?" Kansas asked.

Flashing blue lights promised that, if the cops weren't close, they weren't far away either.

"I've run you through this drill every day since we got here. They want us on the street. The gas and all the noise down below are to flush us out. They're waiting at street level."

"You're paranoid," McKensie said. "They're searching everywhere. Maybe they're just going through the motions here."

"With poison gas? Not likely. Some of that stuff could leak out and kill a ratepayer. Nuh-uh. They wouldn't have launched that kind of attack against the sewer system if they didn't *know* we were inside."

"They couldn't possibly. Besides, we can't just stand here and wait."

"Who's staying?" She hadn't stopped moving even when talking and she didn't now.

McKensie shook her head. "If we climb up the building, we'll really be trapped."

"You guys hired me to be the security expert. So, I'm telling you, our only chance at security is straight up. So follow me."

McKensie looked out at the streets, then let her shoulders droop in mute resignation. Finally she followed.

The elevators required RFID authorization, but the building was a holdover from the twentieth century when people worried about fires. Back then, stairs had still been built into even tall buildings. Following an architectural diagram of the building Julia had located, Olivia cut through the latches that held the stairs door shut and led the way upward.

McKensie was groaning by the time they hit the second floor.

For climbing, as for so many things, bulk muscle cost more in weight than their strength benefits. Even Julia and Kansas were wheezing by the fifth floor.

"We're going out on the rooftop?" Julia asked. "We might be able to swing across to another building. They're close together in this part of the ancient downtown."

"Top floor for now," Olivia answered. She hadn't told them this part of the plan because she'd known they'd object.

"That's the Chairman's zone. All sorts of security," McKensie argued.

"We'll just have to see how good your designs are, then."

"Jeez. Our designs against the best security systems the T-50 can make. You're pretty brave."

"I have an idea," Julia grabbed Olivia's arm as she reached for the door that led into the top floor of the office tower. "I designed a little something nasty. It's a self-replicating eater. It'll dissolve solar panels into their constituent elements. If we release it from the rooftop, it'll spread through centercity. By dawn nobody will have power beyond what's stored in their fuel cells. Talk about a major distraction."

Olivia let herself be tempted for a moment. Not only would it distract the cops and ratepayers, it would disrupt the electronic systems that monitored access to centercity.

"Cool," Kansas said. "Too bad you didn't mention this before we climbed seven flights of stairs."

"Isn't it dangerous?" McKensie asked. "What if it mutated to eat things other than solar panels? What if it ate people? The gray ooze thing may be a paranoid fantasy, but that doesn't mean an eater couldn't be deadly."

"I've put in double-tests for accurate reproduction. It would require a simultaneous triple-mutation to do any damage. And it's generationally limited and susceptible to gamma rays. Everything should be finished by daylight, anyway, when mutation is most likely," Julia answered.

Olivia opened her mouth to tell Julia to go ahead, then thought about how her parents would react to an eater destroying their solar panels and homespace.

They, and just about every other citizen in Dallas, would blame free-code for the destruction. Even if they eventually re-created their environment, and that was far from certain given the way ratepayers insisted on encroaching on citizens in the close-in rings, they would never trust a design based on free-code. Julia's eater might save their lives, but it would eliminate Martin's dream that everyone could become designers. It would do so more permanently than anything the T-50 could hope to accomplish.

"We can't do it," she said.

Julia didn't seem to get it when she explained her reasoning, but Olivia remained obdurate.

"Okay, so what's *your* plan?"

"Watch."

She slapped an override on the alarm system and opened the doorway from the stairs to the executive suite.

The contrast between the ugly concrete stairs and the elegant corporate offices was stark. Breathing clean air for the first time in a week practically intoxicated her.

She caught herself staring at actual tree-wood-paneled walls covered by human-made paintings dating from medieval times. Gold leaf glittering in diffused NaturLight™ shining from everywhere and nowhere.

Cowskin-covered sofas and chairs showed a level of opulence Olivia had never seen, even when she'd worked with high-end ratepayers in property dispute resolution. The hum of a chilling system indicated that the corporate executives who made this their business center didn't bother constructing treats on the fly. They kept them stored for later use. Or maybe they had grown or animal-produced treats. She had to swallow hard at that thought. Ratepayer habits were just a little too over-the-top for her to understand.

What she didn't see was extensive security arrangements. She didn't bother holding back her grin. This was going to be easy.

That sort of thinking brought its normal consequences. Thirty seconds after they'd left the stairwell, a security bot challenged them, sending both an audio alarm and probably radioing police central for backup.

Olivia uploaded a, sadly outdated, police override and it hesitated, its programming clearly warring with itself.

McKensie jerked a steel rod out of one of the cowskin chairs and bashed the thing over its head, smashing through its plastic helmet into its AI.

"That was brilliant," Julia said. "Why didn't you just phone police central and tell them we're here."

"Olivia's override wasn't working."

"Come on," Olivia said. "We don't have long. Kansas and McKensie, I need you to find us a constructor. Julia, help me hack into a computer. I've got to reprogram building security and upload some code."

An ancient law of computing is that executives are too stupid to be trusted with anything sensitive, but that they nevertheless insist on having access.

Olivia was relying on that law, and was relieved to find it held true in the offices of the Enhanced Industrial Seasonings Coding Corporation, which was the T-50 group who had taken over what had once been the old Public Library.

Breaking into the security director's computer was a simple matter of running a dictionary against his password. He'd selected a woman's name, not his wife's, as the password. Idiotic. And the biometrics were disturbingly easy to bypass.

Olivia reset the building's security system, canceled the alarm the security bot had sent when McKensie had bashed it over the head, authorized full bot defense of the lower floors and disabled any future police override. The cops could battle the building's security if they wanted access. Since property rights were the basis of the Corporate Consensus, Olivia hoped Shenker would also have to go back to the T-50, in the middle of the night, for permission to violate the headquarters of an autonomous corporation.

"Accessed a constructor," McKensie reported.

"Is it powered?" In the middle of the night, solar power was not exactly abundant. But a T-50 corporation should hold a rich supply of hydrogen for its fuel cells. Olivia was counting on it.

"Seems to have plenty."

"Great. Kansas, keep looking—I could use another. McKensie, here's the code I want you to construct."

She charged the download to the security director's account, then transferred the design to McKensie. She watched carefully as the designer fed it into the constructor. If McKensie was the spy, this would be the perfect time for her to introduce a little sabotage.

To Olivia's surprise, McKensie passed the code through unchanged.

Seconds later, the constructor started feeding out massive quantities of wormspit-like fabric.

"We going to play dress-up?" McKensie asked. "I don't think we're going to fool anyone into believing we're fairy princesses."

"Found another constructor," Kansas reported.

"Good." Olivia fed Kansas the code for carbon-fiber tubing.

"What's this for? A cannon?"

"I don't want to fight them. Just get away."

"For someone who doesn't want to fight, you do a lot of it," Julia observed.

"Just carry the fabric upstairs."

"There is no upstairs."

"Then cut through the ceiling. We need to be on the rooftop."

"I thought you said—" Julia's voice trailed off when she considered the fabric, together with Olivia's request. "Oh, shit. You're kidding, aren't you?"

"Please."

"Right. I can do this." Julia didn't sound convincing to Olivia. Olivia suspected the designer was really trying to convince herself.

"I figure we have—" Olivia checked the director's security system, "ten minutes before all hell breaks loose."

"On my way."

Julia elbowed Kansas out of her way, programmed a set of plastique explosives into the constructor, set them, and blew a hole three meters in diameter through the ceiling and roof.

"You aren't making any friends in the T-50," McKensie sniped. "Talk about property violations."

"I'm crying about that."

Olivia rammed one of Kansas's carbon tubes into the hydrogen storage system's emergency outlet, then up through the hole in the ceiling. That in place, she pulled a chair onto a genuine tree-wood desk directly underneath Julia's hole in the ceiling, climbed up onto chair, and pressed herself through onto the roof.

Far below, police lights were still dispersed. A small group of cops gathered near the Trinity River, congregating where the sewer outlets promised to dump wastewater and fleeing free-cits into the safety of the river. But police cars and armored investigators were gathering around the former library building, probably in response to the alarm message the short-lived security bot had sent. It wouldn't take long before helicopters gathered as well, which would definitely cause problems.

"Hurry," Olivia ordered, as if nagging the women might make them move faster.

"They're onto us," McKensie moaned as she joined Olivia on the rooftop, huge wads of fabric in her hands.

Shenker

From the sewers below him, Interfaith Enforcers reported running into weird animals, blocked passages, and traps. Despite his warning, many of them hadn't constructed proper filters and were suffering from the gas he'd released.

They were taking casualties although they hadn't caught even a glimpse of the four women they were after. Shenker's pity was highly limited.

"Hiring those IE guys as subcontractors was a stroke of brilliance, Chief." He might be sucking up a bit, but he wasn't lying. He'd needed a bunch of idiots to run around down in the tunnels under the city and Vinson had wanted both to co-opt the Interfaith's leadership and to show that there could be more profit in working together than in competing. Thinning out their ranks wouldn't hurt either, in Shenker's judgment.

"Don't celebrate until you've found the women, Lieutenant."

"We've got them located, sir. They're in the Enhanced Industrial Seasonings Coding Corporation building. A security bot transmitted a high-res vid of all four before they smashed it."

"They smashed a security bot?"

"It was McKensie, sir. She's strong."

"And you don't think there's any way they can get away from EISCC?"

"I'm betting Olivia has a plan. I trained her, sir."

"You seem pretty happy about it."

"Since we didn't waste any cops in the sewers, we've got manpower to spare. I've got cops on the street around the building, cops in all of the surrounding buildings, and I'm bringing in helicopters to make sure their Corporate Houston friends don't try a rescue. I'm pretty confident."

"What about my present?"

"Thanks. I've got Sammy Jardan on standby."

Vinson was silent for long enough that Shenker wondered if he'd said something wrong. After all, Vinson had a family, presumably would do stupid things to protect them.

"Just bring her in, Lieutenant. I want the locations of the Corporate Houston spy centers and I want them in police central AI by this evening."

"You're aware that Olivia has received the standard police security scrub. Our interrogation drugs won't work on her."

"I'm counting on you to figure out a solution to that problem. Unless you aren't up to the challenge."

He hated this, but it was part of the job. "I'll do it, sir."

"Better get back to work, then, Lieutenant. I've got Rev. Ariel on the line complaining his men are taking heavy losses from your gas."

"Plus shooting each other. Make sure to share my condolences, sir."

"I'll do that." Vinson might have snickered as he cut the connection.

Shenker checked the identify friend/foe map on his phone. With the four women firmly trapped upstairs, he didn't need the Interfaith Enforcers in the sewers any longer, tempting though it was to let them stay and take a few more casualties from clumsy steps, trigger-happy men shooting each other when someone took a wrong turn, or from angry rats.

He resisted the temptation, and ordered the IE forces take over street patrol, freeing up his cops in case Olivia got clever and doubled back on her trail.

He ordered a couple of hundred cops to search every closet and every office in the EISSCC building. Then he signaled for a helicopter for himself.

Although he had to go through the motions, he didn't think Olivia would hide—that plan was a loser. She'd try something clever, something an ordinary person wouldn't even consider.

"Security bots aren't responding to police override," a desperate cop cop called.

"Take them out."

He grinned as his helicopter took off. Olivia would try to fly away, right over the heads of the hundreds of cops he'd mobilized to stop her. Unfortunately for her, she'd fly right into his grasp.

"Prevailing wind direction and speed?" he asked police central.

"South-southeast at ten kilometers an hour."

"Okay. Any cop not assigned to search the building and who doesn't have a helicopter ride, I want them to head south-south-east. Keep me posted on any change in wind speed or direction. Set up a rally-point about five kilometers in that direction."

"Message sent."

He grinned at the helicopter pilot. "I see you've got a sniper rifle in there. Do you have anything that fires tracers?"

"I can construct that load in a few seconds."

"Do it and fly straight up. I've got a rendezvous a half-mile above the city."

Julia

Even though she'd been through some hairy times with Olivia, the ex-cop surprised Julia again. Before, when they'd been in trouble, Olivia had been reacting. Here, she was following through on a plan. It made a big difference.

"Give me the bag," Olivia demanded.

McKensie stared at her. "Huh?"

"The fabric you extruded. I need it."

McKensie still looked baffled so Julia grabbed a big wad of the constructed fabric and dragged it toward Olivia. After a moment, McKensie snapped her mouth shut and pitched in.

"Hold on to it," Olivia said. She crammed in the hydrogen-bearing tube into the building's massive fuel cell.

The fabric puffed up as lighter-than-air hydrogen flowed up the tube and into the bag.

The balloon, because that was what the bag Olivia had constructed was becoming, puffed out, a light breeze tugging it away from Olivia's grip.

Rather than explain to the others what needed to be done, Julia grabbed tethers, found places to hook them, and made sure their escape route didn't escape without them.

"Thanks," Olivia said.

"You did stealth that balloon, didn't you?" Julia strapped herself into one of the belts hanging from the bag. "We float away invisibly, right?"

"Not exactly."

"No?" McKensie's moan had turned into a whine. "We'll be sitting ducks for every police helicopter in town."

"Shut up and strap in," Olivia said. "Come on, Kansas. Get your butt in here."

Kansas tried to back away when she saw what they were doing, but Julia grabbed her and snapped her into the harness.

She hadn't felt a breeze since she and Olivia had last looked out the storm sewers into the Trinity River. A hundred-plus feet above the police-filled streets of Dallas, the wind was more than a breeze. It yanked hard on the balloon, pulling against the few tethers they'd snapped in place.

"Grab something and hold on," she shouted. "We don't want to blow off this place until we have positive buoyancy."

McKensie was still complaining, but she followed orders. Kansas didn't, but Kansas wasn't strong enough or heavy enough to make much difference anyway.

Highly compressed hydrogen filled the balloon more quickly than Julia could have imagined although Olivia seemed to have planned for that, too.

"You're kidding me," McKensie said when the balloon threw off its last wrinkles.

The corporate logo for the Enhanced Industrial Seasonings Corporation, a huge saltshaker dumping chemicals into an old-fashioned constructor vat, covered the entire balloon in dazzling animated glory.

The wind caught the balloon and yanked, jerking Julia's arms so hard they felt like they'd be pulled from the sockets.

"I'm not going to be able to hold on much longer," she admitted. "And the tethers are ripping."

"Okay, we have major buoyancy. On three, I'll cut the tethers and let go," Olivia commanded. "One, two, three."

Julia shoved off with her hands and untangled her legs from where she'd had them wrapped around an old air conditioning duct.

Kansas, still not with the program, tried to grab the building at the last minute but McKensie followed orders letting go and the pipe Kansas had grabbed slipped from her grasp. The four women and the huge hydrogen balloon shot upward, drifting to the south, a beacon to everyone below them.

"This has got to be the dumbest escape in human history," Kansas said.

Olivia

The balloon's buoyancy accelerated them upward quickly until they found equilibrium a couple thousand of meters above the city. Olivia felt both exposed and terrified as she swung wildly below the enormous gas sack.

The wind, which had pulled on them while they'd huddled on the Enhanced Industrial Seasonings Coding Corporation rooftop, seemed to have died completely. When she forced open her eyes, she saw that was an illusion. They were heading south at a fairly good clip. Other than the sound of retching from one of the designers, probably weak-stomached McKensie, the silence was almost complete.

"A couple of minutes into their flight, when it became obvious that they wouldn't crash to the ground or fly so high that they would all suffocate, Julia finally spoke. "Remind me why it's a good idea to fly something with no power and that's designed to be seen for maybe fifty miles?"

"We talked about this. We're an advertisement, paid for by the Enhanced Industrial Seasonings Coding Corporation and advertising their product with their official corporate logo."

Kansas laughed. "You know, that's pretty smart. If the cops shoot us down, they'll be violating the Freedom of Corporate Speech part of the Consensus. You didn't tell us about that. You just said we'd be above helicopter range."

Maybe it was the altitude but Olivia's cheeks burned a little. "I hoped that, too. This thing really went up."

"You hoped? As in past tense."

"I still hope." Mostly, she hoped Shenker wouldn't guess they'd be dumb enough to float off in an unguided, unpowered explosive-hydrogen-filled gasbag.

Below them, the skyscrapers of downtown Dallas retreated and they drifted over thousands of acres of solar panels and ratepayer homespaces. A few lights showed that some residents were up late, working on projects or so caught up in entertainment sims that they'd lost track of the time. The silence remained almost complete, broken only by the harsh buzz of bat wings.

They weren't alone, of course.

Freedom of Corporate Speech meant that Dallas's skies were always filled with advertisements. If Shenker gave them just a few minutes, they'd blend in with the others, pass unnoticed over the border of centcity, switch their ad to one for High-Efficiency Solar, land in the outer rings where they could rejoin Martin, Justin, and the others.

Luckily the wind was blowing from the north, which meant that it took them almost no time before they were past the Trinity River, taking them outside the privileged centercity enclave. They might actually—

"Looks like you were wrong about how high helicopters can fly," Julia observed.

"Oh, shit." The glare of a dozen searchlights reached them simultaneously, the clear silence disrupted by the roar of helicopter turbines.

"They found us. How do we get this thing to the ground?" McKensie demanded.

Olivia had hoped that coming down would sort of take care of itself. "Oh, shit."

* * * *

The first shots were warnings, flaring white phosphorus tracers fired well in front of their balloon. If one of those hit the hydrogen bag, they'd go up like the Hindenburg dirigible in the old sim.

"So much for Freedom of Corporate Speech," Julia observed.

"What are we going to do?" McKensie demanded. "We've got to get down."

"Maybe we should surrender," Kansas argued. "What could they do that would be worse than falling a couple of thousand meters? Oh, except for being on fire when we fall."

Giving up might have been the best idea, but there was a slight problem. How do you surrender when you're floating in an unpowered balloon?

"See if you can phone them, Julia. Tell them they're violating Freedom of Corporate Speech. Tell them we're a fully paid-for advertising stunt and vehicle."

"You think they'll believe me?"

"Sure." Being a cop had taught Olivia how to lie. "The accounting is right. Industrial Seasonings is definitely T-50. I used a valid account and we're flying a trademarked corporate advertising design."

"They'll wake up the chairman and find out that your approvals are faked."

"He'll probably have to call some flunky in the marketing department to know. That'll take time. Buy us some time, Julia."

"I'll try."

Olivia didn't need the Freedom of Corporate Speech bit to work forever, just long enough to get down and away.

And speaking of getting down—

When she'd been in police training, she'd thought the rope-climbing test had been one of those silly residuals from the old days. She was glad now that she'd trained for it—and kept up her training.

Her muscles screamed and her shoulders, still sore from when the wind had nearly torn them off her body, shook, but she wouldn't let herself give up now.

Cat, held in the harness attached to her stomach, wiggled and made pathetic meowing noises—the animal wasn't comfortable, but it couldn't be as uncomfortable as Olivia.

Centimeter by centimeter, she and Cat went up the tether. Twice, she had to stop, wrapping her legs around the line while she fought to gain what oxygen was available this high off the ground. The bag swam in her eyes and she had to shake her head to get that dizzy feeling to go away.

Police helicopters, veering ever-nearer, gave her the motivation to keep climbing.

Hand-over-hand, she fought the last inches until her fingers brushed against the bottom of the bag.

A helicopter swept near, wind from its rotors shaking the gas bag and sending the entire balloon plunging maybe twenty meters—just as another helicopter opened up with white phosphorous tracer shells.

The burst of bullets cut a hole through the air where they'd been only moments before. That hadn't been a warning shot.

Olivia pulled the diamond knife from her tunic, leaned out as far as she could away from where her tether was secured into the fabric of the carbon-fiber bag, and sliced. The diamond cut through the tough but ultra-thin fabric like a laser through the fog.

Hydrogen rises.

If she'd cut the top of the bag, the hydrogen that gave them their lift would have flowed through the hole and they would have plunged two thousand meters straight down.

Cutting the bag a meter or so from the bottom meant they'd lose a little hydrogen at a time. Good from the standpoint of not dropping from the sky. Less good in the interests of quickly getting away from the helicopters.

Abruptly, though, the helicopters backed off, keeping the balloon in their sights but no longer attacking.

Olivia considered cutting the balloon again, but decided against it. Hydrogen was difficult to keep contained at the best of times. Any more damage and they'd probably fall hard.

She tucked away the diamond knife and released her death-grip on the tether.

Falling felt like flying. Then the tether caught her, jerking her to a stop perhaps five meters below the balloon.

Cat meowed again, complaining about the mistreatment but evidently okay.

"I notified the Marketing Speech group in the police corporation of the perceived violation," Julia reported. "Looks like it made them stop shooting."

The cops weren't shooting, but they weren't going away, either. Olivia looked downward and saw that the balloon was already distinctly lower than it had been. If the cops in the helicopters waited, they'd be able to pick up the women when they hit the ground. Whether they'd pick up whole women or just pieces depended on whether Olivia had been overly energetic when she'd cut the bag.

She got on the phone herself and let Martin know what was going on.

"Thanks for finally giving me an update."

"We really don't need sarcasm."

"Sorry. I gathered that something was happening when your buddy Shenker pulled every single cop in the entire Corporate Dallas area into centercity. He even brought in Interfaith Enforcers to help and the rumor on the street is that they and the cops are practically gunning for each other. Shenker is playing for all the marbles."

"He's tracking us with helicopters now. I don't think they're going away. Any ideas?"

"Give me your GPS."

She uploaded her coordinates and looked around. They were already miles beyond the centercity boundaries. If Shenker had pulled in *all* of the cops, they'd gotten away from most. The only cops who could catch them when they landed were in the helicopters circling their stricken balloon. Olivia supposed that was good news, but the dozen or so helicopters would hold more than enough cops to do the job.

She waited another thirty seconds, uploaded new GPS coordinates to Martin, then had Julia use her phone to send them automatically every half-minute. That way Martin could plot their trajectory, bringing any assets he or Justin might have into play.

"You're falling pretty fast," Martin said.

"Yeah? Well, driving this thing isn't an exact science."

"If you don't lose any more hydrogen, I think you'll survive but it's going to hurt. Do you have anything you can dump? You did carry ballast, right?"

Like she was going to have McKensie lug bags of sand up the eight stories of the old library building. "I'll check."

"Do that. I'll see if I can think of anything to help you get away if you can get down safely."

A couple of the helicopters flew ahead, landing in an open field a few miles south, letting the cops inside fan out, weapons ready.

At first, Olivia wondered if they'd run out of fuel. When she saw the line of ground cars heading out of centercity, she realized Shenker had done the same calculations that Martin had. Rather than wait for the women to land, they were converging on the predicted touchdown point.

"Maybe the wind will change," Julia hoped.

"If the weather forecast said the winds would shift, they wouldn't be down there waiting for us."

"What do we do now?"

Going up in the balloon had been Olivia's idea. Unfortunately, her plan had ended with them drifting safely and invisibly out of reach.

They drifted lower. Details on the ground were clearly visible now. Outside of the highly populated inner rings, trees and other growing plants mixed with scattered solar panel grids and homespaces.

Thanks to the thicker air this close to ground level, their fall slowed. Maybe they wouldn't be hurt when the balloon drifted down. Not hurt by the fall, anyway. Because the wind continued to carry them directly toward the reception planned by the cops climbing out of helicopters now.

They *really* needed to miss that reception.

Olivia ran through the calculations in her head, but always came up with the same answer. The cops had them dead to rights.

"When we get a little lower, dump everything we can. We need to reduce weight or we're going to crash right in the middle of a hundred cops."

McKensie shrugged. "For sure we can drop some books. I don't know why Julia had us bring them along, anyway."

"Because those books just might be the solution to our problem," Julia fired back. "We *can't* give them up."

Four books per person, with eight for Julia made twenty books, about twenty pounds. Not nearly enough.

Olivia stripped off her pack, already loaded with the books Julia had made her carry, and stuck in the weapons she'd made over the past week. Carbon-fiber blades don't weigh as much as steel, but they weren't exactly light, either.

She thought hard about the diamond knife. She'd carried that from the very beginning and it had been incredibly useful. And it only weighed a few ounces. Still, she was asking Julia to give up her treasures: it was only fair that she do the same.

The diamond knife went into the pack.

"Get ready to throw everything at once," she said. "We need a bounce, at least an extra half a minute of positive buoyancy. But if we start tossing too early they'll just recalculate."

The other women went through their packs, gathering what they could spare, definitely including the books. Even Julia got with that program.

A hundred meters short of the field where the cops waited, Olivia shouted to release it all.

The books and equipment fell like missiles and the balloon flexed a bit, falling even more slowly but still falling.

Almost instantly, Martin's voice sounded in her phone. "I've got some free-cits with cars in the area, but they can't get close. You're still going down near the initial target zone."

Considering how much they'd dumped and how little impact it had on the descent, Olivia figured they could all get naked and it wouldn't make enough of a difference.

"Olivia, help me!"

For a moment of confusion, she thought the sound came from her phone. But the voice wasn't Martin's, it was Sammy's.

"They've got some poor sucker staked out down there," Julia reported.

"Olivia, help!"

She squinted her eyes to bring that sucker into focus—and saw Sammy, his limbs tied to trees.

"They're going to kill me," Sammy said.

Olivia had rationalized that the cops would leave her family alone, that her parents and brother would be safe as long as she made sure the cops couldn't communicate with her. But the cops had figured a way to use them. And Shenker would know how important her family was to her.

That made up her mind. She grasped the tether lashing her to the balloon. "I'm going to jump."

"You'll kill yourself," Julia protested.

"That's not the plan. But even if I do, it's better one die than all of us. I'm leaving Cat, so take care of her." She latched Cat's carrier to her tether and unhooked herself, holding on with bare hands, waiting for her chance.

With a whole lot of luck, the tree she was aiming for would break her fall. One way or the other, she'd make sure they couldn't hurt Sammy.

"You be good," she instructed the little critter. She looked around at the women and tried to think what to say to them. A knot in her throat cut off anything. So she turned back to Cat. "I'll do my best to see you again, soon."

The small predator taken care of, she waited, swinging slightly under the huge balloon canopy, until she'd judged the trajectory and was directly lined up on the tree. Then she jerked the release handle of her harness.

"I don't know what you just did, but the balloon just jumped five meters. That might be enough." Martin's voice warbled in her phone as air roared past her ears and she plunged downward.

Shenker

He'd hoped staking her brother in the middle of the landing field would shake Olivia up.

He hadn't dreamed it would work as well as it did.

She actually let go from her balloon, plunging downward toward a tree.

"Go," he commanded the two carloads of cops who'd just arrived. "Don't shoot her, capture her."

Loss of her weight altered their calculations and he shouted orders to the sergeants assigned to him. "Take fifty cops and follow that balloon. I want all the women wrapped up. Without Jardan to guard them, that should be fairly straightforward."

Olivia's plunge had ended in a huge tree at the north end of the field.

Branches cracked at her impact and he had to hope they wouldn't impale her. Police tunics were tough, designed to stop bullets or blades, but even they have their limits.

He broke into a jog as she dropped through the tree like a meteor through the atmosphere, each impact tore at her, slowing her, but also injuring her.

Poor Olivia. She was hurting now, and things weren't getting any better for her any time soon.

She'd tucked her head, put her hands over her eyes in an attempt to protect them from the grasping branches, and finally crashed to the ground, landing flat on her back, the wind knocked from her lungs.

She gasped for breath and thrashed a bit, but it was too late. After way too long a chase, Shenker had her.

"Nice of you to drop in on us, Jardan." Shenker heard the fatigue in his voice and realized it wasn't just because he hadn't been sleeping. He was already tired over what he'd have to do.

"Let Sammy go. He has nothing to do with this."

"Okay." He looked over to the cops holding the ropes that appeared to keep Sammy in place. "You can let him go now."

Without waiting for anything, Sammy popped up and walked over. "Sorry we had to do this to you, Olivia. But you were playing on the wrong side. I made a deal with them, though. They're not going to kill you."

"You," Olivia seemed to be searching for words. "You weren't being tortured?"

"It seemed to be the best way to get your attention," Sammy said. He gave her a little grin that had probably infuriated her since they'd been kids together. "Chief Vinson and Reverend Ariel together persuaded me to volunteer."

"Volunteer?"

"As Luke said, 'the word shall divide families.'"

"Who?"

"Chief Vinson made a special point to befriend your brother," Shenker explained. "He thought Sammy would be helpful, and he has been."

"But—"

"Let's get a stretcher over here, people. We're taking Ms. Jardan back to a police hospital."

Senior police officers joked about his failed efforts to catch Olivia, but the cops on the spot responded to his orders. He'd proven, once again, that he knew what he was doing.

"Go easy on her," Sammy said.

Much though he wished he could, that wasn't going to happen. "I'll do what I have to."

"You promised, Shenker."

Shenker just nodded. He didn't want to hurt Olivia but he'd do his job, do whatever it took to learn what Olivia knew.

"Disable her phone," he ordered the medic who'd arrived with the stretcher. "I don't want her communicating with anyone but me."

"I'll come along," Sammy said.

Shenker shook his head. Sammy wasn't a cop. And Olivia had almost certainly protected him from the reality of what they did. The least he owed Olivia was to let Sammy keep a fraction of his innocence. Letting him continue to think of himself as a tough guy wouldn't hurt anyone. Shenker had left his own innocence behind long before.

"Don't give her anything for the pain," he said when the medic pulled out a pair of NanoApplicators. "Just disable her damned phone."

"But—"

He sighed. "Do it."

Martin

"**She** did what?"

"She jumped." Over the remote phone connection, Julia sounded shell-shocked, practically incoherent. "Her brother was calling to her and she jumped."

Martin checked his map. Justin's assets had already picked up and hidden the three designers, but Olivia was gone. He was surprised how much that felt like a kick in the groin. After all, Merryweather's plan depended on designers, not cops, and Olivia's sacrifice had let them get away.

"I hope you've got your stuff packed," Julia added.

"What?" It took him a moment to realize what Julia meant. "Come on, Julia. Olivia wouldn't betray us."

"If she survived, the cops will work on her until they break her. I'm not an expert, but I've seen some of their pain meds. It's only a matter of time—and not much time at that."

Martin knew Justin and some of the others thought he was naïve. In his heart, he'd thought of himself as a realist who just happened to have some good ideas. Julia's certainty about torture made him wonder if the others had been right all along. If so, he'd been not just naive but criminally stupid. To think that he'd called Justin paranoid.

He looked around the test lab he'd set up. In the three weeks since he'd brought Olivia and his family here, it had turned into a real city—with its own public constructor, its own solar panel farm, even a deep well as a water source. He was going to miss it, but he'd rather miss it than wait for an army of cops or Interfaith Enforcers to come down on him.

"Time to move out," he told Angie. "Wake up your brother."

"What about the others?"

"I'll broadcast the message. From now on, only Justin and I know where everything is. Stay off your phone with anyone who isn't part of the compound where we're going."

Angie shook her head. "But I've made friends."

Which was a problem. The larger their group got, the more likely someone would let something slip.

"I'll try to figure out a way to allow secure contact," he promised. "But first we have to stay alive."

"Is Olivia joining us?"

Martin's jaw spasmed.

"Oh, dad. She got caught, didn't she? That's why we're running."

"We needed to run anyway. But yes, she got caught."

"They'll kill her."

He considered denying it but couldn't. "Probably. Police don't believe in second chances. She's already cost them more than she could ever hope to repay."

"That doesn't make me feel better. I liked her."

"I liked her too." Until he realized she was gone, he hadn't realized how much he'd liked her—even if she thought he was living in some kind of opium dream of optimism.

Olivia

Shenker climbed into the helicopter and sat next to Olivia's stretcher.

She shifted her weight, discretely yanking on the thick plastic bands that held her limbs in place. But no. She wasn't allowed the easy suicide available to those tied up with the monomolecular police ties. Shenker didn't want her dead, he wanted her to talk.

"Congratulations, Paul. You caught me."

Shenker nodded. "Yes."

"And you made Lieutenant out of it. That's got to be a big step toward your dream of moving to centercity."

"You're right. It's something I thought would never happen to me—things like that don't happen often to ex-citizens like you and me, Olivia."

He didn't seem as happy about it as she'd thought he would be. Surely he didn't have problems with questioning her. A cop wouldn't survive long if she couldn't handle an interrogation.

"You're pretty smart," he continued. Aren't you? Hiding in places where normal detectors won't work, taking advantage of the luxuries ratepayers just won't give up no matter how impractical they are. I'm proud of you. I taught you well."

"Obviously you didn't teach me well enough, considering you caught me."

"You were outnumbered. And your 'blend in with night traffic' trick was right out of my book."

She shrugged, then regretted the movement when her cracked ribs and damaged shoulders protested. Ever since she'd been chased from her homespace, she had been fighting long odds. Still, Shenker and the consensus hadn't given her much choice. Once she'd opened the Pandora's box of looking more closely into Merryweather's murder, there'd been no way of backing out.

"I'm looking to make a deal," Shenker said.

"We already know you're going to kill me. You showed me that when you unleashed the eaters on my homespace. Seems like you don't have much to offer."

"Things have changed. You don't have to die."

"What changed?"

Shenker gave her the avuncular grin he'd so often shared when she'd been his star pupil. "The Interfaith Enforcers have completed their roundup of the free-coders, for one thing. Those who didn't run, that is. So, we don't have to worry about you giving them warnings."

"But they still want the ones who got away."

He nodded. "Of course."

"That's the deal? I tell you and you let me go?"

He shook his head, his face serious. "You misunderstand me, Olivia. You are going to tell me everything you know. We're negotiating over how much damage it takes. Since you've got the standard police interior-sculpt, we can't use truth-drugs on you. But I will get the truth. You can save me some time, and yourself a great deal of pain. I've got a lot to gain here. Once I finish this job, I'll finally have enough money to move to Centercity, start dating women who wear natural fibers and leather, chicks like you've been hanging around with over the past couple of weeks. My children aren't going to be cops like me, they'll be designers or corporate managers. If you help me get what I want, I'm prepared to be generous. I'll make sure you stay alive, let the medics give you something for your pain, and make sure you get the best nanobes for healing."

She'd shared Shenker's goals, once. Do well as a cop, be accepted by the real ratepayers, discover a way to raise her hypothetical children in a world where they'd be accepted, have opportunities beyond those available to a jumped-up citizen.

"Not going to happen, Shenker. I've been living with high-class ratepayers for the past couple of weeks. Living and learning. And one thing I've learned: money won't buy your way into their circles. They think of cops, all cops, as citizens, no matter how much money they have or how much insurance they buy."

She took a breath to continue with that thought, but Shenker smashed a backfist into her already bruised mouth, followed by a solid shot to one of her cracked ribs.

"Once you give me the coordinates for where the Corporate Houston spies and the renegade designers are hiding, I promise to listen to your political posturing. Coordinates first, though, please."

He rubbed his knuckles, then withdrew a pair of padded gloves from under the stretcher. "You know you're going to talk, Olivia. Spare both of us some pain."

If she'd been a sim star, she would have come up with some bravado, like telling him how sorry she was for bruising his knuckles. As it was, she kept her mouth shut and tried not to vomit. Shenker was right—she would break. She just had to hope she could last long enough for Martin to get the others to safety.

* * * *

Like a river piling behind a dam after the spring floods, Olivia's pain piled up, waiting for the moment when it could escape control, flood the banks and wash everything away.

It seemed that Shenker had been questioning her forever. With no clock on the wall and her phone disabled, she couldn't tell exactly. But it was less than the days or months it seemed because Shenker's fatigue and the shadow of his beard were only somewhat darker than they had been. *One more minute,* she promised herself again. *Surely you can survive another minute.*

It got worse when they took her from the helicopter to the hospital. There, they pumped her full of pain nanobes that rendered her so sensitive her heartbeat hurt. Shenker only had to brush a knuckle across her lips to create agony greater than what she'd felt when she'd fallen a hundred feet into a tree.

She babbled incoherent nothings, coughed up fake GPS coordinates, screamed obscenities.

Shenker saw through every trick and kept questioning.

One more minute, she told herself. Surely she could keep quiet for another minute.

Then they walked her brother in, strapped him into the second gurney, and hooked him to his own set of IVs.

"I don't understand," Sammy protested. "I've been helping you. I'm on your side. I understand how the free-coders are destroying everything."

"And you're going to keep on helping us," Shenker promised. "You're going to persuade your sister to stop her foolish resistance. Think of what you're going through as a sacrifice for the Interfaith."

"That's blasphemous."

"Really? Too bad." Shenker patted Sammy on the head, adjusted the flow of nanobes, then turned back to Olivia.

"This is an experiment." Shenker turned her own pain up just a notch, to some level between suffering and babbling idiocy. "I know you're probably angry with your brother and figure it's fair that he share your pain. So, that's what I'm going to do. What you feel, he'll feel. I'll do my best to keep the two of you perfectly even. If this experiment works, I'll bring in your parents next and hook them up as well. All four of you can join in suffering. Very bonding, won't it be?

"You're a jerk, Shenker. I thought you were smart, but you're just a sadist."

"A sadist would enjoy this and I don't. I wish you'd talk, spare yourself and your family. Now I'm raising the brother to level one."

Sammy screamed and Olivia hissed in a breath as what felt like an acid burn spread over her skin.

Shenker was right—her brother had betrayed her. She *should* be happy he was suffering. But he was still her brother. She and Sammy were young and could endure the pain. Her parents were more fragile. They couldn't stand the agony and would rather die than lose their homespace and turn into free-cits.

One more min—

Then, abruptly, without any obvious trigger or anything approaching a conscious decision, she was babbling out the information Shenker demanded. Their plans. The status of free-code. The coordinates for every one of the free-code labs they'd set up, including the dummies and the actual.

She'd betrayed everyone now, had no place to go. But the pain stopped.

Vinson

The traditional cop tunic, in citizen-black, felt uncomfortable to Vinson, but the cameras were out and he was intent on demonstrating that the Dallas Police Corporation could do the job.

"No signs of life inside," Sergeant Smythe reported. She drew herself to her full height, pulled off her helmet to show off long red hair, and stuck her chest out so far he was afraid she might topple over.

He'd selected Smythe based on her looks rather than her employee records. The Police Corporation needed to show up on the Infoweb, and show up in as favorable light as possible.

"Helmets down. Breathe filtered air only," he ordered the hundred or so cops standing by. "We're going in."

"What about traps?" one of the reporters demanded. "Our reports indicate that dozens of cops were injured during the raid that led to Officer Jansen's capture."

"Ex-officer Jansen," he said. "The injured were Interfaith Enforcers, working with the police force. While we appreciate their support and the close working relationship between cops and IE, we overestimated their training. Its lack put them in danger. And second, we've got to take some risks. If we simply deconstructed this unauthorized homespace, we might miss clues to where the Corporate Houston spies have fled."

Smyth tightened her tunic, not accidentally showing off a figured honed by nice sculpts and hard exercise. "Follow me, chief."

"I'll lead the way."

"But—" What an acting talent. He just had to hope his own little speechmaking was up to her standard.

"Those are your orders, Smythe."

"Yes, sir."

He manhandled a police ram, smashed it through the protesting greeter, and plunged into the abandoned homespace.

It would have been nice if the spies had dropped a map with their new locations carefully marked on it. Vinson didn't think it likely.

Still, he had to look. And he'd keep looking. From now on, he'd send cops out to check every time a solar panel showed up where it hadn't been before, every time a shadow changed shape in the drone-based photography. He'd push the designers and the Corporate Houston spies so far from centercity that they might as well have stayed in Houston.

Beyond the Corporate City limits, he'd happily let the Interfaith Enforcers waste their time hunting them. The designers, after all, were the Interfaith's problem, not his.

An alarm jolted him from his contemplation. Sure enough, the spies *had* left a trap.

"High explosive shaped charge," his scanner reported through his phone. "It appears sensitive to local vibrations only."

He gestured to Smythe. "Jell it. But take it slowly. I want this caught in 3-D for the Infoweb."

"Yes sir." Moving almost infinitely slowly, she lowered a protective outer shield over the charge, then pumped in the jell that would capture the force of the explosive, protecting both people and the rest of the building from the destruction it would otherwise create.

"Ready to detonate," she reported.

He checked his helmet to make sure it was secure. "Detonate."

Instead of a huge roar, the explosion was muffled. Still, its force shook the homespace, knocked a couple of reporters down, and jammed Vinson against a wall he had thoughtfully pre-scanned.

"Are you certain this is safe for a person of your status?" Like all reporters, this one wasn't immune to taking the odd bribe, and Vinson had prepped him with some softball questions.

"This is our job." He kept his voice deadly serious. "Corporate Houston has stooped to new lows with this attack. But the Police Corporation will respond to their tactics."

It was, he decided, a nice newsbyte.

As he'd suspected, that newsbyte was the best thing that came from the outing. The spies had left their homespace in a hurry, but they'd ordered it to cannibalize itself before they'd left. Any furnishings, computers, AIs, or biological evidence had long-since been consumed.

Which was fine with Vinson. He'd discomforted a Corporate Houston project and stuck a thumb in Rev. Ariel's plan to compete with the Police Corporation. All in all, it was a fair day's work.

Martin

"**Can't** we stop moving all the time?"

Martin ruffled his hand through Jimmy's hair. "They've got us on the run, buddy. So we have to keep running."

"How come nobody else is running?"

"A bunch of us are. Justin and his gang are setting up camps everywhere. Then there's the three of us."

"What about Julia and those others? They get to stay in nice homespaces and don't run at all."

Martin nodded seriously. He'd been so sure he was doing the right thing that he'd just assumed it would be the right thing for his family as well. Now, with Angie getting interested in boys, and five-year-old Jimmy in danger because of Martin's big dreams, he had to reassess his actions.

"You and Angie can stay with Julia if you want to," he said. "We've analyzed the police attack pattern and they're ignoring everything outside the tenth ring."

"But *you're* going to stay inside?"

"For now. I need them to think they have us flustered."

"I don't know about that, but they sure have me flustrated."

"What did I tell you about twisting words," Angie warned.

"I just—"

Jimmy's explanation was interrupted by a proximity alarm.

"Into the shelter. Hurry."

"Oh, dad," Angie whined. "We get into the shelter every time. They're just flying around." Despite her protests, though, she bundled her brother and herself into the shelter.

"So far." He climbed in afterward.

Before, the drones had flown overhead, then moved on. This one, however, circled around, apparently content to wait.

"They must see something they like."

"Can I shoot it?" Jimmy's face flushed with excitement.

That did it. If he survived today, he was going to make sure Jimmy and Angie stayed someplace safe.

Unfortunately, the drone circling overhead had to mean there were cops on the way—probably close. They needed to move and they couldn't move with the drone in the sky. "Go ahead, Jimmy." He sent the authorization code to his son.

Five seconds later, an explosion rained chunk-o-drone down on a homespace they'd only halfway fabricated.

"Switch identity codes and let's move." He dragged his children out of the shelter. "This time we're going to put some distance between ourselves and the cops."

If they managed to get away at all, of course. Because this wasn't a sim, there weren't do-overs, and his children were in danger. What the cops had done to Olivia was an ever-present reminder that they were playing for real.

Perhaps the worst thing was that he couldn't even contact Olivia to let her know he cared. If he made contact, they'd trace the call and he'd be in trouble. Even if the police eventually let Olivia go, they'd reprogram her phone to keep it permanently linked into police central. She was poison to him.

"Should we leave a trap?" Angie hefted a bomb with a casual disregard that he should have noticed before. Clearly she'd spent too much time in danger.

"Leave it but don't bother arming it," he said. "It'll slow them down just as much that way and there's no risk of some citizen kid wandering in and getting hurt. Now let's move."

Olivia

"**You're** out of here, Jardan. Get lost."

"Huh?" Olivia couldn't believe Shenker would just let her walk away after. Promises or not, cops terminate any citizen who costs them too much money. And she'd cost them plenty.

"I got what I wanted. If you'd had any more secrets, you'd have babbled those as well. So, what am I supposed to do? Kill you?"

"That would be normal. Uh, thanks, Shenker."

"Don't thank me. I'm doing my job." He stepped closer to her gurney, bringing her face near hers. "One thing you didn't know. We were tracking you from the beginning. Want to know how?"

"One of the designers is an informant, right?"

Shenker's mouth was already open to tell her just that. He snapped it shut. "How'd you guess?"

"I apprenticed under you, Shenker. Of course the cops have informants in a group like the free-coders. Code is what it's all about, what the whole corporate consensus rests on. You wouldn't just let a bunch of young designers run around rocking the boat without at least watching them."

"Want to know which designer?"

She didn't, really. Julia had been a fighter, including fighting with Olivia when she could. McKensie had been annoying. Kansas had been too cowardly for words. But she didn't want to think of any of them as her enemies.

"No."

"Okay. It was Kansas."

Kansas? Whoever had hired her as an informant had scraped the bottom of the barrel. "Considering I just spilled everything I know, I guess I'm as much a traitor as she was. I can't feel superior or angry."

Shenker shook his head at her. "Remember your Economics? The corporate system is self-regulating and self-reinforcing. Fight the system and it will grind you like a nanobe-eater."

"Yeah, yeah. I remember all of that junk."

She also wondered if she was channeling Martin. Since when did she argue with the corporate system?

"In this case, the profit motive, in the form of me and Kansas, prevailed over your utopian dreams."

"You did say I could leave, right? Or is listening to you gloat part of the deal."

"Get the hell out of here before I change my mind." He unstrapped the cuffs that had held her firmly in her hospital bed.

She sat up. Or rather, she sent a signal to her abdominal muscles to pull her up. Nothing happened. The nanobes blocking her pain also blocked conscious muscle control below her neck.

"I don't seem able to move."

"Good thing you've got your brother here to help you, then."

"Come on, Olivia." Sammy's voice sounded ancient, trembling and weak. "We'll get you hooked up to the Interfaith. They'll get you pumped full of healing nanobes. Let's get out of here before these bastards change their minds."

* * * *

If she hadn't been so weak, Olivia would have argued that seven days tuned into the Interfaith was worse than letting her body heal itself. Her brother overrode her objections, though. After taking her home and dialing up the nanobes to re-establish her identity, he piped her into the Interfaith and made sure she didn't deviate from their healing sims.

Her parents checked on her occasionally, bringing her the nearly tasteless meals that the Interfaith coded, each one filled with whatever healing nanobes her attention to the doctrines had earned her.

Although she had her identity back, Olivia's account had been emptied. She'd cost the Police Corporation and they'd claimed everything to cover their losses.

Still, she had access to the phone. Recognizing that the police would track her calls, she still tried to connect with Martin, Justin, Julia, McKensie, even Kansas using all the faked identities she was aware of. None of their codes responded.

Not surprising, since she'd blurted out their codes under torture. If they hadn't changed them, they would have been captured.

So she left general posts on the Infoweb letting them know what Shenker had said about Kansas. She couldn't be certain he was telling the truth, or whether he was just trying to stir up dissention in the design community, so she left that in her posting as well.

After a full week, the Interfaith healing nanobes seemed satisfied with what they'd done and abruptly her body started responding to her commands again.

Sort of.

She'd lost a lot of weight.

Nanobes use what they have. From her, they'd used calories and material from the food she'd eaten and from her muscle mass to heal her injuries and put her back together.

Healed or not, she could barely stand. She lurched down the hall to the kitchen.

Her brother met at her at the table. He was eating what looked like eggs, bacon, and biscuits.

"Interfaith?"

"You bet. The word made flesh."

"That's not blasphemous?"

"Not at all. It's doctrine."

She searched the kitchen constructor and came up empty. Interfaith specials were the only things available programmed in and she couldn't stand another. She downloaded citizen slop and coded it in.

Sammy watched curiously as she withdrew the steaming bowl from the constructor. "Seven days of continuous participation in Interfaith sims has built you up some credit. Use some of that credit and fix yourself a treat."

"I don't really want—"

He grinned at her, put his lips together and blew a few notes.

Her mouth salivated as mind instantly supplied the rest of the tune. It was one of the earworm hymns the Interfaith pumped out between boring sims teaching the virtues of obedience to the rules.

That tune, and whatever suggestions went with it, had been packed into her brain during a solid week of continual bombardment.

She stared at her brother, suddenly hit by a horrible realization. She'd bought into Martin's dream of letting every citizen become a designer. A dream that people like her, like Sammy, people who weren't born with the advantages that centercity ratepayers enjoy, could somehow regain the ability to create their own futures.

She could see why ratepayers would resist, but she'd been certain the Interfaith would share their goals. Obviously, she'd missed something important.

"What?" her brother demanded. "You're looking at me like I just grew devil-horns."

"Do you remember how it was when we were growing up? I was going to be a cop, and we were going to save the money we needed to turn you into a designer."

He shook his head. "I was stupid. Those reality sims mom was always watching confused us. They don't let citizens become designers, Olivia. No matter how much money their sisters earn. Besides, you never earned that much."

"I couldn't. It seemed like every time I turned around, they cut the bonuses or added an additional charge for something. But imagine if you could. Wouldn't it be cool to design your own stuff rather than just download what the Interfaith thinks you need?"

He shrugged. "There are smart people and smart AIs on the Interfaith, Olivia. You've got to let go of this feeling that you're better than other people. There's a reason things are set up this way."

She wanted to scream. Sammy was twenty-six, still living with their parents, and hadn't had a non-virtual girlfriend in years.

It seemed to her that he spent his days staring, slack jawed, at nothing at all, watching the sims his phone projected across his optical nerves and playing out meaningless scenarios that the Interfaith had constructed for him. Yet he wasn't alone.

Olivia didn't know any way to let Sammy share her experiences. In the country of the blind, the sighted woman was insane.

Their father stepped into the kitchen, ending Olivia's attempt to communicate with her brother. He kissed Olivia on the back of the neck and told her how happy he was that she was feeling better.

"Thanks, dad."

"Sammy tells me you've built up some positive credit with the Interfaith."

"He told me that, too."

"So, how come you're eating citizen slop?" He constructed himself an Interfaith breakfast combo.

"I felt like something different."

He looked at her like she'd spoken in a foreign language.

They ate in silence, Olivia trying not to taste the horrid flavor of the citizen-slop. For the first time, she saw that its horrid taste was a feature, intentionally designed. Considering the lack of opportunity for who ate citizen-slop, the goal wasn't to persuade citizens to work harder to pay for ratepayer food. The total economic market represented by citizens was hardly a blip on the profit-and-loss statements of the major corporations. Citizen slop tasted bad to encourage citizens to turn to the Interfaith for everything. Perversely, from everything she'd been taught, corporations kowtowed to the Interfaith.

Her father finished eating before looking up from his plate. "So, you're better now. Have you thought about what comes next?"

She'd done nothing *but* think over the previous week, though the bombardment of Interfaith programming and twenty hours a day of sleep had slowed her thought processes. "No jobs are available to a disgraced ex-cop."

"I've been thinking about that," her father said. "One thing for sure, I don't know how we're going to pay maintenance fees on this place without your income."

"The Interfaith will provide," Sammy stated confidently.

Sammy deserved it if they did.

"I guess you could stay until we get kicked out," her father conceded, apparently not as certain as Sammy that the Interfaith would take care of everything. "Your mom might like someone to share her sims with—for a while, anyway."

His tone, even more than his words, let Olivia know exactly how little he welcomed that. Home might be where they had to take you, but they didn't have to like it.

"I'll get out of your way."

"The cops aren't going to lay off us as long as you're here."

She realized her father had misunderstood her words. "I don't mean I'll lay low *here*, I mean, I'll move on."

"What, and be a free-cit?" He loaded the term with scorn.

"That's what's left, isn't it?"

"You don't have to do it." His protest was for his own benefit. He could assure himself he'd given her a choice.

"You say I have some credit on the Interfaith, Sammy. I've got an idea, but I need your help."

Shenker

"**I** know you. Oh my gosh, I played you in *Hunting the Rogue*. You're Lieutenant Shenker, aren't you?"

Shenker forced a smile while he scanned the ratepayer who'd approached him. Considering the sculpts available to high-status ratepayers, she could have been anywhere between seventeen and a hundred and seventeen, but the scan indicated it was closer to the former. The giggle and hand clutched on her girlfriend's arm confirmed it.

"I am Lieutenant Shenker, Holly. But call me Paul."

He was at another of Maudie Vinson's parties, surrounded by the kind of ratepayer crowd he'd always dreamed he'd mingle with. It wasn't as satisfied as he'd imagined it would be.

"My girlfriends and I wondered something. It seems that female citizens always look beautiful."

Beautiful but boring. Ratepayers paid for custom enhancements to their natural appeal. Citizens couldn't afford custom work and went with cheap makeovers.

"Many citizens take advantage of low-cost full body sculpts," he explained. "There are only a few basic models available, but all of these are quite attractive."

Holly giggled again. "We heard that the males do full sculpts, too."

He shrugged. "Of course. Again, there are only a few base types. It would make police work more difficult if—"

"What I'm asking is whether they sculpt particular parts of their body to be unusually, well, large."

Shenker choked down the bile that threatened to spew from his throat. He hadn't really believed ratepayers were so much different from citizens, but he had fantasized they'd at least practice basic manners.

"I'm sure many common sculpts allow the customer to select specific size attributes," he suggested. "Wouldn't that be good design practice?"

Holly giggled again. "If it were my design I'd only bother with extra-large."

"I'm sure many citizens select that option."

Holly sidled closer. "I wonder whether you're talking about yourself. My girlfriend thinks you're an extra-large sort of guy. What should I tell her?"

The worst nightmares can be dreams revealed through another light. Shenker had never been especially prone to introspection, but he was getting it shoved down his throat. Holly was the kind of rich, centercity ratepayer he'd fantasized about. A relationship with her could open centercity to him. If the relationship grew from casual and exploitative sex to something longer-lasting, she might even give him the children he so desperately craved. Although he had no illusion that Holly would stick around to be a good mother, just by being who she was, would assure her children of every advantage growing up.

Shenker could deliver her fantasy while she delivered his. That she considered him a lower life form really wasn't the point.

Shenker didn't think of himself as a snob. He was a cop, which meant he spent his time with people (mostly citizens) who violated code or failed to respect property. Snob or not, he couldn't make himself carry on with this conversation.

"I'm afraid I've got to go," he said. "Busy day tomorrow."

"We could make it a busy night." Holly upped the transparency index on her gown, proving she wore nothing underneath.

More than anything else in the world, he wanted to tell her he just wasn't interested. But angry centercity ratepayers, even angry ratepayers who needed to do a lot of growing up, could destroy a career—or a life—without any more effort than it would take to stomp a garden snail.

"I can't tell you how tempting and flattering this is," he lied. "If Chief Vinson hadn't requested me specifically, I'd take you up on your offer. But I've got to go."

Shenker caught the rail out to the first ring where he lived, alone, in a homespace that he'd thought of as classic and elegant—until he'd gotten a better look at the way real ratepayers live. He wondered whether someone like Holly would see it as more than an animal's den.

They thought of themselves as superior, but Shenker wondered how long they would have lasted if he'd been hunting for them rather than for Olivia and Julia. They couldn't have done as well, yet the corporate consensus had decided that Julia and Olivia were permanent exiles and that Holly and her friend would get all of the advantages.

It wasn't fair. If Shenker had been left with any illusions, he had lost them by the time he threw himself down on his futon. But it couldn't matter. Knowing that centercity was rotten didn't change his desire for it—the alternatives were worse. But he no longer had a plan to get there. Finding the perfect female ratepayer to hook up with simply wasn't going to be happening.

Olivia

Minutes after she'd left her parent's homespace, Olivia knew she'd made a mistake.

Not that leaving was wrong. Shenker had let her go, but police central would ultimately realize the lieutenant had made a mistake—and would send another cop to clean up the mess. Still, leaving with nothing but an old police tunic, leggings, and Interfaith code hadn't been Olivia's brightest move.

After wandering vaguely south for a couple of hours, testing out her legs and realizing how far from fit she actually was, Olivia got in the line at a public constructor.

"You look familiar." The guy in front of her weighed his voice down with accusation.

"You don't look familiar to me." Then again, he hadn't been the designated victim for a search and kill sim.

"Well, you don't look so good. Maybe you should go in front of me."

"That's very kind. But—"

He ignored her protests. Speaking to each person in line, her new friend shoved her to the front, until she faced the constructor on her own.

Which was odd. Citizens learn to hold onto what little they have. Compassion was not something sims ever taught.

Olivia wouldn't have been surprised if an idealist like Martin had given up his place in line to help someone else, but these people didn't have the luxury of a ratepayer background to look down from. Besides, Martin was weird, a utopian. Both citizens and ratepayers were trained to pursue their self-interest rather than naive charity.

"You probably need more than one thing," the woman scheduled to use the constructor next said. "Go ahead and program everything. Nobody here minds waiting, do you guys?

She might have heard a mutter, but nobody objected out loud.

Olivia programmed the code for high-protein citizen bars—another free offering guaranteed to keep her alive. At the woman's urging, she added an Interfaith solar blanket—something that would let her stay warm at night and also power the mini-constructor she built next. Finally, she constructed an Interfaith bicycle.

With power, a constructor, transportation, shelter, and enough food to last until she found a place to settle, she could be independent. She couldn't risk joining Martin and Julia, but she might still be able to help them. She hadn't forgotten that Martin's plan still depended on getting registered, getting authorized, getting validated—or that it was up to her, the ex-cop, to figure out how to do it.

* * * *

Public constructors are slow—intentionally slow as they worked great when presented with the police override Olivia no longer possessed.

It took the better part of an hour before she had her food, blanket, miniconstructor, and bicycle.

All the while, the citizens waited, offered her advice on where she could go, what she could do to create a new life since it was obvious to everyone that her old one was over.

None of the advice was especially useful, but all of it came from the heart. Nobody in that line knew her but they still cared.

She had tears in her eyes when she finally loaded down her new bicycle with her stuff, climbed on, and headed straight south, directly away from where she'd last seen Martin.

Built on the shores of the Trinity River, Dallas was a part of the great flat prairies of the American heartland.

Which made it perfect for a bicycle.

Centercity was barred to her and her legs remained weak after a week of torture and another week of nanobe-enhanced recovery, but she was in no hurry. She munched on energy bars and detoured around the ultra-rich enclave, remaining in the first couple of circles until she crossed over the Trinity River.

She remembered the GPS coordinates she'd read out to Martin and had, if not a plan, at least the faint stirrings of a hope—assuming that Julia hadn't been pulling her leg.

The sun was low in the sky by the time Olivia found the exact spot where the police helicopters had waited for their balloon to descend.

The tree she'd smashed through on her way to the ground was a highly visible landmark, broken branches marking the scene of her plunge.

Her body screamed for rest as she dismounted the bicycle, but she had more to do first. After a couple of weeks, one more night probably wouldn't matter, but Olivia didn't want to take that chance.

Leaving the bicycle and miniconstructor leaning against the tree that had broken her fall from the balloon and nearly broken her, Olivia branched north in search of everything she and the others had thrown as they'd tried to lighten the balloon in their desperate attempt to escape Shenker's trap.

Olivia wanted to believe Julia was right about the books. That part wasn't hard—Julia was smart and generally knew what she was talking about. Olivia also had to believe that if the answers were there, *she* could find them. That part was tougher because Julia hadn't had time to teach Olivia how to read. Olivia recognized individual letters but hadn't learned put them together in words. Reading entire books frightened her almost as much as her concern that police central would eventually track her down. Still, finding the books, learning to decode them, and discovering what secrets the books held was Olivia's plan. That these books could be found nowhere on the Infoweb meant might mean that the Corporate Consensus didn't want anyone to know about their contents, or it might just mean they were so worthless no one had bothered scanning them in.

Olivia desperately wanted to believe that those particular books, books Julia had gathered, held something forgotten, something important, something that would allow her to solve the problem of overcoming the project's problem.

* * * *

She found the books she'd been carrying first, still wrapped in a police tunic along with her diamond knife.

Falling a couple of hundred meters hadn't done anything to help the already ancient books. They were dirty, the bindings were broken, and a few pages had blown around, getting stuck in the shrubs and weeds nearby.

Still, Olivia felt she'd accomplished something.

She grabbed the pack, slipped her diamond knife into a pouch in her tunic, and gathered up as many pages as she could.

When she ran out of loose pages to pick up, she stared at what she'd found.

There were no pictures. Page after page was a squiggle of characters marching across the page. It seemed endless.

Julia

Julia studied the code.

Most of design was high-level stuff. You took existing modules, access published properties, link to pre-defined interfaces, then added a bit of logic to manipulate run-time events.

But Merryweather's project involved reconstruction of the blocks everyone took for granted. Not many designers knew how to produce the kind of tight code that made for high-quality and reliable modules.

She'd been surprised when she'd turned out to have an aptitude for that kind of design work herself—it was something she'd never have tried if she hadn't gotten into this mess, no matter how much Merryweather had encouraged her.

"You look tired." Martin padded into her lab, his feet bare, his face showing a couple of days' worth of beard, and his body thinner than it should be.

"You don't look so hot yourself."

"I, uh, didn't mean to be critical."

"Oh, jeez. What idiot…"

"What?"

"This segment doesn't call its destructor. No wonder it's got memory leaks."

Using a stylus and an old-fashioned whiteboard AI, she dragged the offending code to the trash and formulated a correct destructor function.

"I'm worried about Olivia," Martin admitted.

"Me too." They'd tracked her down and were watching her, but she was just hiding in the woods. "Maybe we should bring her in."

Months had gone by since their ill-fated balloon flight. The Corporate Dallas police had pushed them back, well away from even the most remote zones, into land that had been unoccupied for generations. But they'd been left alone for weeks now. Apparently Corporate Dallas was spending its energies on the economic war with Corporate Houston rather than chasing a few renegade designers.

"They'll have traces on her."

Martin paced Julia's lab. She knew he was torn, but she wished he'd go be torn somewhere else. She had designing to do, then there was the entire training program waiting for someone to tackle it. Watching Martin stew about the same old things didn't help.

"Until she decides to come in herself, as long as she's not in danger, she's safer by herself than with us."

They'd had this conversation at least once a week since the cops had let Olivia go. Martin was wasting time.

He cleared his throat. "Now what's this about you giving Angie a birth control nanobe?"

"I've designed a new security bot." Julia ignored his question. "Why don't you go and construct a few hundred of them. I think this one is smart enough not to go falling down holes."

"About Angie—"

"She's a woman, Martin. That means some personal stuff is off-limits for you. If she comes to me for help, that's between us."

"She's my kid."

"So what—you want to drive her away? Now let me get back to work."

Martin clearly wanted to take out his frustrations on her, but Julia didn't have the time or the energy to deal with it. He sputtered a bit, then left.

"You could be easier on him." Angie had vanished into the bathroom a second before her father had appeared. Which said she had made progress on the spy warning design she'd been messing with.

"You don't understand guys yet," Julia said. "They really want to be told what to do, they just have to put on an act."

"Really?"

Julia grinned. "Of course." She tapped the whiteboard to bring up a design she'd recently debugged. "Now, tell me what's wrong with this code."

Angie studied the electronic whiteboard, then wrinkled her nose. "I don't need to learn low-level stuff if I just want to make cool things."

"You have to learn it if you want me to teach you how to make cool things. Come on."

Angie looked more closely at the code, changed one property, then nodded. "Fixed."

"Really. Compile it."

The electronic whiteboard included a virtual constructor—which was handy when making sure beginning designers didn't accidentally gray-ooze the world.

Sure enough, Angie's design crashed the constructor halfway through.

"It would have eaten a real constructor." Julia called back the code. "It's never just one problem. You've got to learn to see the whole system."

"Speaking of seeing, are you doing my dad?"

Julia laughed. She'd first joined free-code to meet guys. So, she'd met a perfectly nice guy—a guy who, if he just cleaned up a bit and wasn't a

Corporate Houston spy, her mother would definitely approve of. For whatever reason, there'd never been a spark of chemistry between the two of them.

"I'm still waiting for my prince."

"I think McKensie is making moves on him."

"McKensie would be more likely to make moves on you."

"But…" Angie's eyes widened. "How come I never noticed that before?"

"Because you're worried about protecting your dad, not about what McKensie does in her spare time."

"Someone has to worry about him," Angie said. "Because he's not exactly a hundred percent there all the time."

"Your dad's a dreamer. Without dreamers like him and Merryweather, we never would have gotten this project off the ground. But you're right, dreamers need regular people to keep them from wandering too far off."

"I wish Olivia were here. She could keep him straight."

Julia grinned. "You heard what your dad and I were talking about. But I can take a hint. I'll see if I can bring her in."

Vinson

"**War** is Hell," some ancient philosopher had said. Vinson figured that philosopher was still right.

Because war was now run for profit, it was conducted on a more affordable scale than those in the ancient past. The goal of the economic war was to determine whether Corporate Dallas or Corporate Houston would control the road between them and who could expand franchises into each other's territory. Wholesale destruction was unprofitable and avoided. Still, while neither Corporate Dallas nor Corporate Houston actively tried to kill each other's ratepayers, Houston had made Dallas life miserable—and done so in a way more unpleasant to ratepayers than mere citizens.

Vinson poured himself a cup of constructed coffee, then winced as he sipped the bitter brew. Who would have guessed that Corporate Houston controlled both the gateway to actual grown coffee imports and the design modules that made TrueBean™ Coffee an acceptable substitute?

Maybe nobody would surrender because they couldn't get an adequate cup of coffee, but it lowered spirits around Dallas.

He took a second sip of the harsh liquid, then poured what remained back into the constructor reservoir when his phone rang. Nobody was rich enough to waste water.

Because he was grouchy from his lack of coffee (although his Med implant claimed it had automatically delivered whatever essential antioxidants his system would have absorbed from the coffee), he took the call.

"This had better be important."

"Chief Vinson, this is Julia Turnboldt."

"Turnboldt the traitor?"

"You might call me that."

"You giving yourself up? I'll cut you a deal if you help us track down the Corporate Houston spies."

He didn't have much hope of tracking the call, but he set his AI working on it anyway. Better a long shot than no shot at all.

Turnboldt laughed. "I *am* looking for a deal, but not the deal you have in mind. I'm looking for Corporate Dallas recognition for a new design corporation."

"You finally realized how stupid free-code is, did you? I'm afraid you're not asking for anything I can deliver."

"Our friends tell us that Dallas ratepayers are getting antsy about not getting decent tequila, coffee, or vanilla."

"Gloating is not attractive. And I'm sure Corporate Houston isn't exactly celebrating their shortage of TrueBeef™ or UltraSculpt eye scrubs."

"No gloat—I'm prepared to help you." Turnboldt smiled into the phone. "I'm uplinking limited use code to you now. One million single-serving licenses each for tequila, coffee, and vanilla."

"How will I know this is safe?"

"What? Don't tell me you killed all the designers in Corporate Dallas."

"I didn't kill any designers."

"Any still alive after your massacre can check this out."

Vinson's phone acknowledged receipt of full code for three designs and he forwarded all three to the analysis AIs at police central. A million doses would last the ratepayers of Corporate Dallas for months, assuming Turnboldt's code was usable. She had been voted Dallas's top young flavor developer for two years running, so it was possible she could churn out decent code. Of course there was the little issue of intellectual property. He wasn't about to let anyone steal code, not even if doing so would hurt Corporate Houston in the short term. The chief of police needed to worry about the long term and destroying the basis for the economy was too high a price to pay for a decent cup of coffee—although the decision was close.

"Enjoy your coffee, chief. And look into what it would take to allow us to establish a recognized corporate entity."

"So you've abandoned the crazy free-code ideas Merryweather introduced?"

"Not at all."

He sighed. He couldn't have let Turnboldt and the others incorporate anyway.

The problem, like so many others, came from the Interfaith. They didn't care whether ratepayers got their coffee or tequila. They wanted to make an example of those who threatened their control over the cits.

"I'll see what I can do," he promised. If Turnboldt heard that as a bit of encouragement, that was her problem. He'd see he could do nothing and that's what he'd deliver.

"There's more of this coming, Chief Vinson," Turnboldt promised. "Want to try a self-heating pizza?"

His mouth watered. "I'd better pass on that until central gets back with an analysis of what you already sent me. For your sake, I hope you haven't violated copyright. You know the penalty for that."

"Termination," she said. "Considering I'm a designer, I guess I should approve of that."

"Frankly, Ms. Turnboldt, your approval isn't high on my priority list."

"It should be, Chief. Because Corporate Houston is putting the love on Corporate Fort Worth, Corporate Oklahoma City, Corporate Austin, and Corporate Midcities. You're about to be squeezed."

He nodded glumly. His own spies in those cities had picked up on the vibe. Corporate Dallas had launched into economic war with high hopes. Then reality had hit. With things going badly, ratepayers were looking for someone to blame. T-10 CEOs were too highly placed to take the fall, which meant someone else, namely Police Chief Harles Vinson, would likely be tapped to throw himself on his sword for the public good.

Assuming Turnboldt's designs were any good, she might have bought him a couple of months of grace.

"Thanks for the warning, Turnboldt. I mean it about protecting you if you surrender."

"I'm not ready to give up yet."

"I'll hold the offer open as long as I can."

"You know, Chief, you're not a bad person for a hypocritical lying cheat."

He laughed. "And you're not bad for a traitor, Turnboldt. Thanks for the coffee. I need it."

"Gotta go, chief." She blinked out.

Vinson immediately put through a call to Shenker. "Did you pick up that conversation?"

"I got most of it. She was scattering signal all over the place. Way beyond what the network normally does."

"So you can't do anything with it?"

"I didn't say that. I'll analyze the background noise, shadows from the sun, signal strength, and fade. I can't guarantee anything, but you managed to keep her on the phone for a good while. That'll help."

"I know you've taken the pressure off since we ran them out of the neighborhood, but I want you back on this full-time."

"Me and how many others."

"Just you, for now. We need brains more than feet. When you're ready to move, I'll free up some help for you."

Shenker didn't look happy, but Vinson couldn't remember Shenker looking happy since he'd made lieutenant. "I'll do my best, sir."

"From what Turnboldt said, they've created some critical designs. If we could get our hands on those, it would help us in the war effort. So, find them. But no killing designers. If you want to gray ooze the spies, feel free."

"I'll get to work on it."

Vinson disconnected, then put through a call to central. Status of analysis?" he demanded.

"Analysis shows valid design. A coffee dose level caffeine is the only clear risk factor."

"What about patents."

"No violations detected—but analysis is proceeding."

Vinson decided to take the chance. "Download a hundred-copy license to my constructor now."

"But—"

"That's a control override, central."

The AI wasn't happy, but making AIs happy wasn't part of Vinson's job description.

He constructed an oversized mug, sniffed cautiously, then took a sip.

Damn, it was good. While central analyzed possible patent violation, Vinson would get politicking. Once they heard he had coffee available, he suspected he'd have no problem getting key corporate executives to see things a bit more his way.

Olivia

Olivia had spent the first night under the tree that had broken her fall. The next morning, she'd hunted down the rest of the dropped books and equipment, then rode to the site where the balloon had finally come down.

After salvaging what she could, she'd continued south, away from Dallas and away from where Martin and his free-cits were probably hiding. To learn to read, she needed time and space.

About twenty miles south of centercity, she found a place along the banks of a tiny creek where no free-cits had staked a claim, and where enough sunlight got through to power her blanket—and the solar panels she'd eventually build.

Sunsets were beautiful, the sky turning orange and purple as the huge ball of the sun descended through high-level clouds and into the vast open plains of Texas.

But it was daytime when she got most of her work done. Her first need—learning how to read.

She'd thought she'd find plenty of training material on reading. After all, once even young children learned to read. There must have been millions of teachers back in the days when education was provided by people rather than sims. Surely someone had videoed that instruction and placed it on the Infoweb.

To her surprise, all reading training was coded as ratepayer-only, with prices high enough that she could have bought her parents' homespace for less.

On the Interfaith, she found nothing at all. It was almost as if they'd conspired to keep reading out of the hands of anyone who wasn't already from a centercity ratepayer background.

* * * *

Something warm nuzzled her one morning as the gray dawn persuaded her to open her eyes.

She relaxed her mind, not fully connected, imagining the familiar growl of Cat.

Until some synapses closed and she realized she'd left Cat with the designers long before.

She jumped to her feet reaching for a weapon—and Cat dug her claws through Olivia's armored tunic and leapt away.

"What are *you* doing here? You're supposed to be with Julia."

Cat looked a bedraggled. A couple of stickers from some nasty plant clung to her fur and she limped as she crept back toward Olivia.

"You ran away, didn't you? Julia would have taken care of you, you know."

Cat gave her the same answer she always did, rubbing her gums on Olivia's legs and purring, which was what the vague growling was called. Cat never talked. She did limp, though. Poor thing.

Olivia reluctantly carried her blanket outside of her tent and spread it to capture sunlight rather than huddling under its warmth.

Then she Googled the Infoweb for information on cat health.

Although Olivia had thought cats were mythical and reading just rare, cat-lovers had posted tens of thousands of sims demonstrating exactly how to handle a cat under virtually any circumstance, including circumstances Olivia definitely didn't want to imagine. Sorting through that long list of sims was challenging, but Olivia's cop training proved useful once again and she was quickly sorting, discarding, and tagging.

She nearly discarded a nursery sim called 'C is for Cat' before she realized that the 'C' in the title referred to the character 'C' and that the character stood for a sound.

She downloaded the sim, and played it through her phone.

It wasn't easy, but the sim identified sounds with characters. Identified as pet-related material, a reading sim had slipped through the cracks.

An hour, and some major cat scratches later, Olivia had made sense of an entire paragraph from one of the books.

She hoped her reading would get faster. She also hoped that the book would get less boring.

At this rate, it would take her decades to get through the first book. But she'd made some progress—she'd learned that the book was about politics. Politics, it turned out, was how people had resolved disputes before the Corporate Consensus.

So, how the heck could that help?

When her stomach gurgled, Olivia ate more food bars, and drank more water. When she got tired, she slept. When she got antsy, she improved the alarm system she was gradually putting in place around her camp, or used the miniconstructor to make the camp a bit more permanent. And she made sure she spent an hour a day on exercises, gradually completing her healing. Mostly, though, she read.

* * * *

Piecing out the letters in each word, sounding the combinations and trying to fit the resulting sounds into the patterns of known words provided a challenge similar to the puzzle-sims Olivia had played when she'd been a kid, or to the more adult versions that had been part of her police training as a young adult. It was slow, but kind of fun.

The subject matter was something else. Olivia wondered if Julia had played an elaborate hoax on her, tricking her into spending so many hours decoding a few paragraphs of content into something that was clearly incorrect.

She tried to keep an open mind. After all, politics had been important for a long time before it had been replaced by economically efficient systems. Earlier philosophers might have achieved some insights that could open the doors to a different future. Still, the notion that voting would be based on just being a warm body rather than on economic contribution seemed positively backward. How could property rights be maintained if citizens could just vote themselves all the code they wanted?

The challenging part was, Olivia didn't know if the answers she needed were there or if she'd recognize them when she saw them.

A couple of times over the weeks, she had visitors.

A male couple waited politely outside the boundaries of her site until she could invite them in. They warned her about roughing it through the Texas winters and introduced her to the concept of barter, trading small amounts of trace minerals she needed for her diet for a pair of solar blankets.

The next visitor didn't want to barter, he wanted to take. He set off a whole set of alarms as he crashed through her warning system and pulled a projectile weapon on her, demanding that she strip down and get naked for him.

She did a strip—plucking his weapon from his grip and walloping him with it.

When she'd been a cop, she would have either mind-altered or terminated him for his attack. But she'd done a lot of things when she'd been a cop—things she no longer felt comfortable with.

She settled for giving him a couple of serious bruises and a warning that she'd come hunting for him and finish the job if she heard of him attacking any other women in the area.

Then she physically threw him off of her site and into the filthy stream— the runoff, she'd earlier learned, came from an upstream cow-farm, the corporate owners clearly using the stream to reduce the energy demand that recycling cow-dung would have created.

As she watched him struggle out of the icy water and run full-speed away from her while keeping his face turned to watch that she wasn't coming after him, she realized that she'd done something different. That she'd changed.

Her initial self-defense had been pure cop. Her decision on punishment hadn't come from cop training at all. It had been influenced by what she was reading in that crazy politics book. Discussions of justice and justifications for forceful behavior had seemed bizarre to her when she'd first read them. In her world, everything rules were based on property rather than ethics. Crazy or not, new concepts resonated in her brain and become a part of her thought process.

They weren't memes. Not like those Interfaith viruses Sammy had planted in her. But thousands of years of political thought, going back to the ancient Greeks of all things, were so compelling that they stuck in her brain and changed her, even if the logical part of her brain refused to accept them.

After all, why should *she* care whether the creep preyed on some *other* free-cit female? She had no property connection to those other women, didn't know them, wasn't in some corporate arrangement. They weren't paying her for protection.

* * * *

Winter hit in earnest before Olivia had finished reading even her first book, but things started making sense to her.

She didn't have a solution, but she thought that Julia was right. Something in those books, combined with the type of training in contracts she'd been given as a cop, might give free-code a chance.

It was time to get in touch with her friends, to come home.

Unfortunately, she didn't have a clue how to do it.

She posted cryptic messages on the Infoweb, hoping her carefully selected tags would jump out at Martin or Julia.

If they were still free, they weren't responding.

Not a huge surprise. Shenker had broadcast her betrayal, complete with 3-D of her rattling off GPS coordinates and badmouthing free-code. Of course they'd steer clear of her.

Given that the police had planted bugs on her, she couldn't just go searching.

She needed help if she was going to connect with them—someone they would trust. She wasn't sure, but she had an idea of where she could get it.

She grabbed the *Texas Code of County and City Governments* text, replaced the slim high-pressure tires on her bicycle with knobby things that would provide at least a bit of traction in the muddy and icy mess that was a Dallas winter, and headed off across the tundra-like grasses of the area she'd picked for her refuge. It was time for her to visit the neighbors.

Shenker

Olivia was moving.

Shenker suppressed his urge to get up and dance. Over the weeks since he'd interrogated Olivia, he'd divided his time between watching her and searching for the free-coders and spies. His gut told him that Olivia would be back in contact with the others, that he could follow her and use her again, to unravel the entire system of betrayal. As weeks had turned into months, he'd started to doubt those instincts.

He'd forgotten how patient Olivia could be. She'd waited to see what the Police Corporation would do, hoping she'd slipped off the radar screen.

She couldn't know was that he'd planted a bug on her, that he could watch her from miles away.

He rigged a proximity alarm to warn him if Olivia returned unexpectedly, then called up a ground car. He didn't know how long Olivia would be gone—or even if she planned on returning to the homespace she'd built—but getting caught snooping would undermine his efforts to fool her into believing she was unwatched.

He almost expected her to double back, but she kept moving south, and he moved in.

Olivia's alarms were perfectly laid out, but they were cheap Interfaith models. A call to police central got him the override codes and he walked in right past them.

Her next guardian was tougher, though. A furry little mammal, brown and gold, with sharp claws and teeth, attacked him as he pushed aside the solar panels and stepped into the homespace.

Shenker barely resisted the urge to kick the thing as it worried at the tough buckyball construction of his trousers. But his AI identified the animal as a domesticated mammal. Apparently Olivia had adopted some ratepayer habits and was keeping a pet.

Instead of hurting it, he bent down and held out a hand to it.

Big mistake. The thing jumped at his face, ripping those sharp little claws against his nose, barely missing his eyes.

He got out of the way in a hurry. "You're a protective little critter, aren't you?"

The animal made a strange moaning sound, but didn't seem inclined to speak English. Which was lucky for both of them. If it could speak, Shenker wouldn't have been able to leave it behind.

The cat kept worrying at his legs, but her teeth and claws didn't penetrate his pants' armored fabric, so he ignored the animal and turned his attention to Olivia's homespace.

A couple more traps, one electronic and one purely mechanical, guarded obvious hiding places. They would have caught a less wary spy but Shenker disarmed them carefully, only to discover Olivia had nothing hidden behind them.

The homespace's AI resisted at first, but finally coughed up the information that nobody but Olivia and the furry mammal had visited in weeks.

Given her time with the free-coders, he expected to find something subversive—or at least intellectual property violations in the A.I. or constructor. Instead, the only designs registered on Olivia's constructor were publicly available Infoweb stock, or paid-for Interfaith models.

The stack of paper books had been printed before the consensus took over and he didn't recognize any of the publishers as current corporate entities. Someone might make a case that reading hundred-year-old books without paying for them was an IP violation but Shenker didn't think it would fly. Besides, Olivia couldn't read, so how could she have been violating IP? Those had to be decorative, or fuelstock for her constructor.

He flipped through the books, which came from something called the Dallas Public Library, but couldn't make any sense of them, not even when he had central scan and translate into speech.

He was set to go when he noticed the little animal still gnawing at his leg.

A quick search told him that the animals had a chemical dependency on a drug called catnip. He uploaded a catnip design into Olivia's constructor, produced a small amount as he winced at the price, and tossed it at the animal.

The cat lost all interest in him and blissed out, rolling and wallowing in the little ball of catnip he'd produced.

Which gave him time to make his escape.

He'd been certain he would discover something important, convinced that Olivia and the free-coders were somehow in contact. It saddened him that Olivia had lost so much, had apparently reconciled herself to subsistence. On the other hand, that might be the only way she could stay alive.

He was so certain she'd given up, he almost didn't bother setting the cameras. But Shenker believed in overkill.

Olivia

The male couple Olivia had bartered with over the months were both outside their geodesic dome of a homespace, tossing a bright red floating disk into the air for a large yellow animal to chase.

She froze when she saw it, quickly Googling for some reference.

If the reality of Cat was different from the sim version, the reality of the dog was even more dramatically at variance. This animal had only the vaguest resemblance to the bouncy and fluffy talking animations that she thought of when she considered the word. It also had nothing to do with the cat-sized animals she'd seen ratepayers carrying.

One of the guys, Pete, spotted her and called for the dog. Like the dog, Pete's hair was reddish-blond, but she didn't recognize the almost bear-like body sculpt. Mike, in contrast, was shorter, slender, dark-haired, and had blue eyes that wouldn't quite meet hers.

"Hey, Olivia," Pete said. "Great day to be out and about, huh?"

"If you like it cold. From the frozen stuff on the ground, it has to be below zero."

"Like I said, it's great. Say, I hear you were bothered by that Charles jerk. Mike and I chased him out of the neighborhood but if you hear from him again, let us know and we'll make sure he regrets coming back."

If Charles was the wanna-be rapist, Olivia didn't think he'd be back. Still, she was curious. "Why should you care? Not that I don't appreciate it, but it isn't as if he'd be interested in you." Both because they were male, and because they had a large dog to guard their place. Cat might be deadly against small rodents, but she wouldn't exactly frighten human-sized invaders.

"You haven't been a free-cit long, have you?"

"Just since I moved here a couple of months ago. Why?"

"Most of us, the ones worth knowing, help each other out. What goes around comes around, right?"

That didn't make sense. The chances of needing help from someone she'd helped herself seemed incredibly low. Still, it gave her an excuse to bring up what she'd wanted to talk about.

"Speaking of help, there's something I need help with. I've been trying to get in touch with some friends for months now, and I can't seem to get through to them through the Infoweb. I thought you might be able to do something I couldn't."

The dog and Mike approached her and Pete, then the dog ran over to Olivia, sniffing at her as if she was the most delicious thing he'd ever inhaled.

She inched her hands toward her weapon belt, not wanting to do anything dramatic while the two men seemed unconcerned, but thinking that a weapon might just be the thing if the dog decided she was a tasty morsel packaged in a ready-to-eat format.

"Come on, Max," Mike said. "You're making Olivia nervous."

Max, the dog, gave Olivia a couple of looks, but finally responded to Mike's instructions.

Which surprised her as much as anything. Cat never responded to her orders, except to stick its nose in the air and deliberately do what she'd told the animal not to do.

"Olivia, tell us more about your friends. How do you expect us to contact them if you haven't been able to?"

She couldn't think of a reason not to tell them the whole story. Considering what Shenker had broadcast, it wasn't like she had any secrets. She started at the beginning, her cop background, Merryweather's murder, and then her fortuitous meeting with Martin, Justin, and the others.

"So you see," she concluded, "they probably think I betrayed them but I really need to get back in touch with them."

Mike nodded sympathetically but Pete's forehead wrinkled. "Why?"

"Why what?"

"Why do you need to get in touch with them? Wouldn't you just be putting them in danger?"

She hadn't told anyone about her discoveries and she wasn't going to start with guys who seemed nice but who might just be police spies.

"Because they're my friends."

"Friends are based on shared interests," Pete quoted from the official educational policy of the C.C. "You were friends when you shared an interest in free-code. Now that it's over, what's the shared goal?"

She wrung her hands. She'd thought she had already questioned her basic beliefs, but Pete made the dissonance between what she'd been taught and what she'd learned so much stronger. "Shared experience. Shared hopes. Shared loss."

"None of those sound very economic, Olivia."

She stuttered a couple of times, looking for a way of disagreeing before she realized they were right—and she just didn't care. "So?"

Mike laughed. "She got you there, Pete."

"I was wondering if she got it herself."

This was amusing for the two men. It wasn't that funny for her.

"I don't know what you're talking about. I came to you for help, not so you could give me a bunch of tests."

"Well, we're not going to help you track down fellow free-cits if you're going to turn them over to the police."

"The police won. Shenker got his completion bonus and the T-50 is still on top of the world."

"Did you know that two corporations fell out of the T-50 last year? Another three were acquired by other T-50 members."

"No. I also don't know what that has to do with anything."

Pete nodded. "I'll explain it then. The T-50 is self-sustaining because corporations who don't look to the future don't stay in it. If I were a betting man, I'd put my money on someone in the smarter companies in the T-50 worrying that somebody, someday, might be able to figure out a solution to the free-code dilemma. That smart exec is still looking, still hunting, still worried. Not worried enough to spend a lot, maybe. Not worried enough to shut down access to centercity the way Shenker did. But how much could it cost to hire one broken-down failed ex-cop to track down the people she claimed were her friends?"

"That's crap." Unfortunately, Olivia couldn't argue with Pete's logic. The harder she looked, the more it would seem that Pete's theory was right and that she was just a cop after a target. And there was no way to win. If she gave up looking, Martin and the designers would figure she was baiting a trap for them, expecting them to walk into her den. Either way, she'd never see her friends again.

"Is it crap, Olivia?"

"I see where you're coming from, but that isn't true of me. I'm definitely not with the cops and I'm definitely not interested in betraying my friends, even if the cops are still looking for them."

"I wish we could help you," Pete said. "But it just doesn't make economic sense."

"Come on in and have lunch with us, though," Mike added. "Just because we can't trust you doesn't mean we aren't neighbors."

Did she want to eat with people who didn't trust her, wouldn't do anything to help her? To her surprise, Olivia discovered she did. Weeks with Cat as her only companion, made her yearn for human conversation.

She couldn't remember having that kind of need for human company before her adventure with the designers. Under the Corporate Consensus, social contact came from family and from sims so hyper-realistic that almost everyone spent their free time in created worlds rather than in the physical one. Hanging around with friends, sharing meals with them, was something you left behind by the time you were ten.

"Sure. Lunch sounds great."

It was great.

Mike and Pete gardened.

Olivia tried not to think about food as actual plants grown in actual dirt and given nutrients, if she could believe the guys, by actual animal waste. Instead, she pretended they were pulling her leg and had downloaded ratepayer-quality meals.

The men entertained her with stories of their near escapes from police raids, of sneaking into long abandoned gardens to gather seeds, cuttings, and roots, and of their communications with fellow free-cits from other areas. Not just free-cits from Dallas or nearby corporate cities like Fort Worth or Austin, but those from near-mythical corporate cities like New York, Los Angeles, and Chicago.

Oddly, because they hadn't served anything alcoholic or hallucinogenic, Olivia's brain started feeling woozy before Mike brought out his piece de resistance, a lemon chiffon pie.

"I'll have to tell Cat about this," she murmured… just before she lost control of her body and her face smacked directly down into the slice of pie Mike had set in front of her.

"Really bad timing," Pete observed, his voice sounding like it came from a distorter. "And we'd better do something about her animal."

"I guess. But how was I supposed to know she'd like the broccoli so much?"

Martin

"**Olivia's** ready to come in." Justin burst into Martin's lab, followed by Julia and Angie.

Relief surged through Martin. He'd worried that sending Pete and Mike to watch Olivia had just put more people in danger, but he owed her a lot. "Finally. Do we know what happened?"

"She got in touch with Pete and Mike—asked for their help. Well, they're helping."

"We need to get a move on it," Julia said. "When we sent Vinson the coffee and stuff, we were taking a risk that he'd come after us. They'll be watching Olivia. The longer we wait, the more likely they'll get suspicious."

"Justin and I will go," Martin said. "I want you to stay here and watch the lab."

"You can stick your lab up your intestine. Olivia is my friend. I'm going."

"You already mentioned we're under some time pressure here." Martin spoke as calmly and soothingly as he could. "Arguing will slow us down."

"I'm not arguing, I'm coming."

"Perhaps you should both go," Justin said. "I'll shut down the lab and prepare for a move."

"You think the cops will follow."

Justin shrugged. "They will if they can."

Martin looked around. He'd spent more time in this lab than he'd spent anyplace since he'd left Corporate Houston. It had become, if not home, at least a place he was used to, a place that represented safety and security to his children.

"Watch over your brother," he instructed Angie. "And follow Justin's directions. I'm counting on you."

"Okay, dad."

"Julia and I are heading out, then." He changed identities, set synchs with Justin and Angie, and headed for the door.

Julia matched him step for step.

"Don't you have to, you know, get ready?" he asked.

Julia glared at him. "I've been ready to help my friend for months now. So let's do it and not talk about it."

* * * *

Despite the burning need to hurry, Martin drove slowly, taking care not to destroy the solar grids that extended into the narrow streets. It took hours for them to cover the distance, and he begrudged each instant.

Julia didn't help. She'd brought a hand slate and was editing designs as he navigated, but he suspected she'd have to redo everything she touched today.

Pete and Mike kept them current, let them know how much of the narcotic they'd administered, and informed them when Olivia finally fell asleep.

He would have laughed at the 3-D of her face falling into an untouched orange chiffon pie if he hadn't been afraid he'd puke instead.

"I've sent Pete to gather her animal," Mike reported a few minutes later. "Shouldn't take more than an hour so he'll be back about the same time you get here."

"Are you kidding? Someone may be watching her homespace."

"You don't abandon a pet." Mike's voice was as cold as the Texas winter. "But—"

"She'll need Cat," Julia put in. "Don't argue with what you can't change."

He just gritted his teeth and drove.

Mike had moved Olivia to a stretcher and, sure enough, Pete arrived with Cat minutes after Martin and Julia had gotten there.

Together they bundled Olivia into the back of Martin's truck, put the little feline in her arms, and headed due west.

They needed to confuse the trail, and Julia needed to give Olivia a good scanning to discover what the cops had planted on her. One thing Martin was certain of—Olivia was marked, and with high-quality spy gear rather than standard ID tags. Until they could scrub her system, she was a ticking time bomb.

Olivia

Her head hurt.

Olivia struggled for consciousness trying, and failing, to remember when she'd gone to sleep.

Cat's reassuring purring assured her that all was well, that she was safe and at home. Some vague near-memory denied that possibility: warned that things were out of control—again.

She opened her eyes and saw darkness so complete it could only be artificial.

She tried to clutch Cat to her, but her arms didn't respond. Still, her spasm of movement got her noticed by the little carnivore, who rewarded her with multiple claws digging through her tunic and poking her skin. Ouch.

Think, Olivia. Scan your systems. Don't panic.

Scanning, though, scared her even more. Her phone failed to respond and her mediplant didn't register. She was as empty as an Interfaith sermon. And with the absolute darkness around her, she suspected she was permanently blind.

"Looks like she's coming back to life. Guess your broccoli wasn't fatal after all."

Pete's voice sounded like it was coming from a long way away, but at least she could hear it. She should have realized she wasn't deaf from hearing Cat purr, but she still felt perversely grateful.

"So you guys are no different from Charles after all?" she demanded. "You drug me and then hold me as a sex slave?"

She'd picked up the word 'slave' from her politics reading. It wasn't a word she had found anywhere on the Infoweb and she'd had to guess its meaning from context.

"A sex slave," Mike protested. "What a charming idea. The only problem is, Pete and I wouldn't have much use for a female sex slave. Now if you were a cute boy, I could—"

"You can sell me though. So it…" She mentally cursed herself for blabbing. If they hadn't thought of it on their own, only an idiot would give them the idea.

"Oh, Olivia. You are so untrusting. Why do you believe the worst about us?"

"Maybe because you drugged me, ripped out my implants, cut my optical nerves, and are holding me captive."

"She has a point, Mike," Pete agreed. "That would make me suspicious too."

"Surely she understands we're doing it for her own good."

"Would you guys cut the comedy act and tell me what's going on?"

"You asked for help and we're giving it to you."

Starting with blinding her? She didn't think so.

Cut off from her nanobes, she took a purely physical approach to preparing herself for whatever would come next. She had no way of knowing whether one of the guys was checking on her so she tried to move as little as possible while she stretched each muscle in her body, used physical effort and strength of will to send blood into every extreme end of her body so that, when the time to move arrived, when she had that momentary opportunity to escape, she wouldn't be convulsed with cramps.

Cat walked across her stomach, clearly disturbed by her small muscle contractions.

The vehicle the guys were using to transport her was practically soundless, the ride smooth. Still, Olivia picked up the sensation of acceleration when they went around corners, the smallest change in pressure in her inner ear as they climbed a hill or descended into a valley.

After what seemed like multiple hours, the vehicle slammed to an abrupt stop.

"We're here. Everyone out."

Cool air invaded the cabin and outdoor sounds and scents broke into the silence and filtered air that had cocooned her during the voyage.

She recognized Pete from the sound of his breathing as he fumbled with her bonds. Mike must be at the door.

If she was going to escape, this was her chance.

She uncoiled.

A backfist toward the sound of Pete's breathing caught him in the face, distracting him and propelling her toward the door.

She kicked toward where Mike's voice had last sounded—and connected with nothing but air. Without pausing, she retargeted and kicked again, this time connecting with something solid. A head, maybe, from the way it snapped away from her foot.

"Jeez, Olivia. That hurts."

She hadn't killed him—which was okay. But if he could talk like that, she hadn't disabled him much, either.

Still, she didn't have time to play. The men were both bigger than she, and neither was blind. Cop training wouldn't protect her indefinitely.

She sniffed the air, detected a breeze, and sprinted directly toward it. If Mike and Pete had parked their vehicle outdoors, one direction was as good as another to a blind woman. If they'd stopped inside a structure, the wind might indicate a path toward escape.

She was running full speed when she hit a wall, splashed, and collapsed.

"Guess we didn't persuade her we were harmless," Mike observed. "You okay, Olivia?"

She tried to scan again, forgetting they'd ripped out her phone. "I think I broke something."

"You were running pretty fast. Good thing you just hit solar panels."

She sat up. Yep. More cracked ribs. This time she couldn't count on her brother and the Interfaith for a cure.

"You could have killed yourself, idiot. Even a citizen should know better than to run into the walls." The voice was familiar but so completely out of place it took Olivia a second to recognize it.

"Julia? What are you doing here?"

Julia

Julia had learned more about bio-sculpting and nerve-nanobe interface in the three hours she'd worked on Olivia than in all of the lectures she'd attended.

Body-scrub and Body-sculpt designers tended to hold themselves apart, as if they weren't like other designers, as if they worked magic while mere flavor enhancers wasted their time. From what Julia had seen inside Olivia, they had a right to be elitist.

For sure, whoever had implanted Olivia knew their job. While Martin had driven around Dallas, switching vehicles, staying under foliage and in radio-occluded regions, Julia had probed deep into Olivia. It had taken her two hours just to scope out the extent of the probes and beacons the cops had hidden inside of Olivia's body and assess the triggers and traps they'd left to protect them. Anyone who'd yanked them out with something as simple as Martin's phone-busting technology would end up with one dead ex-cop.

By the time she'd finished modifying Martin's scrub, her code resembled a cobweb more than clean structured design. If Julia hadn't had access to the entire free-code library, she couldn't have done it at all. As it was, she'd collapsed into unconsciousness when she'd finally completed her design, constructed a half-liter, and introduced it intravenously into Olivia's system.

Which is how she'd missed Olivia's panic-stricken entrance into their makeshift lab.

"I'm blind," Olivia said.

Julia handed Olivia the next stage of her scrub.

"Why not just upload to my mediplant?"

"Because your 'plant is shot. Now swallow every drop.

Julia had been pretty proud of the chocolate flavor she'd constructed to hide the ashy taste of nanobes, but Olivia swallowed with a distinct lack of enthusiasm.

The ex-cop perked up, though, when her vision returned.

"I thought they'd cut my optical nerve."

"Signal blocking," Julia explained. "Your fellow cops embedded really deep beacons."

Once Olivia could see, and once her completely reinstalled mediplant reported she was okay to walk, Julia took her on a tour of the complex.

The lab was identical to dozens of others they'd scattered well outside Corporate Dallas. Mostly underground, with discreet solar panels linked at a distance far enough to keep them safe if police drones fired missiles at them, it was ugly and only marginally functional. A couple of security bots, their heads protected by far more armor than the one they'd smacked in their escape from the police, checked on them but Julia ordered them away.

"What about Kansas?" Olivia asked when the two of them were alone. "Did you get my messages that she might be the traitor?"

"We got the message," Julia said.

"You didn't kill her, did you? You know Shenker could have been lying to me, right, trying to make us fight among ourselves?"

"We didn't kill her. She's still working on the project."

"But—"

"We told her what we knew and let her decide whether to go back to centercity or stay in one of the labs. McKensie persuaded her to stay. The two of them have their own little homespace a hundred kilometers from here, out near Corporate Mineral Wells. They're working on special projects."

"Special projects? That sounds scary."

Julia laughed. "We set up a fake design company for them, registered through Corporate Mineral Wells. Their designs make most of the money we're taking in these days. They design sculpts, fashion attire, and footwear for ratepayers. Not just in corporate Dallas, either. They've got orders coming in from all over the world. You'd be surprised how much a ratepayer will pay for a one-off designed pair of shoes."

"Oh." Olivia looked uncomfortable, as if she'd been asleep for the months she'd been gone and the whole world had changed in her absence. "This will probably sound like a shift in direction, but that reminds me, I found your books. You know, the ones we took from the Dallas Public Library and that you thought would help us figure out the solution. They're mostly okay, considering they fell for a couple of hundred meters. I brought some, but maybe Pete and Mike know where they ended up."

Guilt squeezed Julia. "Oh, Olivia—are you still worrying about that stuff? McKensie had to be right—how could old textbooks do anything for us?"

Another thought added to her guilt. "That's why you stayed away, isn't it? You thought you couldn't come back until you'd figured it out?"

"It's my job."

Julia threw her arms around her friend. "We've had to lower our expectations. Even Martin is starting to come around to the fact that we can't just change the world, we have to live in it."

Olivia couldn't have much strength, but she pushed Julia away anyway. "That's gray ooze, Julia. There is a way. You just have to look at things differently."

Okay, so Olivia still had those inadequacy feelings. Julia knew how to deal with those. "What we really need is more security. With the constant moves, we haven't been able to get control of ourselves. I was hoping you could take a look at our communications systems, and maybe help us design some new security bots."

"Don't patronize me, Julia. I spent the past months learning to read and going through some really boring politics books, but I've got an idea now. Do you know that the old cities were really corporate structures?"

"As in Corporate Dallas? Everyone knows—"

"Not that," Olivia interrupted. "The old-time cities were legally corporate, themselves, but they weren't run by shareholders."

"How else."

"See. We need the books to see possibilities."

Julia was happy her friend was back, but she had enough to do with the project not to want to spend hours discussing Olivia's discovery of ancient philosophy. "You can keep working on that old stuff in between helping with our security. I sort of bribed Vinson to back off, but I've got a feeling that's wearing a bit thin and he's going to come looking for us soon."

"Speaking of which, where are the others?" Olivia looked around. "I'm really happy that you made it out alive, but what about Martin and his kids? What about Justin?"

"The cops caught a couple of our coders a few weeks ago. Fortunately, they were ratepayers for Corporate Fort Worth and Corporate Dallas is having enough problems without yanking Fort Worth more into the act. So they're treating them like visiting guests in centercity. And Martin, well—"

Martin

"**Martin** is fine." He decided to join the conversation before anyone said anything he didn't want to hear.

He'd navigated the truck twenty kilometers from the makeshift lab, stripped it of anything that might lead the police to him, and sprinkled it with eater nanobes, and bicycled back.

He'd hoped to be there by the time Olivia came out of her coma, but police roadblocks had delayed him.

"I've been worrying about you." Olivia looked around. "Where are Angie and Jimmy?"

Well, that showed where he stood on the importance meter. "Angie has been doing a design apprenticeship with Julia. Jimmy has been blowing things up—which is about as perfect as life gets for a five-year-old boy."

Olivia gave him a tired smile.

She looked a bit shaken up—with blood oozing from a cut on her face, and scrapes on her knuckles. But a few months of living in the wild had given her confidence she hadn't had before.

"I don't have the entire authentication problem figured out yet," she said, "but I'm onto something. I'm going to need some help, though."

Out of sight from Olivia, Julia rolled her eyes. Apparently he'd walked into the middle of a conversation.

"Speaking of help, I already told Olivia we need her to beef up our security," Julia said.

"If there's a solution to the authentication issue, we need that more than anything," Martin said.

Olivia nodded, then slanted Julia a 'told you so' look. "The old cities and towns were corporate entities."

Olivia seemed to think that meant something, so he waited.

Clearly that wasn't the response she was looking for. "Don't you get it? They may still be out there."

"Like Shangri-La?"

"Huh?"

He shook his head. "Never mind. I don't know what you mean, still out there. The corporations took over everywhere."

"But did they terminate the old contracts."

Okay, now he thought he was tracking. "You're thinking that if we could somehow lay claim to one of those, we'd have a valid corporation structure. So what, though? We already have several corporate structures registered. If we authenticate on those, the local consensus will just cut us off. Believe me, we've thought of—"

"What is a consensus?" Olivia interrupted. "It's the group of corporations controlling a corporate city. But if we took over a city, *we* would *be* the consensus."

That rocked him on his heels. The beauty of free-code was that it opened the doors for anyone to be a designer. Citizens and ratepayers alike could create, and the huge waste of ninety percent of North America's population would end. Because he distrusted the corporate structure, he'd never even dreamed of setting up an entire consensus. Even incorporating had pushed at his ethical boundaries.

"If those city corporations are still valid, they still have shareholders," Julia said. "Heirs of the original owners. And no way are those shareholders going to roll over for you and just give up their ownership."

Olivia's laughter reminded Martin of sweet warm peaches picked right off the trees that had grown behind his homespace in Houston centercity. "You know who owned the old-time cities, Julia? Citizens."

"Citizens? But that's redic—"

"The city's citizens elected representatives, sort of like the board of directors of a normal corporation, but working for the citizens rather than for shareholders."

"So you're thinking—"

"I'm thinking we need to find a deserted old-time town with a still-valid corporate charter, set our labs and homespaces there, and have an election. Once we've elected our representatives, we'll hit Corporate San Jose up for the documentation, and register as a Corporate Consensus."

Julia looked as shell-shocked as Martin felt. "How did they decide how many votes each citizen got?"

"Everyone got one vote."

"Even the kids." He hadn't seen Angie arrive, but apparently she'd been listening.

"I think you had to be eighteen."

"Unfair."

"Maybe we can change the rules once we get things going."

"Sweet."

"Of course that would take a majority of the votes so you'll want to make sure everyone understands how mature you are."

"I guess that leaves Jimmy out."

"Jimmy's been doing a lot of good," Martin said.

"Anyway," Olivia looked around, then met his eyes directly. "Those old books told me about the way things used to be organized. I need help, better access, and some certainty that the cops aren't bugging me so I can figure out whether my theory is right, and which, if any, of those old corporate charters may still be valid. Which is why I needed to come home."

Martin's throat threatened to choke him. He swallowed, hard. "I'm glad you're back with us, Olivia."

"Come on, dad." His daughter's voice sounded in his head, through his phone, although she barely moved her lips. "You can do better than that."

He shrugged. Angie kept pushing her romance idea and, frankly, Olivia was even more appealing to him now than she had been before. But they were too much alike—both people motivated by missions, driven by something that went way beyond the basics of creating a home and family. Olivia deserved someone with a permanent home, someone who could balance her rather than someone who would only encourage her flights of fantasy.

One thing was certain. The cops were still coming and unless they figured out a way to hold them off, they'd both be dead before they got romantic.

Olivia

"**Sunnyvale's** charter was canceled as well." Justin rubbed his eyes, then sent Olivia the updated database of one-time communities in the Dallas area.

As Olivia scrolled down the list, a sea of red check marks overwhelmed her. It had seemed like such a brilliant idea, but those long-ago corporate types hadn't been stupid. Someone must have realized that citizen-controlled cities might rise again.

A few flashes of yellow showed that they hadn't gotten conclusive answers on every old-time community, but Sunnyvale had been a major hope. The town had been small enough, back when the corporations had won, that she'd let herself hope it might have been ignored.

"We might as well keep looking," Justin said.

She scrolled through the list one more time, then froze it when her eye caught one of the names in yellow. *The Colony.*

From her political reading, she knew that colonies had been sent to North America and had broken away from their economic and political masters in England more than three hundred years earlier. Once they'd gotten their independence, they'd created something different from the old system. Olivia didn't want to carry that analogy too far—after all, what they'd created had ended up in the corporate consensus. Still, the symbolism seemed promising. And she didn't have anything else to go on.

"What about this The Colony thing."

Justin went blank for a minute as he reviewed his notes. "I haven't found any reference to a canceled charter."

"Meaning it might still be valid."

"Even if it is, unless we produce the actual articles of incorporation, I doubt we'd be able to persuade anyone of it."

She stood. "Well, what are we waiting for? Let's see what we can find."

Olivia

Neothermite was a great example of the kind of thing they'd have to be careful with when they opened code to everyone. A child with a design set and a constructor could destroy half of centercity in a few hours.

For opening an ancient armored-steel safe, though, Neothermite was just the thing. Julia had happily cooked up the formula and constructed them a couple of tubes of jell-like cutters.

Olivia edged past a rusting steel door, brushed dust off the ancient safe still in the wall of what had once been city hall, and carefully molded a tube of Neothermite around the locking mechanism.

"Close your eyes," she said. "It'll flare up faster than they can polarize." Waiting only to make sure Julia and Martin followed her instructions, Olivia fired the igniter.

Free-code neothermite was good stuff—at least as hot as police issue construct. The meter-cube safe had been built to protect its contents against ordinary burglars, vandals, and such threats as building fires. It rolled over for the neothermite like a chick-bot in a males-only entertainment sim.

White-hot droplets of steel still fell when the cutting explosive flared out but Olivia couldn't make herself wait for it to cool. She pulled a hunk of iron rebar from the building's deteriorating roof, knocked off the safe's door, and pulled out the sheaf of papers before oxygen could flood in and heat-flare the safe's contents.

"Well?" Martin looked over her right shoulder and Julia over her left as she spread the papers over the tree-wood surface of the executive desk.

"Don't rush me, and don't elbow me."

Feeling like an archeologist in a classic sim, Olivia neatly sifted through the papers.

A stack of bank statements showed the town's income and expenses. A significant part of the revenue came from things called 'vehicle registration' and 'vehicular violations.' Olivia hadn't thought old-time vehicles were smart enough to violate anything. Modern vehicles certainly couldn't become ratepayers no matter how intelligent their AIs. The idea of vehicular ratepayers struck her as funny but explaining the joke to the impatient duo at her side was hopeless.

Further down in the stack of documents, she found discussions of zoning variances, all of which seemed to be pure violations of the sanctity of property.

She had almost given up hope on finding anything important when she turned over a fancy engraved document.

"That's it." Julia's voice was a mere breath.

"I guess so. We might as well—"

Whatever else she'd planned to say vanished when Martin put his hands around her waist, tossed her up in the air, then caught her and kissed her on the mouth.

"You are an incredible woman, Olivia. For the first time, I actually think we might win."

A rush of pleasure shot through her before she realized Martin was simply exuberant about their findings.

"Don't bet on it, Martin." She reluctantly extracted herself from his grasp. Sure, his hands felt great on her body, but this wasn't the time to let her brain get all mushy. Finding a hundred-year-old piece of paper might help, but it wasn't going to keep free-coders alive all by itself. That piece of paper hadn't saved the life of a single free-coder or free-cit in all the years it had been sitting there.

Still, the paper held what she wanted.

The State of Texas, an ancient jurisdictional authority that had apparently included Corporate Dallas, Corporate Houston, Corporate San Antonio, Corporate Austin, and even far-off Corporate El Paso, granted official corporate recognition to the City of The Colony.

"How do we appoint ourselves its board of directors?" Julia cut right to the chase.

Olivia scanned down the document. "I don't see anything about that here."

"There have to be rules." Martin didn't seem bothered. "A corporate charter wouldn't include Board of Directors election details. That would be in bylaws. Modern corporate charters are the same."

"So we've got to find bylaws." She pawed through the stack of papers she'd rescued from the safe.

"I sure hope wishful thinking works, because that's all we're going on." Julia paused a beat. "Oh, crap."

Taking a chance, they'd already moved a big chunk of the free-coders within what had once been the city limits of The Colony.

Before they'd gone on their archeological dig, they'd laid intrusion sensors everywhere around the place.

And one of those alarms had just triggered.

Shenker

They hadn't gotten sloppy, exactly, but months had passed since the police had raided any of the free-code labs and repeated incompetence by the Interfaith Enforcers and continued conflict with Corporate Houston had pushed the hunt for free-code into the background.

Still, Shenker kept up the hunt. Olivia's escape directly under his eyes pissed him off, made him question his talent.

No organization, though, can continue indefinitely without leaks. Olivia would warn the coders, cajole them, threaten them to make them keep their covers, to encrypt everything they sent, to hold traffic down to a minimum. But people are social animals. They spend their lives communicating. In modern times, communicating meant phones.

Even police central's quantum computers couldn't dependably or quickly break modern public key encryption, but Shenker didn't care what they were saying, just that they were talking. When a surge of traffic had popped up in a desert area northwest of Corporate Dallas, Shenker guessed it wasn't some new clan of free-cits settling down. Or maybe he'd just hoped.

Now that he saw the defenses, he knew he'd guessed right. No free-cits had design access to the sensors and active bots guarding what was supposed to be abandoned ruins. Only the free-coders had that abundance of design skill.

Which meant he'd found them.

His course of action was clear—notify central, call for a major bombing strike, and get on with it. But bombing Olivia warred with his sense of completion. He wanted her to know that he'd won.

So, he kept radio silence and picked his way through the obstructions. He intentionally let one of the sensors pick up his movement, but only for a moment. The security bots roaming the perimeter looked nasty and he didn't think they'd respect a police override.

Once he'd triggered their defenses, he pressed forward, using his peripheral vision to check for movement while keeping his focal vision firmly in the ultraviolet range to pick up any active sensors. His camo-suit was designed to be optically inert and emit zero infrared energy, but smart ultraviolet devices could pick up the tiny fluctuation of a suit adjusting itself to new light sources.

He'd penetrated almost all the way to the region where phone chatter had originated when he sensed movement.

It was smooth, practically invisible, low and mean.

Well, she should be. Olivia had been his star student. He was going to have to demonstrate that she had more to learn.

Olivia

Olivia didn't have much hope for an escape. If the cops had arrived in force, no one would get away.

And the intrusion had to be cops. The triggered alarm was three layers deep in her zoned security. Whoever had slipped in was good.

She scanned the mostly open desert to the south of their newly constructed lab complex. As far as she could tell, nothing moved. There was no roar of helicopters, no shadows cast by high-flying drones, nothing to show that anything had changed.

Nothing but the memory of that one alarm.

"We could head toward the violated sensor." Julia waved in the direction from which the alarm had come. "How about I walk in front like we did in Dallas? You know, bait for a trap."

"No point."

"So, what are we doing out here, then? We might as well be helping Martin evacuate our labs."

"If you were good enough to get through the first two rings of sensors, why would you set off the third?"

"Got careless?"

Olivia shrugged. Even cops, especially young cops who hadn't been given the type of apprenticeship Shenker had given her, *could* get overconfident. But triggering exactly one alarm out of the dozens didn't sound careless, it sounded deliberate—a message.

"Do you see anything?" Julia asked.

"Shhh." Not that they were going to hear anything. An intruder good enough to make it this far wouldn't crash around the underbrush.

"Pull up the satellite imagery," she whispered, "and wrap it over the current view. Let me know any discrepancy, I don't care how small."

This was the kind of job *she* should be doing, but Olivia couldn't immerse in satellite imagery if she wanted to stay combat-ready.

"It looks pretty much the same," Julia reported.

"Compensate for shadows. There's got to be some change."

"Like there's a little black stone in yesterday's but it isn't here today? So what? It could be—"

Olivia froze. "Where?"

"Twelve point five meters to the south-south-west."

Olivia launched herself immediately… and ran into a hard fist to her gut.

The black stone came into view as whoever stood on it moved. A kick to her head told her where that foot had gone.

She oriented enough to shift away from the third attack rather than taking it full-on. She grabbed the wrist behind the fist, pulled and twisted.

The faintest blur of a stealth-suit trying to keep up with fast motion told her that her assailant had performed a mid-air flip, easing the pressure on his wrist.

She dropped her grip, got her guard up, and stepped back quickly. Not quickly enough or far enough. A stealth-booted foot connected with her knee.

Her peripheral vision picked up Julia, a large rock in her hand, moving closer.

"Stay back, idiot," she shouted. "You'll get yourself killed."

"Like you wouldn't help if it was me who was getting beat up."

Olivia *was* getting beat up. But an untrained attack by Julia could get the woman hurt and was more likely to distract Olivia than her attacker.

Another blur, followed by a ridge-hand to her temple, proved that Julia had already been too much distraction-for Olivia.

She managed a snap-kick to where the attacker's knee should be and barely connected with something.

Not enough, by a long shot, as an ax-kick to the top of her head proved.

So, he was a headhunter. Over-reliance on a single target could be a weakness. She'd have to hope so, because that last kick made her knees buckle and her brain seemed woozy.

Julia swung her fist-sized rock wildly, missing everything. On the backswing, the rock got away from her, clipping Olivia on her shin.

Instinctively she grabbed at it. Realizing her mistake, she threw a high guard that, for a change, actually managed to block her invisible assailant's attack.

She recognized the snicker and stepped back.

"Shenker?" she groaned. "I thought you'd be living in centercity, flirting with rich ratepayers and making plans for your babies."

The barely visible blur of motion at the boundary between the stealth suit and the greater universe faded as her attacker froze in place.

Then the suit morphed into the dull black of solar-collecting fabric.

Shenker pulled the hood back from his face. "You're still dropping your guard. It'll get you killed some day."

She knew Shenker was on the other side, but she still felt defensive. "I haven't had time to train."

"That's why they invented *Kata*. You can train by yourself, in your own time. It only takes a few meters of space."

"Ohmigod, it's the wanna-be ratepayer with the tongue hanging out of his face." Julia headed toward Shenker with another rock. Unfortunately, she was trying not to be obvious, making it fifty times more obvious than if she'd just strolled up to him. "The jerk who tortured you into giving us away and tried to make us think that you'd betrayed us."

"Tell your little friend," Shenker said, "that she makes me nervous."

"I think she can hear you."

"She's a ratepayer. I don't need the stealth suit to be invisible to her kind."

"Oh." Olivia paused a beat. "Sounds like your move to centercity didn't go as well as you'd hoped."

"What move? When they found out I was a cop, centercity ratepayers refused to go to contract. I even offered more than the asking price for a couple sweet little homespaces that would have been perfect. And the women? They only thing they'd talk to me about was whether I sculpted myself to extra-large size. I'm not about to be the cute new animal in some ratepayer's zoo. For sure they weren't going to have kids with me and let them grow up to become designers or anything important."

"So you decided to come back to work and get another feather on your cap with the destruction of the project, huh?"

Shenker's laugh was bitter. "That's what Vinson wanted. Thought we'd talk first. That's why I let you find me."

Olivia gently rubbed the throbbing knot on the top of her head. "You want to talk, so you clobbered me?"

He shrugged. "Who attacked first?"

"There is that."

"Given our differences, I wasn't sure I'd survive walking up to your compound unstealthed."

Julia dropped her rock and stepped closer. "I might be able to help you get what you want if it's important."

Julia was negotiating, but Olivia couldn't see why. How could Shenker help them?

Shenker's eyes crinkled with humor. "You? Your insurance is expired. You're a free-cit and a renegade now, Julia Turnboldt."

"Being a real ratepayer isn't just about insurance—you and Olivia are living proof of that. But that's not what I'm talking about. Help us and I'll not only make sure your kids can be designers, I'll help *you* become a designer."

He stared at her. Olivia noticed the slightest dilation of his pupils.

Olivia's mind spun like wheels not finding traction. She didn't want Shenker anywhere near her, and certainly didn't want him anywhere near her friends. But he could help her and the project could offer him a way to get what he really wanted. After all, there was only one of her. Shenker had more experience, more access to central, more knowledge of the kind of equipment and resources the Police Corporation could throw into any eventual attack. If Shenker wanted to switch sides, they needed him. If he wanted to destroy them, he could already have done so.

She wouldn't have minded, though, if he'd broken a few ribs or suffered from some tragic pain on his way in.

Martin

Martin had a hard time believing the cop.

Shenker had hunted Olivia and the design team down. He'd tortured Olivia for lab locations. He'd planted her so full of bugs, removing them had nearly killed her. And he'd practically destroyed the project.

But Martin couldn't figure the logic for Shenker to let himself be captured.

If Shenker had told his bosses where he was going, he would have come with a thousand cops—and terminated the project. Which had to mean he was telling the truth.

Just to be sure, Martin had injected him with phone-destroying nanobes.

He stepped back from the now-sleeping cop when he heard footsteps behind him and turned around to see Justin arrive.

"What's up, Justin." He'd been expecting Olivia—or maybe he'd just wanted Olivia. Come to think of it, he never heard Olivia's footsteps. She just appeared.

"You know what Olivia was saying about elections?"

He nodded.

"I just might have something for you."

"Really?"

"Me and the other free-cits aren't helping much on the project, other than eating some of the stuff the designers make us and occasionally setting out some solar panels. So we looked for more old books."

"And?"

"We found something called 'city ordinances.'" Justin held out a filthy and rat-gnawed volume. "It includes rules on who gets to vote and when."

Martin had expected 'bylaws,' but he'd settle for what worked. "Let me get Olivia."

Three minutes later, Olivia, Julia, Angie and Jimmy joined Justin and Martin in his lab. He and Martin had wheeled Shenker off to sleep off his phone replacement.

"You found something about elections?"

Justin handed Olivia the book.

She scanned through it.

If Olivia could teach herself how to read, maybe a lot of citizens could learn how to design. Maybe he and Merryweather hadn't deluded themselves. Then again, Olivia was special.

"It says here we need thirty days notification of an election," she reported. "There's something called a mayor, who is like the board chairman. And city councilmen, who are like board members."

"So who do we run for mayor?" Julia demanded. "Martin?"

Martin let himself consider the possibilities. As head of a corporate consensus, even a tiny one, he could set some standards, create rules that made life worth living. Yeah, he could get into that. "I think—"

"Bad idea," Jimmy said.

"Yeah, dad," Angie piped in. "Everyone would say Corporate Houston is setting up some scam."

"But—"

"They're right," Olivia said. "Run for one of the city council slots. I think our mayor should be a real citizen, not a renegade ratepayer. Someone who understands what it's like to survive with nothing to hope for."

"You aren't talking about yourself, are you?" Julia arched an eyebrow.

"Of course not. I'm a renegade ex-cop. I'm talking about Justin."

The older man sputtered. "But—"

Martin nodded firmly. "Excellent. Justin has leadership skills that, frankly, I don't. And Olivia's right, he understands what it's like to be a citizen. When he talks, other citizens will understand that he's not tossing them a sales pitch."

"But—"

"Justin's running for mayor." Olivia announced it as a done deal. "Martin can run for council. Or maybe you should, Julia."

"I just want to design."

"Okay, Martin runs. We need a couple more. At least one more citizen and one more designer."

Twenty minutes later, Olivia had delegated, decided, and sorted out an election process.

While she did that, Martin got the city ordinances document back and looked through. "In the meantime, we need a chief of police."

"Shenker's got the knowledge and seniority," Olivia admitted.

Julia wrinkled her nose as if her nanofilters had stopped working. "Don't be silly, Olivia. You're it. If you want to hire Shenker, that's between the two of you."

Vinson

"**Corporate** filing anomaly in the Dallas Economic Interest Zone." Police central's AI never showed emotion. But this was an alarm Vinson had never heard before.

"What the heck does that mean?"

"Stand by for data transfer."

Vinson scrolled through the documentation. Clearly the Houston spy was up to something; why wasn't obvious.

He put a call through to Shenker—and got nothing.

Which was weird. Cops respond when they get a call from the chief, and he didn't even get an autoanswer. Come to think of it, he hadn't gotten any reports from Shenker in a week or so.

Something was going on. Which meant Vinson had to get to work.

First, he called his wife.

"I'm working." Like most designers, Maudie thought her job the most important thing in the world.

"I need your help."

A sigh. "All right, Harles. Go ahead."

"Can you think of any reason the free-coders would want a city of their own?"

"That doesn't even mean anything. You don't own a city, you own corporations that, in turn, form a corporate consensus within a city."

Maudie was partially right, but corporate cities were legally corporate entities in their own right. "Suppose you could own a city, though. What could you do with it?"

"Include and exclude corporations, I guess. Define rules for minimum ratepayer requirements. That sort of stuff."

That didn't sound too dangerous. "Tell me more about including and excluding corporations."

Another sigh. "Corporations get their charters from the consensus. The consensus validates them with the verification authority, which allows them to get their public key, which means they can provide validated design code, sims, or other intellectual property. The corporate city's ability to rescind charters is what gives them their leverage. Come on, Harles. You know this stuff."

He did. But he hadn't really thought about what it could mean before. "You're a lifesaver, babe."

"Can I get back to work?"

"Do. I might be late for the next few days. Things are about to get hairy."

"Is it that stupid war? Since we have coffee again, I'm not really that worried about it."

He disconnected and had central pull up everything it could on the ghost town of The Colony.

The Corporate Houston spy was clearly out of control. Even Corporate Houston wouldn't approve of a competing consensus. Free-code was a feint, a tool, not an objective for Houston. Letting renegades have their own pet consensus was insane.

He ignored his phone for the next couple of hours while he researched how a corporate consensus could be created—and almost had a heart attack over the sheer balls of the spy's thinking. Calming his pulse, he turned to historical records of property ownership within The Colony.

He was making slow progress into ancient database records when Louis Brandon overrode his phone block.

"What the hell are you up to, Vinson? Ariel is shitting bricks."

"I'm doing my job, sir." Manipulation of the little gifts from Julia Turnboldt had helped Vinson keep his position, but Ariel kept pushing to have Interfaith Enforcers take over the police contract.

"According to Ariel, while you're 'doing your job,' those free-code freaks have set up a complete operation just outside Dallas."

"I'm on it, sir."

"I don't want you *on* it, I want you *closing* it. Those morons are out in the open now. So, do something about it."

"They've registered as a corporate consensus, sir. Until we find a way to invalidate their charter, anything we do will make us guilty of violating corporate sovereignty. Every consensus in the southwest would terminate their relations with us."

From the silence coming from his phone, Vinson could tell he'd rocked the chairman on his heels. "You're planning on letting them get away with it?"

"Not at all." He suppressed the "you idiot" he desperately wanted to add. He outlined his plan to Brandon. As he did so, he queried central. How the devil had Ariel found out about the registration?

"Sounds like you've got it under control," Brandon finally conceded. "I want this to happen soon. As in, tomorrow."

"Yes, sir."

"Oh, and don't look to Ariel for help. He says you deliberately led his enforcers into traps when you sent them into the sewers."

"We warned them to pack police-quality equipment, sir." He didn't have to mention that Lieutenant Shenker had warned them in a way that made packing police equipment seem a threat to their masculinity.

"Anyway, you're on your own."

"Doing it tomorrow will cost—"

"We pay our premiums, Vinson. If you can't manage your company on that, maybe we accept competitive bids."

"I see."

"Keep me posted, Vinson."

Vinson disconnected, tried another call through to Shenker—with the same lack of result—then went back to his plan.

The free-coders wanted to game the system, but Vinson had been gaming the system when Olivia and Martin were wearing diapers. Now they were playing his game with his rules. And he was going to string them up by their balls.

Olivia

The election had been a piece of cake. Justin was elected Mayor in a landslide victory over Travis, an Elvis impersonator. Martin, and a couple of free-cits Olivia didn't know were elected city councilpeople. To Julia's surprise, Julia was also elected to the council as a write-in sponsored by Kansas and McKensie.

The new city council quickly confirmed Olivia as chief of police and set her in charge of security.

It took Olivia a while before she could look at Shenker without panicking and suffering residual twinges from his beatings. But she forced herself to spend time with him, interrogating him for hours.

Against her will, he convinced her that he was telling the truth. Ironically, Chief Vinson's inviting Shenker to ratepayer parties he'd before only seen in sims, had turned Shenker off, rather than securing his loyalty.

Her gut clenched, but she asked Shenker to be the other half of the human side of her police and defense team.

The non-human side, an ever-growing array of sensors and security bots, was much larger. With Shenker's help, it created a border a lot more secure than the perimeter Shenker had penetrated.

Nobody was going to just sneak in. What would happen if someone wanted to launch a major attack was a different question.

Two weeks after the election, Shenker and Julia stepped into the homespace Olivia was building in what had been a courtyard outside the old police station. Both wore grim faces.

"Corporate Dallas finally got word of what we're doing," Shenker announced.

"We had to register the election results," Julia added. "Martin thought Corporate San Jose might ignore the requirement to notify Corporate Dallas, since they lean toward Corporate Houston in the war."

"But?"

"He was wrong."

"Corporate Houston doesn't want free-code any more than Corporate Dallas does," Shenker reminded them.

"Someone did some research," Julia said. "They turned up legal ownership documents for all of the property in The Colony. And they've just filed notice of eviction."

She uploaded the documentation into Olivia's phone, replaced since they'd completely stripped her of police bugs. "They say that our police must enforce their rights, under the North American Umbrella Consensus Agreement of 2024.

"Oh, shit."

Shenker nodded. "I checked out NAUC-2024. Failure to enforce property rights is grounds to invalidate a consensus charter."

"Those property documents valid?" she demanded.

"I haven't done all of them," Shenker acknowledged.

"Then let's take a look. If even one of them is incorrect, we can hold up the entire thing."

"And the point of that would be what?" Julia demanded. "A day or three isn't going to make any difference to the project."

"It'll give us time to think of something more permanent."

Unfortunately, despite the age of the certified documentation they'd been sent—many of them actual scanned in images of paper documents—everything looked valid to Olivia.

"Keep checking," she ordered Shenker. "And what do we know about this Colony Holding Corporation?"

"It's a registered subsidiary of the Dallas Police Corporation. My old *friend*, Chief Harles Vinson, is on the job."

"Even if they evict us, we'll still be the elected officials," Julia said. "Right?"

"You have to live here to be a representative. And if you're evicted, you don't live here. They'll have a new election, pick new representatives, and shut the consensus down."

"Maybe we can claim that the consensus owns the property," Shenker suggested.

Olivia strained to remember what she'd read about governments taking over property. It hadn't been easy. Something about eminent domain, serving the public interest, and fair compensation. As little money as they had, *any* compensation was more than they could afford.

"How did cities get money back in the old days?" Julia asked

"Something called taxes," Olivia answered. "They just told Corporations and people what they had to pay."

"Brilliant. Have the city council post some taxes and we can—"

"We don't have time to introduce any taxes. Besides, Colony Holding will argue we had no right to do so for long enough to finish evicting us. Then they'd just pay the taxes to themselves."

One of the intrusion sensors chose that minute to alarm.

Olivia pulled up satellite imagery and saw what she'd feared. The Dallas Police Corporation didn't trust her to fulfill their corporate responsibilities.

Ringing the ancient city limits of The Colony were a host of police vehicles, many of them disgorging cops equipped not with stealth suits, but with hardened combat suits. They looked like they meant business.

Shenker

"**Shenker**," Olivia said, "delay them with whatever line of bullcrap you can come up with. Tell them they're violating property rights and corporate freedom of speech. Julia, program the security bots to keep away from the cops. If they have the slightest excuse, the cops will rule us renegade citizens and move directly into avenge mode."

Shenker was tempted to ask Olivia what she was going to do, but she was no longer his trainee-she was his boss.

"Got it." He grabbed a bullhorn from the stack of police equipment he and Olivia had constructed in their scarce spare time and headed for the door.

Olivia was on the phone putting together an evacuation plan by the time he stepped outside the temporary police headquarters, Olivia's homespace.

Julia touched his cheek. "Be careful."

"Taking care of myself is what I'm best at."

"And don't talk yourself down, either."

He had no idea where he was going with Julia. Just when he'd decided he had no use for ratepayers, that he was a citizen and needed to associate with other citizens, he'd stumbled onto her.

Maybe Julia thought of him as a citizen-toy like the women at Vinson's party had, but that wasn't the vibe Shenker picked up.

He shook his head. Olivia needed him to run interference, create a distraction, and that was what he planned on doing.

He strode toward the biggest concentration of police vehicles. Vinson would be there.

Because he'd changed identities, Vinson's autoanswer didn't let him through.

That's why he'd brought the bullhorn. "Vinson. You are dangerously close to a violation of corporate sovereignty."

Even if they had declared corporate war, using police to physically invade was beyond the charter limitations of the Police Corporation.

Speakers projected the voice of Chief Vinson. "Citizens of Dallas. You have trespassed on property owned by The Colony Property Holding Corporation. You have ten minutes to vacate. Violation of this eviction notice is punishable by all necessary force."

"The police force of The Colony has received and is processing your eviction request," Shenker said. "Please back off and let us do our job."

"Is that you, Lieutenant? What the devil are you doing with the spies?"

"It's a long story."

"Then don't bother, because your ten minutes is ticking."

"Why not send your cops home and we'll sit down, have a beer, and work things out." Julia had designed Shenker a beer that was supposed to taste like the old nineteenth century dark ales of England. Shenker didn't know about England, but he certainly knew that Julia's beer refreshed like nothing else on a hot Texas day. It also packed a kick.

"Your corporate registration is flawed," Vinson stated. "Since your supposed voters were squatting, they weren't authorized residents. Therefore, you have no protection under the Corporate Consensus Agreement."

Shenker had thought Vinson would use that argument. "Corporate The Colony is prepared to accept arbitration by a mutually agreeable Consensus. Shall we say, Corporate Fort Worth?"

Martin broke in by phone. "If we go to arbitration, we'll lose."

"Olivia told me to delay things as much as I can and that's what I'm trying to do."

"Five minutes." Vinson ignored Shenker's suggestion.

"Turn down your spam filters for a moment," Shenker said. "I'm uploading a single-use beer design."

"That won't help."

"You liked our coffee." Shenker was still in awe over that. When it came to food and flavors, Julia was a genius.

"Shenker, I like you. But I'll do my job."

"Ten minutes isn't enough. Tell you what, I'll make it a ten thousand unit design. You can give a beer to all the cops you have waiting and still have enough to sell or throw a party with back home."

"You trying to bribe a police officer, Shenker?"

He grinned. "Sure."

"You've bought half an hour. That's all I can do."

He transferred the design. Okay, he'd added twenty-five minutes. He sure hoped Olivia could figure something to do with that, because he didn't think Vinson would bend any further.

Julia

"**I'm** just a cop," Olivia said. "You're the City Councilperson. This is a City Council problem."

"I was a write-in," Julia said. "I didn't ask for the job."

"Well you got it."

"Okay." Julia tried not to think about Shenker, about the way he'd responded when she touched him. It was weird a nightmare had turned into someone funny, interesting, and sexy.

"We've got a couple of corporations in the consensus already. McKensie and Kansas's purse design outfit, my flavor and food corporation. We could hit the corporations up for early rate payments and then do your eminent domain thing."

Olivia shook her head. "Not enough."

Julia shook her head. "We can't go with taxes. Everyone knows taxes were why corporations rebelled against the old system."

Olivia got that clever look in her eyes, the same look she'd had when she had programmed in the corporate free speech balloon. "If I understand this right, most of the old municipal funding came from taxes on property value. So, what happens if property owners didn't pay their tax bills?"

Julia pulled up the old city documents she'd scanned into her phone and did a search. "If they don't pay their property tax assessments, the city has a right to seize those assets and sell them at auction."

Olivia grinned. "I'll bet nobody has paid on any of those old properties in a long time. Time for an auction."

"But were there taxes to pay? Didn't they all get cancelled when the corporations won?"

"Find out."

Outside, Shenker was promising Vinson a whole bunch of beer, which made Julia a little quivery inside. How cool was it that he thought one of her designs, something she'd tossed off in an evening because he'd complained about the flavor of the Interfaith brew, was good enough to work as a bribe for even a minor CEO like Vinson?

Julia tuned Shenker out and called Martin. Julia, Olivia, and Martin had all searched for a ghost town with a still-valid corporate charter, but Martin had developed a knack.

"What do you need, Julia? I'm sort of busy."

"Find out if the old The Colony had property taxes on record when it went dormant."

"Who cares?"

"You do if you want this project to stay alive. Not to mention the couple of thousand free-cits you've got living here now."

"I'm on it."

"Shenker bought us a few minutes," Olivia reported when Martin hung up.

"We need it."

"Start setting up an auction," Olivia said. "I want everyone to win the bids on their own homespace sites. I don't want Kansas and McKensie buying up everything just because they've made money from that purse thing."

"That doesn't sound like a very fair auction."

"If we get into an argument about fair, that'll mean we survived the day."

Julia got digital signatures from the other council members and the auction was ready to go—if Martin came through with in-place taxes. Then she did a bit of research and found that Olivia didn't have to bid for police property. Some of the land was owned by the city itself—and wasn't subject to taxes.

"Just about everything was canceled," Martin finally reported. "City taxes gone. County taxes abolished. School taxes wiped out."

"You said just about."

"There is something called a flood abatement tax. Hardly anything. But it's still on the books. Everyone's about a hundred years behind."

"Good enough. Launch the auction."

Olivia

"**Auction** complete," Julia announced, just as Shenker reported that the cops had given up listening and started moving forward.

"Let's see if they buy our story." Olivia didn't have much hope. She also didn't have another plan—except a deadman drop she'd given to McKensie. And trusting McKensie went against her grain.

She headed out to the front line to join Shenker.

Vinson must have been scanning, because he greeted her well before she made it to Shenker's side.

"Jardan. I told Shenker he was making a mistake in not terminating you when he had the chance."

"Nice to see you, too, Chief Vinson." He was a good half-mile away, standing in the command position of a heavy assault vehicle built of actual steel. Olivia hadn't even realized the Police Corporation had any of those ancient things. They must have had to research the code for diesel fuel because the vehicle was spewing out partially consumed hydrocarbons and particulates. Nobody had built a vehicle like that in better than fifty years.

"The Colony Holding Corporation," Vinson announced, "has authorized me to allow any free-cits currently squatting on their property to vacate without fear of retribution, so long as they leave undamaged any improvements to the property including, but definitely not limited to any computer servers and any data or programming modules stored on those computers."

"That's extremely generous."

"You have a smart mouth, Jardan. I really don't think you want to show it off, now, though. I've already wasted too much time listening to Shenker's stall. We're coming in but we'll take it slow. Anyone who isn't vacating will be termin—"

"That," Olivia interrupted, "would be an extreme violation of property rights. The property deeds reportedly held by this The Colony Holding Corporation, even if such a corporate entity exists, are unlawful. Due to nonpayment of taxes over the past seventy years, Corporate The Colony has seized all of these properties and auctioned them off for back taxes. The new owners have been registered by the registering authority of The Colony and copies are being filed at the Regional Registration Authority in Austin."

Vinson hissed. "That's bullshit, Jardan. There haven't been any taxes in seventy years. Not since the companies won."

"Flood control taxes are still in effect." She uploaded him the scanned documents.

"You'll note that at least one of the property owners listed, one Mr. Paul Shenker, is a currently registered ratepayer within the bounds of Corporate Dallas. Your police responsibilities should include protection of his property, not an attack on it."

"You asking for police mediation in a property dispute?" Vinson sounded shocked.

"Thank you for the offer but Corporate The Colony has instituted its own police force. They have arbitrated this dispute and ruled in favor of the current residents. I'll note that some of your officers are currently violating property rights, trespassing on registered property."

Even a kilometer away, Vinson's face looked purple with rage. "All right, joking's over. We're coming in. Maybe you'll embarrass us a bit with the big boys in Austin and San Jose. But you won't be around to enjoy our humiliation because you'll be dead, the way you should have been if Shenker had done his job right the first time."

"Oops." Shenker winked at her, as if he'd wanted her to get away the whole time he'd chased her, held her captive, and tortured her for information.

Considering how close she'd come to death several times, Olivia didn't want to think that. On the other hand, he *had* let her walk.

"It won't be limited personal embarrassment," she said. "And it won't even just be that every Corporate Consensus in North America will sever ties with Corporate Dallas. We have something special for you, Vinson. I've got a deadman plan aimed directly at Corporate Dallas. We've prepared a special version of free-code including exclusively free-code versions of every major module produced by corporations taking part of the Corporate Consensus of Dallas. We're advising all other corporations that the Dallas Corporate Consensus has illegally seized property, denied corporate freedom of speech, and used police powers in a manner outside the boundaries established in the Consensus. We're recommending that they declare economic war, raise royalties on any modules they have currently in use within Dallas C.C. designs, and substitute the free-code replacements for all of their code currently using Dallas modules. Stand by for an upload for verification."

Olivia sent him the package she'd had McKensie working on ever since they'd discovered the city charter. Corporate entities competing with Dallas would be reluctant to touch free-code without the excuse of Dallas's violation of property rights. But they'd line up with Corporate Houston in a minute if they thought they'd be able to get all of Corporate Dallas's intellectual property for free.

Vinson had raised his hand in preparation for signaling the police advance into The Colony. He dropped it pathetically. "You're kidding."

"Run it by your A.I. You don't think we'd try to take Dallas with us if you attack?"

"I need to let some experts have a look at this and verify that it is what you say."

In addition to police central, he'd probably run the IP Bomb by Dallas's corporate big-boys. It was their businesses Olivia threatened.

"Take as long as you need, but do it outside of our registered property. When you come back, come back with someone authorized to accept our terms."

"If I don't come back with a nuke."

"You know I'm recording, don't you? Corporate Dallas is downwind from here. I don't think many ratepayers will enjoy seeing that sim."

"I'll be back in half an hour."

Vinson

Brandon wasn't happy.

He was even less happy when Vinson uploaded the code modules Olivia had dumped on him.

"How'd they do that?" the consensus leader demanded. "We're talking about IP it took us decades to develop. How'd they just hack it together? They had to be reverse engineering and that's morally repugnant and a violation of intellectual property."

Vinson wasn't going to suggest that Merryweather's free-code project had developed better code than a few decades of corporations kludging one layer of code on top of another, but he didn't have to. "Who cares? If we attack, they'll release the code and Corporate Dallas will be an instant backwater."

"They'll release it anyway." Brandon had insisted Rev. Ariel conference into the call. "Once you acknowledge them as a sovereign consensus, there'll be no stopping them."

"Maybe." That was the point of a free code project, after all—to produce code that people could use for free, without paying licensing fees for each application. "But a lot of our designs are protected by patents. Without a valid excuse, the other corporate entities wouldn't dare touch it."

"We can surround the so-called city with jamming equipment," Ariel promised. "Like we did in centercity when we were searching for the designers. Kill them while we're jamming."

"They'll have thought of th—"

"Do it," Brandon ordered.

Vinson shook his head. "I won't take that order just from you, sir. I'll raise an exception to the entire T-50. You're talking about a major violation of consensus."

"Screw the consensus." Ariel practically screamed. "We need to take them down."

Vinson ignored him. Ariel was blind to it and Brandon apparently hadn't caught on yet either, but Vinson saw they were playing the wrong game, chasing the wrong enemy.

"Suppose free-code were limited to base modules only," he said before Brandon could give any more orders he'd be reluctant to rescind once he'd blurted them out. "Ninety percent of our base modules are imported from other corporate entities. A lot of it is ancient—way out of patent. Imagine if we could give our Designers nice clean base code, and that they could use all of their energy creating new stuff."

"But The Colony—"

"We have what, ten thousand designers in Dallas. How many do you figure Corporate The Colony has? Fifty, tops. And some of them will have to do maintenance on the code base. Don't you get it? We'll validate the code for them and they'll give us something that we're paying for now."

"They'll give it to Corporate Houston, too," Brandon objected. "And they're bigger than we are."

Vinson forced himself not to grin. Once Brandon was making objections, they were negotiating and he was halfway sold. "I still have a couple of hundred cops outside The Colony. I've even got Ariel's threat to block their communications. Those give me negotiating room. What do you say I cut a deal that gives them what they need, and gives us preferential treatment in the release?"

"Why would they do that?"

"Truthfully? With a pet consensus, they've got the basic requirement for authentication, but they're still high-risk. Nobody knows who they are, whether their code is any good. They need beta testers to validate it, and that could be Dallas."

"But—"

"Also, they don't want me to fly my drones over and drop eaters on them."

"See what kind of deal you can negotiate, Vinson. But if it isn't good enough, I'm going to let Rev. Ariel here attack. We could blame the Interfaith and Corporate Dallas would be off the hook."

"If we do that, they'll use the IP bomb."

"Sir—" Rev. Ariel sounded desperate. Vinson couldn't remember him calling anyone 'sir.'

"Shut up, Ariel. We're talking money here."

Ariel's face turned purple. "Who cares about money? They're threatening the Interfaith. If we don't keep the citizens in line, who will?"

"The day I worry about citizens is the day I turn in my resignation," Brandon said.

It wasn't much of an attitude, and it wasn't even realistic—Vinson's experience with Olivia Jardan and Paul Shenker had taught him that much. For now, though, Brandon was going where Vinson wanted him to, so he didn't argue.

Now he just had to cut a deal.

Martin

The deal tore at his beliefs.

He wanted his code to be free, to break down the barriers. He certainly didn't want to favor Corporate Dallas after all they'd done to him, his friends, and their own coders.

Giving even a temporary exclusive to Corporate Dallas felt like treason.

"Our security bots could hold them off for maybe thirty seconds," Olivia said. "Wake up and smell the TrueBean™ Coffee."

"Essentially they're just signing up to be beta testers," Julia observed. "There's nothing unusual about that."

"They'll have a six month exclusive advantage for deployment of product."

Olivia shrugged. "Better than letting them kill us."

They went round and round, but Martin had to cave—especially after Jimmy hugged him and told him he'd support his dad no matter what. No way would Martin let his pride get in the way of a deal that gave him most of what he wanted and protected his children.

Still, his negative attitude wrung some concessions Vinson had originally demanded a two year exclusive.

With the intellectual property agreement complete, giving Corporate Dallas along with Corporate The Colony a six-month exclusive 'test period' on release of any new free-code modules, he and Shenker negotiated the purchase for any residual rights for properties claimed by The Colony Property Holding Corporation, to be paid over the next five years.

In return, the Dallas Police Corporation backed off, Corporate Dallas and all of its C.C. withdrew any further property claims on The Colony assets, and the Dallas C.C. agreed not to block, spoof, or otherwise interfere with the release of free-code, once the six-month period of exclusivity had expired.

The agreement validated with the double-key encryption of the two corporate entities, Martin and Justin shook hands with Vinson. The Colony was now an officially recognized corporate entity under the questionably protective wing of the much-larger Corporate Dallas. Dallas would pretend The Colony was a normal corporate entity, ignoring its heretical position on equal voting.

After signing the deal he called his control back in Corporate Houston.

"You signed what? Are you insane, Reynolds?"

"Possibly."

"You know we can't support this. It'll take a few minutes for me to make it official but believe me, you're no longer a ratepayer and your children are no longer eligible for ratepayer entry to any C.H. programs."

"I suspected that would be the case."

Control paused, just for a moment. "Why'd you do it, Reynolds? You could have evacuated your family, even saved the free-cits if you'd felt some weird sense of guilt. If you'd just let Corporate Dallas invade and destroy a registered corporate entity, they would have been finished."

"They would have terminated the designers."

"Corporate Houston is always hiring."

That was true. But Corporate Houston wouldn't hire anyone to build Merryweather's dream. And that dream meant more to him than being a Corporate Houston ratepayer.

"Sorry things didn't work out."

Control said nothing for a moment. Just when Martin was about to kill the call, though, Control broke in. "The thing is, Reynolds, we don't feel that your venture is in Corporate Houston's best interest. We'd rather have it shut down than continue. Giving Corporate Dallas an unfair competitive advantage only makes things worse."

"Sorry, sir."

"I'm not looking for an apology. I'm looking for a reversal."

"I can't do that."

"Then let me tell you something. If you won't shut it down, we will."

"I see."

He broke the call and went to warn the others. They wouldn't be happy to hear it, but they deserved to know. Martin didn't know who or where they were, but one thing he did know was that he wasn't the only spy Corporate Houston had in the area.

Julia

"**Come** on, Shenker. We're going to celebrate." She grabbed him by the hand and headed toward the tent the free-cits had erected once they'd gotten news about the deal.

"We've got to reprogram the security system," he protested. She noticed, though, that he didn't pull away from her. Considering that he'd trained Olivia, she was pretty sure she wouldn't be able to hold onto him if he didn't want to be held.

"Program it tomorrow. We've got beer."

"You can't just bribe me with beer, you know."

"Yeah?" She put her hands on her hips. "Well, what is it going to take?"

For a moment, she thought he was going to turn and run. Instead, he pulled her to him and kissed her.

Nice.

"This doesn't mean you don't have to come to the party with me." Her voice might have been slightly breathless, but she figured he wouldn't notice. It wasn't like he wasn't breathing hard, too.

"I don't really like—"

"I saw you at Maurissa's party. I know you like to have a good time. So, let's go and have a good time."

"But I was—"

"We'll talk about that kiss later, all right?"

She knew about citizen Puritanism, preached by the Interfaith—and perversely twisted to the opposite extreme by free-cit sims. It surprised her that someone as sophisticated as Paul Shenker would fall for the puritan line. But she wasn't worried. She didn't know that she wanted a forever relationship with him, but he was fun and she did know she wanted to party. She'd put in a lot of twenty-hour days working on the code, working on the political stuff Olivia had come up with, running from Shenker, then running after him. All of the designers from all of the labs had come in to celebrate their final victory. Her parents and some of her former co-workers from Dallas Universal Flavors were coming out to help celebrate. She wasn't going to let them down by not going.

Besides, she had one of the sexiest guys in their entire town on her arm and there was no way she wasn't going to show him off. Going into free-code had been her mother's idea, after all. Her mother had promised she'd meet a guy that way. Well, she had. The fact that it hadn't been a guy her mother approved of, or at all the kind of guy her mother expected she'd bring home from a designer meeting wasn't the point.

"Do I have to dance?"

"Some." She'd taken to setting her phone to wake her early so she could sneak to the window of her office/homespace and watch him doing his martial arts drills. They looked a lot like dances to her, and she'd dreamed of sharing that dance, feeling the movement of those hard muscles in her hands and against her body. "I won't make you dance all of the tunes," she promised.

"Good."

"Just the slow ones."

Olivia

Olivia's sense of accomplishment vanished when Martin reported the Corporate Houston threat. Sure Houston was a long way away, but a parabolic rocket could complete the trip in ten minutes, dumping either explosives or eater nanobes that would destroy their dream.

She skipped out on the party, choosing instead to walk through the security ring she and Shenker had built around their town, making sure the Dallas cops hadn't destroyed the calibration of any of their sensitive instruments.

After eight hours of that, she returned to her homespace and brewed herself a huge cup of Julia's super-strong coffee.

When Shenker walked in with a big grin on his face, she couldn't help snarling at him.

"Something wrong?" Shenker uploaded a new code to her constructor and generated a couple of steaming cups.

He handed one to Olivia and sipped on the second. "Good stuff."

It was Julia's special secret formula. She claimed she was still working on it, but Olivia thought that was just her excuse not to share. So what was Shenker doing with it?

"The best thing to go with coffee is donuts," Shenker said. He opened her constructor again and pulled out a plate containing two of the fat-filled pastries.

"Donuts are something I am intimately familiar with."

"You've got to try these, though."

"I'll bite. What's different?"

"*I* coded them."

She stopped with the donut in her hand, halfway between the plate and her mouth. "You? How'd you do that?"

"Julia showed me how to use the modules. She might have helped a bit with the flavorings."

"So you and Julia..."

Shenker's grin came back, doubled.

"I don't want to hear any more about it." Olivia nibbled on a donut. It wasn't bad. In fact, it was better than anything she'd gotten from the Interfaith, although not up to ratepayer standards.

Still, Shenker had coded this himself. If he could do it, maybe she could too. So could Sammy. She couldn't wait to tell him he could finally come home, have a place of his own, finally become a designer.

"This is good."

"Yeah." Shenker gave her an evil grin. "You know cops and their donuts. Could be a bit lighter. I've still got a lot to learn. Anyway, tell me about your worries." He pulled up a chair, turned it around, and straddled it, looking the very image of a sim cowboy in a sim bar scene.

Olivia hadn't realized she was sending out worried vibes. "I'm not—"

"Come on, boss. If you can't tell your deputy, there's something really wrong."

She took another sip of that really superior coffee-coffee designed by a woman she'd spent days annoyed at. "Everyone seems so sure we've won, but Martin's control wasn't just harassing him. There's another shoe waiting to drop."

"We're working on that."

"I know, but I'm revving my engines with no place to go."

"Want to take a look at the training sims Julia and Justin are working on? Won't take you more than a couple of weeks, I'm betting, before you'll be the one designing us breakfast. And you'll probably come up with something a lot fancier than donuts and coffee. Me, I've always had a hankering to try biscuits with cream sausage gravy. What they call 'saw-mill gravy' in the western sims."

Olivia sighed. She could look at the training sims, share them with her brother. It might even help to get her brain out of the ruts it had fallen into as she obsessed about Houston. "Sure, upload me the first of Julia's training sims. If I ever design anything, I'll ride my bike into the zones and construct it for my parents. You know they won't believe it without seeing it."

Julia

Scripting training sims wasn't the most fascinating job in the world. And it took time away that Julia could have used to experiment with new flavors, new ways to make some money.

Still, the look on Shenker's face when he'd pulled a batch of really horrible donuts out of the constructor had been precious beyond words.

It also highlighted areas where her sims needed improvement. Donuts needed to be better than that.

So she looked into the camera array and smiled.

"Manipulation of carbon, oxygen, hydrogen, and nitrogen involve use of specially designed cyanobacteria within each constructor. These split apart molecules of water, oxygen, and carbon dioxide to create the organic compounds that form the building blocks of life. RNA molecules serve as messengers, activating particular activities, leading to the creation of the specific complex molecules desired by the designer."

She pulled up a sim of the RNA molecule unzipping itself, using parts of it to express proteins and carbohydrate mixes. "Proper design of the RNA molecule allows construction of the base material for your construction."

Back to her face. "Of course, if you don't want to end up with a soupy mess at the bottom of your constructor, you'll also need to learn how to use nanobe machinery to manipulate the base material stock into the shapes and texture of real food."

She tried to remember how her own instructors had explained things. Designers tended to mix pure cookbook with hand waving, leaving theory for the student to figure out on her own—if it happened at all. But understanding theory was essential if someone wanted to get beyond plugging together a couple of prefab molecules. Still, beginning designers would get bored if they couldn't design something pretty quickly.

"Let's consider the design for a simple high-carbohydrate snack, the donut."

She viewed the sim, then toned down the grin she'd made after the word *donut*. God, she looked like a woman who'd just gotten laid. That was so not the image she wanted to send with these sims.

"For our first donut, most of the base work has been done in free-code. Module F-327-00006 creates sucrose, using CO_2 from the air or from organic material plus directly applied water. The CO_2 provides the carbon. Both water and CO_2 provide oxygen, and water, of course, provides hydrogen. Module F-301-00195 creates a complex carbohydrate that serves as the substrate for your design—an analogue, if you wish, to flour. Please unpack these two modules now."

She paused the sim, then considered how she could add a strawberry frosting that would actually taste like the wild strawberries she'd picked a couple of days earlier, growing outside a long-abandoned garden. The tart burst of flavor and slight crunch from the seeds would add a definite zing to the ordinary cake donuts this sim used as an example design. Of course it would be a long time before new designers would be ready to try that.

She would have to try strawberries out on Shenker next time she saw him.

Olivia

Proximity alarms pulled Olivia out of a sugar hangover. She'd tried out Julia's latest sim and her own donuts were even better than what Shenker had managed.

"Shenker, anything to report?"

"Sorry," his voice sounded weird, like he was talking through a pillow. "I was sleeping."

Never mind. I've got it. Oh, shit. Security bots are reporting substantial life-form intrusion from the southern sector S-202. Oops. Looks like it's spreading. We've got—"

"An invasion," Shenker echoed her thoughts. "It's the other shoe you were worried about. I'm on my way there."

Olivia didn't wait. Vinson had, reluctantly, given her an override as a fellow police chief. She woke him up. "I thought we had an agreement."

"Is this Jardan? Do you know what time it is?"

"Don't play games with me, Vinson. I've got, what, maybe ten thousand human signatures intruding around our perimeters and I've got hundreds of vehicles with Dallas Transport Corporation registration dumping more off. This is clear provocation."

She didn't like Vinson's pause. If he'd been behind the invasion, he would have a story prepared.

"I've got it traced. It's not police or any corporate entity. It appears you're being invaded by citizens. Every one of those vehicles was legally hired. Funding is through Corporate Houston but indirectly."

"Those bastards. Are you still—"

Vinson took a deep breath. "If any of your locals are still paying Corporate Dallas insurance, I can authorize force against the citizens. There'd be a surcharge back to you." He paused a moment. "I could have a squad of cops there in twenty minutes. If the citizens are on a rampage, I'm afraid we'll likely be avenging rather than protecting."

Twenty minutes was as bad as twenty hours.

"Never mind. I'll handle this." Olivia signed off, pulled on her police tunic, and headed out.

Citizens didn't mob. From time to time, a group of older citizens might get together to play soccer or something, but Olivia had never seen more than twenty citizens in one place before, other than at a public constructor.

In violation of everything Olivia knew about them, these citizens *were* mobbing. Clearly they'd learned their technique from sims. They carried constructed pitchforks and constructed torches that actually burned, occasionally scattering flaming hydrocarbons around and dripping them on the citizens carrying them.

She hoped she could disperse them, but sent out an emergency evacuation broadcast to everyone in their town. This mob looked destructive and she didn't think they'd stop short when it came to taking lives.

Once she heard the acknowledgements coming in, she stepped closer to the mob. She phoned into the loudspeakers designed into every security bot and spoke.

"Citizens. You have entered into the security zone of Corporate The Colony. Please state your business before—"

She stopped talking when hundreds of the citizens pulled faux-wood clubs from their tunics and smashed every security bot they could identify.

She sent frantic orders to all surviving bots to pull back, to monitor but not to obstruct.

That was a mistake. The citizens surged forward after the bots like floodwaters behind a bursting dam.

Olivia grabbed a portable powered speaker and went to meet them.

Blood-red skies to the east promised that the sun would soon appear, but the mob's torches still burned brightly.

A couple of them tossed their torches into the ruins of ancient homes, constructed in the days of brick and wood frame. Plenty of others held onto their firestarters, looking for flammable hydrocarbon-based homespaces Olivia and her free-cits had constructed on an emergency basis.

* * * *

"Police. You are violating property rights." It was so easy to slip back into her old habits, to think of property as more valuable than people's lives. She wondered if she could kill to protect a few homespaces that could be reconstructed in a couple of days of work. She also wondered if destroying the homespaces was really what the mob intended. Corporate Houston wanted more revenge than that.

"Olivia, why are you protecting this evil? You should be with us."

Her subconscious reacted more quickly than her conscious mind, sending a surge of adrenaline through her system. "Sammy?"

A couple of young punk-types ran out ahead, tossing torches at anything constructed, then dashing back to the main body of the mob. Most everyone stopped as Sammy, equipped with a speaker similar to hers, stepped out from their midst.

"Olivia, you want to help these people, not their enemies."

"What are you talking about, Sammy? You're being used by Corporate Houston. We're the ones who are helping. We're letting everyone become designers. If *I* can learn how to design, anyone can. In just a few months, we'll release our first complete set of modules. You won't have to be a ratepayer to be a designer any more. Even if you don't want to design yourself, people will make their designs available. Nobody will have to eat citizen slop again."

Sammy shook his head, then whistled a couple of bars from one of his hymns.

Her body twitched in a response conditioned by all those days of Interfaith healing.

"Can't you see that you're playing the devil's game, Olivia?"

Her brain felt woozy, as if this was one of those dreams where she ran and ran and never got anywhere. Harmonics in Sammy's voice triggered controls in her mind.

She struggled to keep her brain from disintegrating into randomness. "There's no devil here. I'm helping people, Sammy."

He whistled another couple of notes and Olivia's mind supplied the remaining chords. "Are you saying that citizens can only find fulfillment by being designers?" He asked. "That they are inadequate if they lack the capabilities to design stuff? Don't you think there's plenty of material goods already designed?"

Another of the punks ran out and threw a torch, this one directly at Olivia.

She stepped to the side, caught it, and extinguished it in the ancient concrete roadway they hadn't yet covered with solar collectors.

"Join us." Sammy reinforced his message with another whistle. "The Interfaith was, and is still, the only true way for a citizen to achieve happiness. So what if you educate a citizen to make his own food? You've done so by cutting him off from true sustenance. Remember, man does not live by bread alone."

"You're tools of Corporate—"

"Suppose you do teach a citizen to code? What can he design that isn't already given him by the Interfaith?"

Dozens of hours of programming from countless Interfaith sims she'd participated in while healing reverberated through Olivia's mind. Her brother's voice and the notes he whistled triggered memories the Interfaith had planted in her.

"Consider the lilies of the field," Sammy reminded her.

"But—"

"They do not work because their father provides for them. With the Interfaith, people are provided for. But you want to make citizens work to eat. And you say you're freeing us."

"We are—"

"You're giving people the devil's choice, Olivia. It was the choice men made when they built the Tower of Babel. They used science and technology to scale the heights intended to be reached by faith alone. Creation is for faith, not for humans."

Olivia knew Sammy was wrong, but her head pounded with the sounds of a hundred hymns, every one of them getting in the way of any serious thought. If she hadn't spent the past few days developing concentration through Julia's sims, her focus and will might have been swept away with the flood. As it was, her brain had problems synching up with her mouth, thoughts transforming to words at only one or so per second.

"Faith is about choice, too."

Sammy laughed. "We made our choices a long time ago, paid in full, sealed in blood. And now, you're trying to void the contract, pretend like there was no past, like you could just start over, debt-free. It doesn't work that way, Olivia. It doesn't work that way for corporations and it doesn't work that way for the faith. The Interfaith healed you. The Interfaith fed you. The Interfaith gave you the blankets that kept you warm, that gave you power, that hid you and your friends from the police. It gave to you when you asked, and now we're asking for repayment."

The mob, still swelling from hundreds to thousands of citizens, roared their support. "You owe us."

The sun pierced the horizon, dimming the light being shed by the torches. But Olivia didn't doubt that they would still burn, could create a holocaust out of her friends' dreams.

"Is that what this is about, Sammy? I took from the Interfaith, so I should have to give back to it. Is this about me?"

Sammy laughed.

"They aren't going to settle for that," Shenker's voice said. "They're going to try to shut down all of us."

Olivia's brain had been so frazzled by the worms the Interfaith had left behind that she hadn't even noticed her deputy and Julia beside her. Shenker carried a load of weapons stuck in his belt. Not that weapons would do much good against a mob this size. Unfortunately, he'd also brought Julia. And putting a pretty ratepayer female in front of this mostly male mob was like throwing gasoline on a raging fire.

Sammy nodded. "You're my sister and I want to help you, protect you, Olivia. But you've fallen in with bad company. If you want to join us, you can. Either way, we're not going to let this modern-day Tower of Babel continue."

"The Interfaith has coexisted with corporations for decades," she pointed out.

"The Interfaith and the corporations won *together*. The corporations were for the rich, the Interfaith was for everyone else. That was the bargain, the great compromise. So, now you're trying to strip that from us? But it doesn't work that way, sister. We're not going to give up what we earned."

Vinson

Vinson had a couple of drones circling over Corporate The Colony and he watched the images as they arrived.

Olivia and ex-Lieutenant Shenker were in trouble. Despite the Corporate Houston link, Corporate Dallas citizens were responsible. If they pushed her hard enough, Olivia just might drop that intellectual property bomb after all.

Acting on impulse, he sent one of the drones lower-and scanned identity codes. Sure enough, Interfaith Enforcers were out in force. Which made sense. Random citizens had no reason to leave their homespaces. Only the Interfaith could mobilize thousands of them. Ariel hadn't been happy with the deal Vinson had cut on behalf of Corporate Dallas. Clearly he'd conspired with Corporate Houston to take revenge even if it meant taking out Corporate Dallas in the process.

Vinson put through a call to Rev. Ariel, using a police priority code to skate past Ariel's autoanswer.

"What the hell?"

"Doesn't sound like you're sleeping, Reverend."

"Chief Vinson, why don't you just visit that pretty wife of yours? There's nothing going on that the Dallas Police Corporation needs to worry about."

"I'd say your goons costing us the war with Corporate Houston is a concern."

"You don't understand the big picture. Brandon will explain."

A second later, Louis Brandon's familiar voice boomed in. "You rocking the boat, Vinson?"

"I'm doing my job, sir. Ariel's IE enforcers are destroying our deal."

"You don't get it, do you, Vinson? Ariel, explain it to him."

"Free-code undermines the Great Compromise," Ariel said.

On a second channel, audio pickups Vinson had planted around Corporate The Colony picked up Sammy Jardan echoing the same thoughts to his sister.

"When the Interfaith community supported the corporations against governments," Ariel argued, "everyone agreed that *we* would control the citizens. You got centercity with your loose morals and your conspicuous consumption. But we got the people. If you're backing out of your part of the agreement, why should we do our part?"

"But what are you so afraid of? You don't make money from those citizens, anyway."

"Saving their souls is more important than money."

Vinson couldn't hold back a choked laugh. "What's that got to do with the price of code?"

"Think about it," Brandon broke in. "The Interfaith has a veto on every decision we make. They're responsible for keeping the citizens placated. Sure what they're doing in Corporate The Colony is scary. But believe me, it would be a lot scarier if they loosed a mob on Corporate Dallas."

"As I said," Ariel repeated, "it really would be wiser for you to go back to sleep, Chief Vinson. You do your job. My men will do their job."

Olivia

There were thousands of them in the mob and only herself, Shenker, and Julia, along with some security bots to face them. And while Julia was tougher than Olivia had given her credit for, she wasn't a trained fighter.

"Tell me everyone else is evacuating," Olivia subvocalized to Julia.

"Sorry. They've got us surrounded. I've brewed up some eaters. If you and Shenker could hold them up for five minutes, I could load the security bots and spray them. We don't have time to put together an IP Bomb on Corporate Houston and even if we did, I don't think these guys are really under control."

"You'd kill all of these guys? Thousands of them?"

"It's self-defense."

"Our faith will protect us against your science." Sammy sounded smug, as well he should. He shouldn't have been able to listen in on their subvocal conversation. Phone calls were encrypted. On the other hand, Sammy had known her since she was a baby. He just might be able to read the faint movement of her lips as she manipulated her phone.

"You downloaded nanobes to protect you from any possible threat? That doesn't sound likely to me."

"Because your faith is weak."

She couldn't argue with that.

"What are we waiting for?" one of the citizens demanded of her brother. "She isn't coming around. Let's burn them out and go home."

Shenker stepped in front of Olivia, confronting the speaker who'd pushed his way to the front of the mob. "If it isn't my buddy from Interfaith Enforcement. What does IE have to do with this?"

"You're just going to make them mad," Olivia hissed. "Follow my lead."

"And what? Let them run over my town? I don't think so."

She thought about pulling rank on him, but Shenker would just quit and she needed him.

"Come on, anyone out there want to show his faith by taking me on?" Shenker shouted. "Man-to-man, one-on-one."

"Hell, yeah. I'll—"

"Shut up, Commander," Sammy said. "Shenker is a cop. He'd win, but what would that prove?"

"It would prove whether your faith means anything," Shenker said. "Right now, all I see is fear. Fear that if people had some choice, they wouldn't come to you anymore. Maybe you're selling the people short.

Maybe they come to you because they love the content, not because of the trinkets you reward them with. You said it yourself. The content is supposed to be part of the benefit, not what you pay to get your food or blankets or whatever."

Sammy's face relaxed for a moment as he considered Shenker's words and Olivia let herself hope. Could it really be as easy as that?

Then her brother laughed harshly. "I almost fell for that cheap cop-negotiating trick."

He looked at the three people facing him, meeting Olivia's eyes. Then he shook his head slowly. "Don't get close. Stone them."

* * * *

The sun had risen over the horizon, but its long shadows distorted distance, and rocks, falling like rain, caught her by surprise.

Shenker reacted more quickly, dragging Julia to the ground and covering her with his body.

A couple of the large jagged rocks caught Olivia in her protective vest, but one, thrown high and descending, smashed into her head.

Her knees buckled under her, but she forced herself to stand.

"Stoning is the ancient punishment for those who sin against the faith." Her brother sounded truly saddened as his mob launched a second volley of stone missiles.

She was prepared this time, and few of the men in the mob had ever thrown anything in real life. Sim training could only do so much, especially as people often selected sim avatars with different body and muscle types than their own sculpts. Still, out of the thousands of rocks they put in the air, dozens were on target.

She pulled a carbon-fiber police nightstick, blocked those stones she saw descending toward her head, and endured those targeting her body.

Her police tunic prevented any penetration, and did what it could to spread the force of impact across her body, but it could only do so much. Several of the rocks were larger than fist-sized. She sidestepped one, and walked directly into another. It rocked her back on her heels.

In the dawn light, she made out a police drone flying low over the mob. Clearly Vinson was tracking what was happening.

Sammy held up his hand to stop the rain of rocks and pointed at the lightweight scramjet overhead.

"Down it."

Three Interfaith Enforcement goons fired simultaneously, their two-meter-long missiles jumping out from the launchers like greyhounds in an old-time racing sim.

"Some rocks have longer reach," Sammy announced as the drone fired its afterburners, twisted in the air, and climbed toward the sun in an attempt to either outfly the missiles or confuse their heat-seeking sensors with the massive power of sunlight.

It was a good attempt. For a second, it looked as if it might succeed. First one, then a second of the shoulder-mounted missiles hurled past the drone while it continued to gain speed.

The third missile and jet were dots against the sun when the distance between them evaporated.

A huge fireball created what, for a few seconds, appeared to be a second sun.

The sound of the explosion, like distant heat-thunder, rumbled in more than thirty seconds later.

"We came equipped with the tools to get the job done," Sammy stated with a self-satisfied tone. "Torches to burn out the homespaces of those who attempt to undermine the Interfaith. Rocks to shower on those who fight us. And more powerful weapons for those who use technology against us. You didn't think Interfaith designers spent all their lives designing blankets and breakfasts, did you?" He snickered again. "Our faith provides us the tools we need. Which is why I don't fear your eaters. More stones, soldiers of the faith."

* * * *

Olivia smeared blood off of her face so she could at least see, and glared at her brother. She didn't like pain, but at least it had stripped her brain free from all of those clinging worms that the Interfaith had planted in her. Her mind was her own again, for the time being.

"What *do* you fear, Sammy?" she shouted into her portable speaker. "Learning that you didn't have to give up your dreams, you didn't *have* to sell out? Because you did sell out. My team has created something special, and you want to destroy it. Don't give me your crap about the tower of Babel. That's just justification. Weak justification."

His voice still carried the harmonics that had distorted Olivia's brain earlier, but they didn't seem to be working any more. Olivia would hate to think getting smacked on the head was a good thing, but it had its advantages.

"Do you hear it?" She turned her head away from Sammy and the others so he couldn't read her lips.

"Huh?" Julia had gotten up from the ground where Shenker had knocked her, but she was a mud-covered mess.

"There's something in his voice, in those whistles he keeps doing. They're triggering a conditioned response in me. Maybe in the others as well. It's probably not just him. The enforcers are probably using it on all of them."

Julia nodded. "Got it. Buy me some time to work on it."

She wasn't sure she had any purchasing power when it came to time.

"What does police training say to do when you're confronted with a mob that outnumbers you ten thousand to two, and when that mob has surface to air missiles, nanobe protection, and more rocks than they'd need to build a new pyramid?" she asked Shenker, who'd risen from his protective position over Julia and now stood back to back with Olivia.

"That particular question never came up during training construction. But there's one all-purpose answer."

"Attack?"

"Right."

Julia

Olivia and Shenker charged into the crowd, waving club-like weapons police had carried forever.

They created enough distraction for Julia to flee back to her lab.

Martin, McKensie, and half a dozen other designers were already analyzing Sammy's voice patterns and those from identified IE officers.

"Everyone knows that the Interfaith puts triggered messages in its content," Angie said.

She was clearly wrong since Julia hadn't known. But that did give her another broad research area. Which was a pity since Olivia and Shenker weren't going to last long enough for thorough research.

She dumped the previous night's Interfaith broadcasts into her pattern recognition AI, then looked at what McKensie had found. "Echoes of that tune Sammy whistled are continually being broadcast in the 25-35,000 Hz zone," the big designer said. "The mob is mostly controlled rather than voluntary."

"Can we sound-cancel by broadcast?"

Martin shook his head. "They've got multiple sources. We'd need to cancel each one of them."

Ultrasonic command suggestions was so not Julia's field. Letting a bunch of brainwashed citizens destroy everything she'd worked for wasn't her idea of a good time, either. And she had Shenker out there—the man who'd become her lover.

"You come up with the echo cancellation program, I'll figure out how to get at the point sources."

"Deal." McKensie and Martin put their heads together and started hacking code.

Julia got on her phone.

"Vinson."

The Dallas cop sounded tired.

"Got any more drones in the area?"

"Two more. You saw they shot one down?"

"I saw."

"I was going to broadcast a warning."

"Pretty brave, considering you're not getting any support from the high-ups."

"I have a feeling my shareholders are going to boot me anyway."

"I need the exact GPS location of a hundred and twenty-eight broadcasters operating in the 25-35,000 hertz range."

"Those IE ultrasonics? Coming at you."

Thirty seconds later, Julia had both the locations and a crudely hacked design for specific sound cancellation. Now all she needed was a way to apply it.

Olivia

Olivia and Shenker couldn't defeat ten thousand angry men. But standing and letting rocks rain down on their bodies was a surer and quicker way to go. By attacking, they'd be too close to have rocks thrown at them.

Not that attacking would slow the mob for long. A smart leader would hold back a few dozen fighters to control Shenker and her, sending the rest around to burn out the community.

But the mob's leaders had been awake for hours, were tired, just might panic when they were rushed. Olivia didn't know what Julia could do, but her friend had asked her to buy time and she would do the best she could to deliver.

"We've warned you and we've given you every chance to back off." Olivia's police override was working again, locally boosted by her status as official police chief. She boomed her voice over every surviving security bot and broadcast to every receiving phone within two kilometers. "By the powers vested in me by the incorporated community of The Colony, I place you under arrest, Sammy Jardan, subject to full vengeance by the laws of The Colony. We're coming to get you. Troopers advance."

"Yes, ma'am." Shenker snapped to attention, saluted her with his billy club—managing to bat down a couple of thrown rocks at the same time, and instantly moved to the attack.

Sammy shrank into the mob when Shenker and Olivia surged into attack mode. But dozens of heavily muscled types pushed forward, anxious to test their sculpts against police tactics.

Badly aimed rocks hit a couple of them, and the stoning abruptly came to an end. Of course, by then, Olivia and Shenker were in a scrum of hundred-plus kilo men ready to play their testosterone games.

Shenker

As a young citizen, Shenker had lapped up sims about the stand of the three hundred Spartans at Thermopylae. Better armed, armored, and trained, a handful of soldiers had held off a huge army because only a few members of that army could reach them at a time.

He'd never imagined he'd be stuck playing the role of sacrificial soldier but that was all that was left now. He intended to make the fight last.

Unlike a noble Spartan, he didn't fight fair.

The club could be an awkward weapon, but Shenker had spent hundreds of hours in battle sims working with sword, *jo*, nunchaku, and tonfa. The simple billy-club was like a short version of the *jo*—less useful against a sword, maybe, but perfect against thugs with knives and fists.

He kept it in motion, slashing with it more than thrusting, breaking hands, heads, elbows, or anything else the Interfaith Enforcers let get near them.

At his side, Olivia was a buzz saw of destruction and he let himself grin. Of all his students, she was the one who'd learned the most, absorbing what many students believed to be outdated knowledge like a sponge soaking up water.

Those foolish enough to come at him with naked fists faded like cheap constructs chewed up by eaters.

Some of the guys seemed to hold back against Olivia. Whether it was her status as Sammy's sister, because she was a woman, or because they thought there would be more glory in tackling Shenker he didn't know, but he took advantage of the weakness that indecisiveness gave him. As long as she stood, she protected his back, he was free to deal out destruction.

With his free hand, he stripped the torch from a man who swung it at him, giving it back to his face. In the same move he blocked a knife-thrust toward Olivia's back and broke the arm holding it, kicked out the kneecap of an idiot who rushed at him like a Greco-Roman wrestler, and rattled his nightstick off three heads as quickly as if he were playing the drums in a rock-video sim.

During the same few seconds, Olivia disabled at least two more opponents.

Then the easy part was over.

It takes room to fight.

Nightsticks were designed for close-in fighting, but "close-in" assumed the user would have a dozen centimeters or so to swing the weapon, recover from a strike, shift his balance and let the latest victim fall to the ground.

With the first twenty or so guys down, the men at the front of the mob surrounding them didn't seem quite so anxious to get at them, but hundreds of people behind that first group pressed them closer anyway.

Whenever Shenker or Olivia stepped toward them, the men at the front pushed back as hard as they could, which made them sitting ducks for Shenker and Olivia, but the guys behind relaxed and closed the distance. With every surge, a few more of the mob fell, but the two of them had that much less room to move in.

And things were getting complicated underfoot.

Unfortunately, the attackers didn't have the sense Xerxes's Persians did. Instead of falling back and regrouping, they kept pushing forward.

"We need to break out, hit them from the flanks." Olivia's voice sounded hoarse from her repeated kias as she'd surgically smacked bone and nerve points with her weapon. "I'm starting to trip over fallen enforcers."

Shenker nodded, looking around to get a sense of the mob. He and Olivia *needed* to break out. Whether they *could* break out was another question. Still, if they were going to, they'd have to move to the south, where the crowd looked just a little less organized. He gestured that way. "Go first. I've got your back."

Olivia rushed forward like the sharpened blade of an ax. Shenker followed like the axe's heavy head, making sure Olivia's opening stayed open, reaching over and around her to double-team anyone who didn't get out of the way quickly enough.

He blocked one attack, turned to catch a club on his baton, then moved just a hair too slowly as one of the Interfaith Enforcers who'd been with him when he'd hunted for Olivia ducked under his parry and rammed a knife straight into his gut.

His police tunic stopped a knifepoint, but the impact hurt. Shenker rammed a palm-heel up the IE knifeman's nose and stripped the knife, but he'd been slowed. Another attacker, a guy with some training, jabbed with the smoldering point of a gutted-out torch, then reversed his hold, swinging the torch in a sharp arc into Shenker's ribs.

His mediplant toned down the pain, but it didn't dampen the sickening crunch. The jerk hadn't just cracked ribs, he'd shattered them.

Shenker forced a smile and jabbed his nightstick straight into the torchman's throat.

He went down gagging as Olivia turned and drove away the four men who'd tried to follow up on their advantage.

"You hurt bad?" she asked.

"Pretty bad." Lying might lead her to expect more from him than he could deliver.

"I guess we'd better keep moving, then."

"Yeah."

But their attempt to break through the mob wasn't working. Men streamed from both edges of the mob to get around in front of her. For every meter they gained, hundreds more men got in front of them.

"What's Plan B?" Olivia demanded.

"This is Plan B."

Olivia

"**You** ever play those Native American sims, Olivia?" Shenker asked.

"Some, I guess. When I was a kid."

"You know how they say, 'this is a good day to die.' Well—"

"Shut up, Shenker. Think positively." She beaned a guy who flew from the crowd so fast she suspected he'd been thrown.

Shenker's laugh cut off abruptly when Mr. Flying Man was shoved into the already battered cop.

Like a school of sharks, the mob lurched forward, grasping at Shenker as he fought for his balance.

He struck back hard and Olivia half-turned to help, but a howl went up from the mob as if from a pack of wolves and they dragged Shenker down to the ground, knives flashing, then going red as they cut at him.

A switch triggered in Olivia's brain. She didn't know that she had any Nordic ancestry, but she went berserker anyway. Adrenaline surged and abruptly she felt no pain, no remorse.

"Cop down," she shouted into her telephone, unaware that she was still broadcasting until the mob's roar greeted her words with celebration.

She'd see how much celebration they'd have left when they finished with her. While they would take her eventually, she could damn well make sure they would pay a high price.

She beat away anyone close enough to use a knife on Shenker, then stood over his body, and dared anyone with balls to come at her and try to take him from her.

Come at her, they did.

She went to work building a wall of unconscious bodies around her friend, mentor, and former deadly opponent.

Kick, block, throw, break, use one man's momentum to drive him into someone else. Time lost meaning. She wasn't moving now, couldn't take more than a single step from Shenker without letting the piranha strike. Instead, she reached something akin to that state of mindlessness sought by yoga masters, existing in the moment only.

She was going into oxygen debt because the human body, no matter how sculpted and enhanced, wasn't designed for the type of continuous violent movement she put hers through. But she felt nothing-her mind and body both working together as one, yet a part of her mind watching as a disinterested observer.

A dissonant throbbing grew in her head, but the sound, if sound was the right word for the almost unheard vibrations, wasn't unpleasant. If anything, it washed away the last of the brain-worms that the Interfaith had planted in her mind.

Part of the whole Zen thing? There was no one she could ask.

She put extra muscle into her strikes, knowing that each one could be her last. Each time she twisted to avoid a fist, jumped to let a swung staff pass beneath her feet, or blocked a torch, she wondered if this was the one that would get through—or if, perhaps, this one was the feint and the real killing blow would come unseen.

Without the protection of her tunic, she would have been killed a dozen times. With that many people swinging fists and weapons, not even police training and berserker speed could keep everything out. Olivia tried to avoid the worst of the attacks and make sure no one landing a blow could land another.

Sometimes she failed.

A toothless man, his face a mask of blood, shook off a strike that should have rendered him unconscious and stabbed at her again with a long knife just as a shirtless citizen with bulging muscles snapped an elegant turning hook kick into her ribs.

She dropped her elbow straight down into the kick, then drove the splintered point of her buckyball nightstick into the knifeman's hand. He spit blood at her but seemed as berserk as she. Instead of falling, he switched hands and thrust at her again.

Her block kept the knife away from her heart, but its razor-sharp edge sliced through her pants, cutting deep into the muscles of her thigh.

She hit him again, harder, this time on the head, and spun to meet the next attack.

Or tried to spin. She'd damped out all sensation of pain, but that didn't mean she hadn't been injured. Her leg refused to respond to her command.

Only a timely attack by another man, undeterred by the dozens of moaning bodies lying around her, allowed her to remain upright. A nightstick-reinforced fist to his gut aided her balance.

The metallic thrum of sub-sound grew louder, if loud is a word that can be used to describe something unheard.

It wasn't, she realized, a part of her berserker state after all. It seemed to be swell up from all around.

And it wasn't just she who felt that near-sound. Several attackers shook their heads as if seeking to clear them.

Anything slowing them down was welcome, but Olivia needed more than slow. She needed stop, and in a hurry. Because she was already bleeding all over Shenker and it wouldn't be long before even her berserker-side realized she'd been bled out.

Martin

"**Pump** up the volume," Martin urged. "More."

Tears streamed down Julia's face. "I'm giving it everything I can."

Most of the security bots were busy, each running Julia's noise-cancellation program near a point source of Interfaith ultrasonic generators. Others had to be held back as reserves, because it wouldn't take a genius to figure out what they were doing.

Martin pushed the few bots they still had free through the crowds until their cameras brought the disaster into focus.

Olivia looked like someone out of a cheap horror sim, except her blood was real. Only a foot could be identified as belonging to Shenker. The rest of him lay beneath the sprawled bodies of dozens of attackers.

"It's working," McKensie said. "The regular guys, not Interfaith Enforcers, are dropping their torches and heading back for the ground cars they arrived on."

So Julia was a genius. The only problem was, their ultrasound elimination got rid of the citizens who'd come along because they'd been compelled. The Interfaith Enforcers weren't dissuaded and they were the most dangerous.

"I'm going out there to help," he announced.

"Me too," McKensie said.

"You idiot." Kansas had been awful quiet for months now, ever since Olivia had accused her of being a spy. "They'll chew you up."

"Olivia doesn't have to do all of the fighting, you know. Come on, Martin. Let's hit them from the side Olivia and Shenker were heading toward."

"If you go out there," Justin said, "you're just one mob against another."

"Yeah? So?"

"So, as mayor, I officially deputize you and anyone who goes with you as acting police officers. And that includes me. Let's go."

Julia looked up from the trance she was in with her AI. "I'm coming, too."

Martin shook his head. "You need to keep the noise cancellation going." It was one thing to make a pointless gesture. It was something else to let that gesture get in the way of problem-solving. "Don't delay us. If we're going to help Olivia and Shenker, we need to move."

He didn't wait for an answer. He scrambled out from the underground laboratory and gave McKensie a hand up. The two of them tore hunks of rusty rebar out of a disintegrating twentieth century structure, arming themselves and the four other members of The Colony's temporary emergency police force.

Martin took a deep breath, made sure he knew where Olivia was, and charged.

He hoped the others would follow where he led. If not, well, he didn't figure to last long.

Olivia

Olivia tried to keep her peripheral vision open, but blood loss and adrenaline cut down on her capabilities until her eyesight became laser-focused, able to see only the single most pressing threat.

One man down. Another. Despite her berserker-madness, her arms were tiring, her body slowing. Attacks she should have ducked to avoid got through her guard, smashed into her gut or already bruised ribs. She attempted to block a kick, and ended up taking it in the face. The sharp snap of her nose breaking formed a weird counterpoint to the thrum all around her.

Blood from her damaged nose cascaded down her front and abruptly she was fighting for air. Nothing at all came through her nose, and blood blocked her mouth.

Then her brother danced in front of her, clean, unhurt, full of energy. He'd trained with Olivia when she'd studied to be a cop. For a long time, his greater strength and size let him defeat her, but her more intensive training had ultimately left him behind. He wouldn't have been a threat to her if she wasn't already wounded, practically immobile, and struggling to breathe.

As it was, he could kill her.

"You always mess everything up," he screamed.

For a moment, at least, the IE enforcers backed away, either distracted or letting Sammy have his say.

"But—" even to herself, her voice sounded weird, shaky, incapable.

"Not this time, sister. This time you're going down." He didn't wait to finish talking before he attacked.

She blocked his knife with her nightstick, but he'd planned for that, let her entangle her weapon with his, twisted her hand to his chest, then used his free hand in a palm thrust to break her elbow.

She heard that snap as well.

For the first time since Shenker had fallen, pain penetrated. The nightstick she'd held dropped to the ground. As she wrenched free from Sammy's trap, her wounded leg gave way under her.

She took a knee, using her still-working arm as support for her falling body.

Balanced on one leg and one arm, she presented a tempting target to her brother, one Sammy was quick to exploit.

He slapped two crescent kicks, one to either side of her head.

She kept her balance but was in a dazed stupor. She was out of the fight.

Then Sammy drew another knife.

"You could have joined us," he said. "I wanted it to be like it was when we were kids. We used to help each other. It used to be us against the world. But you turned away from me and I never knew why."

"You were the one who changed, Sammy. Not me."

Olivia had an increasingly difficult time telling whether the shaking in her legs came from the ultrasonic buzz, or from the fatigued muscles tightening and relaxing as they reached failure. With the extreme focus given her by adrenaline and blood loss, it seemed that she, Shenker, and Sammy were alone on a bloody battlefield. No one else mattered. Amazingly, no one took advantage of her distraction to attack her from behind.

"The funny thing is," Sammy mused, "you weren't a very good cop. If you'd followed orders, we would have been on the same side."

"If you'd kept your dreams, we would be on the same side. You wanted to be a designer, remember. We're making that possible."

"My kingdom is not of the earth, but of heaven." He puckered his lips, blew, but no sounds came out. Frustrated, he wet his lips with his tongue and tried again. This time, he managed the opening notes of another tune from the Interfaith.

A sense of lassitude descended on her and her eyes blinked. She needed to rest. Surely she could rest here, where her brother could take care of her.

The vibration, like supersonic violins, washed that fatigue from her system, pushed the earworm from her brain.

Sammy had been watching. The second she blinked, he attacked.

She was almost too slow, but good technique works, even when it's slow. Her brother had abandoned technique for the power he found in anger and frustration.

She watched the knife stab toward her, then shifted her balance just enough to let it pass by her.

She trapped Sammy's knife between her hand and body ignoring his frantic attempts to cut his way free of her grip as she drove her shoulder into his elbow.

His fingers spasmed and he dropped his knife into her waiting hand.

Could she kill her own brother?

"Kill her," he shouted to the enforcers. "Get her while I've got her occupied."

* * * *

Olivia couldn't fight them. She looked around to at least see how she would die.

Thousands were still there, but they looked less like a mob. Most had dropped their torches. Many of those who still held weapons were looking at them as if they didn't recognize what they had, as if they'd been torn out of a sim, only to discover that they still stood in the mythical world the sim had created.

"Mr. Sammy Jardan," the voice sounded weird, out of place as it played through security bots. You are under arrest for property rights violations including human injury. Please do not resist."

Security bots were universally programmed to be polite. This bot was certainly doing its best despite having a burned out torch driven ten centimeters deep into the armored helmet that served as its head-and sensor apparatus.

"I thought we killed all of you lousy robots," Sammy growled. "Come on, guys. Shake a leg."

A couple of the younger guys in the crowd pushed forward, but they stopped before they got too close. To Olivia's surprise, nobody seemed anxious to follow Sammy's instructions.

"We aren't going to be able to do it Sammy."

"What's the matter with you guys?" He'd put the harmonics back into his voice and seemed to be sending on his phone as well as just talking to those within audio range.

The not-quite rhythmic vibration from everywhere gave Olivia the answer to Sammy's question even if Sammy wouldn't let himself figure it out. Julia had done something about the Interfaith programming. That, not some great strength of character, was how Olivia had resisted being overcome. Over time, Julia's programming had even gotten through the addled brains of the Interfaith addicts.

"Citizens of Dallas, please disperse and return to your homespaces." The security bot's voice was joined by the robotic voices of the other bots that had survived the initial assault. "If you leave at this time, the Corporate Entity of The Colony will assert no contractual rights to Avenge. If you remain, Corporate The Colony will request Corporate Dallas to assess vengeance penalties for the destruction of physical and human property, and attempted destruction of intellectual property."

The security bot didn't stop talking, but Olivia stopped listening. Blood loss finally overcame sheer willpower and she collapsed.

The last thing she saw was her brother pulling another knife from his pocket and stabbing it toward her heart.

Julia

People carried the Interfaith's ultrasonic generators. As those people left, taking their generators with them, security bots who'd been involved in sound cancellation were freed up-and Julia put them to work doing what they were supposed to do—keep troublemakers from hurting anyone.

Interfaith Enforcers destroyed them with sophisticated weapons, but they didn't have the numbers of the mob. For every bot that went down, a couple of enforcers were incapacitated.

She had to fight the temptation to remove their inhibitors, to let them use their robotic power to crush bones and kill.

Somehow, she managed.

Martin and his little gang hit the crowd like a cloud hitting a mountain. They simply bounced back, getting nowhere no matter how desperately they fought.

McKinsey looked in her element, though. Her RealSilk™ top ripped, exposing a harder, flatter stomach than Julia would have guessed, and she swung a hunk of iron like an old-time sword.

Interfaith Enforcers edged away from her, but not enough to open a path to Olivia and Shenker.

And Shenker hadn't moved.

Julia tried not to think about what she'd do if Shenker didn't make it back. Told herself he'd made his choice, he'd come to them before he'd met her so she couldn't be responsible.

It didn't help.

"Can I do something?" Kansas sounded desperate to do anything at all.

"Call Vinson. See if he'll help." She uploaded the override Vinson had given her.

"Okay." Kansas seemed pathetically grateful to participate.

Which let Julia concentrate on her bots. She released the reserve.

"Move in," she ordered. "Open a path for Martin and the others. Shut down the last of the Interfaith broadcasters—and crush them."

The bots clicked their acknowledgements and moved.

It was increasingly easy to tell the ordinary citizens from the leavening of Internet Enforcers. The citizens looked confused. The Enforcers looked mad.

The citizens tried to get away from the bots. The Enforcers fought back.

It made it easy to concentrate on the ones who mattered.

It took a while, but she finally created a hole that Martin and the others could go through.

She almost deserted her post, then. Instead, she asked Kansas what she'd learned.

"Vinson can lend us some more bots."

"How soon?"

"Two hours."

"Way too late. Anything else?"

"He's got his drones watching. He's letting me tap into their signal."

"Multicast that to McKensie and the others."

"She didn't have to go out there," Kansas said, sobbing. "I don't get it."

"McKensie has power issues. She needs this."

"But what if she's hurt?"

"Shenker is lying on the ground bleeding. I know our lovers can get hurt."

"I ... I'm sorry."

Julia felt about two inches tall. "Me too. It's not your fault."

"Oh. Someone hurt her. That does it." Kansas grabbed a mop and headed out of the lab. Minutes later, she showed up on the Corporate Dallas broadcast, smacking anyone who got close as she rushed to take care of the fallen McKensie.

Julia resisted the urge to follow until the bots confirmed they'd snuffed out the last of the Interfaith ultrasonic generators. She turned them all onto the remaining enforcers.

She didn't grab a mob. She did head out in a hurry.

Olivia

"**Can** you hear me?" The voice seemed to come from a tunnel, echoing weirdly, the words planting themselves in Olivia's brain and twisting around until she began to see all forms of meaning in them.

"Huh?" It wasn't much of an answer, but anything else would be too difficult.

"Olivia? Are you awake?"

Despite the distortion, she recognized that voice. "Martin?"

"We've been taking turns, but yeah, right now it's me. Give me a second and I'll phone the others."

"What happened?"

"Julia came up with a design to suppress IE broadcasts."

That was good, Olivia supposed. It was also good that she wasn't dead. When Sammy had attacked, she was sure she'd reached the end.

"What about Sammy?"

Martin hesitated. "Maybe this isn't the best time to talk about him."

"He's my brother."

Her ears must be learning to hear again, because she made out the sound of Martin shifting in his chair. "He didn't make it, Olivia."

"He's dead? But security bots can't kill."

"It wasn't a security bot."

"Damn it, my brother is dead. I need to know how it happened. What am I going to tell my parents?"

"Might as well tell her, Martin." Julia didn't sound like herself, but Olivia recognized her voice anyway.

Martin hesitated, then pushed ahead. "You killed him, Olivia. He stabbed you and you drove his nose into his brain."

Memories of her brother washed through her. The time he'd given her the design he'd wanted so badly. His patience in drilling her for her cop tests. When he'd protected her from a group of ratepayers looking for a good time.

She'd killed her own brother. What kind of person did that make her?

"What about Shenker?"

"He... trust me, you did everything you could. He would have wanted to go that..." Julia's voice dropped off and she wiped a dripping tear from the end of her nose. She sounded as if she'd gotten a bad scrub and aged fifty years since the last time they'd talked.

Olivia dropped her mouth open, but for a moment, nothing came out. Paul Shenker had been her mentor, her enemy, her ally. Uninvited, the memory of Shenker with his donuts in hand and his loopy grin of excitement at having created something, of reaching a bit of his dream to become something more than a mere citizen, washed over her with a vividness that made it feel as if he were actually with them.

"Oh, Julia. I'm so sorry. I—"

"You did the best you could."

Oh, yeah. She'd done great. In one morning she'd killed her brother with her bare hands and failed to protect the man whose back she'd been guarding.

"I'm going to have Shenker's baby," Julia said. "I'm going to raise her to be the best designer I can, better than me, for sure."

"I wish I'd told Sammy I loved him."

"Yeah. I wish I'd told Shenker that, too."

Olivia finally broke the silence that followed. "So, I take it I'm going to live." She wished that sounded like a good thing.

"You lost almost all of your blood, had multiple fractures in your upper arm and elbow joint, torn ligaments and tendons, more broken ribs, a severe concussion with cracks in your skull, and six breaks in your nose. There's no way you could have stood there as long as you did, defending Shenker."

"For all the good it did."

"You saved us," Martin said quietly. "Those of us still here owe it to you and to Shenker."

Julia

"**And** that," Julia said, is the story of how we recreated The Colony and launched the free-code project."

Her eight apprentices stared at her as if she'd left them hanging. "But that wasn't all," Paula, commonly called 'Little Shenk" complained. "What about the great boycott, when nobody would buy your stuff. What about when Corporate Houston tried to bomb us."

"Yeah, and when mommy's incredible handbag saved the day," Benjamin added.

The eight children, all born in the six years since she, Olivia, Martin, Shenker, and the others had created a new world, all nodded. "You can't leave those off," Paula said.

"Yeah. Those are good stories, too." Martini looked so much like a small version of Olivia, Julia wanted to hug her. But then, she wanted to hug all those little ones, even Benjamin, who was often as annoying as his parents, McKensie and Kansas.

"I'll tell those stories, too. But first, who wants to see if they can construct a cupcake with chocolate that really tastes like chocolate?"

"I think we need to taste some actual, plant-grown chocolate again," Benjamin said carefully. "Just to make sure we have our target flavors right."

The eight children solemnly voted that Benjamin's idea was a good one. To Julia's amusement, not even Benjamin had problems with the concept of one child, one vote.

www.ingramcontent.com/pod-product-compliance
Lightning Source LLC
Chambersburg PA
CBHW070205260626
47160CB00002B/458